Lovely, Dark, and Deep

Lovely, Dark, and Deep

Justina Chen

Arthur A. Levine Books

SCHOLASTIC INC. / NEW YORK

Library of Congress Cataloging-in-Publication Data

Names: Chen, Justina, 1968– author.
Title: Lovely, dark, and deep / Justina Chen.
Description: First edition. | New York : Arthur A. Levine Books, Scholastic Inc., 2018. | Summary: Teenager Viola Li and her sister Roz are selling bean buns at a science fiction gathering in Seattle when she suddenly collapses—she wakes up in the hospital to find that somehow she has developed an extreme case of photosensitivity (so bad that even ordinary lights can cause blisters), and somehow, in her senior year of high school, she has to craft a new life that will still include journalism school, activism, and the new guy who caught her as she fell.
Identifiers: LCCN 2017042553 (print) | LCCN 2017047817 (ebook) | ISBN 9781338134063 (hardcover : alk. paper) | ISBN 133813406X (hardcover : alk. paper) | ISBN 9781338134070 (Ebook) | ISBN 1338134078 (Ebook)
Subjects: LCSH: Photosensitivity disorders—Juvenile fiction. | Asian American families—Juvenile fiction. | Sisters—Juvenile fiction. | Dating (Social customs)—Juvenile fiction. | Families—Washington (State)—Seattle—Juvenile fiction. | Life skills—Juvenile fiction. | Seattle (Wash.)—Juvenile fiction. | CYAC: Photosensitivity disorders—Fiction. | Asian Americans—Fiction. | Sisters—Fiction. | Dating (Social customs)—Fiction. | Family life—Washington (State)—Seattle—Fiction. | Life skills—Fiction. | Seattle (Wash.)—Fiction.
Classification: LCC PZ7.C4181583 Lo 2018 (print) | LCC PZ7.C4181583 (ebook) | DDC 813.6 [Fic] —dc23
LC record available at https://lccn.loc.gov/2017042553

ISBN 978-1-338-13406-3

10 9 8 7 6 5 4 3 2 1   18 19 20 21 22

Printed in the U.S.A.   23
First edition, August 2018
Book design by Maeve Norton

FOR LORIE ANN GROVER
WHO DANCES IN LIGHT EVEN IN
THE GRIMMEST OF NIGHTS

"Once in a while you get shown the light / In the strangest of places if you look at it right."

— GRATEFUL DEAD

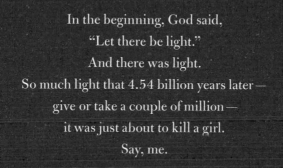

In the beginning, God said,
"Let there be light."
And there was light.
So much light that 4.54 billion years later—
give or take a couple of million—
it was just about to kill a girl.
Say, me.

CHAPTER ONE

"You promised guys," my little sister grumbles as she adjusts the gun belt slung low on her hips.

"And I delivered," I tell Roz, gesturing to the mosh pit of (balding and, hopefully, starving) men congregated before the doors of the Museum of Pop Culture, a full two hours before it opens. They are the perfect, captive audience for my bake sale. "Behold."

"They're *old*. And they're playing dress-up."

"They're in character." I don't point out that so are we. Roz, nice and covered in my original costume: a faux-leather vest stretched to the point of ruin. Me, exposed in a flimsy slip dress I wasn't planning on wearing today.

But Roz is right. Little kids in costume are cute. Girls geared up as some of the most fearless women in sci-fi history? Fierce. Fortysomething men dressed as their favorite characters from a TV show? Vaguely creepy. Even creepier, guys older than our dad are staring at my not-so-little sister, fresh from an elite rowing camp and with the muscles to prove it.

"Everyone here is just . . . ummm" — quick, how would our parents phrase this? — "expressing our appreciation for *Firefly*. Best sci-fi series. Ever."

"You're expressing something, all right." Roz emits a long-suffering sigh. "What's *Firefly* about again?"

"Think hot cowboys who fight bad guys in outer space."

"People actually watched this thing?"

"People are still obsessed with this thing." Like my best friend and me. Ever since Aminta and I binge-watched the entire season on a single snow day back in eighth grade, we've been superfans. Hence, my grand plan: sell out of the bake sale in an hour flat, then head into the exhibit, slap the HoloLens on my head, and compete in the bar fight scene. All great journalists need to be able to hold their own, whatever, whenever, and wherever the fight, on the streets or in a bar. And I, Viola Wynne Li, am that.

Once word leaked six months ago that MoPOP was curating a special exhibit of *Firefly*, I've been prepping my spaceport bake-sale stand to match my costume as Zoë Washburne, she of the fierce leather vest and second-in-command on the spaceship *Serenity*. But then my parents announced last night that they had to be in Portland for an emergency meeting first thing this morning with a client who was having an epic crisis, which meant me babysitting Roz, even though she's in high school. And since Roz hasn't worn a dress in approximately seven years, she got to be me.

"Who am I again?" she demands.

"Zoë," I tell her for what must be the fifteenth time this morning, "first mate and — "

Roz interrupts with a contemptuous sniff. "So not me. I'm going to be crew captain by junior year. And who are you?"

"River Tam, badass weapon in a dress and boots."

"What's her weapon?"

"She *is* the weapon."

Even though my dress is breezy at best, I'm sweating, most likely from dragging the card table by myself from the station wagon parked two blocks away. Call me compulsive, but I straighten the already tidy pile of my latest article featuring today's bake-sale beneficiary, a girls' education fund through CARE International. Now, I set up the sign lettered in *Firefly* font: JOIN THE REVOLUTION: GEEKS FOR GOOD! And at the bottom, in smaller font, is the requisite legalese that my parents insist I include in accordance with King County Public Health codes: BAKED IN A KITCHEN THAT IS NOT INSPECTED BY A REGULATORY AUTHORITY. Perfect.

Roz multitasks in displeasure, picking at the blisters populating her palms (which, hello, is not going to help move a single baked good) and complaining, "It's the last day at Bumbershoot. I could be listening to Black Pink. I could be sleeping."

I choose to ignore her operatic sigh. Besides, in the middle of her woe-is-me soliloquy, I'm suddenly not feeling in bake-sale shape. It must be ninety-five degrees, uncharacteristically toasty for late August in Seattle, but I might as well be in the Serengeti with my aunt, the relentless sun pelting down on us. My forehead leaks sweat, and I feel oddly weak. But who cares if my face is beginning to feel sickly warm? I brandish a copy of my article, complete with my interview with the vice president of advocacy in charge of the education fund, and raise my voice at two oncoming older men dressed as Browncoats: "Buy a bao and help the thirty-one million girls who are out of school around the world!"

The Browncoats veer away from me at light speed.

"You're scary," says Roz, herself moving a stratospheric distance from the table. "I'm getting something from Starbucks."

"By yourself?" I ask, a mini-Mom. "Can't you wait an hour?"

Again with the sighs.

As Roz flounces away, my fingers worry the leather lariat at my throat, Zoë's signature talisman I wear every single day. My right foot taps an impatient beat on the pavement. I was counting on obsession with this short-lived series — just fourteen episodes before it got canceled — for a large turnout of hungry nerds and a rapid sell-out of the bake sale. But there are zero takers for my painstakingly crafted, pillow-fluffy, individually packaged, good-for-the-world red bean buns. In *Firefly*, everyone speaks (curses) in Mandarin. Hence, Chinese dessert: red bean baos. Clever, no?

Apparently not.

I fight a vague wave of nausea. I know one thing for absolute sure: I can't leave my station for some impending cold. Life with my parents has always meant living and breathing these issues, but now they matter even more to me as the next great foreign correspondent.

"Educate girls around the world!" I shout again, and shove an article at another Browncoat who looks shocked, but takes it. Five feet away from me, he tosses my article—the one that took a good ten hours to research, let alone write—into the garbage. "Hey!"

Right when I'm about to stalk over to the garbage can to see if I can salvage my article, I realize, I'm hunting the wrong prey: I shouldn't focus on old geeks, but perpetually hungry guys my age. How hard could it be to find one of those? I rise on my tiptoes, even though my legs are shaky. Miraculously, I spot my target: a broad-shouldered, ridiculously blond, young Thor-gone-lumberman in jeans and flannel shirt.

Before I can yell, "Baos," Thor quarter turns. He should be swaggering around Iceland, circa twelve centuries ago, brandishing a battle-ax, but instead he's making straight for me like he knows exactly who I am and what I'm selling. My flowy dress feels like it's cinching my rib cage. The late-summer sun is burning my face more than ever now. Where was Roz when I needed her?

Thor sets a towering pile of comics next to my articles on the table. The cover on them distracts me from Thor himself—not hard to do because a young woman is busting—and I do mean, busting—out of her stripper outfit (pardon me, *costume*), an obscenely high-cut bikini bedazzled with stars. The title reads *Persephone from Planet X*. More like *Persephone from Planet XXX*.

I glare up at him. He is *so* not colonizing my private bake-sale space with this ode to sexism.

"Excuse me. What do you think you're doing?" I ask, just stopping myself from shoving his comics off. Let them be trampled. But then he picks up one of my articles, skims it, and tucks it in his front pocket.

"Doing what most people do at bake sales. Buying one?" Thor digs out his wallet from his back pocket. "Actually, make it two. My swim coach was in a foul mood today. Super hard set. I'm starving."

"Oh."

"But since when are pork hum baos a hot bake-sale item?"

4

"Red bean baos," I grudgingly correct him when he holds out a five-dollar bill. "The barbeque pork wouldn't make it past Seattle's nonhazardous food code." I thrust two buns at him. As my parents say, the best offense is defense. So I start to gather his comics to hand back to him.

"Take one," he tells me.

"No, thanks."

"Really?" He looks genuinely perplexed.

My silence speaks eloquently for itself, if I say so myself.

Unfortunately, my silence is a foreign language to him. Gesturing to the geeks around us, Thor continues, "A new superhero. Planet X. I mean, come on! This could drive traffic to you."

"'Sir,'" I say as I pass him his change, knowing that the iconic line was going to be thoroughly lost on him, "'I think you have a problem with your brain being missing.'"

"Zoë, I'm desperate," he answers.

I blink up at him in surprise. He speaketh *Firefly*?

"No one wants one. Besides, Aminta texted that I could sell my comic here," Thor announces.

My best friend, Aminta? Aminta, president of the Geeks for Good? Aminta, who conducted a private study proving that our teachers did, in fact, unconsciously call on guys more than girls in our science classes? I eye Persephone's chest, a solar system unto itself, one that defies gravity (not to mention, reality). Whatever universe Thor and his comic hail from, I'm pretty sure that Aminta and I have never seen, heard, or wanted to populate it.

"I'll donate all my proceeds to your cause," he says.

More like he'll drive traffic away from my cause. I prepare to give Thor a polite brush-off, yet, I swear, I've been teleported to the Sahara Desert, the glare is so harsh. Still, it's not harsh enough to stop me from witnessing with my very own eyes the stealth moves that any pilot in any universe would envy. Roz (finally) returns with her iced coffee and maneuvers in front of me. Her back may be to me now, but I can feel the gale force of her eyelashes fluttering at Thor.

"River on Zoë action. Nice," some balding guy snickers as he and his Browncoated buddy pass us.

My hand automatically shoots out to Roz's arm, yanking her out of harm's way, even though she towers over me by a good eight inches. I snap at them, "Yeah, and we can kill you with our brain cells." My outburst saps me. I end up clutching Roz for balance.

From my side, I hear Thor: "Very River Tam."

I try to glare up at him, except that the sun is so bright. I squint, lower my head. Too fast. The planet moves in dizzying circles.

Thor asks urgently, "Hey, you okay? You're really red."

Roz finally acknowledges my presence and frowns. "Whoa, Viola. You really are." Her hands fan her own face. "Like, really red. Really, really red." She looks revolted. "And you're getting puffy."

The familiar hard guitar chords of *Firefly*'s theme song strum overhead. Hundreds of voices roar their approval. The cowboy twang of the lyrics fills the air: "Take my love, take my land / Take me where I cannot stand."

Let's go, I want to tell Roz, except I can't. I don't feel flushed; I feel faint. Not "weak in the knees" faint either. But faint faint. Like "I'm going to collapse in front of this guy" faint. Like I'm going to be trampled by the Great Migration of geeks who are now thundering toward the opening doors. The earth buckles underneath me. I lurch. As I fall, Thor reaches for me, his arms tightening around me.

"Call 911," Thor says, his voice muffled in the ringing of my ears.

"I'm fine," I protest. At least I think I protest.

All I see is the answering blue sky of Thor's eyes. The theme song — *my* theme song — swells, mocking me: "You can't take the sky from me."

The world falls black, and my sky disappears.

WE HAVE A SITUATION

When your company is under cyberattack, the first thing you must do is calibrate the threat. Where is the attack coming from? Who is behind the attack? What is the damage?

— Lee & Li Communications
Inside the War Room: The Crisis Management Playbook

CHAPTER TWO

I shiver, cold with sweat, lion-stalked in the middle of the savanna. My heart pounds. Escape is impossible. My skin itches and prickles and stings, assaulted by legions of mosquitoes and tsetse flies. Waking from a dead faint is nothing like stirring from a good sleep, all groggy and blurry, wispy dream remnants floating away into the ether-space of happy. Instead, think: nightmare.

"Mom?" I whisper. "Dad?"

My eyes blink open, slowly. There are strange men, and we are moving, and I'm lying in a cot, strapped down. For one panicked moment, I almost believe that I've been kidnapped. Isn't this the very situation that my parents warned me about when I turned ten and was allowed to bike down the street by myself for the first time? What was I supposed to do to escape a locked van? But the men are in uniforms: crisp white shirtsleeves stitched with official-looking Medic One patches. One tells me, "You passed out. We're taking you to the Emergency Department."

"Roz?" I ask. "My little sister!"

"She's with your friend."

Friend? What friend? Then I remember Thor and fainting in front of him, not to mention hordes of strangers, and I've just met the guy for a nanosecond and they left Roz with him? There are no words for this crisis. My parents are going to skin me alive when they find out that I've left her behind. As if the paramedics divine my thoughts, the older one with a buzz cut assures me, "Your sister said that your parents are already on their way from Portland." He gives me a grandfatherly pat on the shoulder, and I moan. Who jerks away first is unclear and doesn't matter; I'm relieved that no one is touching me. "Just rest."

I don't need to be told twice. I close my eyes.

...

Where other (normal) parents might hover and fret and liquefy into blubbering pools of utter incompetence in a crisis, mine shine. Of course they do. They're professional crisis managers. Throw in an emergency room? They'd go bioluminescent, glowing at the opportunity to come to my rescue. Only my parents aren't here. Which left me alone to contend with the on-call doctor at the Children's Hospital who ordered approximately a billion and one tests: a CT scan, a couple of vials of blood (!), and an EKG. And now I find myself the lab rat of a pediatric dermatologist, who is hmm-ing and hunh-ing in a not-so-comforting way in my new exam room in a different ward at the hospital. Dr. Anderson looks young enough (no stubble on his preternaturally smooth chin) to be sitting next to me in physiology, especially the way he's worrying his top lip like he's cramming for a test. He very well could be. As soon as I made it to registration in the Emergency Department, the nurse called Mom, who authored and emailed a mini-textbook on my medical history in ten minutes flat.

"Hmm. Are you sure there's no family history of lupus?" Dr. Anderson asks, peering at me like I'm a pickled organ he wants to dissect.

"Pretty sure. Was it just a heat stroke?" I'd seen my Auntie Ruth have one of those during our trail run on Tiger Mountain when it hit ninety-eight degrees last summer. I self-diagnose. "I was nauseous and dizzy, and I fainted."

"No, you have a rash, too," says Dr. Anderson. "Try not to scratch."

Which, of course, makes me notice that I am, in fact, itchy, and I do, in fact, have a blotchy red rash running along both arms. When Dr. Anderson returns to the intake form, frowning because Mom writes at the speed of her thoughts, rapid, dense, and always indecipherable, I surreptitiously check my phone. My parents ought to have all the answers about my condition any moment now. Instead, there's a text from Aminta.

> Aminta: *ARE YOU OKAY?!?!*
> Me: *Where's Roz?*
> Me: *And how's the bake sale?!*

"Could your mom have forgotten someone?" Dr. Anderson asks, looking up with his finger on the lupus question, then frowns at the sight of me with my phone. I quickly pocket it. "Somewhere in your family?"

"Not a chance."

"Hunh."

Obviously, the good doctor has zero clue who my parents are: the principals and cofounders of Lee & Li Communications, who can transform the very worst crises into media-darling gold. All questions are locked down, checked off, and sealed shut with solid answers. So if Mom says there's no lupus in the family, then that is as indisputable as the fact that the sun will always rise from the east.

My phone buzzes.

"Maybe it's my parents," I say. The doctor nods. But it's Aminta again.

> Aminta: *I took Roz to Bumbershoot.*
> Aminta: *WHAT'S WRONG WITH YOU?!*
> Aminta: *LITERALLY! WHO CARES ABOUT A STUPID BAKE SALE.*

I do, because it's never just a stupid bake sale, not to me, anyway. As Lee & Li have intoned through the years, we speak for the speechless. They view their corporate clients as their waiter job to pay for all of their pro bono work for nonprofit humanitarian groups. Well, I bake for the powerless and homeless and everyone in between. But just to make sure that I'm not dying, I ask the doctor, "Lupus isn't fatal, is it?"

"Hmm. Lupus is a possibility, not a diagnosis. Oh, wait!" Dr. Anderson grins as he holds up a finger as if that is good bedside manner and says almost gleefully, "I've got an idea. I'll be right back."

Even before he's safely out of the room, I begin to research my symptoms with the intensity of a scientist on the verge of a major breakthrough, pecking blurry fast on my phone. (BBC reported that cell phones don't really interfere — much — with medical equipment.)

Too soon, the doctor returns; I tuck my phone to my side.

"I don't have any of the classic signs of lupus. No butterfly rash on my face," I tell him and hope I'm right since I didn't have time to fact-check with the mirror.

"Perhaps," Dr. Anderson concedes reluctantly, yet I can see his jaw tighten with frustration, the same way Dad's does when he can't resolve a client's problem. "But being sensitive to the sun is a common sign of lupus." Emphatic tap on the iPad screen he's holding up to me now. "Photosensitivity, which can also be caused by vitiligo, porphyria, maybe xeroderma pigmentosa."

None of these sound particularly benign. What's worse, I'm back to being scared, flailing around without concrete information. So I ask, "Okay, worst-case scenario. Am I dying?"

Just then, a blur of navy blue and motorcycle boots sweeps into the room and stops at my hospital bed. It's Auntie Ruth with her distinctive scent of motor oil and cedar and risk.

"Viola! No, you're not dying," she says immediately, her brown eyes snapping with conviction. It is a very good thing that my skin no longer burns since she wraps her arm tight around me, then glares at the doctor. "Did you tell her she's dying?"

The doctor audibly gulps. How could he not be in awe? Auntie Ruth's wearing her usual uniform: custom-made mechanic's coveralls from Tokyo.

She's got one in every color of the rainbow. Today's front pocket is embroidered with her first name in hot pink, and the back features the winged logo of her auto repair shop. The waist is cinched in to accentuate her curves, and the pant legs are rolled up so you can see her beat-up boots that are scuffed gray from overuse on a real Harley, not distressed at some factory. The uniform is so sexy-utilitarian-cute that Aminta has been coveting one, but Auntie Ruth believes it's important that every woman create her own signature look.

"Sorry, I got here as soon as I could after Roz called," Auntie Ruth says to me before turning her attention back to the doctor. "I'm Viola's aunt. So what's next?"

"We need to run tests," Dr. Anderson says, all clinical efficiency now, not a hmm or hunh in hearing range.

I eye him suspiciously because what tests could possibly remain? Or more likely, is he trying to impress my aunt? (Yes.) Was decisiveness a doctor's way of flirting? (Apparently.) Was it working? (Hardly.)

"I wish your dad was here. He'd know why you'd fainted and what's up with your skin," mutters Auntie Ruth, completely missing how the doctor looks more crushed than offended.

I jump in to explain, to smooth things over with him. "My parents specialize in crisis management for humanitarian organizations. You know, tsunamis, earthquakes, famine, endangered animals. They always know what to do and say in an emergency."

But Dr. Anderson has found his own way to resuscitate his authority and says to Auntie Ruth, "Wait. It says here she was on malaria meds."

"Yeah, for a trip to Ghana," I answer, even though he's addressing my aunt, not me. "And Tanzania."

"With me," Auntie Ruth says.

"Really?" Dr. Anderson asks her, interested, as if that fact has anything to do with my current condition. "I've always wanted to go to Africa. What brought you there?"

Auntie Ruth tells him, "A college friend of mine was filming a documentary on child trafficking, then we went on a short safari."

"That is so cool!" Dr. Anderson's eyes grow appraising, until they drop to the wedding ring Auntie Ruth still wears five years after Uncle Amos died. Under any other normal conditions, I'd shove her number at him myself—"She's single!"—since she looks clueless as ever, her man radar at a permanent loss. But now, I need info.

"I took Doxy for a month," I blurt out, "and finished two weeks ago."

Dr. Anderson blinks as if finally realizing that he's not at a club. I feel at a distinct disadvantage, prone, so I scoot up and swing my legs off the bed.

"Was it the meds?" Auntie Ruth demands, her hands knotting together.

"It's possible she may have had a phototoxic reaction from the meds," Dr. Anderson grants. At Auntie Ruth's alarmed gasp, he adds quickly, "It's one of the known side effects. But two weeks after stopping the meds? That'd be highly unusual, almost impossible."

"Phototoxic?" No matter what anyone could say now, *that* word sounds ominous. Deadly. Something you'd read in an obituary. My legs stop swinging.

"Generally, not fatal," Dr. Anderson says.

My heart goes into double time. Fatal? Fatal as in lethal fatal? Fatal as in death fatal?

"Fatal! Oh, my Lord. This is all my fault!" Auntie Ruth says, folding her arms across her chest. "Why didn't I just listen to your dad? Mick was totally right. As usual. I shouldn't have taken you with me." Her eyes well with tears. "I can't believe I did this to you."

"There's only about a one in a million chance that it's the meds." Dr. Anderson soothes her as if she's the patient with the generally, not fatal diagnosis. "In fact, the half-life of Doxy is no more than twenty-two hours. So it'd be out of her system in two weeks, which means the chances of it leading to death are even more infinitesimally small."

Leading to death!

Auntie Ruth vows, "We are so not going on your graduation trip anymore."

"What?" I ask, startled, because I've been counting on that white-water rafting trip and all the other ones we've planned.

"I'm not putting you in danger ever again." Her intense expression looks eerily like Dad's when he's about to issue a nonnegotiable Parental Veto. My stomach churns in a familiar, doomsday way.

Auntie Ruth can't nix our plans to take clandestine trips (Jordan! Mongolia!) to prep me for my clandestine career (foreign correspondent) after I attend my clandestine college, New York University (in Abu Dhabi) (for four years). That's where I've planned to fulfill my journalistic destiny, since the campus is strategically located so I can travel as fast as breaking news anywhere in Africa, Asia, and the Middle East. Kiss good-bye to embedding myself in Abu Dhabi, learning Arabic, and reporting on that part of the world, if I can't even get into a tiny, little rubberized boat.

"Probably a good idea to stay out of the sun as much as you can until we know for sure what's going on," Dr. Anderson advises. "Wear sunscreen whenever you go out. You're stabilized enough to go home now. We'll get you scheduled for some phototests next week."

"Home," Auntie Ruth echoes, nodding, key fob already clasped in her hand.

Home?

People, people, I want to say, I have baos to sell out, a cause to champion, the exhibit of my lifetime to see, a Thor to avoid.

Thor.

Did I really faint in front of Thor?

My cheeks burn, but my self-respect doesn't matter. "I have to go back to MoPOP." It's true. Thor or no Thor, my bake sale calls.

"Oh, honey, I don't think so," says Auntie Ruth, shaking her head.

Dr. Anderson agrees. "You really want to stay out of the sun for the next couple of days." A lanky nurse comes in with a sheet of paper that he hands to me while Dr. Anderson explains, "That's some info on photosensitivity. I'll give you a call tomorrow to check in on you, especially if you have any questions."

But what if Thor's still trying to offload his misogynistic comics on my bake-sale stand? I get up, grab the edge of the cot, and pretend that my legs aren't wobbly, not at all. Then I catch my reflection in the mirror and freeze.

The rash on my arms may be fading, but this is no ordinary blush on my cheeks. I am not a lovely, demure shade of English rose. No amount of foundation or concealer or special effects makeup artistry could camouflage this: My skin is a field of molten lava. This is "stabilized"?

Auntie Ruth says, "Thanks, Dr. Anderson, we'll book the phototests for next week."

Wait! We're leaving? I have to go outside? I want to protest now. No, more accurately, I want to crawl into a ball, shield my head in my arms, never go out in public again. But the floor is covered in millions of microbes, and the worst thing that could happen is for me to get MRSA on top of everything. Maybe they're right. Maybe the next best thing is to hurry home.

Home where I'll be out of sight.

Home where I can plot my makeup Geeks for Good bake sale.

Home where I can sequester myself in my bedroom while my parents parse my condition to their hearts' content. The elevator doors ping open. Just as I break into a run straight for the parking garage, I grind to a stop.

"What's wrong, honey?" Auntie Ruth asks, concerned.

Do I see my parents, blazing a path across the hospital lobby to quash this crisis? Do I see Roz with Aminta and the rest of the Geeks for Good, beside themselves with worry?

No, instead, it's . . . Thor?

CHAPTER THREE

"Thor? Who's Thor?" Auntie Ruth asks, scanning the lobby until her gaze stops on the blond, broad-shouldered one hulking his way toward us. "Oh. Behold."

Indeed.

Auntie Ruth nudges me. "Just how do you know him?"

I'm still stuck on the fact that I uttered my code name for him out loud. Did photosensitivity fry brain cells along with skin cells? Apparently, not all of them because I recall my lobster skin with perfect clarity. Panicking, I turn my back on all that impending Thor.

"Okay, time to go," I tell my aunt, hoping she'll ignore the squeaky high pitch of my voice, not to mention the inconvenient fact that we have to pass Thor to get to the parking garage.

"Muscles: natural or steroids?" she asks quietly.

"Shh."

Auntie Ruth sidles closers to me. "I'm just . . . I know you were off boys after what Darren did . . ." She lifts her hand to cup my cheek, but thinks better of touching me. "Oh, honey, I'm so proud of you. You're way braver than me. Just like I told you in our tent."

"Auntie Ruth."

"But isn't he a little old for you?"

"Stop!" I cast an anxious glance over my shoulder.

I swear, everyone—nurses, doctors, soccer moms, a pigtailed toddler strapped in her stroller—swivels around to watch Thor stop in front of me. Oversize muscles aren't his only superpower, as it turns out. The mere presence of his wide blue eyes fringed with criminally long eyelashes is enough to erase a girl's ability to form a simple hello.

I really and truly didn't think it was possible to embarrass myself even more. Wrong. Totally wrong. His stubbled cheeks (just how old is he?) obliterate all language skills acquired over the last eighteen years.

I gurgle, "Uhh."

Auntie Ruth, unlike me, extends her hand, all poised and put together as if we're in her auto repair shop, not the Children's Hospital. "Ruth Peters. I'm Viola's aunt."

"Josh Taylor," Thor responds as he shakes her hand. "No steroids. Seattle Central Community College. Eighteen. We just met at MoPOP."

I have a vague memory of getting lost in his big sky blues before I fainted. I ask him, "Met as in: Did you break my fall?"

Josh/Thor shrugs, shoves his hands in his pockets, shifting his weight. He mumbles, "I was closest to you."

"Wait. What about my baos?" I blurt out.

He hesitates. "I've got them in my truck."

"No one stayed to sell them?"

When Josh grimaces apologetically, it's obvious no one wanted to buy them.

"What am I going to do with two hundred red bean buns?" The thought of all those snubbed baos just about demolishes me, and I feel like a failure and my eyes well up, and I want to cry, but I know it'll be ugly weeping, and I already look bad enough as it is without snot running out of my nose, and I've already hit my humiliation quotient for one day.

"Hey, I can bring them to my swim practice tomorrow with your articles," Josh tells me.

Auntie Ruth pipes in, "That is so nice of you." Then, to me, "Isn't that nice of him?"

Exhausted now, I would like to self-immolate on the spot, right here, right now, please. The second-best option is to burrow home, not deal with anyone's curiosity, let alone become a curiosity. And in the way that hundreds of clients before me have raised the red flag—rescue me!—and had their SOS call answered, there they are, my parents, at last.

Lee & Li burst through the sliding glass doors, straight out of a block-buster action flick: Mom, the petite, redheaded queen of the faeries; Dad, her Mongol warrior, who prides himself on being descended from Genghis Khan. (Mom likes to point out that most people today are.)

"Viola, honey!" Dad booms across the lobby, hurtling toward me. Luckily, just as he's about to bear-hug me, Mom touches his arm, a swift warning. He draws back before his protectiveness can inflict damage while Mom scrutinizes me up and down, then up and down again, even as she's digging in her leather tote bag for her water bottle. She holds it out to me, insistent. "Drink. You need to hydrate."

"Mom."

"We got here as soon as we could," Mom says, her voice choked up, "but weekend traffic! How are you doing, honey? Drink! You need to drink."

Mom's eyes may fill with tears, but Auntie Ruth is leaking them as she cries, "It was my fault! Mick, you were right! Africa was a bad idea."

Dad, who is the first responder for crises with just the right calming words, now sighs with nothing to say.

As if Josh is the trained crisis manager, he introduces himself to my parents. A perfect diversion. I chime in, "Josh caught me when I fainted."

"Really?" Dad says, remembering his manners and extending his hand. "Michael Li."

"Really?" Mom says (coos). "Siobhan Lee."

Dad pronounces his next statement in a way that he's never greeted a single guy who's taken me to a school dance, not even Darren, who oozed charm, "Son, you're coming to Souper Bowl Sunday." Then, finally, he says to my aunt, "It's going to be all right, Ruth. We're going to figure this out. Okay, I'm getting answers now." Dad gazes once more at me before striding to the registration desk.

Josh/Thor inclines his head slightly at me: *Souper Bowl Sunday?* Which reminds me of the raw meat condition of my face. I duck my head, wishing my hair was longer so it could shield me. I mumble, "Grab a bowl of soup. Cheer for the Seahawks on game day."

Mom refocuses her attention from Dad, who's interrogating the registration nurse, back onto me. "You know, that could be too much for you, honey. We'll cancel Souper Bowl just to be safe."

Somehow, I have dropped into a time-space-hellhole. Souper Bowl Sunday, Josh, the public, my face. What are these people thinking? Apparently, they aren't.

"Actually, I'm doing great. I should get started on the soups." I seize on that reason to bolt. "Auntie Ruth can drive me home."

"No, I'll take you," Mom decides, overruling Auntie Ruth's feeble protest. Our go-to babysitter whenever our parents are on a business trip or dealing with an emergency has been demoted, and now Auntie Ruth looks hurt on top of guilty.

I can only imagine Mom's hypervigilant hovering over me at home. So I encourage her. "Mom. You should go research with Dad. I can go with Auntie Ruth."

"Your dad's got it under control, but I'll let him know our game plan." Then to Auntie Ruth, Mom says, "Really, Ruth, thanks for being here for Viola, but I got it from here. We'll talk with you later." With that dismissal, Mom sprints over to Dad at the registration desk.

"Okay, then, I guess I'll call you tonight," says Auntie Ruth, hugging me ever so gently. Her sigh is grief-deep. "It's probably a good thing I was never a mom."

"Auntie Ruth!"

But she's already racing out of the hospital, her shoulders hunched. I glance at Josh, who must have some mad superpowers because if my family is weirding him out and my raw hamburger face is disgusting him, he isn't showing it. Instead, he's watching my parents. Honestly, by the time my parents are fully satisfied with the entire medical community's answers, I'll be graduating from college, ready to make the world a more informed place. The skittish way the registration nurse jumps out of her chair to go do something (flee my parents) — one can only imagine what they said to her. Mom flutters her eyes up at Dad. And then they kiss. As in: mouth-on-mouth, my-hero kind of kiss.

Josh clears his throat uncomfortably. I can't even muster a sideways peek at him. Awkward doesn't even begin to describe the moment.

"Well, they sure are into each other," he says.

"That's one way to put it," I tell him.

"It's kind of . . . good."

"If you mean, good like a horror movie can be good, then maybe. I suppose." Then I whack him on the shoulder. "Wait, no! In no universe is this possibly good. You have no idea what it was like to be in preschool when they dropped me off on the first day of school, and then actually made out in the front seat of our car when they thought no one was looking." I pause for breath, my eyes wide. "We were all looking! All of us, noses pressed up to the windows, looking. Crying for our moms, looking."

"Did you all stop crying?"

"Yeah."

"Well. Effective, then."

Crisis contained. That was one way of looking at it. I preferred to look at him and the way his right cheek (and only his right cheek) dimpled with his smile. But what am I thinking? Josh is obviously the same kind of player as Darren. A guy who goes for impossibly proportioned, sun-kissed blondes glowing with health. A hearty and hale Viking woman to his rugged, he-man Thor. See: Persephone. Not me: Pippi. I barely squeak above five feet tall with curves that would be politely called petite and hair that is a confused brown. My one asset are my eyes, large as Mom's with a mysterious tilt, courtesy of my genes from Genghis Khan by way of my dad.

I use that asset now to side-glower at Josh. But my glare is lost on him and his obscenely wide shoulders. He's studying the empty space where my parents had been standing (kissing) at the registration desk as if he were measuring the residual isotopes of their attraction. Whoever they've slipped off to interrogate now, I feel sympathy. Lots of sympathy.

Josh asks, "They're your bio parents?"

"Unbelievably, yes. In a blink of an eye, boom, love." I can't contain my blathering now. "Literally: Dad ran public relations for a pharmaceutical making eye drops, Mom was a crisis communications consultant called in when the eye drops blinded people. And then they bonded over the whole Lee and Li last name thing like it was fate. And then both of them wondered what they were doing, wasting their lives, working for big corporations when they wanted to save the world. I mean, who falls in love and creates a business to save the world together during a crisis?"

"Seriously? They did?" Josh turns a penetrating gaze on me.

All that concentrated male focus makes me nervous. I fidget, not knowing what to do with my hands.

"So." Josh says, "Souper Bowl Sunday, River Tam?"

I'm about to correct him that while I might be cosplaying River the weapon, I'm one hundred percent Zoe the commander to the core, all contained and one hundred percent controlled. But my chest prickles where my shirt is unbuttoned. I tentatively touch my hot skin. I cannot possibly have sunburned—or worse, broken out in another rash—just by standing here in the lobby, could I?

"I'm getting your parents," Josh says, worried.

"No!" Then I'd be dragged right back to the doctors. I just need to go home.

Mom's perpetual crisis echolocation wings her back to my side like she senses my distress. "The doctor warned about this."

Not a moment too soon, she and Josh whisk me outside to her trusty Volvo sedan and buckle me in. I wave good-bye to Josh, (mostly) relieved but also (weirdly) regretful. When I lower my hand, it grazes slick paper sticking out of my messenger bag: a copy of *Persephone*. In thick black permanent marker is a phone number under his message:

River Tam.
My brain will, in fact, be missing until I know you're OK. Text me.

Josh

THE WORST-CASE SCENARIO

The best offense for any kind of crisis is advance preparation. Where are your vulnerabilities? What is the very worst thing that can happen?

—Lee & Li Communications
Inside the War Room: The Crisis Management Playbook

CHAPTER FOUR

Name a cause, any cause, and I have mixed, baked, and frosted for it. Forty-nine consecutive bake sales since fifth grade, all of them successful by any measure: money raised, baked goods sold, satisfaction of beneficiaries. All of them themed: bite-size gingerbread houses that perched on mugs of hot chocolate for a group benefiting refugees. 3-D cookie trees for Treehouse, which supports foster kids. Giant gingerbread people iced in gowns and tuxes for the Exchange, which provides free formal wear to anyone who needs it at school. All of them accompanied with a well-researched article complete with interviews with subject-matter experts. I've never once bailed on a bake sale, not even when I had back-to-back-to-back finals during junior spring. Not even when Auntie Ruth's husband, Uncle Amos, died of pancreatic cancer five years ago. Not until this morning, that is. But a few minutes of losing consciousness and a fading rash are not derailing my track record, not when my future as an NYU-educated and Middle East–embedded foreign correspondent might depend on it.

The moment I spot Aminta's denim-blue Prius in our driveway, back from Bumbershoot, I feel the first sense of calm in this whole, long, tiring day. I will make things right. So even before Mom comes to a full and complete stop, I shove the passenger door open. Or at least, I try to. The door feels like a herd of mama elephants are pushing against it. (Elephant Rescue mission, pecan-cinnamon elephant ear cookies, Bake Sale, 2013.)

"Viola, be careful!" Mom warns me as my boots hit the pavement.

How can I slow down? Adrenaline, sweet adrenaline, surges, so I pound up the three steps to the front door. My house key slides into the lock at the same time the door opens. It's not Roz greeting me—all, how's my big sister?—but Aminta Sarabhai, my big-hearted, big-haired best friend from second grade, who is still in her *Firefly* costume like she couldn't be bothered to change until she sees me.

"I'm sorry about the bake sale!" I tell her.

"Shut up about the bake sale already," Aminta says. While she has many (many) superpowers, what tops that list is her ability to give grandma hugs: warm, encompassing, and reassuring. Only today, my body tenses, my skin supersensitive when she embraces me.

"Careful, Aminta!" Mom cries.

Immediately, Aminta releases me. "I'm sorry! Did I break you?" Then, looking down at me, her eyes grow round. "Oh, my gosh, you're red!"

"Yeah, and I will be for an entire day," I tell her.

"Oh, good. First day of school's on Monday."

"I know. Lucky me."

"You better get inside," Mom says, waving us both into the house. She bolts the front door behind us hastily as if she's blockading an enemy.

Once inside, I peer into the living room and ask Aminta, "Hey, where's Roz?"

"Bedroom."

Which is code for: pouting.

Which is precursor for: getting whatever Roz wants.

Aminta and I learned the early warning signals the hard way. A few big tears rolling down Roz's pudgy cheeks, and my little sister got the first choice, the best portion, the biggest serving. Once when we were six, Aminta openly questioned Roz's right to have the last scoop of chocolate chip ice cream — our fave of the moment — and she split it between our two bowls. Roz's face went horror-movie enraged. I had to get Aminta out of the kitchen fast before Roz cried and my parents intervened. Even though I heard Roz waddling behind us — "wait for me!" — I ran even faster with our contraband bowls. Then Roz stepped on a nail left out from our remodel, it pierced her foot, and she fell. The blood, I'd never seen so much blood. The wails. The wails!

We all thought she was dying, and it was my fault.

A few stitches, one tetanus shot, and a giant cast later, Roz returned home, victorious with not one, but three tubs of ice cream, all Sharpie-markered with her name.

"Sorry," Aminta whispers, shaking her head. "I just couldn't tolerate one more K-pop band at Bumbershoot. I know the tickets were expensive, but I wanted to be back here when you got home. So we left early."

I can only imagine the conniption fit Roz threw. "I'm sorry."

"You should go rest now," Mom tells me.

Irritated, I sigh. "I'm not an invalid, you know." Fighting is futile, though, especially with Mom casting worried glances at the expansive kitchen windows. Anyway, I want to talk to Aminta about our bake sale and Josh. So I grab her hand and we tiptoe past Roz's bedroom, blasting chirpy notes of K-pop. Just to be extra safe from eavesdropping, I whisper to Aminta as I close my door, "We're going to have a makeup bake sale."

"What?" Aminta splutters, then whisper-yells at me, "again, who cares about the stupid bake sale?"

"I do." I plunk myself down onto my bed and scoot back to rest against the wall. My whole body relaxes. "You know our plan. Donate so much to CARE that we might actually be invited on one of their field visits to Nepal or India and get the real scoop."

The grand plan was for me to write about our on-the-ground experience, and Aminta to turn those facts into infographics, complete with her hand-drawn comics and number-crunching skills. We are the Geeks for Good, after all. Geeks who were censored in our school paper our freshman year because the administration refused to allow us to publish our investigative report: Aminta's data crunching that proved — proved! — that teachers unconsciously favored boys in STEM classes. The school did not appreciate her accompanying political cartoon any more than they did my article with interviews with the leaders of the local chapter of the Society of Women Engineers, who had choice words and even choicer examples of institutional sexism. So we decided to go rogue: report on causes that mattered and distribute our articles through innocent bake sales both on campus and off. Can a handheld apple pie have an ulterior motive? You bet, when it includes information about our vets, who risk their lives for the sake of our freedom and return home with untreated PTSD.

"So we'll have a do-over on Friday." I nod my head firmly. Never mind that I have no idea what I'll bake to substitute for the bao failure or that my body feels so achy tired that the thought of making soup in the morning drains what's left of my energy. Tomorrow, I'll be back to baking shape, and this health blip will be history. "Everyone's going to be ready for a sugar high after the first week of school."

"True, the teachers always lay it on thick the first couple of weeks to scare us. Don't they understand it's senior fall? Don't they know how many college essays we need to write? Don't they know — "

"We'll sell out then, especially if we sell before the back-to-school dance. We should make an extra-big batch." I interrupt this monologue because the same one's been playing in my own head this whole summer with one major variation: My parents have no clue that my Early Decision college choice is NYU Abu Dhabi. Not only that, but if I get in, my first step is to snag an internship with a field producer for any of the major news outlets.

"Okay, good idea, but only if I help bake this week," Aminta says. "I know Caresse will, too."

"Nah, I got it. She spent so much time making our costumes for today." My leather vest that I didn't even get to wear.

"You never let us help!"

"I do, too! You guys donate the ingredients. I donate the baking time."

There's a light rap on the door before Mom enters with a tray loaded with popcorn, carrots and hummus, water, and Josh's comic.

"You know," Mom muses as she sets the tray between Aminta and me on the bed, "it's a little weird that the main character is photosensitive, too."

"Persephone? She is?" I ask as Aminta gasps with a loud, "No way! I totally forgot that part of the plot." She leans forward for a better look when I flip through the pages. "We were in the same comic class."

"Remind him about Souper Bowl Sunday," Mom says.

"Mom."

"Well, good thing I did, then."

"Mom! You didn't!" Even Aminta groans, covering her face with her hands. Crisis managers, my foot. My mom isn't smoothing over an incident; she's creating one. "Mom!"

"We didn't give him our address. Just living up to our word, honey. Eat up," Mom says. "You need your strength, sweetie."

That "eat up" is a beacon calling all little sisters to stalk into my bedroom and frown, outraged at the injustice of our tray of food. "Hey! What about me?"

"Rosalind-honey, let's get you something, too." Not a moment too soon, Mom leaves with Roz, thankfully closing the door behind them.

"This is terrible," I say, rubbing my eyes. There is nothing I can do to fix this situation. So I do the next best thing, which is to barrage Aminta with questions. "What do you know about him? And why, why, why would you tell him he could co-opt our bake sale with this?" I jab my finger at the twin peaks on the cover. "This?"

Aminta digs a carrot stick into the hummus and takes a thoughtful bite. "I'm kind of shocked Josh finished it, actually."

The gavel slams in my head: case closed. "So he's a slacker! I thought so."

"Well . . ." Aminta shoves a couple of pieces of popcorn in her mouth like she needs serious reinforcement before answering. "It's just so tragically sad. He and his twin were working on this, and then suddenly, they both stopped coming to camp. And then we heard that Caleb —"

"His twin?"

Aminta nods. "Well, we heard he died."

"That's awful."

"Horrible."

"What happened?"

"I don't know." Aminta studies the cover of the comic. "We didn't keep in touch, not like some of the other kids and I did, but then Josh texted a couple of us late last night and said that he had published *Persephone*. Not just finished it, but actually published it with a short-run press." She shrugs. "I just wanted to support him, and we were having the bake sale, and it was the *Firefly* crowd, and it seemed like the right thing to do."

"Yeah, of course, it was. I'm glad you did." On the wall across from us I've pinned all fifty of our rebel articles. "It's hard to get published."

"As we know."

I pick out my favorite pieces of popcorn, the ones that are shy of burnt, the ones that slipped through the Siobhan Lee carcinogen filtration system. "He waited for me at the hospital."

"Josh?"

I nod. "Isn't that nice?"

Aminta shakes a carrot stick at me. "Oh, no, you don't."

"What?"

"That's code for, 'Isn't *he* nice?' "

I blush. Because. Pretty much, yes.

"Well, all I know is," Aminta says, crunching down hard on the carrot, before waving the remaining stub at me, "he was always 'nice' to a different girl in class, before class, and after class."

"Darren 2.0."

Just what I didn't need in my life ever again: a guy who'd toy with me when it was convenient for him, texting to get his ego fix, angling to get his physical fix. I set *Persephone* facedown on my bed. "Don't worry. Not doing that again." Then I groan. "Wait. Souper Bowl Sunday. My mom texted him!"

"He won't show."

"You're right. He won't." Of course not. Showing up meant following through, which players do not do. Following through is the Lee & Li way,

29

no matter how grueling the assignment. Following through is why I'm insisting on Friday's bake sale. Only now, my body betrays me when I should be charting all the details, researching cookies to make, outlining the signs to create, composing social media announcements to blast. I curl up on my side, a little ball of tiredness.

"Should I go?" Aminta says, concerned. "Get your mom?"

"No." My eyes close, but the sunlight is bright behind my lids. I turn my face to the wall. "I'm just going to nap for a few minutes."

Aminta slips to the ground with the comic. "I'll read. You sleep. Go on. Stretch out."

Instead, I stay where I am, according to my plan.

CHAPTER FIVE

That night, I dream of the Serengeti: endless plains that stretch brittle green and yellow-gold to the horizon and beyond, air steeped in sun-dried heat. There is no drizzling rain, no soft mist, no persistent ceiling of low, gray clouds that is the Pacific Northwest, yet I feel more at home here in the restless savanna than I ever have in Seattle. The roof of the touring jeep is popped up, and Auntie Ruth and I stand in our seats, leaning out and breathing in sunlight and red dirt.

"Ready?" Auntie Ruth asks me, grinning with wild delight, just as she has since she invited me on this trip of a lifetime.

I lift the camera in my hands. "Ready."

After a day on safari, I'd learned fast to be prepared for my shot. You never know what the Serengeti will unveil to you, moment by moment. As it is, the hum of life is ever present: a leopard growling deep in its throat from a faraway tree, hyenas cackling through the tall grass, elephants trumpeting somewhere in the thicket.

"A lioness is hunting!" our guide tells us excitedly. She spins around in the driver's seat. It's Roz in a khaki safari shirt, instead of her usual yoga pants and T-shirt.

I know that I'm dreaming.

As much as I command myself to wake up, the jeep heaves into gear, and we race down the hard-packed dirt road. Roz doesn't warn us about the stream ahead. So the hard jolt as we bump over the lip of the road knocks Auntie Ruth off-balance. I fling my right hand out to grab her, but I lose my grip on the camera. It sails into the long grass fringing the side of the road.

I cannot lose the Nikon, Roz's combo-Christmas-birthday-Valentine's present.

"Stop!" I yell. "Roz! Stop!"

Instead, she speeds down the parched streambed. The next jarring lurch throws me out of the jeep. My shoulder hits the ground first, then my head, my hands. Throbbing, everything throbs. I've watched the drama of the Great Migration, the largest movement of mammals on the entire planet. If I stay sprawled in the hot sun and open wilderness, I am fodder, fresh meat, easy pickings. I've seen what happens to injured wildebeest, the hobbled ones.

"Roz!" I scream, and rise to my feet, but my sister is long gone.

Heart thumping, I spin around in a panicked circle and find myself not in the savanna anymore, but inside the canvas tent I've been sharing with Auntie Ruth. A lion roars breathtakingly close, prowling outside the tent.

"I've got everything under control." Auntie Ruth unzips the tent and shoves me out. "You'll be safe."

Then I see my hands: red, blistered, molting. For once, Auntie Ruth is wrong. I am safe nowhere.

...

"Viola! Viola! Wake up!" A calloused hand jostles me roughly as if my shoulder is an oar. "Where is it?"

I bat weakly at the death grip, but Darth Vader breathes down on me. The Force—my force—does nothing to set me free from my little sister. How did she know that I lost her camera?

"It's in the grass. I'll find your camera," I tell her, yearning to be back in the fading dream. Braving the predators in the Serengeti is preferable to being mauled by Roz.

"Stop faking it!" Shake! "Mom and Dad aren't even here to see your act."

I crack my eyes open to check the time on my bedside table: a few minutes after five in the morning. I groan and close my eyes again. Senior year—and crew practice, criminally early the entire school year—cannot possibly have started already.

Every single syllable is a sound of outrage, as Roz demands, "I got to go."

But I don't.

"I'm not feeling great," I tell her. "You're going to have to ask Mom or Dad to drive you."

"They can't. They're already at work."

I angle a look at her. "Seriously? On our first day of school?"

Roz sighs. "They had to head back down to Portland first thing this morning for the client they had to bail on yesterday for you. They only found out this morning. Something about global pandemics? How am I supposed to know?"

Fine, if my doctor wants me to hide from the light, I will. I throw the covers over my head. Let Roz find her own way to crew. I'm sleeping through the day. "Well, then, you're going to have to take the bus. If you go now, you can probably still make it."

"I'm telling Mom and Dad that you're really sick."

"That's because I really am sick."

"Yeah? What do you think they're going to do if they know you can't get out of bed?"

Slowly, I lower the comforter and feel the slap of cool air, cold truth, and icy smugness.

"I need a latte before crew. And dinner with the team tonight." The blackmailer holds out her oar-hardened hand. "Debit card."

Buying Roz's silence is a small price to pay. "My bag's under the desk. You know, you could always get your license and drive yourself to crew."

"Why should I?" (You are at my beck and call.)

It's true. Six days a week, I am my sister's personal and unpaid chauffeur, hauling thirty minutes north to the school's boathouse up in Kenmore at five thirty in the morning. Such is the price of driving privileges and parents who work around the clock since global crises wait for no one.

33

Without another word, Roz flicks on the overhead light and charges to my messenger bag, where she rummages for my wallet and pockets the debit card. My books, notebook, emergency kit, and makeup bag lie on the ground, detritus from Hurricane Rosalind.

"Hey!" I call as I follow her out my door. "Umm. Mess."

Roz waves a hand carelessly in the air; it's never her mess to clean.

The truth is: I'm unsteady on my feet, not that I'd admit this to myself, much less my parents. Sighing, I tug on a T-shirt since it's supposed to be hot again today. With my hair pulled into a ponytail, I'm as ready as I'll ever be. I'll have plenty of time to do my makeup in the car while I wait for school to start, but my makeup bag bulges suspiciously. I unzip the pink case. My favorite foundation and concealer that I splurged on with my birthday money are gone. In their place are tubes of sunscreen and an SPF-infused foundation brand I've never heard of and will probably clog my finicky pores.

"Mom!" I yell, even though I know she's not home. "Honestly!"

I dig into my trash can. Of course all my things are gone. Grumbling, as I'm about to bend down to repack my messenger bag, I spot the good luck present (scare tactics) my parents have left on my desk: a stack of printouts—full-color—from the Mayo Clinic's website, featuring men and women with photosensitivity, their bumpy, burned skin. The angry red rashes. The chains of blisters. There is only one place for these pages. I gather them up for the garbage can and see my hands.

My hands. It'd be impossible to miss them. Blotchy and red, but how? I haven't even left my bedroom since getting home yesterday. I can only imagine what my face looks like.

Duty calls me away from this nightmare.

From the front door, Roz hollers, "Hurry up. Seat races this morning. Today's important for me."

...

At the boathouse, Roz slips out of our ancient silver Subaru station wagon with her Liberty Prep duffel bag before I can even put the car into park.

34

Within an instant, her posse of muscular friends surrounds her as if she's the senior and I'm the sophomore.

Normally, I head to Auntie Ruth's auto shop after dropping off Roz, not just because little else is open at this hour—not the Northgate Library or Cloud City Coffee. But because she is the refuge of cool, more like a big sister who's planning our next trail run than an adult watching over me. Plus, like me, Auntie Ruth appreciates a quiet, early, and caffeinated start to the day.

But: the dream. Auntie Ruth had pushed me—shoved me!—outside the tent to the lions. Lions with pointy incisors made to rip through skin and scissor-sharp carnassials to tear through muscles—the perfect killing tool. (Yes, I did study up before the safari.) It may have been a dream, but it feels a smidge too close to her shoving our graduation travel plans off the calendar and into my parents' perfect killing tool of a crisis management plan.

So I drive toward school instead, but even as I pull into the empty parking lot, reserved for seniors, images of humiliation keep dancing in my head: There's me, fainting at MoPOP in front of strangers. There's me, hamburger-facing it in front of Josh. There's me, abandoning my bake-sale stand, not that anyone cares. Not even Aminta.

Still.

My hands tighten on the steering wheel before I turn off the ignition. I don't need or want to see a flaming red version of myself, so I studiously avoid the rearview mirror. What I crave right now is the quiet of a trail run—each step demanding every bit of your concentration so you don't trip on a rock or a branch and break a leg out in the woods. But that's not happening right now.

Instead, I can soothe myself with research. According to Lee & Li, knowledge empowers. Data makes you capable of making a good decision in hard circumstances. Say, a catastrophic flood with a thousand competing needs, all urgent. Or a murky situation, like not knowing what the hell is going on with your body. The flimsy page that the doctor handed to me isn't particularly illuminating.

Not to worry; I intend to find out everything for myself. Thanks to the battalion of generous, insomniac parents who work around the clock at Amazon and Microsoft, my school radiates with Wi-Fi power, even out here in the parking lot. I pull out my Mac.

...

(NOT SO) FUN FACTS ABOUT PHOTOSENSITIVITY

Fact 1: Photosensitivity is sometimes called an allergy to the sun. (Yes, the star that's at the center of our solar system. The star that gives off heat and makes things grow. The star that gets you hot enough to dive off the sketchy platform at the public beach three blocks away on Lake Washington. That sun.)

Fact 2: There are also a bunch of different disorders that cause serious photosensitivity, not just the pretty common and temporary photosensitivity you get from taking malaria meds. Pinpointing which disorder is difficult. (Trust me, I tried. But after reading about erythropoietic protoporphyria—which causes sun sensitivity, not to mention severe stomach pain, vomiting, constipation, and oh, yeah, personality changes—I got too scared to play diagnosis roulette.)

Fact 3: The most common symptoms of being allergic to the sun are:

- Redness: check!

- Itching or pain: check!

- Tiny raised bumps that can appear from face to toe: Are you kidding me?

- Blisters: seriously?

- Scaling, crusting, or bleeding of said blisters that will take up to six days to heal: no comment.

- And then sometimes — for the lucky few — you'll feel like you have the flu, go into anaphylactic shock, pass out, and possibly even die.

- Possibly even die (in extremely rare cases) (rare, meaning not occurring extremely often) (rare, meaning that it does occur sometimes).

- Possibly. Even. Die. (Excuse me, did or did not Dr. Anderson say that photosensitivity was generally not a fatal condition?)

- "Generally nonfatal" and "in extremely rare cases" mean possibly even die.

...

For the first time, I wonder if I'll be holding a bake sale for myself. I want to throw up at the thought. But when I wasn't looking, cars have surrounded mine in a cave of metal.

Welcome, senior year.

CHAPTER SIX

It's the early afternoon and there's one more class before my free period, then I can call it a day and tell my parents, *See? Nothing has changed.* In the hall, a jock double takes at the sight of me, then another. Self-conscious, I wrap my arms around each other, rubbing the itchy hives that now blotch my forearms. These raised bumps are supposed to fade within a couple of hours. Still waiting. And how on earth did I get them after being sequestered inside my car and then the back row, the darkest row, in all my classrooms: calculus, Spanish, and the senior seminar I've waited four years to take—Asian American literature to explore my roots.

No matter. New plan: I'll borrow a sweatshirt from the lost-and-found and hide my arms, but halfway to the front office, I realize it's the first day of school. I want to weep. Nothing's been lost—at least nothing that anyone realizes is missing.

I take a deep breath before I approach the double doors, leading to the square. I'll need to run across it to get to the science building, all of a minute, max, in the sun. That couldn't possibly make me worse, could it? I hug myself tighter, then spy familiar khaki coveralls.

Just the person I need. "Aminta!" I call, hurrying to her.

My best friend turns around, but her huge smile contorts into horror. Her wavy hair bobs around her shoulders, like she herself is my life buoy, as she runs to me. "Oh, my gosh, Viola! What happened?"

I duck my head fast at her (loud) alarm, which I know is drawing more stares. Aminta shrugs out of her blue satin jacket and holds it out to me. My first instinct is to tell her no, I don't need it, but I do. Gratefully, I slip it on, welcoming how the billowy fabric swallows me whole.

She asks, "Should you even be here?"

"I'm okay."

"I don't know."

Me, either, to tell you the truth. As if my mom knows how my skin is erupting, she texts me roughly a billion heart emojis, and then a symphony of pings:

> Mom: *Are you okay?!*
> Mom: *Please check in.*
> Mom: *Now.*
> Mom: *Update, please.*
> Mom: *Skin status report, please.*
> Mom: *Love you, honey!*

Before I can even complain about my text-happy Mom to Aminta, let alone share all the gory details about photosensitivity that I've researched, Caresse, the new treasurer of Geeks for Good, strides down the hall toward us. She is a blur of purple bohemian skirt that she's designed and sewed. Every little part of me wants to surge ahead of this moment, this conversation, this attention, but: my future. I say as much. "So we're good for Friday's makeup bake sale, right?"

When I tug my hair out from under the messenger strap, they both get a good look at my hands, one now bubbling with an ice floe of a blister. Aminta actually flings her hand up to her mouth.

"You need to go to the doctor," Aminta orders me. "I'll drive you."

"Yeah," says Caresse, scrutinizing me like she's on a scientific expedition, discovering a new subspecies of teen girl in the wilds of Liberty Prep. She brushes back her black dreads. "Those are hives. An oatmeal bath could help."

Aminta pulls out her phone. "I'm calling your parents."

"No, I'm fine."

"Auntie Ruth, then."

"I'm good."

"Well, there is no way we're having the bake sale on Friday," says Caresse like she's the official Bake-Sale Coordinator, not me.

When I start to protest, Aminta cuts in, "Next Friday, maybe, if your skin clears up by then. Are you sure I can't call your parents?"

"Ack, I got to get to class." I rush out the double doors of Jacobsen Hall as if I'm heading to physiology in Robinson-Iqbal across the square. Once outside, I dash to the senior parking lot to the side of the school. My quick escape is foiled by my messenger bag, which spills onto the gravel. Everything falls out. Everything.

Of course it does.

"Honestly?" I yell as I bend down to pick up my daily planner, splayed open to a hidden note I'd never seen, marking up the very last page.

"SET YOUR LIFE ON FIRE."

— Rumi

Auntie Ruth's handwriting feels intrusive when she herself torched our travel plans. The sun is taking care of my skin. What else could possibly be burned?

CHAPTER SEVEN

Another safari nightmare wakes me from my post-dinner, post-first-day-of-school nap. Unable to sleep and needing to cook something, anything, I creep down the hall past the wall of family photos from our trips to Disneyland, tiptoeing by Roz's bedroom, where she's bunkered down for her mandatory ten hours of sleep for crew.

Personally, I don't understand comfort eating, being more of a comfort cooker myself. Bread bakers can talk all they want about the solace they find in the yeasty smell filling their home. I like baking, too, obviously, but soup is my specialty. I know, weird. For me, there's satisfaction in seeing vats of my homemade soup poured into matching mason jars, all lined up in nice, neat, nourishing rows. On Sunday, the Seahawks are playing the LA Rams. I'd originally planned for Moroccan lamb stew, a kissing cousin to soup. (Rams, lambs, get it?) But lamb is expensive, and anyhow, baa baa black sheep and all. So instead, in honor of LA vegan, antifood, calorie-protesting types, I now plan to prep a test batch of weight-loss soup (aka cabbage). Tomorrow, I'll guinea-pig it on my family for dinner.

The kitchen is too dark to read the recipes I'd printed out earlier. So I flick on the pendant lights over the island.

"Honey, turn off the lights," Dad says, his voice low but urgent.

I jump as if I've been caught sneaking out of the house instead of into the pantry. "You scared me! When did you guys get home?"

While we may not attend church faithfully, my parents honor their quality time religiously, always shutting down work at seven every night with the caveat that they will only respond to true life-threatening emergencies (there must be blood). So tiny alarm bells jangle when I find both of them sitting at command central in the dark breakfast nook, kitty-corner to each other, and not just holding hands. It's a couple minutes past eleven, and the kitchen table is covered edge-to-edge with papers, pens, and every device known to modern man so they can mainline the news as if this is normal. So much for Mom's lectures on good sleep hygiene.

"You were sleeping," Dad says, setting down his phone. "We didn't want to wake you."

"How are you feeling, honey?" Mom asks, her green eyes racing over my body and braking on my bare arms. "Hives! When did you get hives? Why didn't you tell us?"

"I put aloe vera on them just the way I researched, and they're going away," I assure her, annoyed when she leaps out of the breakfast nook anyway to inspect my skin herself. My self-sufficiency doesn't stop Dad either. He barrels blindly past me, keeping his eyes on the overhead lights as if he doesn't trust them. I sidestep out of his way. "What're you doing?"

"Turning off the lights."

"Seriously?"

"Seriously. I haven't had the time to change out the light bulbs yet."

"If we change them out," Mom says, frowning as she lowers her reading glasses to the tip of her nose to peer closer at my hives and notices my hand with the ragged remains of the blister. "Did you pop a blister?"

"Mom."

"We need to sterilize it."

"Mom. I dealt with it and followed the instructions on the Mayo Clinic site."

Thankfully, Dad's hmm, as he glares at the pendant lights, distracts Mom.

"Like I said, honey, Nat Geo's energy blog says that it's a myth that CFL bulbs" — Mom tells Dad, pointing at the light bulbs above us — "emit UVA rays."

I may have researched my potential condition, but my parents have one-upped me with an action plan. Annoyed, I focus on collecting the ingredients for the test soup. I search the freezer for the flour only to find the missing canister against the backsplash along with the sugar, even though I've told everyone a million times to store the flour in the freezer where it'll last longer. I slam the container harder than I intended (sort of) on the counter.

"Roz is sleeping," Mom chides me mildly as she grabs a teacup from the table, but Dad is already sweeping over to her with the kettle. Her answering smile is so sunny, we should check her for UVA emission. "Oh, thank you, honey."

"No problem, but, treasure, the NIH published a study that says photosensitive people" — Dad sits back down and nods over at me as if there was any doubt about who the photosensitive person in the kitchen is — "can get sunburned from those bulbs."

I sigh. Heavily.

"Oh!" Mom cries, forgetting all thoughts about letting a sleeping Roz lie. She scurries away on her tiny, slippered feet, as she does whenever an idea overtakes her. What now? The call of her inspiration is as mysterious as it is indiscriminate — whether chaperoning a field trip to the Pacific Science Center or showering when my friends are here (all true, all witnessed with real live eyeballs, all mortifying).

A tiny prickle of foreboding needles me. I push down my concern and forage in the fridge for the carrots and onions I need to dice, which will be seriously risky given how dark the kitchen is, but if I mention this to my parents, they'll imagine me chopping off my finger and there goes cooking. While some people might classify this as paranoid thinking, I know it to be a real possibility, which is why I haven't been entirely forthcoming about my final list of colleges. If my parents think it's dangerous for me to study at Northwestern, in Chicago ("Have you seen the murder rate?"), just wait until they hear about Abu Dhabi.

I fact-check my father: "You came home from a business trip and started researching light bulbs?"

"Umm, yeah," he says as if it is a perfectly logical thing to do on a week-night. "Maddening. Here we thought we were being so eco-conscious, doing good for the environment, making the huge investment of replacing all the incandescent bulbs with these compact fluorescent ones. Meanwhile, they've been poisoning you."

"Poisoning is a little strong, don't you think?"

A flying saucer crash-lands next to me on the kitchen island, bowling over the flour I've set down. The canister clatters, spilling an avalanche of flour. I flinch. "Mom!"

She tucks her wavy red hair behind her ears, which are the tiniest bit pointy like she's really part Irish fairy. Mom grins at me excitedly. "What do you think?"

Apprehension swells inside me. "What is that?"

"A hat."

No, a hat is a cute accessory, known to punctuate sassy outfits worn by little old ladies at our church on Easter Sunday. This is a UFO, its massive wingspan doubling as a wind turbine. Just ask my hair. I brush the long strands off my face and edge away from the flour-speckled island. Who knows what else Mom will wing at me?

In any case, I should have known to be more specific with a crisis manager who releases facts, and just the sanctioned and preapproved facts. I ask, "What's the hat for?"

Mom is careful not to make eye contact with me. Instead, she glances at Dad to sync their response, as they keep to the script: "The One Where We Turn Our Eldest into a Fashion Crisis." They are a united front of imperturbable, unflappable, unreadable expressions.

"Protection," Mom says finally. "We picked it up in Portland. Do you like it?"

"Protection from what?" I ask.

"Look," says Dad, scooting out of the nook so he can stand next to Mom, his Mongolian warrior to her pixie princess. "We updated this house to be all about daylighting design, remember?"

How could I forget? Thanks to the inspiration of their clean-tech clients, the grand plan was to maximize natural light to minimize our drag on the electrical grid. So now we have eight skylights overhead, picture windows that envelop the breakfast nook, and a bank of floor-to-ceiling windows in the living room, care of a remodel that we pretty much handled on our own. At six, my job was to pick up all the stray nails; unfortunately, I had overlooked one and learned my lesson later about being thorough.

"Glass doesn't filter out the UVA rays, and the research says that sixty-two percent of UVA rays come through windows," Mom says, frowning, as she consults her notepad in the nook. "All the experts agree on that much."

"So? What? I have to wear this" — I grab the hat and shake it — "inside?"
No answer.

"Even at night just because the lights are on? Seriously?"

With a single clearing of his throat, Dad's in Crisis-Manager-Knows-Best mode. "The doctor said to minimize your exposure to UVA rays until we know more after the tests this week."

One hundred and eighty pounds of pure frustration stomps into the kitchen. No light — natural or artificial — is necessary to detect Roz's irritation since her growl says it all: "Did you know that sleep is important for my body to recover?"

"Munchkin," Dad says, rounding the kitchen island to hug Roz. In our family, Dad's a giant at almost six feet tall, and he alone is able to call her by that nickname. "Did we wake you up, princess?"

"What do you think?" Roz's pout turns into a sulk when she sees that the Cooking Fairy (*c'est moi*) is shirking her duty: no freshly made, crisp on the outside, late-night snack waffles? Just as she's about to express her displeasure, Roz notices the hat in my hand. "What's that?"

"Oh, just something Viola's going to start wearing," Mom says breezily. "For now."

"I'm not," I say.

"Good, because that"—Roz points at the offending and offensive hat—"is social suicide."

"But I'd be wearing it," I tell her, "not you."

With a coaxing smile, Mom says, "How about this, honey? Wear the hat tonight with the lights on, and we'll reassess tomorrow. Before school."

Before school. Appearing on the first week of school in a sunbonnet is not the way I imagined my senior year to start. But what if my face becomes as red and blotchy as my arms? Worse, what if my cheeks blister?

"Fine," I say, and allow my head to become the landing pad for this UFO of a hat, but not before I catch my parents' satisfied looks as I run a dishrag over the flour on the kitchen counter. "Everyone out of the kitchen, please. I just need to prep if you want to eat dinner tomorrow night."

"What's that smell?" asks Roz, wrinkling her nose.

I take a whiff of the flour. Rancid. Light has that decaying effect. I would know.

CHAPTER EIGHT

A few days later on Souper Bowl Sunday, I sweep through the crowded kitchen with an empty platter, semi-worried that I'm going to seriously injure someone with my wide-brimmed hat. It's an actual possibility: Our compact, energy-efficient home is as thick with people as it is with the soupy aroma of cabbage and salmon. As much as I hate to admit it, the hat is effective. I haven't broken out in hives or blisters since I started strategically wearing it at home and driving to and from school. Crisis contained; Abu Dhabi, here I come.

My stomach growls. I've been so on the go since dawn, I haven't had time to do more than sip and nibble in between bouts of wondering whether Josh will actually show up today. To be honest, wondering ratcheted up to worrying after Aminta texted thirty minutes ago, apologizing for no-showing since she had to talk Caresse through some relationship issues. Talk about relationship issues: My armpits dampen at the thought of being alone with Josh.

I set the platter down by the last tray of brownies, already cut into candy bar–size rectangles (easier to eat one-handed while socializing), and air my underarms out. Of course Josh won't make an appearance. He's one of those "I'll see you tomorrow" promise breakers. A *Persephone* illustrator.

While I give the salmon chowder an expert swirl so it doesn't scorch the bottom of the industrial-size pot, Dad sidles next to me, or more accurately, next to the brownies. I watch him carefully even as he tries to divert my attention.

Dad points to the breakfast nook. "Your mom's playing Cupid again. Your poor Auntie Ruth."

"Poor him," I say, casting a cursory glance at Mom, who's in deep discussion with the unsuspecting new neighbor (fresh prospect), a silver-haired man who moved into the condo a couple of doors down. More like Cupid goes bad cop, actually: Are you single, stable, and available? Are you gainfully employed or are you looking for a sugar mama? What is your vision for the future? And do you have a weird Asian-woman fetish? That one, I fully approve, because my auntie and I have a healthy suspicion of men with severe cases of AWF.

Just as I suspected, Dad has edged ever so slightly closer to the brownies. "Yeah," he says conversationally, "she pounced the moment she noticed he wasn't wearing a wedding ring."

"Pouncing is so overrated." I body-block Dad from pouncing on my brownies. With a warning look at him, I replenish the dessert platter, reserving a one-inch corner piece on a tiny plate for myself later. Center eaters are a mystery to me. They can talk all they want about the gooey middle of brownies, but the real action is at the crunchy-chewy edges. One hundred percent.

Meanwhile, Dad casts another furtive glance at Mom before he swipes the largest brownie from my perfect display. "Dad!" I hiss as he wolfs down half in a single bite before I can stop him. "Oh, come on, Dad. What are you? Twelve?"

"What? It's your fault," he says, words muffled, as he lifts his eyebrows innocently.

"I thought you're not supposed to blame anyone in the first throes of a crisis."

"Is this a crisis?"

"It will be if Mom sees you."

"I was just helping you out. Quality control." He hastily wipes his mouth free of crumbs. "Did I get them all?"

"As if I'm going to be your accomplice. Do I look like I want to lose my driving privileges?"

"Let's just call this what it is: an act of service." He considers the remainder of the brownie.

"Dad."

"It looks kind of lonely, doesn't it?"

"Dad."

"Cover for me."

"Dad, don't."

Does he listen to me, the voice of nutritional reason? No. Instead, Dad crams as much of the brownie into his mouth as he can and shoves the remaining corner — a glorified crumb — into my hand. His words are muffled but easy to decipher: "See? I didn't eat it all."

"Hmm." I don't entirely blame him for his complete lack of willpower in the face of delicious. Even if I personally go for salty snacks myself, I pop the leftover morsel into my mouth: not too sweet, with just the right touch of smoke from the bacon and heat from a dash of chipotle. Aminta was going to lose her mind over this batch, which is on my short list for Friday. Hello, sell-out bake sale.

As if I've conjured her, Aminta responds to my emergency text: What do I do if he shows?

Aminta: BE CAREFUL. I REPEAT. BE CAREFUL.

She doesn't have to worry. I am not Gretel, laying out a trail of brownie crumbs so Josh can find his way back to me when I haven't even moved. If he wants me, he'll have to come to me. Then I'll be careful.

"Viola, you've outdone yourself!" Auntie Ruth declares as she strides into the kitchen, black hair swinging behind her. She's holding a mason jar that has approximately zero spoonfuls left of salmon chowder.

"Try the brownies," Dad mutters to Auntie Ruth under his breath like he's doing a drug deal.

"I'm watching my cholesterol," she demurs, "unlike some big brothers around here."

"Just one bite."

"And who's going to eat the rest?" I frown at Dad, whose doctor did, in fact, lecture him about his eating habits: *You do not have the metabolism or clean arteries of an eighteen-year-old anymore.*

"Are you kidding me? These" — she says, succumbing to Big Brother. After a rapturous bite, Auntie Ruth closes her eyes while Silver Fox widens his — "are addictive."

"Fatal," agrees Dad.

"Which is what's going to happen to you if you keep eating them," Mom says, plucking a crumb off Dad's plaid shirt and holding the damning evidence out to him. "You promised to outlive me, remember?" Then she orders me, "Stop enabling him."

"Me? I'm just the cook!"

"Yeah, it's the cook's fault," says Dad, nodding vigorously.

"Hey!" I protest.

"Honestly," Auntie Ruth says, "I'd hire you to cater my company holiday party if you wanted to earn money for — "

My eyebrows raise, and I shake my head slightly at Auntie Ruth: Don't leak our trip details!

Luckily, Mom interrupts with her fact du jour, "A quarter of new restaurants go out of business in their first year. The food industry is too risky as a career path."

"Yeah," I say, not that I need Mom to recite dream-ending information when I'd gone on my own fact-finding mission on fare wages for food service workers. Last summer, I'd done a (grueling) four-week apprenticeship at my favorite bakery, Ginny, reporting in to oven duty at three in the morning six days a week before I headed to my parents' office to fill in for their receptionist, who was on maternity leave. If I didn't love the owner so much, I'd have quit.

Except Lee & Li do not quit.

Ever.

Like me, right now.

"Earn money for what?" Dad asks, looking from Auntie Ruth to me, then back again.

"Hey, how's the hat working?" Auntie Ruth asks me in that rare moment when an entire room falls silent at the same time. I'm conscious of all the people surrounding us, Mom and Dad listening intently, but she ignores everything and everyone as if we were back in the savanna and it was just the two of us in our tent.

Only we're not.

I so do not want to have this conversation in public, but where there's an opening, there's an opportunity. So I seize it. "Totally awesome. So we should still be good to go white-water rafting after graduation."

There's the slightest of hesitation before the three adults eye each other uneasily, guiltily, everyone's muteness damning. As damning as the silence nine months ago when Auntie Ruth invited me to Africa.

...

"You know this is my tradition with my nieces and nephews, and you know this is what Amos wanted since we couldn't have kids. What he stipulated in his will," Auntie Ruth had explained to my parents after I opened the birthday gift I'd been hoping to receive: a book set in the exact spot in the world where she wanted to take me, the same way she'd announced the Seventeenth Birthday Adventure to each of her nephews. "A work-and-play trip on the eve of their adulthood. So first, Ghana for a one-week internship, then Tanzania for a fully supported safari."

"Yes, of course, and it is so generous of Amos and you," said Mom, smoothing her hand over Yaa Gyasi's *Homegoing* before turning it facedown on our kitchen table. "But you took your nephews to places like Ireland and . . ."

"Switzerland," prompted Auntie Ruth with a fortifying sip of her after-dinner coffee.

"Not exactly places known for danger," said Dad.

"Ghana and Tanzania are probably safer than some places in the US," I pointed out, not that my parents acknowledged my argument.

Instead, Mom nudged the book to the side and asked, "What happened to Japan?"

"My friend from Ghana called," Auntie Ruth had shot back. "It's not every day that things could change because of a documentary."

"Don't you want me to witness history?" I asked, inserting myself more forcefully into this conversation, knowing better than to ask the question I really want: *Don't you want me to seek the truth?* This was, after all, my secret ambition since fifth grade, when I wrote a letter to the editor of *The Seattle Times* after former congresswoman Gabrielle Giffords was shot in the head. The editor actually called me before publishing my letter about rational gun control and told me that I should consider being a journalist. That prospect so horrified my parents that after instructing me on the death rates of journalists, they instituted my internships at their office: *See, honey? You can seek the truth safely behind a desk. Isn't it fun making an impact?*

"We do. Absolutely," Dad said with a reassuring clasp of my hand. "It's a great opportunity."

Little ripples of warning tripped down my spine. Our family vacations are vacuum-sealed in Disney, all calibrated adventure and controlled risk. Just as I knew, my parents launched on the classic tag-team approach to thwart a bad idea.

...

THE REDIRECT IN 3 EASY STEPS

Step 1: Support the general idea. "We think it's great that you want to end human trafficking," Dad said, looking first at Auntie Ruth, then me. "It's one of our top priorities this year at Lee & Li, too."

Step 2: Deny the specific implementation. "And while the trip to Africa sounds phenomenal," added Mom, "we were thinking you should be open to other locales."

Step 3: Redirect to a more palatable outcome. "Yes, like research the trafficking problem for us this summer. And then, if Auntie Ruth really wants to support her friend this year, you can join her on another trip next summer," said Dad, nodding his head at me, willing me to change my mind on my own.

...

Just then, I had a flash of inspiration. "You know, I could write about this in my college essay. It's a crisis, it's a humanitarian problem, and it's a solution. Georgetown would love this."

Georgetown: the magic key to unlocking my parents' objections. My dad's dream school that he wasn't able to attend. Executing on their plan for me to take over Lee & Li one day meant Georgetown — double majoring in their top political science and business programs, a match made in crisis-management heaven. With an acceptance rate of near-impossible, a killer essay was critical. We all knew it.

Dad leaned forward as if this was a boardroom table, not our kitchen one. "Ebola."

I said, "Not in Tanzania. Or Ghana."

"Not to mention terrorists."

"Dad, not in Tanzania. Or Ghana."

"Malaria."

"I'll take meds."

"I'll make sure she does," promised Auntie Ruth.

"Maybe we should consider this," Mom said slowly. "Georgetown."

But Dad didn't say a word.

"History won't repeat itself, Mick," Auntie Ruth whispered.

There was a collective intake of breath around the kitchen table. Mom placed her hand on top of Dad's. No one ever so much as refers to the freak accident that killed my grandparents on their first vacation together since their honeymoon. Dad was seventeen, and Auntie Ruth was just seven. Their uncle may have taken them in afterward, but even I can see how Dad treats Auntie Ruth like she's his kid, not his kid sister.

So I knew what it must have cost Dad to say, "They went away and they never came back."

"I know," Auntie Ruth answered quietly.

"I can't protect you much when you're that far. Accidents happen."

"I know."

"Buses career off cliffs."

"Mick. I know." After a long silence that was loud with unspoken history, Auntie Ruth finally reached out to my Dad's other hand and said, "You have to trust me."

"I trust you. It's life I don't trust."

Auntie Ruth promised, "I'll have everything under control."

Dad finally nodded, staring intently at Auntie Ruth as if holding her to a long-ago vow: We will stay safe no matter what.

...

As it turns out, some things — sun, skin, your heart, the future — simply cannot and will not be controlled.

Case in point: Auntie Ruth has now ditched our entire secret travel list, specifically curated to get me ready to be a foreign correspondent who's comfortable in any condition. She is actually joining the side of the home-bodies, who consider risk-taking to be riding California Screamin' at Disneyland. She actually sounds like my parents when she interrupts my memories now and delivers the deathblow to the white-water rafting trip: "Traveling could be dangerous for you now. There's really no harm in waiting."

Case in point: The football game kicks off and draws everyone into our living room, where they are all scrunched on our sofa, perched on the arms, cross-legged on the ground. The Seahawks must be off to a rough start because I hear groans. The soundtrack of my life right now.

Case in point: Josh saunters into the kitchen, where I'm tidying up. Thor is here? The guy actually showed up? He might be wearing an "I love Pluto" T-shirt today, but he looks even more dangerously Nordic than I remembered: blond hair, windswept like he's been standing at the prow of a warship. Like any good Viking exploring new territories to conquer, he spies me at once at the stove top.

Steal me away, Viking Boy.

"You look great," he says, then flushes, shoving his hands into his pockets. "I mean, better."

"I'll take great." Especially when I'm wearing a monstrosity of a hat.

He blushes even more. Well, what do you know? There's a certain appeal to a red-flushed face.

"So what's good?" Josh asks, aiming his attention to the stockpots like he's mesmerized by so much soup. He gives one of the pots a stir, which flexes his (well-defined) biceps. "I mean, great?"

You. Me. Everything. Hello. I ladle him a jar of chowder and say, "Come with me."

CHAPTER NINE

Today is the perfect rule-breaking day for a rule-abiding girl.

"Entrez vous," I tell Josh, opening the door to my bedroom and saying *au revoir* to my parents' No Boys Allowed dictum.

What I hadn't counted on was for Josh to hang back uneasily outside my bedroom like this is a hotbed of danger. Hot bed, the precise reason why my parents instituted the no-boy rule. I blush, immobilized with a double dose of awkwardness and uncertainty.

Josh asks, "You sure this is okay?"

"Pretty much." (Yeah, I can pretty much hear my parents' lecture.)

Two days before my thirteenth birthday, Mom's best friend, Jannie, a pediatrician, called, weeping and probably breaking all kinds of confidentiality laws, but she was having a crisis and Mom was the one to SOS. As it turned out, Jannie had treated a ten-year-old girl who was six months pregnant. I can't even imagine. Apparently, neither could my parents. A couple of hours later, both of them pale, had issued yet another Travel Advisory: this time barring male visitors to my bedroom.

Josh shrugs, still staying on his side of the doorway. "Your parents don't seem like the boys-welcome type."

"And you would know from your vast experience?"

"Pretty much."

At that, I should throw him out because a) that was confirmation that he was a guy who had girls on a strict and steady rotation, and b) I was done with being a magnet for those types of guys. Instead, I widen the door.

Josh takes one step inside, and my bedroom suddenly shrinks. My palms sweat. Ridiculous, I know. Even more ridiculous, I'm too self-conscious to wipe them on my jeans. It's not hard to imagine Mom barging in here with her finely tuned maternal radar able to detect the smallest hint of teen boy testosterone. Or more accurately, a surge of teen girl estrogen as I picture him kissing me, me winding around him.

Retreat to the living room is prudent.

All thoughts of safety in numbers vanish, though, when I notice my bedroom is dark. Suspiciously, preternaturally, parentally dark. I frown at the blinds, which have been lowered all the way down. The blinds I had opened partway after cooking this morning to allow the suggestion of natural light into my room because some of us actually love the sun. So while Josh spoons chowder into his mouth, I yank the blinds up. The late-afternoon sun saturates my room in yellow-gold. Nope, my life isn't going to change. Not one iota, not when my skin is back to normal. For good measure, I toss my hat onto my bed and feel both light-headed and lighthearted.

"You made this?" Josh asks, his words muddied with soup. Talking with your mouth full of my cooking is something I interpret as a compliment.

"Thank you," I say. "But wait until you try my Mongolian sheepshead soup."

"Sheeps? Head?" He lowers his spoon cautiously, then laughs. "LA Rams. Got it. That's good. But this . . ."

"Chowder. You're safe."

Josh looks visibly relieved and declares, "Even better than your baos."

"You ate one?"

"Maybe more than one."

"Three?" When he says nothing, I find myself laughing, too, before guessing, "Four? Five? No, not five. Five? Really?"

"I'm going to have to swim extra laps tomorrow." He digs into his back pocket and holds out a wad of cash. "Should be seventy-five bucks. Sorry, it's not what you would have made."

"Are you kidding? I didn't think you'd sell any of them, and this is way more than those *Firefly* guys would have spent," I tell him, and set the cash on my desk. "Really. Thanks! Aminta's going to be so happy. Come on, have a seat."

Josh drops to the floor with his back against my bed, which makes me feel like a self-conscious Goldilocks, not knowing where to place myself: across from him (too patty cake, patty cake). My desk chair (too aloof). Next to him (just right).

"How do you know Aminta?" he asks.

"Best friends since second grade," I tell him. Horrific, but when I lower myself, I misjudge, our hips graze, way, way too close for comfort. I scoot away while he stretches his (long) legs out and crosses them at the ankles, lounging back like he's at some sunny, exotic beach locale, used to girls pressing themselves up against him.

"We were in the same comic class," he says while scraping the jar for the last bit of chowder.

"I know. She loved that class," I tell him. I wriggle a little farther from him, now putting too much distance between us, but I can't possibly adjust again.

"I did, too. My parents forced my brother and me to take it one summer," Josh says as he places the empty jar by his hip. "And we got so into it that we signed up for another class . . ."

I want to ask him about his twin, but know I'd be prying. He clears his throat. "Hey, your foot's in the sun."

"I'm wearing socks. And Converse. My toes are safe."

"Maybe you should move over." Which he does to make more room for me, then angles me a look that is a little uncertain before it vanishes. "So I take it you didn't read *Persephone*?"

"Uhhh . . ." Guiltily, I remember tossing the comic in the trash bin under my desk because I honestly didn't think I'd see him again. Now I panic that he'll spot it in there, but he'd need Superman's X-ray vision to do that.

"It's okay. It's just weird that she's photosensitive, too."

"What are the chances?"

"Yeah, weird, right? She escapes from Planet X to Earth. Her skin's not used to being this close to the sun."

"So she's a refugee?"

Josh looks at me, surprised. "Yeah, I guess she is."

"In a bikini? What happened to make her need to escape wearing only that?"

"I never thought about that . . ."

I raise my eyebrows.

Josh lifts his hands into the air and says, "Neanderthal. Guilty as charged."

"Noted," I say. "So what could have happened to her planet?"

"Geopolitical turmoil. None of the other planets want to take her people."

"Because a faction is extremist and has been doing all these terrorist acts. So the rest of the universe thinks that all of her people are dangerous, even the babies in refugee camps."

He looks at me, impressed. "That's really good."

I shrug. "I wrote about the Syrian refugee crisis for one of our bake sales."

"So maybe she's on a recon mission to Earth to see if it's a friendly environment for her people. And then the sun happens."

"Like, what?"

Josh drums his fingers on the floor. "I haven't nailed down the science yet. But I do know that the sun changes her life."

"Well, this isn't going to change mine," I tell him, myself, my parents' voices in my head, and most of all, my body. The prickling on my arm now is just my hyperactive imagination, right? I tilt my arm subtly: normal. The triangle of light from the window is a good foot away from me. "I'm not going to let it."

"But life happens," he argues. "We think we have control over everything, only we don't. At all."

"But we do. Like, I'm still going to travel, no matter what."

"To Disney?" A smile plays on his lips.

How did he know? Then I remember all the photos of just me, then Roz and me after she was born, hanging up in the hall. Where some other kids have their childhood marked out year after year with their ceremonial photo with Santa, ours are with Mickey and Minnie. Not every year, but practically, because Mom's cousin happens to get free passes since he works at Disney.

"Left to my parents, all our vacations would be in the Happiest Place on Earth," I tell him now.

"I love Disneyland."

"Yeah, me, too, but it's a big world after all, and I want to see it all."

"And report it all?"

I nod, surprised that he understands.

"Could you," he asks, "if you're photosensitive, though?"

"Yes, for sure. Have hat, will travel." To convince myself, I slide my daily planner off the nightstand and flip to the adventure list that Auntie Ruth and I started on our flight home from Arusha. "I mean, how could I not go to—oh, I don't know"—I pick the most outlandish adventure on the list—"Naadam, the Mongolian Horse Festival?"

"Do you ride horses?"

"No." I blush, wishing now that I'd left the blinds down.

"Then . . ."

"Why? Well, we're part Mongolian. Definitely don't ever get my dad started on the whole descended from Genghis Khan thing."

"Genghis Khan, ruthless conqueror?"

"Yup, him." We trade knowing smiles, smiles that say, *I get what you're talking about* and *Parents!* Smiles that say, *We're on the same side.* "Anyway, my aunt thought it would be cool to see our ancestral competitions. Up to a thousand riders. Jockeys who are all kids. And journalists have to be able to fit in anywhere, even yurts, drinking yak milk."

"Yak milk."

I flush. "Yeah. I want to blend in wherever I go."

"And your parents would let you go?"

"My parents would lock me up if they knew I wanted to go."

"What else is on your list?" Josh asks, but he doesn't reach for my planner or even crane his neck to read what I wrote, which I appreciate.

"What's on yours?" I counter.

"Chile."

"You're joking, right?" Without thinking, I place my hand on his biceps — his muscular, buff, defined biceps that could be a body double for the Incredible Hulk. What the heck am I doing? I yank my hand back and run my fingers through my hair as if that was what I meant to do all along. How muscles could possibly get that big (and cut) would demand supernatural, otherworldly, and freakish comic book conditions, like a spider bite or accidental radiation poisoning.

"No. Why? Is it on yours?"

No one aside from Auntie Ruth knows about this list. Aminta is so obsessed with college applications that adventure and anything that remotely hints of senior spring are foreign objects that her body is rejecting to survive.

But now, I set my planner on the floor, a bridge in the space between us.

...

ADVENTURE LIST

1. Snake River: White-water rafting.

2. Chile: Trail running in Patagonia.

3. Mongolia: Naadam and Sunrise to Sunset 42-km run.

4. Paris: Catacombs.

5. Jordan: Bedouin Trail to Petra.

6. Finland: Cross-country ski border-to-border.

7. Botswana: Everything.

...

"Chile!" says Josh, looking at me, astonished. "You know, there's supposed to be epic stargazing there."

"And trail running."

"And a dark sky reserve."

The term alone intrigues me. "Dark sky reserve?"

"Yeah, Atacama Desert. There are a couple of dark sky parks around the world, including Utah. Protected land without light pollution. So the stargazing is incredible. I thought that'd be a cool setting for *Persephone*."

"Maybe where she looks up and literally gets lost in the stars, homesick."

"Yeah." Again with the admiring look. I wonder how many girls have fallen for that very expression. He says, "That's good."

Oh, honey, I haven't even gotten started. Neither, apparently, has he. "Or," he says, tapping the adventure list, "maybe that's where she can read the stars like a map."

"Or a message! Like, turning the horoscope readings into real news from her world."

"So when are you going?" he asks.

"Oh, that." My tone goes flat, and I tuck my knees up to my chest.

"Canceled?"

"My parents thought it would be 'imprudent' to go anywhere until we know more. But, come on, the Idaho rafting trip is nine whole months away and it's supposed to get me ready for the hardest conditions. I sometimes feel like everything for them is a potential forest fire. Stamp out every little spark of fun."

"Sometimes parents are right," he says softly.

That is the last admission I'd expect to hear. I smile at him like he's joking. "Seriously?"

But what's serious is Josh's expression. "Sometimes, yeah."

"But sometimes not . . ." Then I tell him about how once—just once—I had told my parents I actually wanted to be a reporter. That mistake happened right after my high school had brought in Lisa Ling and Lara Setrakian, both journalists who got started not all that much older than us, to talk about facts and the media during my frosh year. That was the confession that launched a thousand lectures just like the one I received in fifth grade: Do you know how dangerous it is to be a journalist these days? Did you know that eight hundred—eight hundred!—journalists have been killed in the line of duty over this last decade alone? Did you know that only eight percent of the cases have ever been solved? Did you not hear what the terrorists did to Daniel Pearl? Heavens no, let others do that dangerous job of being the world's truth-tellers in conflict zones. "So, no, parents don't always get it right. Some things are worth the risk."

"Maybe they have a point. I never thought about it, but journalism does sound dangerous."

"Truth is dangerous."

With a teasing half grin, one that must have been practiced on hordes of girls before me, he taps adventure number six. "Then why cross-country skiing?"

"Why not?"

"River Tam would totally bomb downhill."

"Heli-ski," I correct him.

"True."

"But in the world according to my parents, downhill is too dangerous," I say, then admit, "plus, it really is a little scary. I went once when I was about four, and they thought my lower center of gravity would make it safer. For once, they were wrong."

"Powder pigs?"

"Powder pigs! You were in the class, too?"

"A rite of passage."

"If a rite of passage includes a full face-plant." I mime with my hand, holding it upright and then — timber! — crashing down. "When I got up, my goggles were totally covered in snow, and I thought I was blind. Literally. I started screaming, 'I can't see! I can't see!'"

Instead of mocking me or my parents for playing it safe, Josh says, "That's so cute."

I blush and wish that the blinds concealed the evidence that he and his words affected me. "So, you ski?"

"We used to," he says, then quickly asks me, "so you cross-country instead now?"

"We go up to the Nordic Center once or twice a month in the winter. Just for a couple of hours. Nothing serious. Hot chocolate is always involved. But I love it! Cross-country skiing is pretty much winter training for trail running."

"But Finland sounds serious. Border-to-border."

"It is serious." The skin on my arms breaks into a suspicious prickle. I spot-check them again: nothing. So I continue, "We were on a flight home from Los Angeles, I forget when, and I sat next to a guy who used to be on the US national cross-country team who told me about this event every March and how it's the old ladies who pass everyone on the trails by day, then drink them under the table all night."

He laughs, just as I hoped he would. The patch of sunlight has snuck up on us while we were talking. So I have to move closer to Josh. Oh, too bad.

"But for me, there's nothing" — I gesture widely — "like hiking in the winter with all the massive evergreen trees and the rivers and creeks frosted with snow. The best parts are the frozen waterfalls. You think they're iced all the way through, except you can see and hear the water still running underneath."

He's staring at me, watching me so intently that I shrug. "Is that stupid?"

"Not even close. Where do you go?"

"Franklin Falls."

"I want to see them."

"Yeah, for sure, this winter," I promise. Hang on, I didn't just ask Josh out, did I?

"Yeah?"

I swear, Josh's voice is a shade husky, as if I did just that. Our eyes meet, mine startled, his sultry. His lower to my lips, mine follow to his. But this is Thor, and I am so far from Persephone, with my post-Darren frostbitten heart that kind of likes its shell of ice. I clear my throat with a professional: "So." Which breaks the spell and only goes to show how miraculous it is that our species has survived.

By the time I look back at Josh, he's studying my list again.

"Paris, I get," Josh says. "But what are catacombs?"

"Underground cemeteries in Paris. They've got something like six million bodies under there. Skeletons. Technically, they're not buried. More like stacked."

"And you want to see them because . . . ?"

"Because a journalist needs to be brave enough to face anything, even six million skeletons. If I can't do that, how would I ever be able to go to war-torn places and confront what's going on without running from the story? And if I don't report it, who will?" I stop, shocked with myself, because I have never breathed a word of my plan to anyone besides Aminta and Auntie Ruth.

"So these are training exercises."

I nod.

"Aren't you scared?"

"Well, yeah! But someone's got to report the truth. So I need to be comfortable traveling anywhere, seeing anything, if I'm supposed to get a story and report what's really happening around the world, no matter what. I can't look away. I can't even flinch. And that's hard and scary to do because, well, all I've ever been to, really, is Disney until this last summer with Auntie Ruth. She took me to Africa — Ghana — where one of her friends was making a documentary on child trafficking. And Tanzania, too."

"Didn't that make you nervous?" asks Josh.

"Yeah, but I was with Auntie Ruth." I'm suddenly aware of the itchiness of my arms, and I need to lighten the conversation. "And then there's yak milk. Number Three."

"Seriously?"

"Fermented yak milk, actually. The stuff of my people. Well, half my people. I figure, if I can learn to drink what the Mongolians drink, I'll be able to subsist anywhere I travel."

"I can see that I need to do a lot more traveling and toughening my stomach and a ton more research," Josh says.

Research. If I had one superpower, it's research. After all, that was my main job during my Lee & Li internships. Aside from sitting at the front desk, manning calls, I would hunt down facts that my parents and their associates needed: every single city with a reported case of the Zika virus. Number of people around the world forcibly removed from their homes in conflict zones. Areas with the highest incidence of health centers closing because of strife.

Before I even know what I'm saying, I offer, "I could help. Research."

"Yeah?"

Yeah, what the heck am I thinking? My mouth has mounted a coup to replace my brain as the center of my nervous system. I am literally all jittery, prickly nerves at the way Josh is grinning, not a single hint of predatory player. His warm gaze is my undoing; the lowering of my eyes to his lips is his.

I lean closer to him and promise, "Yeah."

He seals that promise with a kiss so soft, it makes me demand another. And another. My mouth opens. Even if the tiny speck of my (poor) survival instinct reminds me, ever so faintly, that Josh can seriously kiss because he's gotten serious practice, when he deepens the kiss, I moan. He pulls away, and I'm about to protest until I finally open my eyes and see my hands on his shoulders and spot the reason my skin was prickling: I'm pebbled with hives. How the heck could this have happened? The sun didn't even graze my skin.

"What?" he asks.

I have never been more happy to hear Roz bellow, "Viola!" My relief doesn't diminish when she yells, "Mom wants to know if you're wearing your hat."

He rises easily with the empty mason jar in one hand and passes me my hat just in time before Roz barges in. Her mouth drops open when she sees the Y chromosomes in my room. Josh nods at her, then smiles at me. "I'll text you tonight."

Quickly, I plunk the hat back on my head. Roz's eyes narrow, the little extortionist. I wonder what she'll demand for keeping this a secret.

The hat is no protection, after all. I burn.

A LITTLE LIGHT READING

RESEARCH & RUMINATIONS FOR JOSH TAYLOR

1. The colors we see are actually sunlight reflecting off objects. (So it's possible that Persephone has never seen the colors that we have on Earth.)

2. Colors are different wavelengths on the electromagnetic spectrum. (Wouldn't it be cool if Persephone could see colors unknown to humans?)

3. "Visible light" refers to the rainbow of colors we see. (You know: red, orange, yellow, green, blue, violet.)

4. Ultraviolet (UV) rays are the ones that go beyond the violet rays that we humans can see. (Yes, there are colors that humans can't detect!)

5. Some animals can see UV light. Take reindeer: Their ability to detect UV light enables them to spot the white polar bears hunting them. (So maybe Persephone has an epic battle in the snow.)

6. Some kids and teens can actually see UV light. (What?!)

7. UV light includes UVA rays (A is for Aging) and UVB rays (B is for Burning). (Persephone could learn about UVA rays when she suddenly ages in Earth's atmosphere.)

8. When you suntan, freckle, or sunburn, it means you've spent too much time exposed to UV rays. (Hence: Superheroes need sunscreen, too.)

9. Some animals produce their own light. See: biolumi-nescence. (If Persephone and her people live on the farthest planet of our galaxy, then maybe they've evolved to create their own light?)

CHAPTER TEN

By ten that night, there is no trace of our Souper Bowl Sunday: not our friends, not our family, and certainly not any Joshes. I know it's early, but I should know better than to hope that he's going to text me tonight, just the way he said he would. Only a complete idiot would still do a quick hour (or two) of research for him, just the way I said I would. What's pathetic, though, is how I keep glancing at my phone now when my credible source (Aminta) has already confirmed that I shouldn't hold my breath for a response from Josh.

> Aminta: *Did I or did I not warn you about him?*
> Aminta: *He changes girls the way Caresse changes outfits.*
> Aminta: *Let's talk about something really important: sleepover at my place after the bake sale?*

She's right, of course. Josh will probably go as abruptly dark as Darren had. For months, Darren the soccer guy multitexted me all day, every day. Then came the supermassive black hole of not one more peep. Ever.

A RECIPE FOR DISASTER

Serves: 1

Ingredients
- 1 teen boy with a well-ripened ego
- 1 rogue journalist with a malfunctioning BS detector
- 1 ex-girlfriend simmering on the back burner

Directions

- Heat the summer day to a hot, humid, and sultry eighty-nine degrees. Head to Tiger Mountain for a fast run. Wear a skimpy tank top, branded with Liberty Prep.
- Add the entire Liberty men's soccer team, who are running, too. While these guys may hit the flat streets near school, few have trained on rocky, dirt-packed, uphill switchbacks in the heat. You have.
- Race past each and every one of those huffing and puffing soccer players, including said teen boy with the (shall we say) healthy ego.
- Swig your water bottle at the top of the mountain, as the soccer team (finally) makes it to the summit.
- Ignore the now shirtless teen boy with the (shall we say) robust ego, who swaggers toward you, all "Wait, you go to Liberty, too?" Now would be a good time to retort that you've been in the same school with him since ninth grade. You don't.
- At this point, your BS detector should be on high. However: The siren call of six-pack abs is loud and strong. Perhaps you should remember the siren's job is to lure sailors to their death. You do not listen.
- Add his text to you that night. And even more texts and texts and texts. Whisk in your own.
- Wait two full days before he responds. Stir back in his text, text, texting you, multiple times a day. Do not overmix. Yet you speed text, text, text him right back.
- A few days later of intense texting, he reveals that he's never been able to talk with a girl this way. You melt faster than ice on a scorcher of a day. Even faster, you type the fateful words: "Me, too." Immediately, he sends an exploratory "hey, girl, what're you up to now?" Do not say, "Nothing." You say, "Nothing." He invites you over. You drive to his house, hook up, and go farther

than you ever have in the history of you, and drive back alone. There is no text asking if you made it home safe. No text saying he can't wait to see you tomorrow. No text at all. You ignore the slight sense of hurt.

- Wait three whole days for more Nothing.
- Set BS detector to extremely high.
- Just when you near the full boiling point of anxiety and rereading your texts to see if you had said something wrong, he pings you, not one little reference to his days of silence. Instead, he is funny and charming about a whole bunch of nothing. Before you know it, you are doing a whole bunch of something with him in the backseat of his car.
- Wait two whole days before his texting resumes.
- Continue cycle for the entire summer and into the school year.
- Cook's Note: All of his "hey, we should go running," "hey, we should grab some dinner," "hey, we should hang out" rarely turns to reality — aka a REAL date. Instead, those suggestions vaporize like mist in the desert whenever you try to nail down basic details, such as when and where. Do not overheat. But you do. Nothing stops you from hooking up with him in the rare times you see him.
- Pulverize your own self-esteem.
- To make the frosting on this sad, sad upside-down cake: Combine teen boy with superhuman ego with ex-girlfriend who's been on simmer. Bring them to a roiling boil in front of you and the rest of the school in the middle of the hallway.
- Without delay, lower temperature down to arctic cold. Listen. That is the sound of your heart cracking.

...

The next morning, there is still Nothing from Josh.

CHAPTER ELEVEN

I'll research for you. I groan the next morning in the living room. The embarrassing memory of those words is nothing compared to the memory of our kiss. I kissed another player. Why? Why? No, even worse, I spent hours of my own time researching for him.

Done obsessing about him, I shut off my phone and spot one lone cup from yesterday's Souper Bowl Sunday, used and forgotten on the mantel. Snatching it, I march the cup into the kitchen, where my parents are putting away the dry platters. Dad mentions to Mom, "Hey, your sister emailed about Viola's graduation again."

Mom breathes out, irked as usual by this phantom aunt I've rarely seen, the only person who elicits that impatient, verging on hostile sigh. It's an eye roll set to sound. I echo that annoyed sigh now, as I plunk the cup hard next to the sink. My parents startle at the same time, then Mom asks, "Where's your hat?"

"Baseball caps are in the hat family," I tell her, touching the brim.

"Wait! That's mine," Roz says as soon as she looks up from the book of Robert Frost poems that she was supposed to have read over the summer. She scowls, holds out her hand, and wriggles her fingers expectantly. "Did you go in my room?"

"Yeah, it was on your floor next to my *Firefly* vest," I tell her.

"Give it back!"

"Princess, let her wear it now," Dad says.

"But it's special. The Princeton coach—"

"Fine." I barely swipe the cap off my head before she grabs it out of my hand. Of course she does. Roz sets it down, not on her head but next to my dessert plate that, once upon a time, had housed the corner piece of brownie,

72

reserved for me. Empty, of course. What's mine is Roz's, what's hers is never mine, house rules, always has been, always will be.

I ask, more rhetorically than anything, "Where's my brownie? She ate my brownie."

"There's more," Mom says, gesturing to the leftovers, all of them center pieces. It may just be a brownie, but the injustice burns.

Dad leans against the sink and says casually, "So, Viola, honey, we were thinking."

A trickle of dread skitters down my spine at those famous last words: "We were thinking." Those words tip me off that they have a proposal, no veto allowed. Like a meerkat sensing danger, too, Roz jerks her head up from her book. Her eyebrows raise like twin caution flags as she meets my eyes.

Brownie wars forgotten, we are both remembering the infamous "we were thinking" of years past.

...

WE WERE THINKING: CHRISTMAS EDITION

Mom: *We were thinking that since we represent several clean energy companies, we should support a more ecological Earth.*
Dad: *So we were thinking that we won't chop down a Christmas tree this year.*
Translation: *Not chopping down a Christmas tree in the Mount Baker–Snoqualmie National Forest (sanctioned with a tree-cutting permit) meant rosemary plants that went bald indoors, then an olive tree that lost the war with the heater,*

*followed by a beady-eyed, partridge-like bird on
a pear tree that dropped all its leaves (scared to
death, like the rest of us). Our garden outside has
become the burial ground of Christmases past.*

...

WE WERE THINKING:
PARIAH EDITION

"We were thinking that since your skin reacted so quickly to the light again,"
Dad continues as he hands Mom the newly scrubbed cup to dry.

> Mom: *When you weren't wearing your hat yester-
> day. And had your blinds up.*
> Dad: *At this early stage, it's best if we play it safe
> with your condition.*
> Mom: *So we were thinking that it would be wise
> for you to carry an umbrella at school tomorrow
> just in case.*
> Dad: *Better safe than sorry, right?*

...

Flushed as if she's the one who's hypersensitive to the sun, Roz slams her
poetry book shut and huffs, "No way."

"You'll get used to carrying an umbrella. Everyone will after the first day.
You might even start a trend," Dad says as if he, Mr. Khaki Pants, somehow
has become a street-fashion trend spotter.

Roz scoffs; I second that scoff.

"Doesn't that seem a little extreme?" I ask, digging hard in my mental closet
of random but useful scientific facts my parents can't contest or debate.

Victory! "I mean, don't you think we should have a control case to test what my skin can tolerate?"

My parents may exchange an impressed look, but as it turns out, being impressed is cheap. Mom says, "You make a great point, honey, but you've already had a control case. Yesterday afternoon. In your bedroom when you took off your hat and opened the blinds. You broke out in hives."

"But—" Barely in time, I cut off my protest: *But I haven't been wearing my big hat at school and I've been fine.* Instead, I cast around for another mutually palatable solution or, heck, one that wasn't so personally humiliating. "How about heavy-duty sunscreen? SPF 200?"

"SPF only goes up to 100," corrects Mom.

"And only protects against UVB rays, not the UVA ones that you seem to be sensitive to," says Dad.

If my parents can help a world food organization revive itself after a corruption scandal, I should have known they would have complete command over the ins and outs of my (still undiagnosed) condition better than I do. Even so, it rankles. My skin literally heats up. Clearly, I've developed a severe case of parental sensitivity, overexposure causing irritation, loss of temper, and in some cases, blood-red rage.

"We have no idea what kind of light bulbs you have in school," Dad says reasonably even as he aims an accusatory finger at the overhead lights. "They could be fluorescent."

"We should email Dr. Luthra," Mom says to Dad, who nods eagerly as if it's perfectly acceptable to ask the head of Liberty Prep on Labor Day (a public holiday that entails no labor) to specify the type of light bulb installed at school.

"An email, perfect idea. Documentation is everything," Dad agrees.

"Wait. Document what?" I ask.

"Document our first official ask of the school to prepare for your condition," says Mom as if that's logical.

From working summer afternoons at Lee & Li since I was twelve, coupled with osmosis from living with my parents my whole life, I know how crises start. Just one unthinking comment on anyone's part—principal to teachers, teachers to my classmates—and boom! Rumor. As everyone learns in middle school, rumor is the speedskater of information, fast, efficient, and brutal. Then there is Roz, who doesn't look like she is in much of a secret-keeping mood when she just ups and leaves—not my problem!—without putting her brownie plate in the sink.

"We don't even know what my condition is yet," I protest, automatically cleaning up after Roz. I sweep her crumbs onto the plate and rinse it in the sink.

"Which reminds me. Your phototest is on Friday afternoon," Mom tells me.

"But that's the bake sale."

"You're selling in the morning before school and at lunch, right?" Dad confirms. When I nod, he says, "Well, then, the club members can handle the afternoon."

"Plus, it's going to be sunny on Friday. The UV Index is supposed to be six. High risk, honey," Mom says knowledgably like she's become a meteorologist. "We don't want to take any chances."

There's no hope of winning against Mom and Dad. So I place everyone's breakfast plates in the dishwasher and bargain for whatever freedom I can get. "How about I just wear an even bigger hat at school? Table the umbrella for now." Even if I cringe at that concession—was an even more gargantuan hat possible?—it's way more preferable to looking like a sunny-day, umbrella-wielding Mary Poppins inside every class. "Maybe that'll be enough."

"Great plan," says Dad as if this is my idea.

Mom's eyes brighten, which should have prepared me for the hat the size of Starship *Enterprise* that she pulls out from under the breakfast nook table. "Ta-da!"

I have been crisis managed.

CHAPTER TWELVE

No one needs to remind me that there are a billion worse fates—like battling cancer, losing all my hair from chemo and radiation, and needing a hat to keep warm. After watching a child trafficking case in a stifling courtroom in Accra, after driving by some of the ramshackle shelters in Arusha, it's not lost on me that I have a roof over my head to hide me from the sun. I had the luxury of traveling to Tanzania and Ghana with my aunt. My parents have the means to keep me stocked in hats. And umbrellas.

Yet.

Umbrellas.

By Monday night, rage—hot, white, and pure—escalates to UV Index 11+, the most extreme level. I am the sun in all its full, searing, dangerous glory. The unfairness of everything burns in me and through me and over me. There I was, helping Auntie Ruth support her friend in the name of justice, and I might have gotten sick from taking meds that were prescribed to keep me safe and healthy.

I need to parse the last day and a half of my life. So close to midnight, I text Aminta: *SOS. Parents gone crazy.*

More accurately: Girl gone crazy.

For ten minutes, I perch on the edge of my bed, knees bouncing up and down, staring at my screen, willing her to answer.

Anything, anything.

Nothing.

I resort to calling Aminta.

And go straight to voice mail.

My best friend isn't hanging out with Caresse without me again, is she?

What if my stay-out-of-the-sun existence turned into a stay-away-from-me one because I'm no longer fun?

My heart is heaving. Images of impending doom at school tomorrow fill my head. The worst one: I'll be all alone to deal with everyone's stares and snickers, no Aminta in sight. I glare at my own personal canopy, the new sun hat, spread across the foot of my bed. I need something, anything, to take my mind off tomorrow — cooking is outside the realm of possibility since I don't want to be in the vicinity of my crisis-controlling parents, and it would take a miracle for my parents to allow me to go for a run outside, much less hit a trail.

Against all odds, I drift over to my desk, where my Mac awaits my next query. My college essay is already printed and ready to go to school with me tomorrow. The college counselors all "strongly recommended" that seniors return from summer break with good "working ideas." I have a good, working draft, focal point: NYU Abu Dhabi. Except now I've discovered that my dream campus is parked in the desert with roughly 3,462 hours of sunshine a year compared to Seattle's measly 2,044 hours. I yank my hands off the keyboard. (Research is so much more fun when the facts you dig up don't singe you.)

Sighing, I reach up to the shelf for my favorite Tamora Pierce novel, cover lost years ago. That's a world I can get lost in. But *Persephone from Planet X* winks up at me from the trash can, her twin assets gleaming in the dim light. Seriously, this comic is worse than an STD, following me around forever.

Desperate for distraction, I actually pluck the comic out of the bin. My room is too dark to read so I turn on my lamp, then hold still. Was natural light through windows or artificial light from a lamp less dangerous? What if my rash and hives are the least of my worries, and the light bulb triggers an even worse response? I scoot the lamp to the far edge on the desk, then tuck myself into the extreme-most corner of my bed, where the light won't graze me.

Page one of *Persephone* gives me the perfect place to direct my anger.

Meet Persephone, an intergalactic Amazon from the farthest planet in our universe, the so-called Planet X, never mind there are only eight planets in our solar system. I flip another page. So the warrior princess (how many times have we seen that trope?) leaves her besieged planet ruled by a power-hungry dictator who denies the oncoming Ice Age. She speeds light-hours to Earth to find a home for her people and finds herself battling . . . vampires.

I snicker.

Who wouldn't be a little irritated by the time they reach page five? And no, my annoyance has nothing to do with the fact that the author didn't text me the way he said he would. Nothing to do with how this neglect feels so very love 'em and drop 'em like Darren.

What gets to me is how so very wrong — anatomically and astronomically — Josh is about all things photosensitivity. I mean, seriously, Persephone's kryptonite is the sun. Okay, that I buy since she's from the farthest reach in our galaxy. But she's walking around, fighting vampires in broad daylight in her teeny tiny, itsy-bitsy almost-bikini? Right. Talk about dropping straight into a guy's fantasyland.

My critique is far, far more than a single text could ever express. I think about all the extra work my parents do for their clients, telling each other, *Well, this is for clean water. Well, this will help girls get educated in Afghanistan. Well, this will deliver books to kids in Kenya. Well, this will provide dental care to the homeless in the Northwest.*

Well, this will educate a misogynist.

So, no, I'm not sharing the research I've done for Josh, but my parents — lo and behold! — have it so very right about one thing, though: A letter is a fine way to make change. Because of them, I've written missives to companies (please stop using carcinogenic ingredients), my school administration (please stop censoring my articles), my representatives in both Washingtons (please address the growing sex trafficking epidemic). And the comic so very conveniently has a generic email address for the publisher on the back cover.

Even better.

My letter won't go to Josh, but to the publisher. For extra credibility, I'll use my email account with my parents' firm and collect the halo effect of being associated with communications experts.

I grab my Mac from my desk. Fingers on the keyboard, I pound the anger out of me.

From: Viola Wynne Li
To: Publisher@PlanetXComix.com
Subject: (Photo)sensitivity for Dummies

To Whom It May Concern:

I recently read *Persephone from Planet X* given to me by one of your writers. I am quite literally speechless at some of the inconsistencies, not to mention insensitivities, in this work.

Number One: If photosensitivity is triggered by the sun and if Persephone has recently vacated the planet farthest from said sun and has zero sun tolerance built up, there is no possible way that she would be traipsing around Earth in a glorified swimsuit. No, seriously, if she did, she would have melted into a puddle of pain, and her skin would have become an irradiated red.

Number Two: Given Persephone's photosensitivity, how is it possible that she can have a twelve-hour epic adventure in full-blast sunlight without taking any kind of precautions? First, there isn't a single iota of shade for her. Second, where's her hat? For that matter, where are her clothes? (See point

Number One because even if that scrap of fabric had beaucoup UPF protection, its coverage would be—shall we say, scant?) Let's also, for the sake of this thought experiment, believe that Persephone (miraculously) had sunscreen on, she would sweat it off in two hours flat, less than an hour if she were really combating vampires.

Number Three: By the way, I thought vampires self-combusted and incinerated in direct sunlight. So why on earth would they battle Persephone in the daytime? Wouldn't she—a superhero—know that all she had to do was lure them into the sun, then kick back and watch them smoke on their own?

Number Four: Can you say objectification? Why, why, why does a female superhero have to wear barely there clothes? This is not beach volleyball, but frankly, even that sport is a mystery to me since the male beach volleyball players seem to play just fine in board shorts and shirts. Look, I get that aerodynamicity is a prerequisite for superhero uniforms.

But consider this:

Superman: chin to toe coverage.

Batman: head to toe coverage.

Spiderman: face to toe coverage.

And not one of them is photosensitive.

(Incidentally, I highly doubt that any self-respecting superhero of any gender in this current millennium would travel 7.44 billion kilometers just to attract the attention of another being, vampire, human, or otherwise. No one is that desperate.)

These are (all) serious errors, which I hope you'll remedy immediately.

Sincerely,

Viola Wynne Li

Intern, Lee & Li Communications

...

My fingers almost hurt from typing so hard and fast. The smallest, almost undetectable flare of misgivings stops me from pressing SEND. I can hear Mom warn: "Think through every possible ramification before you send anything." Dad would caution, "Give every inflammatory email a good twenty-four hours to cure overnight."

Perhaps I ought to cast a cursory look over my email, but the screen is so bright. My eyes burn. I close them, assuring myself that I've just become accustomed to the dark.

My parents are wrong: In no way will I ever get used to carrying an umbrella — umbrella! — in the sun.

There it is again: rage.

My eyes snap open. I don't want the dark. I want the light.

I hit SEND.

CHAPTER THIRTEEN

After dropping Roz off at the boathouse on Tuesday morning, pure muscle memory speeds me along Lake City Way, and I'm halfway to Auntie Ruth's before I even know where I'm driving. This sketchy stretch of road runs around the north end of Lake Washington, where seedy pot shops and gritty bars mix with truly great hole-in-the-wall pho and Ethiopian restaurants. I yawn, exhausted from my late-night tirade.

My phone buzzes an alert for an email. I tighten my grip on the steering wheel, which stretches my skin uncomfortably. I groan. Blotchy and red, a new blister bubbles on the top of my left hand. I had worn my spaceship of a hat around the house all day yesterday, but I hadn't thought to protect my hands. Or my heart.

As my parents tell their new employees, in this world, there are promise-keepers and promise-takers. After Darren, the one promise I've kept to myself: no more takers. I haven't gone out with a guy for over a year, which is nothing compared to Auntie Ruth going man-free for five whole years. So why the heck had I not only lowered my guard, but thrown down the draw-bridge, rolled out the red carpet to my bedroom, and invited a taker to stroll straight into my life with my offer for free research?

Another alert. I loosen my hold. As much as I'm itching to check the mes-sage, years of cautionary tales of car accidents care of Auntie Ruth do what my parents' lecture(s) don't: I keep my attention on the road.

The phone buzzes insistently, now with a text. There is no possible way that the publisher could have read my email about *Persephone* so soon, right? Suddenly, I'm wide awake. The moment I pull up crookedly in front of Auntie Ruth's repair shop, my phone pings again. Another text. Instead of righting the car, I consider myself parked and check my messages. As it turns out, the cage of metal surrounding me isn't much more protection than a canvas tent, not after I've poked the beast's ego.

> *5 min ago*
> *Hey, it's Josh. I'm glad you emailed. It felt too weird to ask your mom for your number.*

Josh read the email? I blush, remembering what I wrote. And how I wrote it. Let's just say: I did not practice what my parents preach about tone and wording and effective communication. I groan. I cannot believe that I forgot to erase my number in the signature line. And no, this was not a Freudian slip. Another buzz, another message.

> Josh: *You bring up good points.*
> Josh: *So let me know when you can talk.*

Talk? I want to ignore his texts, but as Lee & Li always say, *No ignoring, no ghosting, no pretending about problems.* Willful neglect of an issue is what turns minor concerns into major crises. Yeah, but I hadn't just kissed him; I had lost sleep over him. Out the passenger window, a brown leaf drops to the sidewalk, exactly how I feel as I try but fail to compose a response: parched dry. Someone didn't have the same writer's block. My phone alerts again.

> Josh: *And where.*
> Me: *That letter was for the publisher.*
> Josh: *I am the publisher.*
> Me:

I panic.
He. Is. The. Publisher.

I panic some more. Silence is not an option. Silence signals that I am embarrassed (which I am). Silence signals a tragic lack of ability to compose a creative comeback (which is true). My scalp itches. I take off the hat, wipe the sweat off my forehead, and smash it back on my head.

Anything is better than silence. Anything. So I do the classic Lee & Li maneuver: I deflect to a safer topic, partly to distract him, mostly to buy myself time to think.

> Me: *What are you doing up? Before 6?*
> Josh: *Swim practice.*
> Me: *The shoulders. Got it.*

The moment I hit SEND, I stare at my screen, mortified. What the heck had I just texted? Why on earth isn't there a retract-immediately function? Was there some kind of magnetosphere around this guy that repelled normal, simple, benign conversation?

> Josh: *What are you saying about my shoulders?*

I started it; I had to see it through.

> Me: *Some people might call them otherworldly wide.*
> Josh: *I'll take that as a compliment.*
> Josh: *Unless you're saying they're comic-book wide.*
> Josh: *As in: I need to wear more clothes?*

I can't help it. My laugh sounds suspiciously like a girl who's being flirted with and who likes it. A lot.

Me: *I thought double-texting was a no-no . . .*
Josh: *It is when you're flirting. Which ellipses are.*
Josh: *For the record, you used ellipses first.*
Josh: *And correction: I triple-texted . . .*

No, the guy cannot possibly be flirting with me after my ranting email? And I'm not ellipses-ing flirting with him, am I . . . ? Was he . . . ? Could he be . . . ?

Me: *A sign of desperation.*
Josh: *Desperate times call for desperate measures and all that . . .*

An ellipsis! He ellipsed me!

Josh: *So can we get together? Talk?*
Josh: *Because.*

Wait for it. Wait for it. Wait for it. Forget it. Waiting serves as much purpose as malaria-ridden mosquitoes in this world.

Me: *?*
Josh: *Because if I hurt your feelings, I want to apologize.*

That wasn't what I expected. Stunned, I sink back against the driver's seat as my mind strays to how Darren had trampled all over my feelings like I was his personal practice field. Which, in a way, I was, since, as it turns out, I was just a midseason substitution while he waited for his ex-soccer-star-girlfriend's return to him. After they got back together, there was nothing, not even a single text, to break up with me. Or to apologize for string-ing me along as if that had been his right. My flattened heart, his trophy.

A rap on the passenger window startles me. I'm half expecting a homeless person and automatically reach under the driver's seat for the emergency supply kits my parents keep stocked there: plastic bags filled with socks, two KIND Bars, a Jimmy John's gift card, and the number for the Union Gospel Mission emergency shelter downtown. Instead, I tug out an all-new Sick Girl emergency kit stuffed into a clear pouch: aloe vera, scrunch-able sun hat, sunscreen, and a card with my name, my parents' phone numbers, and contact info for my doctor.

"Viola!" Auntie Ruth's outside, frowning with worry. Dark half-moons under her eyes mean she's slept fitfully like me. "Are you okay?" She opens the passenger door and leans down to conduct a full-body search of me with her eyes. "Is your car?"

"All good." I nod even as I hide my blistered hand.

"Then what are you doing sitting out here? I was starting to get worried." She casts an accusatory glare at the bruised purple sky, looking exactly like Dad declaring war on light bulbs. She frets, "It's going to be light soon."

Hardly. The sun's not going to rise for a good hour, just shy of seven at the very earliest. Still, Auntie Ruth's uncharacteristically cautious, sound-ing eerily like my paranoid parents. This is my aunt, who prepares for adven-ture the way Dad does for crisis. He tucks emergency kits in our cars; she stashes trail running shoes for emergency runs. But now she urges, "You need to come inside. Just in case."

Every single muscle in my body protests. "In a second."

"I feel so terrible, honey. This is all my fault. If you get sicker, I'll feel even worse. So come on in, please."

Coming here was a terrible mistake. My parents' hovering is bad enough, but Auntie Ruth — the coolest aunt under the sun, so to speak — has amplified her guilt with anxiety, and we are now ten billion light-years from cool. I'm way too tired to remind her that the meds may not have caused my condition because that would just invite a dissection of how I'm feeling.

"Then why have you been parked out —"

My phone chooses that precise moment to buzz, buzz, buzz as text messages flood in.

She says knowingly, "Oh."

"No, it's not that."

"Josh?"

Well, two can play this game. Mom had asked me to be the arrow to her Cupid. So I take aim. "Hey, Mr. Silver Fox from Souper Bowl Sunday wants your number."

"Oh." A small dent in the door suddenly sidetracks Auntie Ruth and she probes the nick with her finger. "When did this happen? We can fix it." Her eyes lift, and she catches sight of my uncovered hand. Again with the upset tone. "Is that a blister?"

"Don't tell Dad."

"You know your dad and I don't keep secrets."

That's what I'm worried about. What if my legs got shaky inside? Or I fainted? What if I fainted at school? I hadn't even considered that possibility. My phone buzzes yet again. And again. Seriously, how much does this guy have to say? Was Josh this verbose with all the girls?

Before she shuts the door, Auntie Ruth winks at me and says, "I'm coming out for you in five minutes."

"Yeah," I say with a weak, unconvincing smile. No matter how hard I try to believe that nothing is going to change my plans, everyone seems intent on babyproofing my life. Case in point: Auntie Ruth turns around to check on me, worried, before she finally slips inside her shop.

> Josh: *How does Café Nestor work for you?*
> Josh: *By Liberty?*
> Josh: *After school?*

Texting Josh is one thing, but seeing him in person, something else entirely. My hands, my hat, my fainting, I have strayed far, far away from normal. I stuff the phone into the dark recesses of my messenger bag. My shoulder is against the door, ready to push it open, but for the first time, I don't want to go inside, where I'll be under surveillance. Or worse, pummeled with guilt. That guilt means that I should be wildly concerned about my mysterious condition, a reality I can't deal with right now because my life is not changing. At. All.

My head itches under the hat. Irritated, I swipe it off, feeling ten pounds lighter and ten times cuter. My phone buzzes with a call. I sigh. This could not possibly be my parents, detecting my hat removal, is it? I narrow my eyes, scan the dashboard. I wouldn't put it past them to rig my station wagon with a spy cam even if one of their core concerns is protecting personal privacy.

"Viola," Dad says, his voice urgent in my ear, "there's an opening at the pediatric dermatologist in an hour. Can you meet us at Children's?"

Before I can protest, Mom preempts my refusal. "Honey, we know it's the second week of school. But your health is more important."

Who am I to ignore the perfect excuse to leave Auntie Ruth guilt-free? I text her, Sorry, I'm not up for a visit, which is technically true. Take that back to Dad.

THINGS YOU NEVER WANT THE PERSON YOU'RE CRUSHING ON TO SEE

1. Clipping your toenails.

2. Picking earwax, eye goop, belly button lint, pimples, scabs, tartar, or ingrown hairs.

3. Cheating on tests, board games, or people (say, your
   boyfriend, and you find out that he's back together
   with his ex because you and thirty of your favorite
   classmates catch them grinding in the hall, and he
   never, ever acknowledges your presence again).

After this morning, I can say with the confidence that comes from first-hand knowledge, none of these compare to phototesting.

What I'm talking about is having one-centimeter patches stuck to your backside. (Yes, your buttocks, butt, behind, bum, tush, rump, rear.) And then, aimed straight at said polka-dotted backside are different light sources along the visible light, UVA, and UVB spectrum. (Who knew my research on light for Josh would come in so handy?)

So there I am for an hour, while fluorescent bulbs, a xenon lamp, a boxy device called a monochromator, a slide projector, and good old sunshine are blasted one at a time at my butt. What the medical team is doing is provoking a reaction. They could have accomplished that with their questions alone.

"Are you itchy?" (Yes.)

"Does it burn?" (Yes!)

"Does it hurt?" (You think?)

...

It is not a good sign when the phototest is cut short because your skin has reacted faster than the speed of fear.

CHAPTER FOURTEEN

Weakness is not an option for the Lee & Li clan—we grit our way through headaches, laugh at broken bones, scoff at fevers. Menstrual cramps? What are those? We are the Marines of our lives, letting nothing and no one come in the way of duty and obligation, always faithful to work, school, and bake sales.

So it's startling when Mom asks me once we're headed down to the lobby of the Children's Hospital, "Do you want to go home, honey?"

I keep my hands fisted at my sides, wishing I'd worn a long-sleeved shirt that I could tug over my knuckles. Blister count: now three. Troubling since the phototest was aimed at my rear, not my hands.

Dad chimes in, "Yeah, rest a little? You must be exhausted."

I am, but I won't, especially when their very questions reveal that they're fretting, too. "Fret" is a four-letter word in the Lee & Li world. We lock down. We pinpoint. We plot. We do not worry, considering anxiety an unnecessary waste of precious time and energy. So I shake my head and look stoically forward at the windows, all sunshiny bright outside like there could not possibly be anything wrong in the world.

"Okay, then!" Dad says with the heartiness of a serial attendee (reject) of Santa school. He throws his arm around my shoulders. "We'll get the test results tomorrow. They promised." (Ho! Ho! Ho!)

"They ended the test early," I remind them.

"Meaning they were able to rule out some conditions fast," Mom explains to me like I'm a toddler.

I fume. Another four-letter word in the Lee & Li world. We pitch. We persuade. We produce. We do not aimlessly fume. Yet. Why won't my parents just tell me what they know or suspect? Annoyed, I demand, "Like what? What could they have ruled out?"

"Lupus," declares Dad, all definitive.

"That's what I told Dr. Anderson on Saturday," I huff.

"We know. Auntie Ruth said you did a great job advocating for yourself," Mom says as she checks her phone and frowns.

"What, honey?" Dad asks.

She shrugs. "Just my sister, asking about graduation again." Which should remind Mom that I'm the college applicant, where every class and every grade still counts. Instead, she asks, "You sure you want to go back to school? You can rest in your bedroom. In the dark."

"Ms. Kavoussi is waiting," I tell them, but I've already missed my meeting with my college counselor, thanks to the phototest that was awful on so many levels: humiliation, pain, and fear. What else could possibly go wrong today? Even if I shiver at that thought, I stalk away.

...

So much for the dramatic exit. Sitting in the driver's seat after a phototest can only be described as uncomfortable. No matter how gingerly I shift, how tightly I grasp the steering wheel, how much I try to rest my weight on one cheek, then the other, I find no relief. I need help of the geek variety:

> Me: *SOS. I can't even sit and I have to drive to school.*
> Caresse: *Extra padding.*
> Aminta: *So much for nutritionists saying that cookies are bad for you.*
> Caresse: *Do you have anything to cushion you?*
> Aminta: *Even a gnarly towel in your trunk?*

My eyes drop to the sweatshirt Roz tossed on the passenger floor. When I reach down for it, I find her discarded summer reading, the Robert Frost book, crushed under her feet. I can't help but smooth out the mangled pages, my eyes skimming the poem about woods that are "lovely, dark and deep" and "miles to go before I sleep." After staying home this last weekend, let me tell you: There is nothing lovely about a darkened room. Yet I have miles to go myself if I want to preserve my future.

Even though it's going to hurt, I force myself out of the car, wincing, and rummage for my mud-encrusted trail running shoes in the trunk. I kick off my Adidas. Once my toes wriggle in the familiar footbeds of my thick-soled trail running sneakers, I feel like a semblance of myself. Quickly, I fold Roz's sweatshirt into a small pillow. What more could possibly go wrong today?

In answer, my phone buzzes with a text.

Josh: *So Café Nestor today?*

My eyes blur with tears. I wipe them angrily. What the heck am I doing, flirting with another charming flake? Did I really want to be further humiliated? Did I need to repeat Darren today and have my heart shattered tomorrow? These boyfriend dreams are the ones that should go up in flames.

I type one word.

Fury, grief, regret, the two letters burn: No.

I hit the gas and go home.

CHAPTER FIFTEEN

My best-laid plans to hide at home and get a head start on the bake sale are no match for the Lee & Li Action Plan. An armada of work vans is assembled in our driveway. What are my parents conspiring now? I hated to imagine. My phone pings, and I nervously check it, only it's not Josh asking me why I can't meet, but Auntie Ruth: *Are you sick?! What do you need? I'm so sorry! Call me.*

After that deluge of concern, it takes me a full minute in the station wagon to settle down and gear up for whatever's waiting inside. Even so, I have to suppress a small gasp when I slide out of the driver's seat. Set my life on fire? My rear is taking care of that just fine.

Inside the living room, two older women are so hard at work, measuring the windows, that they don't even notice me walking in until I greet them, then ask, "So what are you doing?"

"Your dad wanted a bid for blackout shades," the woman with a halo of gray hair answers.

Of course he did. My fist chokes the strap of my messenger bag.

A gasp — never reassuring — comes from the kitchen, and I hustle over to find a rotund man with a beard that belongs at the end of a squirrel, balancing precariously on a tall ladder, where he's sticking some sort of film over the skylights.

"Careful," I tell him automatically.

That must have translated into a dare because the Bearded One steps up another rung. "Don't worry. I've got insurance."

Which is so not reassuring. Where, may I ask, are the two resident and professional crisis managers now? I point to what looks like Saran Wrap in his hand and ask, "What is that?"

"Window film."

"Let me guess. It blocks UV rays."

"Ninety-nine percent of them," answers Dad as he rushes in from the back door like I'm the one who's about to topple off the ladder. Sorry, my two feet are planted on terra firma whereas Dad is clearly floating off in space because this in-home invasion of blackout materials is beyond irrational. Nothing about my so-called condition is a fact yet, just fear and speculation. He says, "We've been trying to get ahold of you. Wait, what are you doing home so early?"

I could ask him the same thing if the reason wasn't so obvious: Lee & Li have declared war on light.

Dad shifts the brown package in his arms without moving his eyes off me. "Are you sick?"

"No. I'm fine," I grit out.

"Fever? Vomit?"

"Dad, do you see me throwing up?"

"Lesions?"

Lesions? As in ulcerated, weeping wounds? I swallow. "No, I'm fine." (I was, until now.) "What list are you checking off?"

"Side effects of the phototest. It's all in the sheet the nurse gave us." Dad sets the package down on the counter and slides his phone out of his pocket, frowning, as he texts, no doubt reporting in to Mom: *Baby bat has winged home. I repeat, baby bat captured and contained.*

A troubling banging comes from our basement. Suspicious, I ask, "What's going on down there?" A curse soars up: harsh with a side of terror. I guess hopefully, "Oh, are you getting rid of the spiders finally?" Unless you think Halloween should be a year-round experience, you never, ever, venture down to the basement. Doing laundry in our house is petrifying, an act of supreme courage. It's not a question of what you're going to encounter, but how many and how big (The Invasion of the Wolf Spiders, 2017, 2016, 2015, 2014, 2013).

"Something like that." Dad takes a swig from his coffee tumbler.

Thank you, Bearded One, for showering years of dust from the skylights upon us. I sneeze. Dad, unfortunately, spies my blisters before I can lower my hand from my nose.

"That's it," says Dad. Even if his voice is cool and collected on the surface, anxiety churns in his undercurrent. "The school's getting a letter. Today."

Worried, I ask. "Why?"

"We told the school what the doctors suspected. That you're sensitive to the light," Dad continues, his voice picking up indignation. "And all they've given us is a pat 'we'll look into it.' Sorry, not good enough."

"You can't force everyone at school to sit in the dark because of me. That's not fair."

"You can't serve nuts at school because of peanut allergies," Dad counters, arms spread wide. "No peanut butter sandwiches, a staple of school lunches for generations. That's not fair, but it's right."

"Yeah, but —"

"This is for your own good."

"Dad," I say calmly, then ask, "where's Mom?"

"Your mom who's not going to be happy that you left school early?"

"Yeah, that mom."

Dad checks his phone. "She's on her way home."

It's just two in the afternoon. My suspicion brews, and I narrow my eyes at him. "Why?"

Dad answers, "You'll see why the letter's a good idea. If I pound it out in the next hour, I'll have time to run it by legal."

Legal?

Dad was going DEFCON Three, a slap on the wrist with the threat of a nuclear bomb behind it. It doesn't take a whole lot to picture Dr. Luthra making a public announcement during an assembly: "Little did we know that we have our own resident vampire."

I yank my hat off and swing it, brim and all, dramatically toward the living room. "Dad, what gives? We remodeled this house for the light."

Unhelpfully, the Bearded One on the ladder says, "You'll still get light through this film. It'll just block out the UV rays."

"See?" says Dad, pointing heavenward. "Behold: light. We're just mitigating the danger."

"Dad."

He narrows his eyes at me. "You look really—"

"I know: pink."

"I think your color is more commonly referred to as red," says Dad.

"Pink."

I choose not to hear Man on the Ladder cough: "Red."

The alarm bell chimes loudly: intruder alert. So does the maternal alarm: Baby bat under attack.

"Red? How red?" Mamazon descends, hurtling toward us as if blood is leaking from my eyes.

I shrink back. All laws of normal physics bend. The air thickens with motherly concern. Mom charges in with a bottle of aloe vera in her hand. My mother is not stowing a crate of aloe vera in her purse now, is she?

"Good, you're home. We've been trying to reach you. Here, slather it on," Mom says as she scrutinizes the Bearded One in the kitchen, then the ladies in the living room. Her voice lowers confidentially. "Let's go out to the Shed."

"Here's fine," I say. Privacy may be a virtue in the Lee & Li world, but whatever news she has, I want to hear it now.

For once, Dad agrees with me. "Here's okay, love."

"Honey," Mom says slowly, a new script she hasn't mastered, "the doctor wants to see you. Today."

...

For the record, the third time to Children's Hospital in a matter of days is not the charm, not when Dr. Anderson's eyes are distressingly tender when he breaks it to me, "Your skin reacted so fast during the phototest, it's likely you've got solar urticaria. But because your hands also presented with blisters independently, it's possible that you also have polymorphous light eruption." His voice actually becomes the same nerdy-excited I hear in Aminta and Caresse when they're on the brink of an invention. "I even found one study where almost a quarter of patients with solar urticaria also had coexistent PMLE."

"And?"

Dr. Anderson sidles an unconscious look at my parents as if he needs their moral support, but for once, they don't look invincible. Mom's biting her lip, Dad's worrying the writer's callus on his middle finger. So the doctor straightens his necktie embroidered with helicopters before telling me, "There have only been about a hundred cases of solar urticaria in history, obviously fewer with both conditions, but to date, there isn't a cure."

"You mean, this is lifelong?" I can't conceal the despair in my voice, as I consider hats and blackout shades and hives and blisters forever. Not to mention the possibility of dying.

"Not necessarily. There are too few reported cases to know for sure, but some of those cases resolved spontaneously on their own!"

Spontaneous — nothing in the climate-controlled world of Lee & Li is spontaneous and unplanned. Yet Mom brightens and seizes the word like spontaneity is her new motto. "So it's possible. What were their diets?"

Dad adds, "And exercise programs? How much average sun exposure did they have in a given day?"

Dr. Anderson shakes his head. "We don't know. There's just not enough data."

I swallow and ask the question that needs to be answered, "What's the worst case you read?"

Dr. Anderson says, "Some people can't leave their homes."

"Oh, come on," I scoff, edging off the examination table, and stand with my hands on my hips. "Ever?"

He nods. "For some people, it takes just a minute outside for their skin to react."

I look from the doctor to my parents, but they are frozen in not-so-comforting shock, too. My hands drop to my sides.

Ever.

As fast as I blink my eyes, tears still blur my vision.

"There's a new biologic medication that seems to help with the hives," Dr. Anderson offers.

But Dad shakes his head. "She's not a guinea pig."

Dr. Anderson reassures me, "There are lots of other ways to mitigate — lessen — the triggers." Hastily, he hands me a sheet of paper as if it's a security blanket. All I want to do is wad it up like the wrecking ball that the facts are. "Solar urticaria is just so rare, and the two conditions combined are even rarer. But we can apply techniques from people who've learned to live with conditions like lupus and have to stay out of the sun. That's the key: Keep out of the sun as much as possible. So, for instance, if you want to swim, wear a rash guard and swim pants."

Adieu, bikini summers.

"Was it the Doxy I took for Africa?" I choke out abruptly because I'm not ready for good-byes yet, not when a headwind of "why's" presses hard against me: Why me? Why now? Why is this happening?

"I would have to say no." Dr. Anderson shrugs, then shakes his head in pure regret. "But we don't know what triggered your conditions. Viola, we might never know."

"Could I really die?" I ask quietly.

Again, he gives me an apologetic look: yes. Gently, so very gently, Dr. Anderson says, "In very, very, very few cases, yes, some people with your conditions have died."

The room may fall silent, but that damning statement echoes all around me. Finally, I ask, "What about college?"

"Don't worry. We'll make even more adjustments," says Mom quickly.

Dad agrees, "Absolutely. Immediately. Whatever it takes."

Along with Dr. Anderson, Lee & Li begin to formulate the new Viola Wynne Li crisis plan, but I sink back onto the examination table, unhearing. Say good-bye to Abu Dhabi, desert land of perpetual sunshine. Even wearing my most broken-in pair of trail running shoes with thick soles designed for the roughest terrain, I cannot outrun this avalanche that's burying my life.

CHAPTER SIXTEEN

My bedroom is darker than my thoughts. I can't see anything—not my blisters, not my hands, not my future. Frowning, I flick on the overhead light. My room remains a stubborn black. I fumble for the doorknob and widen the door so light from the hallway seeps into my room. When I look up at my ceiling, I identify the problem: There is no light bulb, just an empty socket.

Without knowing it, I have become the Sleeping Beauty of light bulbs, which have all been banished from this Kingdom of Crazy.

I'd bellow, Mom! Dad! But then they'd tear into my room, where we'd have the dismal discussion I don't want to have—them explaining, explaining, explaining why cave conditions are necessary—when all I want to know is why the hell I have solar urticaria and PMLE. I yank aside the curtains to find cardboard taped over the windowpanes.

I am serious.

Eight panes of glass, eight perfectly cut pieces of cardboard.

I rip off one piece of cardboard to give just enough light to read and settle in the shadows on my floor. Our eco-green house may be an even and pleasant sixty-eight degrees, but I am freezing. I tug the handwoven throw blanket off my bed, brought back from Auntie Ruth's mission trip to Guatemala a couple of summers ago. And then I research.

Greetings and welcome, Viola Wynne Li!

Congratulations! Out of the 7.12 billion inhabitants on Earth, you have been invited to join the rarefied group of approximately one hundred known and verified cases of solar urticaria throughout the entire history of humanity. Even more unusual, you got a double dose of photosensitivity with your polymorphous light eruption. Yay, you!

Membership to this highly selective society of the Dwellers of the Dark includes the following exclusive, lifetime benefits:

- You get to take part in a mystery called the Great Unknown. Because. The cause of solar urticaria: Unknown! The cure for solar urticaria: Unknown! How long will it take you to break out in hives? A few minutes? A little longer? Unknown!
- Your skin is going to swell into hives every time you step into the natural sun or sit under a light source that emits ultraviolet radiation.
- Sometimes the swelling / reddening / hiving will go away in a couple of minutes. And if it doesn't, it'll probably be painful!
- And as an extra-special bonus, you'll get your fair share of blisters, too, thanks to your PMLE!
- You may opt to take preventative measures with treatments like phototherapy (we'll blast you for longer and longer amounts of time to thicken up that skin of yours, but then you run the risk of getting skin cancer), photochemotherapy (drugs

may help, but then you run the risk of getting other cancers), or our personal favorite, plasmapheresis. (Where your plasma is removed, treated, and reinserted into your blood. Seriously.) In all cases, your desensitization to the sun will be short-lived. So lucky you, you get to repeat these nonlasting treatments over and over and over again.

- The best course of action: Avoid any and all contact with light.
- And remember, all members of this ultraselective society get to lead (severely impaired) lives unless, of course, you die.

Good luck to you, and welcome again!

CHAPTER SEVENTEEN

It's four thirty in the morning by the time I'm done learning all I don't want to know about my condition. Sleep is as impossible as hope, even after a long text exchange with Aminta, who is just trying to support me with her every suggestion. I know better, but I become one of those no-no-no clients who hate every idea and find fault with every recommendation my parents propose.

> Aminta: *You can go on night walks with rangers to search for owls.*
> Me: *Since when have I ever searched for owls?*
> Aminta: *At least you can swim in a rash guard, pants, and a hat, right?*
> Me: *While everyone else is in a cute bikini? Even the pregnant moms? No.*

Irritated at myself, I force lightheartedness back into my answers.

> Aminta: *At least you can run in the dark.*
> Me: *I can.*

The truth is: I might not be able to run in the broad daylight now, but no one said anything about running in the dark. However much I'm supposed to impose lights-out martial law in my life, I am not about to go silently into a severely limited life.

One headlamp, a jog bra, and I am out of here. At my closet, though, I stagger back, shocked. While I was at school, my wardrobe became a dead zone of fashion, a place where cute goes to die. My flowy tank tops, V-neck T-shirts, anything and everything that might show a microscopic amount of skin is gone. I push back the (teal! magenta! aqua blue!) long-sleeved, button-down shirts, including an entire zip code of turtlenecks, all with their tags still on: UPF 50+ for sun protection. Of course they provide sun protection. No one would be caught dead outside in them.

A radioactive pink tunic (a tunic!) actually hangs front and center in my closet. The chances of Mom allowing herself to be seen in any of this in public are nil to none. So why would I? I yank the offending tunic off its hanger, wad up the diaphanous fabric in my hands, and lob it at my floor. Even that denies me any satisfaction: It floats down, a bare whisper of a protest.

I can't stand being stuck inside for another minute: not in my room, the victim of Project Uglification, not in my home with parents who are mounting a war I want to fight on my own terms, and especially not in my head, where the diagnosis slithers around, preparing for a fatal strike.

Lo and behold, I have an entire closet of sun-protecting clothes.

Why, thank you, Mom and Dad. A test run outside in my new wardrobe sounds like a fine idea. We're hours before sunrise, and look how over-prepared I will be.

I shove aside shirt after shirt, and finally choose a long-sleeved black rash guard, which is better than anything else, even if it'll cover my *Firefly* lariat. When I open my bureau to rummage for my headlamp from various school camping trips, my hands skim over the khaki trekking shirt I wore in Tanzania.

"Welcome to the land of the sun," Auntie Ruth had announced as soon as we stepped out of the tiny twelve-seater prop plane. Her head tilted back, black hair gleaming, and her arms spread wide like she wanted to scoop up the entire sky and place it in my arms so that I could carry a piece of the sun with me wherever I went.

Little did we know, I would.

...

I rip the cardboard covering off the rest of my windowpanes and shove the window wide open. Cold air blows in. It's a small four-foot drop to the ground, yet when I land, I'm all newborn giraffe, ungainly on my feet. I flail for the flimsy branch of the Japanese maple, which doesn't stabilize me, and land on my rear. Of course I do. It stings. Of course it does. I rub my bottom cautiously, not wanting to inflame that area more than the phototest already has. After I shove the side gate open, I dart down the driveway, hugging the shadows. A quick glance at the front door confirms that all is clear, even though I'm half expecting the parent patrol to stop my escape.

This is the first time in my entire life that I have snuck out. I don't feel so much as a weak flicker of guilt.

City running has never had any appeal for me with its asphalt roads and cement sidewalks, random garbage blowing around, piles of dog poop here and there. Then there's the rumble of cars, the distracted drivers who don't look, stop, or yield for pedestrians or bikers, the constant stench of exhaust and impatience.

Now, I sprint, sucking in deep gulps of predawn quiet. I wish I could run forever, tear down the shoreline of Lake Washington and keep going. North, south, it doesn't matter. But my breathing is off, my phototested butt is aching, and my sneakered feet feel claustrophobic on these smooth, urban flats. So I slow to a walk, promising myself that this weekend I'll hit the dirt trails — Tiger Mountain or Cougar Mountain. No matter what, I can be on a trail at dawn when only a mere hint of light edges the horizon. Who cares if a woman was tasered on Tiger Mountain a few weeks ago? I press down on my heaving chest.

Why do I sound like just the sort of person I despise, all enthusiasm and promises but no intention of keeping my word?

I head to the tiny lakefront park and plant myself on the lonely swing. My legs pump, pulling higher to the purple-bruised sky. My toes tease the vanishing stars. Somewhere beyond the horizon, the sun lurks, ready to singe everything else I love and want: my summer tank tops and denim shorts, running on trails with the sun warming my face, desert oases I've only seen from my computer.

With a deep inhale, I bottle the outdoors, a perfume called Freedom and Future. No matter how long I hold my breath, I must exhale. When I do, it feels like good-bye.

CHAPTER EIGHTEEN

My bedroom window has been closed, cardboarded, and relocked, which can only mean one thing: My parents know I've snuck out. Still hoping to slip inside undetected and unlectured, I skulk around to try the back door on the off chance that my parents might possibly be conspiring over some crisis or another in their backyard office, a souped-up garden shed with electricity and heat. The back door, sadly, is dead bolted against my plan, but does nothing to muffle Mom's worry. From inside the house, I can hear her, agitated: "Where is she?"

Not good.

At the kitchen window, I spy my parents in the living room, waiting for the prodigal daughter's return.

Great, just great. Right as I'm gearing up to face my parents, Roz's window creaks open. She hisses, "Hurry up." Gratefully, I haul myself up to her windowsill and drop inside Roz's bedroom to her scoff: "Don't you know to unlock the back door first? Just in case?"

"How do you know that?"

"Always have an Option B. Don't you ever listen?" (Idiot.)

I shake off my little sister's derision, but get immobilized in the hall when I hear tears clogging Mom's voice: "I should be there with her, wherever she is, helping her process all of this. I should always be there with her. That's my job." Her deep, rattling sigh makes me feel guilty now. "I'm just like Samantha, a leaver. I'm an abandoner!"

"Sweetheart, you're not like your sister at all," Dad tells her, and I creep down the hall to see Dad in the living room, enfolding Mom in his embrace. "You haven't abandoned her to fend for herself with alcoholic parents. And you're not abandoning her now. We will never abandon her."

"It was so scary being left behind. I hated feeling helpless and alone. Hated it."

What I hate is how I can hear the scared twelve-year-old girl in Mom's voice. Like Dad, she hardly talks about her life before us, even more rarely than she drinks, which is next to never. Not so much as a sip of cooking wine. All I know is that my aunt Samantha up and left at sixteen and never checked in on Mom — not a single call, not even a one-line post-card. And then fifteen years later, when Mom and Dad started Lee & Li before they even got married, there she was, asking for a small loan to help her out.

So I announce loudly, "I'm home."

Mom wrests out of Dad's arms and rushes me like she's been training with the Seahawks. "Honey! You can't just be going outside."

I back away and point to the skylights in the kitchen. "Mom. Big, scary risk. It's still dark."

"What if you fell and no one saw and then the sun rose and you were stuck outside? In the sun?"

"I'm wearing sun-gear from head to toe, even though it's basically pitch black." I stretch out my arms, body fully encased in UPF-protective and reflective running gear. "Moonlight doesn't emit UV rays."

"The moon reflects them. We don't know if you'll get a moonburn," Mom says.

Is there even such a thing? I take a deep breath to calm myself. It's futile to fight their superior research and data. The lightning speed of their man-dates for my life has caught me off guard. Rookie mistake, when I know my parents pivot better than quarterbacks with every new circumstance.

Mom's voice goes high-pitched. "Do you know that you could die? Really die?"

"Instead of sort of die?" I ask lightly. Behind me, Roz and Dad chuckle, all of us trying to defuse the tension.

Mistake. Big, huge mistake.

Mom's eyebrows nearly spring off her forehead. "This isn't funny. Do you really want to flush your life down the toilet because you went out for a run that burned your skin and then you died? Isn't that a little selfish of you?"

Alarmed, Roz and I exchange a nervous look: Mom never loses her cool. She channels her anger into championship lecturing packaged as "strong recommendations" and "news you can use."

"Honey." Dad reaches for her hand and he starts to translate: "What your mom means is — "

Mom finishes, her voice back under tight control, "This could get worse."

"It could," I say quietly. "I know it could."

"Death!" Mom cries.

"I know, Mom." Of course I did. Uncle Amos died after a swift bout with cancer. While I didn't collapse during soccer practice like Aneesh, I held vigils along with the rest of Liberty when our school hero had to have emergency heart surgery two autumns ago. My father may not have died of a stroke on a business trip or my mother committed suicide, all of which have happened to different people in my class since freshmen year, but I have experienced the impact of death.

"You can't take any risks. Not anymore." Mom's eyes home in on my headlamp: Risk! Risk! Major risk! Horrified, she snatches the headlamp off my head, a crown of thorns she will not have me wear. "Light bulb, honey!" She shakes the headlamp. "Light! Bulb!"

"Mom, Crisis Management 101. Sheesh," I say, rolling my eyes despite countless parental lectures about R-E-S-P-E-C-T. How about aiming some of that my way? Which propels me to rant myself: "Hey, you wouldn't treat any of your clients this way. I've seen you with my own eyeballs over how many summers? You wouldn't order CEOs around. You wouldn't tell them what to do. You're all about: We're partners. We're in this together. So how come you're not asking me what I want to do?"

"Because." Dad looks perplexed as if it's perfectly acceptable — perfectly reasonable — to bubble-wrap me for the rest of my solar urticarial–impaired life. "You're our daughter."

"But I'm not two." My voice raises three octaves, maybe four, sounding exactly like a toddler in a tantrum when I should be calm, cool, and crisis-containing. So much for that. This comes howling out: "Where are my clothes? I want my clothes back."

"Viola," Mom says softly as if my breakdown snaps her out of her fear and back to the safety of crisis management mode.

No, my parents are not going to legislate away any more of my freedom. Without another word, I temper-flounce into the bathroom I share with Roz and slam the door behind me. I flick on the lights, only the bulbs have now been downgraded to the lowest wattage possible, one that can cast shadows, not much more.

CHAPTER NINETEEN

Fresh from my shower and safe in my new UPF-protective and boy-repellant outfit, the dutiful chauffeur is ready to transport the princess to the boathouse, but Dad raps on my bedroom door.

I sigh as I finish tucking my college essay for my meeting with my college counselor into my messenger bag. "Don't you have someone else's crisis to solve?"

"Well," says Dad, widening the door while juggling a large box and thrusting a sheet of paper at me, "I thought maybe you could read the letter before your mom and I send it to the school."

Conflicting emotions slow my response time: irritation that they went through with writing a letter, grudging astonishment that they actually shared said letter with me.

Dad taps the box in his arms. "And this came for you yesterday. In the middle of everything, I forgot to give it to you after the doctor's appointment. What's Planet X?"

My heart quite literally leaps. All thoughts of proofing the ballistic letter are forgotten. Despite knowing a diversion when I'm on the receiving end of one, I hold out my hands. "Dad, give it to me."

"And what" — Dad pauses theatrically as he holds the box above his head — "is Josh Taylor sending you?"

I lunge for the box, which entails a nonelegant hurdle and a near-stumble when I read the label for myself.

From: Josh Taylor of Planet X

To: Viola Li of the Spaceship SERENITY

Supreme Magnificent Executive Intern

c/o Lee & Li Communications

What the heck required a physical package and not, say, a triple text? Before I can find out, though, Dad sets the letter on my desk. He rubs his nose and says, "We're trying, honey. We're just worried."

"I know, but this is my life."

"I know."

The door swings closed behind Dad. That gentle motion sets off the new, parent-approved night-light in the corner of the room. I draw to the vague suggestion of light, dropping to the floor with the box. Inside is a sheet of bright yellow paper, hand-lettered in black marker to look like a book cover.

(PHOTO)SENSITIVITY FOR DUMMIES

by Josh Taylor

"I highly doubt that any self-respecting superhero of any gender in this current millennium would travel 7.44 billion kilometers just to attract the attention of a being, vampire, human, or otherwise."

-Viola Li

Supreme Magnificent Executive Intern, Lee & Li Communications

You got my attention.

And I hope to prove you wrong on one point.

Tomorrow, travel 2.3 miles to Ada's Technical Books?

Underneath the dummied-up book cover is a khaki hat, the kind that Auntie Ruth wanted us to wear on our safari and I refused on the grounds of because. Now, unbelievably, I laugh and try on the hat. It's a perfect fit, but there's still no way I'm going out with him.

Even so, I find myself putting on makeup. When you add my new SPF foundation and a poorly lit bedroom, you get Halloween, four weeks early. *Don't do it! Don't do it!* Still, I (compulsively) dab on another layer of concealer when I hear Roz clomping down the hall.

"Where is she?" Roz's voice vibrates with impatience.

"Viola, time to go!" Mom calls, then not-so-conspiratorially, adds, "Roz, princess, can you make sure Viola wears her hat at school today?"

I crush the pink makeup sponge in my hand.

Now, indignation rings: "Viola. I'm. Late!"

With one last glance at the mirror, I drop my makeup sponge on my desk. I'd need special effects makeup skills to camouflage my face anyway. And then there's the matter of the Lee & Li letter, a missive to Dr. Luthra and the school board that's so well written, so well researched, and so well reasoned, there's zero chance the school won't blot out the sun with all the measures my parents "strongly suggest." Honestly, I'd be in awe if it also didn't guarantee that everyone will know about my condition before long. Maybe I should just fake being sick, stay home from school, enforce my ban on players. Did I really need to add Josh's expression to my Library of Regrets: Tanzania (regretted), Darren (regrettable). He has other ideas, apparently. My phone pings with a text.

Josh: *Meet at 4:32 p.m. today?*

Tonight is my prep night for the bake sale when I'm supposed to make and bake all the cookies so they're ready to be frosted and packaged tomorrow. But that 4:32 p.m. is catnip with its mysterious specificity. I bite.

Me: *Not 4:30?*
Josh: *Official sunset.*
Josh: *Somewhere*

I admit it: I laugh out loud and on-screen.

My bedroom door thuds under a disgruntled palm. "I knew it! Mom! She's not even getting ready in there!" Another thump. "I can't be late!"

Apparently, the Viola Express runs, rain or shine. News flash: This conductor is taking her own sweet time.

Me: *4:32:05*

CHAPTER TWENTY

The college counseling office on the second floor of Liberty Prep is bathed in soothing shades of maroon and beige, and filled with soft autumnal light, all come-in-and-get-cozy as if it were a log cabin high in the mountains. Looks are deceiving, and not just because invisible UV rays are seeping through the glass. Lurking above are storm clouds of expectation: college pennants, pinned shoulder to shoulder along the tops of the walls. Wesleyan. Boston College. Stanford. MIT. UCLA. Occidental. Georgetown. New York University.

One moment inside Ms. Kavoussi's office, and my stress almost builds into hives. My counselor swivels around in her black chair to greet me by way of opening my file folder. She doesn't even glance at her notes, not one little peek like she's already summed me up. Like it's not hard to sum me up. I lower myself delicately to the wood chair in the corner farthest from the windows. Even so, I hunch my shoulders to tuck as much of myself under my hat, but that does nothing to ease the pain in my rear.

"Viola. I've been looking forward to chatting with you." Ms. Kavoussi smiles and picks up a ballpoint pen as slender as herself, not to jot notes, but to use as a baton to punctuate her speech. *Tap!* "Did you make your preliminary list of colleges?"

Why, yes, college counselor who is dressed for our future success, all East Coast liberal arts college with her tailored gray pants and pearls, I didn't just bring the list of potential colleges, I even brought my full essay. I rummage inside my messenger bag to find it, printed out and filed for safekeeping in my planner, and hand the pages to her.

Ms. Kavoussi now takes her pen to my list. "I love Grinnell. Northwestern and Grinnell could be targets." TARGET! "University of Washington.

I'd say that's a likely for you." LIKELY. "But NYU Abu Dhabi?" *Tappity-tappitytappity. TAP.* "That's an unlikely." UNLIKELY! Ms. Kavoussi raps her pen on her chin. "What happened to Georgetown being your first choice? I thought when the four of us met last spring, your parents said that you were going into crisis management with them."

"Actually, I was thinking about being a foreign correspondent," I say a little shakily, not just because I've rarely declared this aloud, but now I'm wondering whether I'm the one checking into the Kingdom of Crazy for still believing I can report breaking news. Just picturing myself in the middle of a riot, standing in the blazing sun, makes my skin almost prickle now. "An international journalist."

"Ah. Hence, Abu Dhabi. That's bold. Part of the school's winnowing process is to fly out their best prospects for a free campus visit. Do your parents know?"

Even as I'm processing that luscious piece of information — free trip! — I shrug noncommittally: maybe yes, possibly not yet, definitely no.

Her cedar-brown eyes pierce through my hedging. Nervous, I touch my lariat, remind myself that my job in this world is to give voice to the voiceless, to cover the forgotten issues, the ones more convenient to ignore.

Tappity, tappity, tappity, TAP. Ms. Kavoussi, sounding thoughtful, says, "Dr. Luthra told me that you have a condition."

"Dr. Luthra?"

"Are you sure with your condition that you'll be able to go to a school in the desert? Or that being a journalist is really possible?" Ms. Kavoussi asks, her tone now carefully kind like she's speaking to the Sick Girl. If my teeth clenched even tighter, my jaw would break.

...

QUESTION: WHY IS VIOLA WYNNE LI SWEATING LIKE A HUMAN WATERFALL?

a. Anger at her parents for informing Dr. Luthra.

b. Irritation at Dr. Luthra for tattling to Ms. Kavoussi.

c. Climate change is real: Her future plans are melting from sun exposure.

d. Or maybe, just maybe, her father has it right, and the overhead lights are frying her skin.

Correct answer: All of the above.

...

How is it possible that I felt a heck of a lot safer in the savanna, even when a lion's primal roar scared us awake in our (flimsy) canvas tent? I can't shrink from the high beam of Ms. Kavoussi's scrutiny or the reality that being a foreign correspondent might be impossible or that both my skin and my plans feel like they're being rubbed raw.

Ms. Kavoussi continues, "I ask, not because I don't think you'd be excellent as a journalist, Viola, because you would be. A great one. But we have to be realistic and strategic in your college apps, especially since it's so extremely competitive today. If you want to put crisis management back on the table, then Georgetown—which would still be a stretch—should be your Early Action pick."

"I'm absolutely sure I want to be a journalist," I tell Ms. Kavoussi firmly, "and I have no doubt that I'll figure out a way to do my job."

Liar, liar. My skin stings ever so slightly, even though not a speck of sunlight is touching me. Yeah, so how could I stand out in the open to cover a million-person march? Or broadcast in a studio under the hot lights? I scoot my chair farther back even if it makes me feel cornered.

"Okay, fine, so journalism," Ms. Kavoussi says doubtfully. The bell sounding the end of my dreams tolls even louder. "The natural question—the number one question — admissions officers will ask is why you didn't work on the school paper. You'll need to address that in your essay."

"Actually, I've got a first draft," I tell Ms. Kavoussi as I pull her copy out of my planner.

"Fantastic," she says, nodding once, smoothing out the pages. "Tanzania," she reads. "Safari."

"Field experience."

"Entitled."

"But my aunt brought me to — "

"Watch a documentary being filmed in Ghana."

"Yeah, in the courtroom — "

"Observer."

Sweat starts to collect under my arms, and I lift my elbows off my sides to ventilate a little. But the thought of being an Entitled Observer makes me sweat even more. I quick check my body for the telltale prickles of a gathering rash, but all I feel is the rawness of my phototested rear.

"Bake sales," Ms. Kavoussi ponders before her frown deepens. She plays with her pearls like they are a rosary, and I get the distinct sense that I'm the one who should be praying. "You've raised fifty thousand dollars over forty-nine bake sales. That's solid."

Why am I getting the impression that "solid" in college-application speak means inadequate?

"And I wrote about fifty different causes," I tell her, and pull out my copy of the essay, so flustered I barely remember what I wrote. "I interviewed leaders, researched trends, and Aminta drew political cartoons. We distributed our pamphlets through bake sales with even more info online on Medium." Now that I hear myself, it sounds like amateur hour. Maybe I should have stayed on *Liberty News*, writing my way up the editorial chain, censorship and all.

"Yes, my hips are well acquainted with your bake sales. Good causes. All of them" — *tap!* — "but college admissions officers have read about every single issue and every single brownie in the world. They like focus. Focus is good. Being the editor of the school paper would have been excellent."

"I was censored! Don't my articles for my bake sales show initiative?"

Tappity-tap-tap! "Some kids have raised a million dollars for cancer research with their lemonade stands. I'm sorry, but that's the kind of initiative that NYU Abu Dhabi is looking for."

No wonder there's a box of Kleenex on the conference table, ready for the spontaneous combustion of egos and the ensuing tears when you discover that despite what your parents have told you, special you, there are sixty thousand students Better Than You with better grades, better test scores, better brownies.

"But it's all I have," I tell her. From her pursed lips, it's obviously not enough.

"What could be compelling is how you manage your own health crisis." Ms. Kavoussi leans back in her seat to stare at me. "That's unique. What do you think?"

"No," I grit out despite Ms. Kavoussi's lifted eyebrow, "because this is not going to change my life at all."

GEEKS FOR GOOD MEETING

(checked against audio)

SEATTLE— The following is a full transcript of a meeting with Geeks for Good, a community service group sited at Liberty Prep. It has been edited for content and clarity.

Participants: Aminta Sarabhai, Caresse Jackson, Viola Wynne Li

> Aminta: *Caresse and I have been thinking . . .*
> Viola: *[unintelligible sound, possibly a groan.]*
> *[Nervous laughter.]*
> Caresse: *Honestly, we can take a break on the bake sales for now until you get better. Or stabilize. There's no urgent need—*
> Viola: *Not a chance. I need fifty bake sales.*
> Aminta: *That's not going to make or break your college apps. And a bake sale isn't going to make or break one of the groups we support.*
> Viola: *But it'll make or break me.*
> Caresse: *That's the point! We don't want to break you.*

Aminta: *So let us help bake this one time. We can totally handle it.*

Caresse: *And we'll handle all of the setup.*

Aminta: *Not to mention, all of the sales. We'll handle all the table duty, drop-off, lunch, and pick-up.*

Viola: *And what's my role then?*

Aminta:

Caresse:

Viola: *[unintelligible sound, possibly a chair scooting back, sneakers running away, door shutting with a soft bang.]*

CHAPTER TWENTY-ONE

Take an indie bookstore dedicated to geekery, add a café that serves all things buttery goodness, throw in shadow-box tables filled with antique compasses and cameras, and you have one of my favorite places on the planet. One that I need today after my dream-killing meetings, first with Ms. Kavoussi, then with my friends (formerly known as my bake-sale buddies). It's a few minutes after four, and I have hustled from school to Ada's Technical Books for the sole purpose of getting comfortably settled before Josh arrives. My timing may be wrong: be fashionably late and all. But there is nothing fashionable about UPF clothes. Which is why I plan to be parked at a table with as much of me concealed as humanly possible and with maximum time to purge the thought that my life is changing, with or without my consent.

Case in point: Fate laughs at me in the face once again.

Unfortunately, after I wave at the best barista at Ada's—a mermaid on land with sea-glass everything: earrings, necklace, and wispy blue-green hair—I catch the unmistakable unfurling of a hulk wearing a matching safari hat as he straightens out of a gunmetal gray chair. Josh and his (many) (many) muscles wait for me to take my seat before he sits back down at the one table that hugs the wall, away from the bank of windows.

"Hey!" Josh says as he tips his brim in my direction. "The hat looks great on you."

"Thanks, I love it," I say with a shy smile, then bend down to rest my messenger bag at my feet.

"Is this table okay?"

A single exposed light bulb hangs over our table, but thanks to him, my helmet du jour should keep me safe. What could an hour do to me, covered as I am?

"This is perfect," I tell him and mean it, especially when I notice what lies under the glass tabletop: a telescoping spyglass and a chart of the stars.

"It's like — " I start to say.

At the same time, Josh asks, "Do you want — "

We do the whole awkward first dance of conversations: "you first," "no, you first," "no, really, you go."

Somehow, I'd forgotten just how blue his eyes are. I clear my throat and tap the star map. "It's like Persephone is with us."

"Whoa, a little weird, isn't it?" he says, but he still looks distracted and nods toward the back room, nestled dark and cozy on all four sides with floor-to-ceiling bookshelves. "We can go over there if it's better." (For you.)

I hear that silent addendum and add my own silent sigh. Frankly, it's embarrassing that any concessions have to be made for me. More importantly, I don't want any pity accommodations, not when I'm perfectly fine. Liar, liar: I adjust uncomfortably on the hard chair. Recovering from the phototest or from a meeting with Ms. Kavoussi or an intervention from my friends is not the fastest thing I've ever experienced. I assure him, "I'm great here."

"Sorry. You can add me to the list of nags."

"Parents, aunt, doctors, college counselor, and you," I say lightly, even though I feel off balance like I haven't eaten or drank anything in three days, maybe four. "Done." Yes, my future is done. My eyes water, and I bite my lip because I don't want to cry now.

"What?"

"I just got some bad news, that's all."

"Your doctor?"

"No, well, yes, that, too." I take a shaky breath, still hearing Ms. Kavoussi's penetrating questions. "With my condition, I'm not sure I can be a journalist anymore. It's what I've wanted to do since I was a kid."

"That sucks," he says. "Are all your bake sales for causes?"

"Yeah, how'd you know?"

"All your articles hanging on your wall at home. It kind of seems like you do a lot more than just report about an issue. You take a stand and try to make a change, more like an activist."

Was that true? I had never thought about myself that way: an activist. And I hadn't seen my writing from that angle: to create change, not just to document. I frown.

"Something to think about, anyway," Josh says with a slight smile like he knows he's inverted my world.

"Definitely," I tell him, wishing I had something hot to drink now. I feel so cold. "It's just hard to look at my life in a new way. Being a foreign correspondent is what I've always planned to do."

"I know that feeling. My twin died. We fought like you wouldn't believe, but I never thought I'd go through life alone."

Just then, the barista calls Josh's name, and he jumps up. A moment later, he sets a steaming mug in front of me. "I figured all the baristas knew you. Almond milk chai, geothermally hot. Did we get it right?"

It's not just the table location or meeting Ms. Kavoussi or blathering about myself that's thrown me off. It's this guy himself.

"Totally right," I tell him. "Thanks! What do I owe you?" He waves my offer away as I take an experimental sip and sigh. "This drink is a public service."

"What do you mean?"

I wrap my hands around the mug. "Caffeine to get me through homework, more nutritious than a cookie, good for my bones. See? It's prepping me to be a healthy, productive member of society. Public service."

"So you should be paid to drink this?"

"Heck, yeah! Hey, where's yours?"

"I don't drink."

"What do you mean? You don't drink the most amazing homemade chai tea in the world out of, what? Misplaced loyalty to coffee?"

"No caffeine."

"Coffee? Coke? Red Bull?"

He shakes his safari-hatted head (adorably).

"Beer," I crow with a triumphant lift of my mug. "Straight shots of vodka. No, tequila, right?"

"None of the above. Just water."

"Seriously?" I lower my chai, deflated.

Josh's eyes crinkle at the edges. He doesn't even attempt to conceal his not-so-subtle smugness. "Surprised you, didn't I?"

I blush because it's true that I've judged and convicted him of being one of those guys who views flirting and partying as professional sports. I mean, those (broad) shoulders, those light blue eyes. How could they not be weapons of female destruction? Plus, Aminta had warned me about him. "You just kind of seem like the partier type."

Instead of being offended, he simply says, "I was. Until a car accident after a party."

He looks lost in a bad memory, and I ask quietly, "What happened?"

"A truck T-boned us."

"That's awful. Were you hurt?"

His hands knot together on the table. "No." (I wish.)

I hear that silent "I wish" loud and clear. How many times last night did I yell the same thing in the privacy of my own head? "I wish this hadn't happened to me. I wish things were different. I wish I were Roz instead." And his? How much did it cross over to "I wish I were the one who died?" because I swear, I hear that, and I hate it.

Finally, Josh says, "I was too drunk to drive home after a party last summer. So my girlfriend called Caleb. My parents would have flipped out since they'd given me an ultimatum. I'd partied through junior year, and this would have meant the end of my car. I was worried about my stupid car. What an asshole, huh?"

"I'm sorry."

"I can still hear the metal crushing in the driver's side."

I grimace. His eyes are hot when he catches my expression before dropping his gaze back down to his notebook covered in scribbles. I tell him, "If I can still hear my diagnosis, I can't imagine a car accident."

His words are barely discernible. "It's my fault."

It is, he said, not it was. As if the accident is happening real-time in his head. As if his guilt is a gathering storm. Our silence fills with the sharp angles of his grief, all the "what ifs" and "only ifs" that are crowding us out.

"You know, I almost killed my little sister once." Then I tell him about the day Roz stepped on the nail, following me and Aminta and our ice cream, and I have to believe that he's paying attention even if he's not looking at me. Finally, I share what I've never told anyone, not even really remembering it until now. "That night, my dad came into my room and made sure I knew my job as the Big Sister is to protect Roz until death do us part. So it was my fault that she fell."

"Your dad actually told you that?" Josh asks, indignant. His eyes finally raise to meet mine. "He blamed you?"

"Well, he didn't say that it was my fault exactly, but—"

"Well, good! It wasn't. You didn't make her step on the nail."

I want to take his hand in mine, but I don't. Instead, I hold his gaze steadily. "You weren't in control of that other driver."

A waiter with a trimmed goatee chooses that precise, awkward silence when I wonder if I've said way, way, way too much to drop off a thick, gooey grilled cheese sandwich. How could I have compared Roz's couple of stitches and cast-wrapped foot to his twin's death? Correction, Ms. Kavoussi: I am an Entitled Unobservant Jerk.

Instead of grabbing his stuff and leaving me the way I thought he would, Josh slides the warm plate across the table. His tone is light when he says, "Public service, right?"

"No, personal gluttony."

Josh busts out laughing, and I can't help smirking back at him.

"Hey, so my letter," I say apropos of nothing but nervous energy, and not the way I had rehearsed in my Subaru: all calm and cool and uncaffeinated. I place one of the wedges on the extra plate and nudge the other back to him. Even though he's stopped laughing, the afterglow of his smile softens the guilty edge in his eyes. I'm relieved. "So I'm sorry."

"Sorry for what? That you made good points?" He rubs the side of his nose self-consciously and pushes his textbook to the edge of the table. "Math and science aren't my strong suits, obviously. I didn't think the second time around would be so hard, though."

"You look like you're studying your brains out now."

"I better be. I've got four years of high school to make up in a year."

"How come?"

He flushes. "I owe Caleb."

That's when I decide to share my research on light with Josh, after all. I pull out my Mac to airdrop the document to him. "Well, then this is your lucky day."

"Because you're here?"

See also: player.

"You say that to all the girls," I chide him, yet I actually up the ante (see also: idiot) by telling him, "because it just so happens that I am a great researcher."

"I could tell."

"How?"

"Your article."

"You actually read it?"

"I actually did." After a moment, his phone pings. Josh immediately skims the research document, frowning in concentration. He finally looks at me, appraisingly, and asks, "So are you one of those girls who's really good at math but pretends not to be?"

All thoughts of calm and cool go by the wayside of uncaffeinated. I narrow my eyes at him. "Do you have a problem with smart women?"

"No, smart and strong is a total turn-on. It's why Persephone is a rocket scientist. Literally."

"I must have missed that."

"It's going to be in the second issue." Josh drops his eyes back to his screen before training his big sky blues on me again. "I really like the idea of her being bioluminescent. What would trigger it? I mean, what if she goes bright at the wrong time?"

"Because she can control it on her planet," I theorize, then I clap my hands together. "But there's sunlight here, and she's not used to that. It's like driving a new car for the first couple of times when you don't know how much acceleration you have."

"Or braking power."

"Yeah, so think about her skin suddenly going all twinkly in the snow at the wrong time —"

"Like right before a battle. She betrays herself."

"And the people she's fighting with. They all die."

We both look at each other, knowing we've struck a plotline of gold. Josh strums his fingers on his calculus book, while my mind charts its own constellation of possibilities: Ms. Kavoussi's idea to write about a capstone experience, my crisis slaying of solar urticaria. Maybe I didn't need to speak out for my condition. Maybe Persephone could.

Josh tilts his head to the side and studies me like he's Caresse, designing a costume for me or Aminta, only he's marking all my points, physical and personal.

"What?" I ask.

"Nothing."

It makes me nervous, all this attention: the chai tea and grilled cheese, his stare, my corresponding one. Even when I lower my gaze and tuck my hair behind my ear, I can feel him searching me. Was my face getting red with a rash? I cup my cheeks. No, just an old-fashioned blush.

Josh finally takes a bite of his sandwich. I take a companionable bite of mine when he says, "So."

"Yeah?" I ask as he sets down the crust on his plate.

"All the best stories begin with so."

"So," I say, pause, and smile at him.

He laughs, then says, "Why don't you enlighten me?"

"About what?"

"Whatever your doctor told you."

So. I find myself telling him about the phototest, solar urticaria, the rarity of also possibly having PMLE, the symptoms, the treatments, the lack of a cure. It comes out all clinical and antiseptic like I've gone to medical school and I'm talking about someone else, someone I don't know. That is, until Josh makes it about me: "That's tough — the sun making you sick. It really sucks. Should you even be out now?"

"Well, yeah. I'm covered up." I frame my hands around the hat and flutter my eyes. "See?"

"But what are you going to do if you can't go outside anymore?"

My mouth opens, then closes, a fish trapped in a faulty aquarium. My brain is nothing but white space, devoid of words or ideas or answers. The fact is, I haven't let myself consider being locked in the dark forever, which is weird because I've spent my entire life listening to my parents coach executives to be prepared for the worst-case scenario. How else can you protect your company unless you identify the very worst thing that can happen? How else do you build the best security system? The ultimate safety plan?

I just hadn't thought I would ever need to construct a worst-case contingency plan for myself at eighteen.

"I don't know," I finally confess, "but I think I miss trail running the most. I miss running in the woods. That's a little treacherous in the dark."

He nods. "I'm really sorry. That must be tough." We're both quiet for a long time until Josh says, "There are so many layers we didn't put into *Persephone*."

"So am I just research?" I ask. "I'm not going to read about me in an issue, am I?"

He doesn't even hesitate or lie. "Maybe. You muses inspire just by being."

Muse? I'm his muse? Both of us flush, avert our gazes as if we've shared too much. Josh tilts his seat back, stares up at the funky light fixture above: a galaxy made of pages taken from technical manuals. Suddenly, the front legs of his chair crash onto the ground. People spin around to look at us, but he doesn't notice them. All he notices appears to be me. His gaze is steady, unrelenting.

Did I have a stray nose hair? A bread crumb wedged between my front teeth? Were my cheeks blistering now? I gently wipe my face on my shoulder and, thankfully, don't feel a single suggestion of soreness or bumps.

Josh says, "So."

"Story time?"

"Ultraviolent Reyes."

"Ultraviolet rays," I correct him.

"Ultraviolent," he intones like he's an announcer at a Seahawks game. "Reyes!"

Everyone stares at us. Again. Not that he cares. Apparently, Josh does not do subtle. He says, "Could be the name of a superhero, right? Or Persephone's best friend?"

"Or her archenemy."

His eyes widen as he nods with increasing speed. "Yeah. Her enemy. Her superpower are her UV rays, right?"

"It doesn't matter as long as she's dressed in real clothes."

Another loud bark of his laughter annoys the woman near the water station in the back of the coffee shop. I smile benignly.

"So." Josh leans forward, hands clasped, Dad's classic closing-the-deal position.

"This better be good."

"Oh, it is. We should work together."

Which was exactly what I had been thinking. No, what I was thinking: He is awfully cute when he gets all worked up. But what I was really thinking: I want to date him, not just work with him as if that ever stopped Mom and Dad.

Hang on.

How on earth did I promote someone I've known for all of a few hours—some of that when I was unconscious—to boyfriend potential? A guy who imagines a planet filled with scantily clad Persephones and (probably) equally clothing-challenged Ultraviolent Reyes. I can't be associated with either comic or comic book creator.

His fingers play a nervous drumbeat on his notebook, open to a page of calculations mixed with doodles: the spaceship *Serenity*, a safari hat, the frozen icicles of Franklin Falls. Doodles like he had been possibly, maybe, hopefully thinking about me, too.

"What do you think?" he asks.

All of my yes-no-I-don't-know answers get clogged in my throat when—seriously—Death Cab for Cutie starts playing "I'll Follow You into the Dark" as if we're on a movie set of a romantic comedy, but this can only end as a tragedy because what chance do I have of a boyfriend with my condition? *Oh, never mind me, honey, while I explode into hives in front of you.*

"It would never work," I murmur.

"Why not?" he counters.

Wait — what? What did I say out loud? I take a hasty sip of my chai as I instant replay the last ten seconds. To buy myself even more time to think of a comeback, I spoon a dollop of cranberry sauce on the remains of my sandwich.

"Why wouldn't we work together on this?" he persists. "We brainstorm great. You obviously can research. I know how to get it printed."

A smear of bloodlike red is all that's left of the mound of cranberry sauce. I feel nauseous and push the plate away from me.

"What?" Josh says. "I can feel an entire monologue going on in your head. Tell me what you're thinking."

I breathe out, not realizing until that moment that I'd been holding my breath. Yeah, right, tell him. Not a chance of that when I don't want to acknowledge my own (uncensored) thoughts: I want my old life back, all safe and sunshiney with boyfriend possibilities.

So I tell him, "I guess, maybe, if Persephone wore some clothes."

He looks away from me and shakes his head. "Her uniform's not changeable."

"Everything is changeable."

"Not this."

In our silent impasse, it finally occurs to me that the V of my neckline tingles. Oh, no. No, no, no, not again. I duck my head, worst-case scenarios spinning in my mind. But I'm armored in UPF clothing, I'm not sitting in the sun, and even if there is a light bulb above my head, a hat shields me. Yet prickles spread up my neck, and I want to scratch my skin so badly. Instead, I stand and tell him, "I got to go."

"Already?"

In my head, I answer, confidently, *Text me later.* In my head, I stride out to my car as he watches me, intrigued. In my head, I'm perfectly normal. As it turns out, my nerve endings have gone berserk. Unbalanced, I grasp the edge of the table, and Josh jumps up to steady me.

"Ultra," he says. "I'll drive you home."

"You say that to all the girls. I'm fine."

"It's either me or call your parents."

I narrow my eyes at him, but I'm not sure I can let go of the table or him. Who knew his negotiating skills were on par with Lee & Li? All I can do is nod. What the hell is going on with me? He slips one arm around my waist as he lifts my heavy messenger bag off the ground with enviable ease.

"My truck's just a block away. Can you make it?" he asks, his breath warm on my cheek.

Speaking wastes energy. I nod. One step, then another, until we stop at a fiery red pickup truck. It's too much effort to snark about his macho road machine when the step up is so high it could be a hurdle. Somehow, I hoist myself into the passenger seat without help. As soon as Josh is inside the cab, he glances at me, then gently rights the safari hat that's slid off-kilter on my head. The sunroof is open, exposing us to the insistent sun through the clear glass.

"Sorry, the cover was busted when I got the truck." Even after a cyclist passes us, Josh waits a beat, and then another before maneuvering into the street. "For the record, Ultra, you're the first girl I've wanted in here."

CHAPTER TWENTY-TWO

The real emergency this afternoon wasn't my near faint at Ada's, which I've since — thankfully — recovered from (more or less). The real emergency is unfolding right now on the dining room table, loaded down with large plastic mailers. No doubt, the rest of my sun-blocking wardrobe bought on extra-super-special-clearance has arrived. I can only imagine what these will look like. (Puce! Tan! Mustard!)

Let me pass out now.

My parents have a different plan, of course. As soon as the house alarm alerts that Josh and I have come home, they emerge from the kitchen, Dad clenching a (filched) Minecraft Creeper cookie, snagged from the batch I decorated last night for the bake sale. I'm too preoccupied by this imminent parental crisis to grill Dad on how much inventory he's consumed.

"What's wrong?" Mom asks, eyes boring into every visible pore on my skin.

"Nothing," I start to say, because it's true (more or less). I feel eighty percent better now, but I know my pat answer will never satisfy my parents. To conserve energy, I sink onto the plush sofa in the living room and tell them, "What I mean is, I feel a lot better now. And I already talked to Dr. Anderson." See? Crisis handled by yours truly, no parental intervention needed.

"About what?" Dad flicks off the light switch as if a single moment under the lights will kill me. Thirty minutes ago, it felt like the one above me at Ada's just might. Even though I feel mostly better, I sag against the back of the couch and bask in the darkness, blessed darkness, that now floods the living room.

"You're red." Mom stands in front of me and asks, "Do we need to take you back to Children's?"

"No!" I sigh, and straighten immediately. Of course my parents would choose this day to leave work at the exact same time. I make a note to tell Josh that pre-crisis cognition is the superpower Persephone ought to have — the ability to sniff out a crisis before it even happens.

"We were at Ada's," I tell my parents, "and I just had a . . . thing."

"A thing? What kind of thing?" Mom asks, snatching her water glass from the dining table and shoving it at me. "Drink."

"Mom."

Dad directs the question at Josh. "What kind of thing?"

Josh responds to my parents easily as if he's known them his whole life, "Viola felt a little sick. So I drove her home while she called her doctor."

"Oh, honey," Mom says, sitting next to me.

"Then she started feeling a lot better," Josh continues, "but her car's still parked there. I can drive one of you back to pick it up?"

"That'd be great, later," says Dad before dropping into the armchair across from me. "How are you feeling, kiddo?"

"Fine, now." Except that Josh is standing by himself. So I scoot to make room for him and pat the empty spot on my other side.

"We should call Dr. Anderson," Mom suggests, already pulling out her phone.

"Already done," I repeat with, I admit, satisfaction that grows when my parents look stunned. "I read the information that Dr. Anderson gave us at the hospital" — (correction: *finally* read the information, after exiling the sheet to the crumble-covered bottom of my messenger bag) — "then I called him to fact-check, and he agreed that maybe driving could have triggered my . . . episode. So I'll use all my birthday and Christmas money that I've saved up to tint the windows. He agreed that made sense, and he'd be happy to sign whatever medical form I need to turn in to the state. I'll ask Auntie Ruth, who can do the work. Done."

My parents exchange a look, half-impressed, but still mostly anxious. What more can I say to reassure them? Josh squeezes my hand. That unexpected touch so completely blindsides me, so completely distracts me, I literally have to catch my breath.

Despite my plan, Mom still embarks on her own fact-finding mission. "How much time did you spend outside?"

I sigh. "Seriously?"

"Seriously."

"I walked, like, a couple of steps, then I drove," I say. "And then we were inside at Ada's for about an hour. I wore a bunch of layers, and I had my hat on, too. Everything UPF 50."

"Hmm." Dad's leg fidgets up and down.

What now? Seriously, what now? Whatever plans my parents are conspiring, Dad just says, "Well, you should go rest now. I'll get your car with Josh."

To his credit, Josh looks like he wants to say a thousand things to me, but not one of them is panic to be driving alone with my dad in his pickup. Out of nowhere, Mom does her "oh!" thing and tears out of the living room for reasons unknown. Thankfully, Dad follows her, leaving the two of us alone.

"Doing okay, Ultra?" Josh asks.

"Mortified."

"Don't be. My parents can't say two sentences without getting into a fight. It's, like, tension, all the time. Yours are actually partners, like, they really work together. I mean, not just work work, but—"

"Parenting together? Nagging together? Publicly humiliating together?"

"Caring." His hand touches my knee. Then stays on my knee. That touch, that nickname, accomplish what ten hours of sleep, followed by gallons of chai tea could never do: They vanquish all signs of weariness.

My own words, I don't trust, not when my insides are warm and discombobulated. So I simply hope he's engaged in the same silent planning as me. *Why, yes, kiss me, Thor.* To prod him to this logical conclusion, I look straight into his eyes and hold his gaze, one second, then two. My lips part. His eyes dip to my mouth. I sigh. And there it is: The Moment. Anticipation itself has weight and heft and four dimensions: here, now, you, me. In The Moment, time itself becomes part of the kiss, a prelude to our yes. Josh leans in; I do, too. I can almost feel the kiss before it happens: now, now, now.

And then, wouldn't you know it, my parents clatter down the hall before returning to the living room, deforesting The Moment of any sign or sigh of life. In our own silent partnership, Josh and I rear from each other at the same time.

"Ta-da!" Mom says, brandishing a zippered pink pouch of an emergency kit. An emergency kit. She bestows said emergency kit on Josh. "For you."

I.

Kid.

You.

Not.

"Talk later," Josh says to me, gamely holding the kit bulging with I'm-afraid-to-know-what.

As soon as Dad and Josh leave, Mom plunks herself down on the sofa, unintentionally bouncing me on the seat cushion like we've hit a pothole. I stifle a groan because only now do I notice that my body does, in fact, hurt.

"He seems like a great boy. See, honey?" Mom smiles radiantly bright, inflicting damage without even meaning it. (An emergency kit!) She says, "See? Not everything needs to change."

But everything has. I feel it deep in my bones, which now ache like I've aged eighty years.

CHAPTER TWENTY-THREE

"Honey!" Mom cries out as if we've been separated for seven long years instead of seven short hours with me tucked in my bedroom exactly one floor beneath theirs. Her voice lowers to a whisper and she asks, "What are you doing up?"

"Why do you think?" It's four in the morning, and the night has been, shall we say, restless? My bedroom door has been opened and closed no fewer than three times with one or both parents checking in on me like I'm a newborn on the brink of SIDS. Multiple awakenings, though, have the productive side effect of bonus text checks from Josh. Like now. I check my phone.

Still nothing, nothing, nothing.

Whatever happened to "talk later"?

Mom squints at my face. Even though the only light comes from the tiny motion-detecting one out in the hallway, she proclaims, "You aren't as red, I think. That's progress."

"I know, right?" I say, playing along, because if I'm not all hearty and hale now, she'll shift into Crisis Overdrive: *A date at a coffee shop is too dangerous!* I can't even pretend to go to sleep again. So I slide the phone back under the covers and sit up, managing to conceal my wince. My body feels tenderized like I've spent a few too many hours in the weight room. I tell Mom, "I'm starving!"

Instead of lecturing me on the perils of late-night snacking, Mom lights up. "Me, too! Almond butter on a rice cake?"

"Suddenly, not so hungry."

"Kettle corn?"

I shake my head and counter, "Jalapeño cheddar?"

"That sounds surprisingly good," she whispers, then wrinkles her nose. "But messy."

"I'll wash my sheets tomorrow if we goop on them."

"Deal." Mom grins and scoots off my bed. "Okay, baby, cue up *The Great British Baking Show*."

The suggestion to watch our all-time favorite show isn't even out of her mouth before I reach for my computer, only to have my phone ping. My body does as well. Expectant, I grasp the phone. As much as I hope it's Josh, it's not. Insomnia must run in the family this morning, because the text is from Auntie Ruth, who tells me that she's called in a favor with her window tinter of choice, but it'll be at least two weeks before that shop can fit me in.

> Auntie Ruth: *I'm so sorry! But Mary is worth the wait! It's so easy to screw up tinting, kind of like eyebrows. (Never wax them. Ever.)*
> Auntie Ruth: *Hey, I miss seeing you and your eyebrows around here.*
> Me: *Me, too.*

The truth is: As much as I do miss Auntie Ruth and I appreciate her help with the Subaru windows, her outpouring of guilt makes me feel worse about my condition. I'm not ready to face her alone quite yet. In the kitchen, the microwave alerts: The popcorn's done. In another few minutes, Mom creeps back into my bedroom and snuggles next to me under the covers, resting the popcorn bowl on a kitchen towel between us.

"Ready?" Mom asks.

"Always." I hit the space bar on my Mac to start the show while Mom plumps a pillow.

"Actually," she says, placing the extra support behind me. "Now we're ready."

Since discovering the baking series, I've rationed the episodes, hoarding each one like they're the last remaining sticks of unsalted butter on our planet. In middle school, I'd actually bake along with each episode, a virtual contestant, participating in all the challenges from making my signature dish to architecting my showstopper. I swear, watching the show is how my baking improved astronomically beyond mere chocolate chip cookies. Tonight, though, I can't concentrate on the anatomy of a light, airy pâte à choux, my mind springing instead from thought to thought: Josh's silence to Auntie Ruth's disappointing text to the parts of my conversation with Dr. Anderson that I'd chosen to deny.

"Too much jalapeño?" Mom asks, worried, a few minutes into the episode when I still haven't eaten more than two pieces of popcorn. "I always mess up the proportions."

I finally tell her, "Dr. Anderson said that some people can't even tolerate the light through tinted windows."

Mom nods. Of course she'd known that already.

"What if I can't drive anymore?" I ask, keeping my eyes on the screen between us, but all I see is another piece of my freedom vanish. It's not like riding a bus would be any safer, surrounded as it is with four sides of light-welcoming windows.

Mom sighs. "We'll figure something out."

"Until then, no driving, huh?"

She shakes her head, then nestles me against her, perching her chin on the top of my head. With a sigh, Mom adds the refrain that the Sick Girl will hear for the rest of her life: "I'm sorry, honey."

CHAPTER TWENTY-FOUR

Silence is, in fact, golden.

Golden as the sun, punching through the barricade of clouds on Friday morning. Funny, my skin's just fine, it's my life that's being fried alive. That's the way I feel, sequestered all day yesterday "to recover" and now cornered in the back seat of my parents' Volvo sedan, silent and hidden under the thickest blanket Mom could find at home. Because my parents can't reschedule the conference call addressing global pandemics like Ebola and because there is no safe spot for me in the boathouse, our parents made the executive decision that my sister will miss crew practice today. The wails. The wails!

"Wait," says Roz, leaning toward the front seats, where our parents are rehearsing their call strategy. "How am I supposed to get to crew for the next two weeks? And back home? Or from now on if the tinting doesn't work?"

Curious about how they're going to answer that, I lower my blanket shield. Mom and Dad exchange glances at this unexpected question, not a surprise, because most of my sister's transportation questions have been dealt with by yours truly since the fateful day I passed my driver's test. Dad must have lost the ro-sham-bo of meaningful stares with Mom, because he is the one who answers: "Plan B. The bus."

"The what?" Roz looks genuinely confused.

"The bus."

On the Scoville scale of anger, Roz reaches the habanero level: blistering. She hisses at me, "You're ruining my life."

Do my parents say anything? Well, yes, if you count their mild, "Rosalind. Honey."

I hadn't known what a relief it would be to retire from being my sister's keeper. I huddle under the blanket again.

Roz starts furiously (literally) texting, punctuated with sporadic muttering: "You know, *some* people want to be crew captain by their junior year." Then, "How does anyone expect me to be *crew captain* if I don't show up on time at practice every day, every season, every year?"

Meanwhile, I sink deeper in silence, shrinking from any real and imagined fractal of light. The sun grazes the tips of my fingers. I yank them back under the cloak of darkness because I don't want a single hint of a rash, not even the subtlest reddening of my skin before school. Then, what would I do next? I wipe the sweat off my nose. Boiling, I'm boiling alive under this woolen tent for one.

Finally, after an eternity and a half, we reach Liberty. I lower the blanket and drink in fresh air as we pull in front of the Quad, the square surrounded by the main office and chapel turned performance hall. The square flanked by the redbrick library and science buildings. The square occupied by Aminta and Caresse, sitting at the bake-sale table.

The bake sale.

My stomach craters.

"Whoa!" Roz snickers at Aminta in her steampunk outfit, complete with a stovepipe hat, and Caresse in her latest creation, an eggplant-colored maxi dress with a cowboy hat. "What are they wearing?"

I have eyes only for the empty bake-sale table.

The bake sale, where I was supposed to provide the cookies. The Minecraft Creeper cookies still on our kitchen counter, individually wrapped and tied with maroon ribbons and labels that read: GEEKS FOR GIRLS AROUND THE WORLD! The bake-sale table decorated with my articles and a six-foot-long banner.

Our Volvo barely has time to stop before I bolt out of the car, tugging my messenger bag after me.

"Hey, Viola!" Aminta waves to me. "You're here!" (Finally!)

Caresse stands up, eyebrows furrowed. "Where are the cookies? Everybody's been waiting for them."

"I'm sorry!" I try to explain the morning: Losing my driving privileges made me lose my memory.

"It's okay." Aminta nods emphatically. "You have a lot going on."

Caresse half-shrugs and studies the tips of her boots. No one gets mad at the Sick Girl.

"I'll ask my parents if one of them can drive the cookies over," I say, knowing that the chances of that are nil, but I walk back to the car. Mom's already rolled down the window, shaking the blanket like a matador as if anyone can miss seeing it. The conference call has started, but both of my parents are mouthing to me while gesturing: Go inside! Hurry!

Not until I salvage this second bake sale for Geeks for Good. I whisper to Mom, "Can you go home to get the cookies? Please?" For good measure, I take the blanket from her, as if I'm really going to drape it around myself while I'm in class.

She shakes her head regretfully, but then her mouth shapes into a victorious smile. "Auntie Ruth!"

But no, I don't want to see Auntie Ruth. Her guilty texts alone drown me in her anxiety—*I am so so so so so sooooooooo sorry!* What would her in-person presence do to me?

"This is no big deal," Aminta assures me as my parents drive away. "Maybe you really should get out of the light?"

I've become the ghost of bake sales past, haunting unwanted.

THE RACE IS ON

After a story breaks, reporters will race to get the story out. It's fast and (usually) straightforward. They'll describe just the bare bones. But be prepared for misinformation.

—Lee & Li Communications
Inside the War Room: The Crisis Management Playbook

CHAPTER TWENTY-FIVE

You know that feeling when everyone is staring at you, and you tell yourself that you're imagining things because it's just absentee cookies from a bake sale, after all? Only you have inconvertible proof that people are, in fact, staring at you because your little sister confirms it with her text to STAY AWAY from her at school.

Seriously, they're only cookies, people.

Somehow, some way, you—the person who has shied from being the center of attention—have become the center of your high school's universe.

The sideways stares, the scandalized murmurings, all the signs of impending crisis.

It can't get much worse, you tell yourself.

Only it does.

CHAPTER TWENTY-SIX

A lifetime with my parents has trained me to scan the environment for even the slightest signal of change, the smallest disturbance of the field — really no different from being on Pimple Patrol like every other teenager. Was my nose reddening? Was there an ever so subtle pain on my forehead? Did a pore on my chin look a tiny bit inflamed?

That was my face then; this is it now.

So when people's eyes flit away guilty-fast, I know it's only a matter of moments before I find out what the hell is going on, because, really, how many people can possibly be upset that my cookies no-showed? My skin feels clammy-damp, but I force my arms to stay at my side instead of touching my cheeks. Still, the stares. It almost makes me want to throw the blanket over myself. Almost.

There is no possible way that the (slow-moving, censorship-happy) administration could have answered the missive my parents have composed, fact-checked, and legal-approved to UV-proof the hell out of every speck of visible and invisible light at school, could they? As I hurry down the hall, heading for history, where I can hide for a few minutes, a couple of kids swivel to stare at me. There is no mistaking the ultraviolent rays of their collective curiosity. I tip the brim of my hat lower, wishing that I could do a Persephone and vanish to another planet.

"So is it contagious? What she has?" asks Brian, a guy I've known since fifth grade, field-tripped together countless times to the Pacific Science Center, and even ate fried silkworms with side by side at an assembly. As soon as he started high school, though, Brian jockeyed his way out of nerd-dom and into popularity with his new six-pack abs.

"Slug-brain, no," says Aminta, my defender who's followed me inside the main building. I think everyone in the hall is as startled as I am by Aminta's harsh tone. This is the girl who's been voted Most Likely to be Emma Watson in the UN and who's slated to fast-track at MIT, where she'll invent some groundbreaking contraption that will change the emerging world. "You can't catch solar urticaria. It's not like the flu."

"What?" scoffs Brian, his lip curling. "You Doctors Without Borders or something?"

Aminta's cheeks flush like she's the one who's been out in the sun for too long. Forget hiding. No one messes with my friends. I march over to them, a blaze of red. It is a tiny bit satisfying to see Brian cower, even if he's not intimidated so much as he is revolted. There is no mistaking that people are staring.

Let them stare.

Hands on my hips, I demand, "If you have something to say, say it to my face." (Slug-brain!)

"You're all over YouTube," he tells me, smirking.

Uneasiness takes root. I ask, "What do you mean?"

"*Firefly* fan films." Brian (gleefully) cues up the one episode I have never seen on his phone.

"You are such a jerk," Aminta tells him, trying to drag me away, but I can't take my eyes off my solo performance.

There's so much of me and only me, front, center, full zoom. The footage turns to the moment lost from my memory when I am prone on the ground, my eyes closed, my cheeks disturbingly red. Even if I cannot bear to watch this in full view of everyone at school, I'm statue-still, riveted by what I see: I am drooling.

Drooling.

"Stop it," Aminta orders Brian.

"Fine." He lifts his phone to shoot new, raw footage of my face. Aminta grabs for his phone. Brian body-blocks her, indignant. "Hey! Personal property. Touch it and you're going to be so busted by the judicial committee."

"You are so going to be busted by the police," Aminta shoots back.

"Yeah," he sneers, "for what?"

Aminta is silent, at a loss for words. Brian's smirk deepens.

"Not the police, the FBI," I say, my voice so much stronger than my marshmallow legs feel. "Filming with the intent of doing harm." Who knows if that is true, but the threat sounds real. More importantly, I do not quaver, and I do not lower my eyes one single degree. Instead, I go full-on Genghis Khan and stare that boy down. Journalists never cower, not in the face of an authoritarian tyrant in government, not in my school hall.

Caresse joins us on my other side. She tosses her long dreads and wriggles her own phone in the air. "I got the whole thing. I'm sure Dr. Luthra and the judicial committee are going to find this highly interesting."

Brian vanishes, grumbling about girls on their periods and entrapment. Mr. Bluster, that's all he is, the bully who can dish it but can't take it. Even if I know that, I'm trembling. Ms. Bluster, the kind who can dish it but can't stand afterward.

"You okay?" Caresse asks me, frowning with concern.

I cannot even nod to thank them for being on my side because I'm heaving, somewhere between throwing up and weeping. The bell rings. I spin around and run. The hall teems with people who turn to gawk at me. The cloud of gossip hangs low and heavy. I can't breathe. I've become a mutant species, never before seen and intensely scrutinized now. I barge into the bathroom. Every single stall is occupied. There is nowhere to hide and regroup.

"Honestly?" My uneven breath battles my sobs for control of the conflict zone that is my body.

Aminta and Caresse follow me inside.

"Viola, do you want to go to the office?" Aminta asks, anxious.

That—that concern—is almost as bad as Auntie Ruth's guilt. There is a reason why I haven't answered any of her texts. Not for days.

Shaking my head, I race outside into the brilliant sun and sprint toward the parking lot. The stupid blanket drags behind me, but I don't slow down to bunch it into a ball. A few stragglers are crossing the square for their science labs in the Robinson-Iqbal Building and their free periods in the library. I keep my head down. For a school that touts that every place on campus is a safe space, there's no place to go.

In the middle of the parking lot, I want to screech into the wind. My car is at home.

Escape. I have to escape. Since Aminta's concern borders on pity and Auntie Ruth's guilt is cloying and my parents' overprotectiveness is one crisis away from martial law, who can I possibly call?

As if my subconscious knows, I hardly even realize who I'm texting until I press SEND. But Josh hadn't responded to me last night and hasn't reached out this morning. If I didn't think I could feel worse, I am wrong. I ám such a fool. Why did I keep pursuing the impossible?

CHAPTER TWENTY-SEVEN

Under the library's overhang, safe from the sun, I am trembling with anger, indignation, shock—name an upset, I'm feeling it. Even if I could find a backup getaway ride now, even if I want to ignore the humiliating video, I have to watch every single frame again. Enough crises have been dissected at my kitchen table for me to know that the longer you ignore a problem, the more aggressively cancerous it will become. So I force myself to hold my phone, surprised that I don't drop it, I'm shaking that badly.

"Get it together," I mutter to myself and find the video.

While I'm expecting myself on-screen, I'm startled to see me and just me and so much of me again. Deathly comes to mind. I lift my eyes across the square to the empty running track. I've never wanted to be in front of the camera. My safe spot—my sweet spot—is in front of a computer. I'm the researcher, the interviewer, the reporter. I like the backstage, not the podium.

I click PLAY.

It's as if the cinematographer has choreographed the entire production: the swell of the *Firefly* theme song, the slowing of the Browncoats as they gather around me, fallen on the ground. Enter Thor, dropping to one knee, ready to hoist me over his shoulder and fly me to safety. I wish he had. Firefighters storm-troop toward us and transfer me to a stretcher. The camera zooms onto my face, an ugly red. My mouth gapes open, and then the thin, unmistakable streak of drool.

Really, whoever posted this couldn't have cut that millisecond?

> Cue: *the repeat loop of my painfully red, unconscious face.*

Cue: *the stretcher.*
Cue: *the drool.*

This is all my fault: These twenty thousand views driven by my fellow obsessed fans, the Browncoats of *Firefly*.

If only I hadn't insisted on hosting the bake sale on the opening day of the *Firefly* exhibit.

If only I hadn't gone to Africa.

If only Josh would answer an SOS for a girl he just met.

It's been a full ten minutes since I texted him. In crisis time, that's an eternity. I shiver, unsure if I'm distraught or cold or remembering how Lee & Li never dwell in If. Instead, we sequester the If with concrete contingencies and clear options. And always, always, always, we have a solid Option B backup plan.

I have nothing.

Then a text pings.

Josh: *Almost there.*

Two minutes later, a red pickup truck rumbles into the school's long driveway, then curves around the circle. I step into the sun. My heart lifts at the driver wearing an unfortunate safari hat that matches mine. I have never been so happy to run to If.

CHAPTER TWENTY-EIGHT

I fidget on the passenger seat, the phone uncomfortable beneath me. If I could only smother the memory of Brian's smirk and the video. At least there's one indignity I can dismiss: I shove Mom's ridiculous blanket to the back seat, where it falls on top of Josh's textbooks, all of them winged with Post-it notes. Josh is putt-putting down the street despite the small fact that we're in a vehicle designed for off-roading over muck and boulders and river-beds. Ninety-year-olds in rain-blinding deluges drive faster than us. Slugs on hot asphalt crawl faster than us. This, while I am having my first-ever primal need to comfort eat: Must. Have. Poke.

"Persephone would die of old age before we get there," I grumble.

"She's immortal. She doesn't age," says Josh. "Or eat."

"Or wear clothes."

"Okay, what's going on?" Josh finally asks as he continues to refine his octogenarian driving skills, which I didn't fully appreciate driving home from Ada's. Honestly, he slows a full fifty feet from the traffic light that is still green. Until now, I've kept my commentary to myself, grateful that Josh hasn't pressed me to tell him why I SOS-texted him. Instead, he's given me space to think, so different from my parents, who would have invaded my privacy, (mis)translating and (micro)managing every particle and nuance of my fear, anxiety, and shame.

"Fainting in front of complete strangers was bad enough," I say, sounding way too emotional, knowing I should modulate my voice like the best of crisis managers. I can't. Indignation makes my voice rise. "But did some stupid *Firefly* fan really have to post a video of it on YouTube for the entire world to see? Did the biggest jerk at school have to show it to everyone? Oh, look, the Sick Girl goes down! You know what? At least when it was happening, I had no idea what I looked like."

"The video was a total asshole move," Josh spits out.

I lift my eyes to him, startled. "You saw it?"

Josh nods.

My eyes sting with tears. I didn't think I could possibly feel any worse. Yet again, my body proves me wrong. I hug my arms around my stomach. Josh saw me drooling. Well, of course, he did. He hovered over me, up close and personal, making sure I didn't clobber my head on the concrete. My drool probably dripped onto him, a baptism of weird.

"I just didn't want everyone to know!" I cry, dropping my head to my knees. "I don't want people to think of me and have that image stuck in their heads."

He doesn't deny the horror the way Dad would — "What's a little faint? Who cares about a little drool?" — or minimize the video the way Mom might — "In the scheme of things, not *that* many people saw it." Instead, Josh lays his hand on my back and says, "I'm really sorry."

"I know this isn't cancer, and I know I'm lucky not to be dying, but . . . did I have to become school news?" I bite my lip to stop from crying and draw a shaky breath. "Did I have to totally forget that today was the bake sale and leave everything — everything! — at home?" Oh, no, I am on the brink of ugly crying. I pause to collect myself. In a low voice, I ask, "Did I have to have some weird skin condition for no reason at all? I didn't do anything but live, and then this happens! And my plan was to go to college in Abu Dhabi! To cover wars and peacemakers and famines and refugee camps and Ebola and the first female fighter pilots."

"This really and truly sucks," Josh agrees, his hand moving in slow circles on my back. Slow, mesmerizing circles that gentle my heaving breath. I sniff. Slow, delicious, distracting circles. He says, "I get it. It sucks to have people talk about you. Stare at you. Feel sorry for you."

"I don't want to be pitied! Or gossiped about! Oh, Viola, the Sick Girl." I wail, "I don't want to be the Sick Girl."

"Pity is the worst," he agrees flatly.

"Is that why you came to get me? Because I'm the Sick Girl?" I ask quietly, not daring to lift my head yet, not even if I've had a lifetime of coaching to scrutinize body language: Sometimes, involuntary expressions can reveal more than words. "Because you pity me?"

"No." His hand loses momentum until the dizzying circles stop. "Because I hated it when people pitied me when my brother died."

Finally, I straighten. Josh is staring out the windshield, out past the horizon, out into another universe, far, far away. His hand rests flat on my back, dead still.

"I was The Guy Who Killed His Twin. I don't know how many times I've asked myself, What if I didn't get drunk? What if my girlfriend hadn't freaked out because I had passed out? What if she hadn't called Caleb, who was home studying the way I should have been?"

"I'm so sorry," I tell him, my voice hushed as I think about his brother, the accident, the aftermath. "You must miss him."

"My parents miss him more."

"Josh, they'd have missed you, too."

"I don't know about that. Life afterward was never the same. Everything Caleb loved, we stopped doing: no more skiing, no more family vacations, no more family. My parents got divorced." Josh shrugs, no big deal. Like a crisis management pro, he deflects neatly away from the crisis he no longer wants to relive and asks, "Do you pity Persephone?"

The superhero's clothing choice aggravates me; her exile from her home makes me feel bad for her. But pity?

"No," I tell him, but my mind keeps wandering back to his accident. Did his parents really blame him?

"How come?" he asks.

"Because even though she's barely wearing any clothes . . . " I angle a smirk at him.

He snorts. I smile.

". . . she's strong," I continue, "and I know she'll figure something out to save herself and maybe even the world." It's true: Persephone is nowhere near weak.

"I rest my case, Ultra. Like I said, we should work together."

"Do you have a girlfriend? Or a thing for Asian girls?" I blurt, then blush. What the heck was coming out of my mouth? I mean, I think of myself as both Irish and Mongolian, not that that would stop me from being the object of some creeper's Asian Woman Fetish. But that wasn't Josh—at least I didn't think so. Which means: Have I, horrifically, become my mother, interrogating a guy? Or even worse, have I become Auntie Ruth, seeding a minefield with potential issues? Always pointing to the guy, always saying *look, it's him, not me.*

"Um, no, she broke up with me a couple of months after the accident."

"I'm sorry."

"Don't be. It wasn't working. She knew it, and honestly, I did, too. And for the record, aren't you mixed race?"

I nod. "So?" My eyes narrow. "Do you have a fetish for mixed race girls?"

He smiles. "No. I like strong girls, no race requirement."

We both go quiet, the uncomfortable kind of silence after you've said too much, revealed too fast. I'm relieved to notice that Josh has parked on a side street. Even better, the clouds are clustered into a heavy, gray shield in the sky.

Before the sun can batter its way through that defense, I fling my seat belt off. "Come on. Paradise awaits."

Josh remains in his seat, eyeing the 45th Street Stop N Shop and Poke Bar with more than a healthy dose of skepticism. Not that I blame him. From the outside, the plain box corner convenience store looks sketchy, the last place you'd expect to find culinary nirvana.

"You have no idea how good this is," I assure him. In troubling news, though, two more people disappear into the dismal-looking shop. How long was today's line? "This poke is going to change your life. Let's go."

"Poke?"

"You don't speak Hawaiian sushi?" I ask, genuinely appalled.

"I've never had it."

"But sushi-sushi you have, right?"

"Ummm."

"Seriously? No coffee. No sushi. No poke. You sure you're from Seattle?"

"I feel more at home on Planet X."

"Time for indoctrination, then. So here's the plan: We'll grab our poke, then eat it at home where it's darker." Specifically, my bedroom, the darkest place at home. "Come on." Really, my urgency has nothing to do with the high kissability factor of my plan.

Still, Josh lingers in his seat. Honestly, I have never seen a guy move with such sloth-like speed. Did the weight of his formidable muscles slow him down? His face tilts sunward. "Tell me what you want and I'll get it for you."

"A kiss?" I can't believe I said those words.

He doesn't answer, just turns to study me with that half smile of his, the one that dimples his right cheek. His hand may cup my face, but he doesn't move an inch closer. Instead, he promises, voice low, "I *am* going to kiss you." Liar, he only caresses my cheek, a slow trace of his finger down the side of my face, the length of my neck, the outline of my clavicle.

"I like your necklace," he murmurs, "even though I still think you've got River Tam in you." My breathing speeds as he (finally) leans toward me. He's right: I feel wild, untethered. His hand wanders to the back of my neck, and his lips hover over mine, making me wait.

"Josh." His name is a moan low in my throat. I can't wait a second longer. "Now."

"Time for indoctrination?" he whispers. Only then do his lips touch mine, moving softly, then more insistently. I sigh. He pulls me closer to him as my lips open, and he tastes me, slower, deeper. "Indoctrinated?"

"Not yet."

Darn it, I've made him laugh, then I laugh, too. The mood changes, but sultry or silly, both are good.

"My turn to be indoctrinated?" he asks, nodding toward the convenience shop.

"You won't be sorry."

Josh slowly nods, then — wonder of wonders — he sprints to my side of the car like he can move (when he wants). Clearly, as his hand grazes my lower back and stays there when we dash across the street together, he wants. I do, too.

...

Seven people are ahead of us in line: three construction guys in orange vests. An old couple holding hands. Two yogis carrying matching black-and-gray mats. What catches my attention, though, are the fluorescent lights dangling above us. Every inch of my bared skin is slathered with sunscreen, the rest armored in sun-blocking clothes. There is no way a single UV ray is penetrating me. Even so, I lower the brim of my hat, burrowing deeper into my own private shade.

"I can order if you tell me what you want," Josh offers again.

"I'm good." To distract both of us, I say, "I dream about this place." (And your kiss.)

"How'd you even find out about it?" Josh asks.

Valid question. Shelves of candy bars, Ding Dongs, and potato chips line the aisles, and cigarettes and booze fill the back wall. Above the miniscule kitchen is a chalkboard listing the limited menu: five choices of fish, edamame, avocado, crabmeat, seaweed salad, rice. Finito. That's it.

"Oh, my gosh! It's her!" exclaims the slender, thirtysomething Yoga Woman with long hair dyed an indigo purple and tattoos running up and down her ropy arms. Of all the tattooed yoga practitioners (of which there are many) in Seattle, we get the one who's inked with the spaceship *Serenity* followed by a jet stream of words: "You can't take the sky from me."

Hate to break it to you, Yoga Woman, but yes, in fact, life can.

Yoga Woman now confides to her companion, the equally fit Yoga Man, about the YouTube video, featuring me. (News flash: We can hear your "inside" voice.) I duck my head, entranced by the new scuff on my once-white Adidas sneakers.

"I've watched *Firefly* since I was, like, fifteen." Yoga Woman then informs me conversationally, "You know, acai, algae, and ginseng could help your skin."

"Uh, thanks," I say, looking in her general but not specific direction. Eye contact only encourages further conversation. Yoga Woman, unfortunately, is not so easily deterred.

"Hmmm . . . you should really get started on the regimen," she says, frowning prettily. "Like, pronto. You're starting to get a rash. If you keep getting sunburned, it's going to age your skin. A lot."

"Okay," I say briskly, glad for all the press conferences my parents took me to over the last few summers for my "personal edification," because the ready answer comes to me automatically: "I'll look into that right away."

Even so.

Humiliation, as it turns out, comes in infinite gradations of awful. There's the lifetime mortification of being The Girl Who Drooled. Then there's the very exquisite shame of having your personal business aired out in front of the one guy you might possibly want to date. Like now: Yoga Woman actually lifts her tattooed fingers (L.O.V.E.) to touch my cheek. Deflect! I pivot to face Josh and ask apropos of nothing, "Do you want to hear what I think Persephone needs to do?"

"So you decided to work with me?" he asks, grinning, even as he angles his body so he blocks me from the Yoga Couple's view. My view, I would like to state, is appealing: a Seattle Central College T-shirt hugs his wide chest and accentuates the blue of his eyes. He says, "So, partner, give it to me."

"Editorial consultant," I correct him.

"Is that so?"

Words, sentences, and coherent thought vanish when Josh leans down to me. I can smell wood chips and smoke on him like he's been out throwing his hammer in some forest or chopping wood or feeding a fire or whatever it is that a Thor does when he's not with me.

"I'm curious, potential editorial consultant." He nudges me. "What should she do?"

"Wear some real clothes." (Kiss him.) I want his eyes to drop to my (kissable) lips. Mine drop to his.

But instead, my neck itches.

So does my chest, the sliver of bare skin above my lariat.

The problem with an adrenaline cocktail spiked with oxytocin — the love hormone — is this: It has masked my body's protests against the sun. I fist my hands so that I don't scratch and scan my body now. My skin stings under my clothes. I can feel welts forming and want to shriek: Seriously? I've taken the proper precautions and then some. We've been in this poke shop for all of ten minutes. Psychosomatic or not, I can now feel the coil of UV tentacles tightening around me.

My eyes tear up. What the heck is going on with my body?

"I need to go," I whisper urgently, ducking my head and tugging my sleeves over my hands. There is no denying it: Even my cheeks are prickling. I have to fight from itching them, my neck, my arms.

Concerned, Josh takes my hand. At the door, I inhale sharply like I'm girding for battle, only I'm not afraid of the sun. It's my own skin that scares me.

"Wait," calls the Yoga Woman, following us outside.

What now? Honestly, what now?

Yoga Woman hands Josh her brown bag of poke bowls. "Take ours."

That unexpected kindness crushes me in a way that the video hasn't, Brian's taunts didn't, and my pain couldn't. There is no denying that I am the Sick Girl. I weep.

CHAPTER TWENTY-NINE

"Okay, Ultra, almost home," says Josh. He, the slowest driver in the universe, actually accelerates.

Warp speed, please. I just want to be home.

The blanket mummifies my body, yet I continue frying from the outside in. Every year at the Washington State Fair, I have always wondered about the appeal of deep-fried Twinkies. There is none.

Josh swerves into my driveway like a stunt driver. Before he can dash around the truck, I've shoved the blanket off and pushed the passenger door open. That alone winds me. The walk to the front door might as well be an ultramarathon in the desert. Dad rushes out of the house to me. I can tell he wants to shove Josh away, all hands off my girl.

I tell him, "Dad, I'm not that sick."

Even I hear the betraying "that"—the caveat, the concession, the conclusion.

It takes every bit of my focus to walk up the stairs to the threshold, shaking my head for all offers of help. Even with the UV filters shading the windows, I can feel the sun scraping along my skin.

"Bedroom," I gasp, and that startles an "oh, honey" out of Dad.

Not soon enough, I'm in the dark, blissful dark. My eyelids shutter the moment I lie on my bed, body aching as if I've swum the entire stretch of the galaxy to reach this safe cave. The door closes gently, and I am glad to be left in the dark, even when the cross-examination begins in the hall: "Where did you take her? What do you know about the video?" And then the death knell for any possible future relationship: "Don't you know that she's sick?"

CHAPTER THIRTY

Monday dawns way too bright, way too early, and way, way too loud with Roz banging on my bedroom door, yelling like she's rowing on Lake Washington, "We're waiting!"

No matter how hard I try to get up after an entire weekend of rest, no matter how much I tell myself that I can't miss class during the all-important senior fall—when grades really matter—I stay in bed. Calamine lotion and antihistamines hadn't relieved my itchiness, neither had hours soaking in oatmeal baths. Regardless, the angry red hives blotching my face and body faded by Saturday night. I'm exhausted, even though the Seahawks weren't playing and I had no vats of soup to prepare. It doesn't help that my brain has been flipping somersaults, day and night. If my skin had erupted after just fifteen minutes under fluorescent lights, what the hell was it going to do next? Not to mention, after Josh's Friday night check-in—a single "hey, you okay?" and my, *yes, still alive*—his only response was fade-out: going, going, gone.

There's a soft knock on my bedroom door before Mom walks in, leaving the door wide open. My room glows from the bright hallway light.

"Mom! Lights!" I cry as I dive under my blanket. Welts on my arms are one thing, but I refuse to go to school with hives lumping my face.

"Oh, honey!" Remorse coats Mom's voice. She immediately flicks the light off in the hall.

Dad joins us in my bedroom, assessing the situation swiftly, then says, "That's it."

"What?" I ask, worried enough to leave the safety of my cave of blankets. I prop myself up on my elbows. "What's it?"

Dad's only answer is to take Mom's hand, shutting my door behind them, as if I'm a client whose latest outburst needs a new strategy. Yet now, my parents seem to forget all their operating procedures, which is never, ever, to conduct a meeting within hearing distance of listening ears. Never.

Out in the hall, Dad says, "No school this week, not until they can promise that she'll be safe."

"Safe from lights and bullies," I hear Mom agreeing as they walk toward the kitchen. "I'm going to take another look at the Disabilities Act."

Of course my parents would ferret out the bully episode from Aminta or maybe even Josh, not that it matters. What matters is that my parents cannot escalate this with Liberty. If it's hard enough to imagine returning to school, just thinking about bumping into Dr. Luthra or my teachers after a lawsuit almost makes me break into hives. While I don't exactly leap to my feet, I inch off my bed and out my bedroom. After a weekend stuck in a darkened room, I'm not used to the natural light that filters stubbornly inside our home. I squint down the hall.

"Hello? Crew practice!" Roz growls.

I'm shocked to hear Mom snap, "Rosalind Phoebe Li. Wait your turn."

Dad chimes in, "This is important."

"It's always about Viola," Roz protests. The door to the garage slams shut.

I near the kitchen, staying in the shadows. From there, I watch Dad handing Mom her steel travel mug, steaming with fresh coffee. "I'll work from home today."

"I can." Mom is already unpacking her tote bag. "I want to."

"We've got the new business pitch at ten, and you're better at it. You know you are." Dad tugs Mom in close to his chest at the kitchen counter. "Besides, I called dibs first."

"It's a mom's prerogative to be home with her sick child," she protests, leaning her forehead against his chest. Mom resorting to gender stereotypes? Now I know she's really worried.

"Honey," Dad says softly, "going into work isn't the same as abandoning anyone. You know that, right?"

"This isn't about me trying not to be my sister." She lifts her head and sighs. "Okay, maybe a little, but you never get between a mom and her baby. Never. This is primal."

"I know, honey."

She sighs. "I still need to do the pitch, don't I?"

"Bring home the bacon, baby." Dad lifts her chin and kisses her. "I'll stay home today."

Today? As if there will be future days of me staying home? I manage a scoff that comes out a half-baked cough nobody but me hears. Sorry, let's not forget my one and only sanctioned sick day five years ago (The MRSA Episode). A boil the size of a marble sprouted on my jaw. A call to the CDC (Client #38) and one dermatologist visit later confirmed the treatment my parents had already lined up for me: drugs, bleach baths, surgical soap. Even though I protested — "Mom, creepy" — I was secretly glad that she slept on the floor in my bedroom the first three nights.

Just as I'm about to lodge a formal protest, I stop myself. Staying home means that I don't have to face every single person at school who's watched the super slo-mo of my drool. No pitying looks. No rude questions. No ignoramuses who think my disorder is contagious. And most of all, absolutely no kneejerk SOS calls to Josh and missing his texts and yearning for his touch and remembering his attention.

Famous last words.

Exactly two hours later, I am so bored in my bedroom, I check my phone, half hoping to find a message from Josh — a "hey, you still doing okay?" or even just "hey!" Then, I can craft a comeback line, ask him about his weird pullbacks, allow myself to dwell in If.

All continues to be quiet on the Josh front. There is nothing to come back from. For that matter, it doesn't look like there's anything to come back to either.

...

164

Another two hours later, my bedroom has transformed into the island of misfit projects, a jumble of starts and stops. In the north sector of my rumpled bed, my Mac is open to my old college essay, but how do I revise when I'm wondering whether I can even report the news if I can't embed myself in the news. On the western coastline of my bed, Post-it notes with ideas stick to the first five pages of *Persephone*. Lost in the Arctic on my nightstand behind me is my makeup bag, unzipped but not unpacked. Why bother even swiping a little lip gloss on?

There's a rap on my door, and I'm grateful for the distraction because the eastern front is causing me a lot of trouble. There, my daily planner is open to a page with Josh's question: Where would you go if you couldn't go outside anymore? Not one answer.

Dad pops his head in. "Hey, pumpkin, you need anything?"

"A skin transplant," I tell him.

"Other than that?"

"Time travel via Tardis to MoPOP and stop the video of me."

"How about popcorn?"

"Okay."

Even though Dad returns to the kitchen, I can hear Lee & Li in my head: *What's your Plan B?* Dad's phone rings with Auntie Ruth's special ringtone: "Brothers and Sisters" by Coldplay. Like clockwork, a few minutes later, I receive a text from her.

Auntie Ruth: *Keep resting!*

The old Auntie Ruth would have written: *Keep resisting!* But the Sick Girl gets *Keep resting*? Conspiring to go to NYU Abu Dhabi feels like an entire lifetime ago when the sun was still benign, and Thor was just a myth. Slowly but firmly, I finally cross the mirage of my dream school off my list in my planner. I recompile a new list of colleges with two criteria: the best journalism programs far from home with the least amount of sun.

So the Sick Girl is taking her college counselor's advice. The Sick Girl is going to write about how she wasn't just her own investigative journalist, but she became an advocate for her condition. Sorry, Josh, but the road to my college success now hinges on my new best friend: Persephone, my mouthpiece for the photosensitive.

I set the planner in my lap to jot a new topline strategy:

1) Research the Persephone myth.

2) Deluge Josh with so many ideas, he's convinced we need to work together.

3) Keep the relationship purely professional (i.e., no more kissing).

"Popcorn delivery!" Dad calls from down the hall. Seeing me propped against my pillows must make him think I'm five again, home sick from kindergarten. His face softens. "Maybe you should rest some more, pumpkin."

No more resting. I am not an invalid. Watch me head off to college in exactly ten months and counting. I chirp, "I'm doing great! Thanks!"

Dad sets down a bowl big enough to feed three hungry crew girls at the foot of the bed, then hovers. "What else do you need? Is that enough light to read?" Answering his own question, Dad raises the blinds about five inches, then thinks better of it and lowers them for just a sliver of light.

Forget a skin transplant; I'm planning a life transplant.

"I think I'll do a little more research," I tell him, and place my Mac on my lap. "Ms. Kavoussi thought a college essay on solar urticaria would be compelling."

Dad grins his approval. "Great idea. Fight fire with fire."

You have no idea.

BRIEFING DOCUMENT:

PERSEPHONE

Meet Persephone, goddess of the spring. There she was, picking flowers with her besties on a bright and sunny afternoon when Hades snatches her down to his lair in the Underworld. His (lame) excuse: He was "in love," and he "needed a queen," as if that justified the kidnapping.

Hell hath no fury like a goddess-mother whose daughter is stolen. Demeter, Persephone's mom and the goddess of the harvest, refuses to let any crops grow while she searches for her missing kid. (Now, there's a goddess who knows a thing or two about negotiating from a place of power: You want to eat? You better help.) Hunger on earth ensues. Humanity's cries rise heavenward. The sun (finally) tells the heartbroken mom exactly what it saw. Zeus (finally) orders Hades to free Persephone. Which Hades (finally) does — after he feeds a starving and unsuspecting Persephone three pomegranate seeds. Because of those tiny seeds, her fate is sowed. The Underworld becomes her winter home for eternity.

What does the name Persephone mean? To bring or cause death. (Could Persephone be an intergalactic bounty hunter?)

Why would Persephone bring death? According to one interpretation, Persephone is responsible for the first growth of spring, which means the death of winter. But it's also possible that with her so-called coronation as queen of the Underworld, Persephone's job is to carry out men's curses upon the souls of the dead. (Could she be chasing Ultraviolent Reyes across the galaxy, intent on bringing her to justice?)

What does Persephone look like? She's mostly portrayed at the moment of her abduction, limbs flailing. (Since I doubt she'd want to be defined as a victim, I hope we can rethink her uniform. Maybe we can preserve the best elements of her current one, such as the constellation of stars?)

Where was Persephone abducted? The Necromanteion, in Greece.

What is the Necromanteion? It's the entryway into the Underworld, where Hades lived and where the Oracle of the Dead prophesied to the living under special circumstances. (Could the modern-day Oracle of the Dead be a crisis manager? Let's just say I have a lot of material to draw from.)

Who else visited the Necromanteion? Odysseus. Although, if you want to be technical, Persephone didn't visit the Necromanteion, not unless you define kidnapping as an unplanned trip. And prison as your vacation home.

Has the name Persephone been used elsewhere? In the days when Pluto was a planet, scientists once thought there might be a tenth planet in our solar system. They preemptively named it Persephone. (Josh must have known that already.) (See also: chagrin.)

CHAPTER THIRTY-ONE

As tempted as I am to text Josh about this research the next day when I'm still homebound from school, I call on every last one of my Genghis Khan genes to protect my future and nudge the unnecessary temptation of my phone to the far recesses of my bed. Flirting with a boy (who regularly drops off the face of the planet) shouldn't break my top one hundred priorities, let alone be my top communication priority. The key is to work-zone him. Keep it purely professional, none of this heart-palpitating, sweaty-palm, fantasy-kissing nonsense.

"Viola!" Dad calls from the front door, "your friend is here!"

Friend? What friend? Josh?

In one crazy, irrational moment, all thoughts of work-zoning him vanish: Heart palpitates! Palms sweat! Kissing memories ensue! I swing myself off my bed. As soon as I open my bedroom door, I squint. The darkness takes the shape, not of Thor but of my best friend, floating in a froth of silver tulle and anchored to earth in floral Dr. Martens. Aminta envelops me in a soft hug like she's afraid a single touch will shatter me.

"I am an emissary from Liberty, bearing good tidings," Aminta says as she lowers her tote bag to the floor and drops onto my bed. She tips up her black top hat, corset tied all the way up to the crown. "I've missed you! Texting isn't the same!"

"I know it. Hey, so what happened to boho? And steampunk?" I ask, gesturing to her outfit.

"It's all about pixie punk today." Aminta shrugs.

I haven't just holed up inside my cave for the past couple of days but have slipped into a Rip Van Winkle black hole. Everyone has moved on without me. I don't even recognize my best friend.

"You know what I finally figured out after interning at that start-up?" she asks me.

"You love to code."

"Nope, already knew that. But did you know that no one knows or cares about who we are or what we were at Liberty? Who cares if you were the nerd? Who cares if you were slut-shamed? So the corollary is: Throw everybody at school off, especially all the Brians of the world. Be unpredictable. Shake up their expectations. Like, that way, you don't allow anyone to label you."

"Like, the Sick Girl."

"Like, the Geek Girl. My mom is all, 'You need to code and only code. That's job security.' And Dad's all, 'Do what you love! Fashion design!' Okay, fine, who says I can't be a geek with seriously good taste?"

"You sound like Auntie Ruth, who's all, 'Asian women ride Harleys.'"

"Thanks." Aminta beams because who wouldn't want to sound like my auntie? "I am so going to own Silicon Valley in style." She bumps her shoulder against mine, then remembers my skin. "Oh, my gosh! I'm sorry! Did I hurt you?"

"I'm totally fine. I've hermited all weekend."

Aminta plucks at my shirt, which I've buttoned all the way to the top. "I can tell."

"UPF clothes aren't exactly fashion-forward."

"Yeah, but you don't have to give up." She removes her hat and plunks it on top of my head, leans back, then nods approvingly. "Better. Okay, so thanks to you, the predance bake sale sold out. So guess who's making a huge donation to the girls' education fund?"

"What bake sale?"

"Someone dropped off all your cookies."

"They did? Who?"

Aminta stops fluffing her hat-flattened hair. "Wait, you don't know?"

I shake my head. "My parents, probably." But after my body's freak-out at the poke shop when Josh brought me home, Dad was there. Had Mom brought the cookies over? Or could it possibly have been Josh? (Heart palpitates! Palms sweat!)

"Well, whoever did is awesome." The bake sale is forgotten when Aminta seizes *Persephone* by my Mac. "I still think this is so weird."

"Yeah, totally weird. Just look at her boobs."

"Well, it's not like Josh could have changed them. His brother was the illustrator, right?"

"Caleb was the illustrator? But Josh draws. I've seen his doodles."

"Yeah, but Caleb thought he was better."

I drop my head into my hands and groan. Could I have been more insensitive? Of course Josh wouldn't have wanted to alter a single stroke of his brother's work.

"I made such a big deal out of how sexist this is!" I confess. "I'm a jerk."

"You had a point. But what I meant, though, was" — Aminta taps Josh's handwritten message to me — "what are the chances that you and Persephone are both allergic to the sun?"

"Weird, but it doesn't matter. I haven't heard from him in a couple of days." (Four days and thirteen hours, not that I'm tracking or anything.)

Aminta snorts. "I warned you to be careful."

"I just thought that . . ."

"What?"

"He picked me up when I had a panic attack at school," I tell her.

"That was nice, I guess."

"And remember? He waited for me at the hospital. And he drove me home from the poke place and Ada's."

"Do you think he brought the cookies to school? Text him. Let's see."

"No."

"Think of this as a test of his interest level."

171

"It's nonexistent."

"How do you know?"

"He hasn't texted." Just to be sure, I sneak a peek at my phone. Nada.

"Whatever happened to journalistic pride?" Aminta sounds horrified as her arms splay wide. "Finding out the truth no matter what? Even if it hurts?"

"Well, when you put it that way . . ." So I type.

> Me: *Hey! If you brought the cookies, thanks for saving the bake sale!*
> Me: Persephone *research is going super well . . .*

"Wait, you double-texted," Aminta says, worried, reading over my shoulder. "And you ellipsed. You shouldn't do that."

"That was purely professional. It was the I-have-more-to-tell-you kind of ellipses, not the I-want-to-kiss-you-again kind."

"You kissed him?" Aminta groans. "I told you to be careful!"

If it's possible to feel more anxious, I don't think so. But it's not like Josh is going to answer — "I'll text you" (Darren, Disappearing Act, 2016) and "I'll talk to you tomorrow" (Josh, Fade-Out, 2018).

My phone pings. (Heart palpitates!)

> Josh: *Tell me everything . . .*

"He brought the cookies! He didn't deny it." Aminta leans over my shoulder. I can smell the peppermint on her breath when she gasps. "Whoa! And he ellipsed you."

He did, indeed. (Palms sweat!) I reach for my Mac to send him my research brief. (Kissing memory ensues!) But now, I'm freaking because, according to my plan, he needs to be work-zoned. Work-zone him, I order myself. Work. Zone.

From: Viola Li

To: Josh Taylor

Re: Research Brief

Dear Josh,

Please find attached some background research on Persephone.

Best,

Viola

"Don't send—" Aminta says as I hit SEND. "Oh."
"What?"
"What happened to your inner flirt? It's like she atrophied or something!"
"Because we are working together. I'm going to channel everything I want the Brians of the world to know about photosensitivity through *Persephone.*"
"Okay, not a bad idea. We could sell it at the next bake sale. But back to your inner flirt."
"Really?"
"It's like Darren silenced her. It's like your heart's been mummified."
"Wait," I point out, "you said to be careful with Josh." For good reason, I should add. Just consider my research on the Necromanteion. Orpheus descended to the Underworld to rescue the love of his life. He got to escape; she was imprisoned in hell. That's what this whole last year was for me, replaying my stupidity for not reading the obvious signs the summer before: Darren's sporadic "let's hang out" texts with him never asking me out on a real date, while somehow always finding the time for us to hook up.

His "hey, girl" that never materialized into "my girl." His acknowledging me for that last entire school year with a jerk of his chin — if that. Josh was one thing I did not want to regret because my heart shattered into a billion pieces of Hades-hot ashes.

"Well, yeah," says Aminta, "that was before I knew he bake-saled you."

"You're hurting my brain. You told me he was a player."

"Maybe he's reformed."

"What?"

"No one drives over cookies for just some girl."

When my phone pings again, Aminta scoops it off my comforter before I even reach for it.

"I rest my case. More ellipses," she says, holding the screen out triumphantly. She scoots off my bed. "I've got at least ten hours of Latin to do. So I got to go. Flirt, but cautiously."

No, I will work-zone him. Josh has other ideas. My phone pings. He ellipses. Flirt cautiously. Will do . . .

CHAPTER THIRTY-TWO

Josh: *Ultra . . .*
Josh: *Maybe Ultraviolent Reyes is a guy who
wears ample clothes.*
Josh: *Maybe he's murdered Persephone's best
friend or sister.*

My mouth curves into a reluctant smile. I love these ideas, which is a whole lot safer than loving the unwanted warmth from that nickname: Ultra. This melty, bubbly ultrarcaction to Josh should be the last thing I crave. Of course it isn't. I practically buzz along with my phone.

Josh: *Time to talk?*
Me: *Yes, as your editorial consultant.*
Josh: *Is that a fancy way of saying muse?*
Me: *It's the salaried way of saying muse.*

And then, putting me in line to win this year's Darwin Award, do I stop? No. I cautiously flirt even more.

Me: *Which you need:*
Me: *Photosensitivity expert.*
Me: *Encyclopedic knowledge of crises for plot
twists.*
Me: *Exceptional fact-checking skills.*
Me: *Friends with superhero fashion sense.*

Josh: *You quadruple-texted me.*

Josh: *I have it from a good source that's a definite no.*

Me: *Excuse me: quintuple-texted.*

Me: *Lucky you. I consult on math and science, too.*

Me: *My schedule happens to be open for the next couple of months.*

Me: *Which is a job proposal.*

Me: *And public service.*

Me: *For the record, this is a sixth text. Call me an overachiever.*

Josh: *Apparently.*

Me: *So. I'm hired. Right?*

Josh: *Well, that all depends.*

Me: *On?*

Josh: *Your interview.*

I'm about to fume: *Excuse me? An interview? Haven't I already proved that I have scintillating ideas? That I can research? That I can —*

Josh: *For purposes of gauging your creativity.*

Josh: *And whether you have the Risk Gene.*

Josh: *Persephone is a superhero after all.*

Me: *OK. Fine. Fire away.*

Josh: *Name the trip you'd take if you had one day left in the sun.*

Speechless, I lower my phone to my lap. It isn't as if I haven't thought of my travel adventures. My planner is open to that very unanswered question, after all. I just haven't allowed myself to spend a single moment thinking about a sun-less existence. If I did, that would be admitting that I might be trapped in darkness for the rest of my life.

Josh: *So far? Interview not going well.*

Oh, yeah? I think to myself, but beads of sweat collect on my forehead and I'm probably leaving sweat marks on my phone. I'm relieved Josh can't see me.

Josh: *?*
Me: *Necromanteion. Clearly.*
Josh: *Wow. That's commitment.*
Me: *I take primary source research seriously.*
Josh: *Hired.*

Not many messages warrant an escalation to a phone call. As in: actual person-to-person voice contact and verbal exchange. This last text did. I tap Josh's name on the screen, my heart beating fast, and I calm myself: *This is just a call. One simple fact-checking call.* Besides, all I had to do was shimmy up a mental image of Mom and Dad, who never betray nerves before a call because they rehearse hard conversations together — Wait! Should I have rehearsed?

Too late.

"Hey, Ultra," Josh answers smoothly like he's fielded dozens — hundreds — of calls from girls. "Multiplatform communication, nice."

Multiplatform flirting, even nicer. What is it that makes me want to not-so-cautiously flirt back? So antsy, I stand up to pace the room as I force myself to use my professional voice that I've perfected at Lee & Li. "Are you serious about hiring me?"

"Well, that depends. Are you serious about the Necromanteion?" he counters.

"Well, that depends on two things," I fire back. "Are you serious about *Persephone*?"

Josh is so quiet, I wonder if our connection has been lost.

"Hello?" I say. "Josh?"

"Yeah, I'm here. I flaked on *Persephone* with Caleb for two years. We'd do these epic brainstorms late at night. He'd illustrate his part a couple of days later, and I'd blow off mine. Parties to go to, right?" His chuckle is wry, punishing, harsh. "After he died, I promised myself that I would finish *Persephone*, no matter what. So, yeah, I'm serious."

"But you finished it. You don't have to continue."

"Yeah, I do."

"Why?"

"Because it makes it feel like he's still alive."

"Oh." I sigh and lean against my desk. "I get that."

He clears his throat. "So how about you? You serious?"

"Me?" I know a redirect when I hear one, and remember how intense our last conversation was. Was that why he had pulled back? "Yeah, I'm serious. Working on *Persephone* kind of helps me deal with my condition. I don't know why, but it's easier to process everything my body is going through when it's one step removed."

"A superhero surrogate."

"Yeah, and it gives me a real voice for my condition. That guy who made fun of me?"

"Yeah, the jerk who showed you the video? I could take care of him for you."

"You are not beating him up, but I'd be open to putting him in *Persephone*."

"I'll zombify him for you," Josh offers gleefully, and I laugh (cackle). He continues, "Our first casualty."

"Okay."

"Okay," Josh echoes. "So work together?"

My parents always say that professional relationships are like marriages with ups and downs. When things fall apart, the divorce can be just as painful. So I want clean, clear, reliable communication, the kind I didn't get from Darren, who was so slippery, I could never nail him down on basic details: What time were we getting together? Heck, were we even getting together?

"Only if you call me when you say you will." I pause, shocked I dared to say that to him, shocked even more when I ask him point-blank, "So what's up with that?"

"Because you scare me."

"Me?"

"I haven't felt this comfortable—felt like me—with anyone since I can remember." (Since Caleb.) "It's a little scary."

I understand him perfectly. So I tell him, "A lot scary. I let in a guy, like, really let him in. We texted pretty intensely for about five months, but in the middle of that, he'd just go dark and then reappear a couple of days later, no explanation. No I miss you. Nothing. But I honestly thought we were going out, otherwise I wouldn't have, well, you know, with him . . ." I sigh. Admitting all of this is hard, but even harder is keeping the truth pushed down inside like my history never happened. "And then he got back together with his ex and I never heard from him ever again. Like, zero. He just disappeared on me even though I'd see them in the hall at school almost every day."

"Awkward."

"Totally. It would have been so much better if he had even just texted me that he was moving on, that he was going back to his ex instead of having me find out when I saw them together."

"What a coward."

That startles a laugh out of me. "He is."

"You'd never be happy with a coward."

That statement yanks me back onto my feet to roam my room. Was it true? Cowardice is the opposite of reporting the journalistic truth.

"So," Josh says, "no ghosting on *Persephone*."

That qualifier — "on *Persephone*" — stings a little, if I have to admit it. I've been work-zoned right back, which is what I wanted, right? But I agree, "No ghosting."

"So tell me more about the Necromanteion," he says.

It takes me twelve circuits around my bedroom to give him more details about the place of the dead: how it's located at the confluence of three rivers (woe, fire, and wailing). At that vortex of pain, you could commune with the dead. Josh is so quiet afterward that I begin to have second thoughts: Was I stupid in thinking that there was a story possibility based on the Necromanteion? I'd never worked on a comic before. What did I know about fiction when I've only dealt with facts that could be checked and verified and used to help people see the truth?

Josh says thoughtfully, "Santorini is where vampires were taken to be buried."

"Santorini?"

"Greek island."

"So if vampires are the undead — "

"And if they kept reanimating like that asshole you were pseudo-dating — "

" — then that might be what Persephone found as soon as she dropped into the Mediterranean," I finish, triumphant. "Near the site of the Necromanteion."

"She'd have to battle all the vampires that are reanimating. Should he be the first to get a stake in his heart? A stake made from a meteorite?"

"Ha!" But I'm too engrossed in our brainstorming to dwell in sweet revenge (much). "And they're all sucking down innocent tourist blood. So she'd totally feel honor bound to protect earthlings before she could hunt down Ultraviolent Reyes — "

"And head back home with him to Planet X. Hang on a second," Josh says hastily. "I'll FaceTime you in five minutes."

FaceTime means we can see each other.

We. Can. See. Each. Other.

Panicking, I brush my knotty hair off my greasy face. Why hadn't I bothered showering? Why didn't I learn from Mom and always look camera-ready?

I rush to my bedside table and grab my emergency makeup kit that Mom insists I always carry, updated for my condition: hidden stash of twenty bucks, dental floss, tampon, Advil, SPF 100 sunscreen, extra hat, aloe vera, and the all-important lip gloss. Some color on my lips might make me look more living and less living dead. My phone buzzes. Answer it or be counted lame.

Be counted lame!

I have lip gloss to put on.

Finally, I accept his call, placing the phone as far as humanly possible from me on the base of my bed, only to realize: Josh is young and healthy; his eyesight is good. There's no disguising my shapeless, dowdy shirt or my hair that's a nest of coppery-brown confusion. I stifle a groan and smile gamely at Josh. "Hey!"

"Love your idea." Josh looks at me admiringly, which makes me question his eyesight. "And the Necromanteion is safe underground."

"In the dark."

He grins widely. "I like it. A lot."

I like his smile. A lot.

"Hang on a second," he says, pulling out a sketchbook. His pencil moves quickly, and we're both silent for a few minutes, him sketching, me writing, before he lifts up his drawings, each panel showing a different part of the action that we've just brainstormed. "Our first storyboard."

"Whoa . . ."

"So. Ultraviola Adventure Numero Uno," he says, nodding as if he approves of that thought.

"What's that?"

"The Necromanteion. Research trip." His expression is serious. "When?"

181

"Ummm . . . like how would I ever get to Greece? Money, for one," I tell him, now holding my phone high for a better angle. "School. Parents." I shrug. "My parents would freak out if I went to the land of the Mediterranean sun. Wouldn't yours?"

"Mine pretty much let me do what I want."

"Well, mine don't. Mine have me on lockdown. Mine see crises when I'm just crossing the street by myself."

"O ye of little faith," he says, shaking his head sadly.

"Seriously?"

He nods like money and timing and parental permission are easy obstacles he's overcome countless times. Somehow, I don't doubt it. My arm trembles so I lower the phone to my knees.

Josh explains, "So we got a huge settlement — huge — from the insurance company for pain, suffering, death. As if money will wipe out what happened."

"I can't take your money."

"It's blood money. Which is why the Necromanteion is a real possibility. I got at least the money part covered."

"I can't take your money," I repeat.

"Why not?" (Because you blame me, too.)

"Because I'm an independent woman, for one. I pay my own way. Two, my parents would never allow it. Oh, my gosh, I can just hear them now: You can't just take someone's money."

"You're not. You're taking Aetna's."

"I can fund-raise for myself."

"Bake sales?"

"Okay, that seems self-serving." I run my free hand along my ponytail before coiling it around my fingers. "I'll figure something out. And three, you should save your money for college."

"I go to community college." Josh looks away from the camera.

"Which is awesome," I tell him.

"Sure." (I am a loser.)

Josh is right about one thing even if it's taken me some time to admit it to myself: I am the master of the censored phrase. That's how I translate his silent statement, flat and damning and self-incriminating.

So I continue, "It is, if that's your plan. Is it?"

"Caleb had it all figured out: go to Seattle Central to save money, transfer to CalArts, then intern at Marvel, where he'd work on — "

"*Thor*?" I ask hopefully.

"No, *X-Men*. Then pitch *Persephone*."

"That sounds like what you're doing," I tell him softly. "Are you sure that's your plan?"

"It is," he says immediately. He clears his throat, then says, "Add twenty-five bucks to your Necromanteion fund."

"So I'm hired?" I ask. A Lee & Li mandate: Close the deal as soon as a client expresses interest.

"That depends."

"On what?"

"Your commitment to research."

I sit up straighter. "But you said: Hired."

"That was for a researcher, but if you're wanting byline credits . . ."

"I don't."

"You should."

Which is what my parents would say, too. Especially my dad: Don't let anyone take credit for your work.

"Well, we can't go to Greece!" I protest.

"Why not?"

"I told you. Money, timing, parents."

"And the problem is?"

"Money, timing, parents."

"Then let's find a research trip that doesn't entail money, timing, or parents," he suggests.

For a weird, brief moment, I'm disappointed that I can't race ahead to twenty-three, have enough money banked so that we can book a real research field trip to the Necromanteion and travel to Greece together.

"You sure you'd be up for my kind of research trip?" I ask. When he nods — of course — I say, "Nighttime polar dip in the lake."

"Too cold."

"What happened to your creativity and risk gene? How are you going to draw how it feels to crash-land from a meteor into a body of water?"

Josh laughs. I swear, my dad in the kitchen can hear every last note of that booming laughter. For a moment, the dark feels a little less lonely. I can't wait to make him laugh again (for purely research purposes) (of course).

CHAPTER THIRTY-THREE

Even though it's five thirty in the morning and I can't drive Roz to crew anymore (hallelujah!), I'm up and dressed for a full-frontal sun attack on my predawn jog despite it being completely dark. That's what I intend to tell my parents when I get to the kitchen: *I was fine during my last jog. I'll bring my phone in case of emergency. I'll run laps around our block so I won't be more than three minutes from home. Plus, I rested all yesterday* (never mind that I stayed up until three, multiplatform "working" with Josh).

Halfway out my bedroom door, smoothing my hair back into a ponytail, my fingers graze my blistered cheek. I want to scream. Maybe I do.

Footsteps thud to me.

"What's wrong?" Mom demands before she looks scared, then cries, "Mick. Mick!" An instant later, Dad is standing next to Mom.

"Oh, honey," he says, worried, as he inspects my face.

"How bad is it?" I ask, looking between them.

These are not the poker faces of world-class crisis managers who are trained to be the still point in every chaos, the voice of reason, the center of calm. Tears well in Mom's eyes. I'd check the mirror above my bureau, only I'm too afraid to look at myself.

"Aloe vera," Mom says, holding her fingers to her trembling lips as she speeds to the bathroom.

Even Roz — she with the highest tolerance in our family for blood-and-gore on Netflix — grimaces when she joins us in my bedroom. "You know that scene in *Star Wars* where Anakin Skywalker falls into lava and comes out like a slab of barbequed meat and Darth Vader is born?"

"Seriously?" There is no disguising the panic in my voice.

"It's not *that* bad," says Dad, but his expression remains concerned. "Did you go outside yesterday?"

"No, I was working inside," I answer. "And I was wearing everything: hat, clothes, everything."

"Did you stand by the windows?"

"No."

"Did you bake under the skylights?"

"Dad, you were home. Did you see me baking?"

"Did you walk outside?"

"Not even for a second."

"So," says Dad, worrying his jaw, "what have you been doing?"

"Just work," I wail, "on my Mac."

"Your Mac," repeats Mom from the bathroom. When she hurries back to us, aloe vera forgotten, she asks me, "Texting? IM'ing? Phone and computer?"

"Ummm . . . why?"

Mom is relentless like I'm a witness she's cross-examining. "Your blisters are mostly on the left. Your phone, right?"

"Well, yeah, but then I was on FaceTime. The phone wasn't even on my face."

"Hmmm," says Dad. My parents exchange a meaningful glance.

Years of hearing that contemplative, gears-turning, theory-generating *hmmm* puts me on edge. That *hmmm* has been the harbinger for all kinds of sad verdicts. My favorite purple dress when I was five: junked (because, *hmmm*, Mom read an article about lead in the zippers of kids' clothes). The crew carpool that Roz could have been in so I wouldn't have had to drive her: deal voided (because, *hmmm*, Dad wasn't convinced that the coxswain drove cautiously enough).

I tell them, "But my research showed that screens don't emit UVA rays."

"Or UVB," Mom adds. She stares up at Dad. "What did we miss?"

"It could be that your condition makes you extra sensitive to any light," Dad says. "We'll figure it out. In the meantime, no going out again today."

Wait. Any light?

Any?

Light?

That would explain how a few minutes under any kind of light bulb and driving in the daytime could inflame my skin. Could screens? How was I going to research local field trips? How was I going to "work" with Josh?

"I'm calling Dr. Anderson," I say.

Before I can dial, Mom cries, "No phone!"

"Mom, chill," Roz says as I scowl wordlessly. I'd aim a smile at Roz for her unexpected solidarity, but any facial movement makes my face burn like I've sunbathed in the Sahara Desert without an umbrella, sun hat, or sunscreen for two days too long. This is much worse than I thought. I chance a look in the mirror.

A chain of blisters. Darth Vader. Slab of barbequed meat.

NOT SO FUN FACT FROM A NIGHT OF MULTIPLATFORM "WORKING"

What happens when you spend thirteen straight hours in front of a computer and phone and you've got a more extreme case of photosensitivity than you, your parents, and the medical community realized? You get burned.

CHAPTER THIRTY-FOUR

That evening, as I'm starting a test batch of this week's Souper Bowl Sunday offerings (Seahawks vs. Buffalo Bills), Mom says casually, "So we were thinking, honey, about your phone."

Oh, no.

No, no, no.

The emergency appointment for a second opinion with a different dermatologist today was demoralizing enough with the doctor's murky answers. I rest the heavy knife on the cutting board, drained of all hope that I could lose myself in this new and intriguing recipe for buffalo chicken wings soup.

...

HOW TO ANSWER WITHOUT ANSWERING: A MASTER CLASS

Q: Could my skin be allergic to plain old visible light, not just ultraviolet rays?
A: Perhaps, but it would seem so.

Q: Screens don't emit UV rays. So is my skin supersensitive?
A: Unclear, but it's a possibility.

Q: How bad will this get?
A: Uncertain, but it could possibly worsen.

...

I'm not prepared for one more piece of my life to be stripped away when I would so much rather stay in the land of denial, pretending this is just another normal day prepping for yet another normal Souper Bowl Sunday and waiting for another normal text or two from my friends and the strong-and-oh-so-very-silent Josh.

But no.

I can't handle my parents' new plan of doom, whatever it is. So I host my own intervention. I face my parents, a united front of Lee & Li "We Were Thinking" dictums. Well, this Lee & Li has her own thoughts, too.

...

I WAS THINKING:
THE HIJACKED EDITION

Me: *Funny, I was thinking, too.*

Mom (eyebrows lifting):

Dad (eyes widening):

Me: *How about I shut down my devices at midnight? That'll give me enough time to do my homework, and I'll use them in ten-minute intervals until we know for sure if the screens are triggering my skin.*

Mom: *Oh.*

Dad: *We'll all shut down at the same time.*

Mom: *At eight o'clock.*

...

"Excuse me?" Roz clutches her phone to her chest like it's a flotation device and snarls, "Take Viola's."

"No, princess," Dad says, his hands spread out in a way that's authoritative, "we all stick together. No one's taking anyone's away, but Viola's got a good plan. We can limit everyone's nighttime usage."

"At eight," Mom repeats.

"Eleven thirty," I counter.

"That's not fair!" Roz protests as she slips her phone underneath herself at the breakfast nook.

Everyone turns to me expectantly: Mom, Dad, Roz. In my head, the soundtrack for the tragicomedy of my life swells. Except my movie got hijacked, and I no longer know the screenwriter or the director, and certainly not the actress or plot. Still, I've memorized the old script, the one with my cue to play the Good Girl, the one who sacrifices. The one who dutifully offers, *No, just take mine. Roz shouldn't suffer.*

I don't say a word. Instead, I let my chopping do the talking. My butcher's knife guillotines three stalks of celery. Off with their heads!

"Whatever," Roz grumbles, and a moment later, her bedroom door slams shut.

"Actually, honey." Dad sets his ankle on top of his other leg. "We were thinking about That Boy."

Mom adds for clarification, "Josh."

"That Boy who waited for me at the hospital? Who brought me home twice?" I'm Josh's advance PR team, already guessing what's about to come next.

"That Boy who doesn't seem to have your best interests in mind." Dad's voice flattens, a single note of grim. "He's a rule breaker."

"You're the one who thought he was great," I point out to Mom before I narrow my eyes at Dad. "Is this about him going to community college?"

"Not entirely," Dad says, sounding reasonable, even though his face is getting flushed.

"Dad, isn't that a little elitist of you? I mean, you don't even know his story."

"We know enough," Mom says, slipping her hand back into Dad's. "You should only surround yourself with people who want to protect you, who put your best interests ahead of their own, even if it hurts them to do so."

For the record, anger cooking is not nearly as satisfying as anger baking. Fists or rolling pin, I've punched down plenty of dough with both, but I can't possibly wait hours for dough I haven't even made to rise. The next best thing: I dismember the next batch of celery.

"Umm, honey, don't you think you should be a little more careful?" Dad asks uneasily.

"Hello, I've been cooking since I was four," I grind out, and whack the stalks into tidy quarter-inch segments, but when I almost nick my thumb, I force myself to take a deep breath. Ignoring my parents, I crouch down to pull out the slow cooker and bang it on the counter. Perhaps all this unusual aggression scares my parents away.

Carrots and potatoes have never been peeled and diced so vigorously (violently). I dump them all into the slow cooker. The chicken breast I'd roasted earlier needs to be hand-shredded, but I tighten my grip on the knife handle and mince the chicken. Sour cream? I bypass Mom's fat-free container of choice in the fridge and go for the full-fat one. Calories? Who cares? What the heck, let's add another whopping spoonful. Or two. I slam my finger down on the on-button for the slow cooker.

Breathing hard, I glare at the aftermath of the Category 5 hurricane that's gusted through the kitchen, because someone, c'est moi, has not been cleaning as she cooks. Bits of celery leaves and potato peelings cling to the counter. Wait another thirty minutes, and they'll be encrusted on the surface. The cutting board is clogged with chicken bits and coagulated fat. Blue cheese is smeared on the fork I'd used to crumble the wedge.

I sweep out of the kitchen. Let someone else clean up for once.

To quote Roz: Whatever.

CHAPTER THIRTY-FIVE

It could be Christmas morning, me creeping down the hardwood floors before anyone else has woken up, except there are no presents to break into, just my jailed phone. Apparently, I'm not the only one suffering from tech withdrawal. Roz is crouched behind the kitchen island, rapid-fire texting in the dark. She drops the phone behind her back when she feels my presence, not that that hides the evidence. The phone glows in the dark.

Roz whispers, "Oh, it's just you."

"Just me," I say, drawing to the basket of impounded goodies.

"You won't believe what Mom's done this time."

This conspiratorial tone I haven't heard since we were little, sneaking into the Girl Scout cookies. A placard in beautiful calligraphy is tied to a basket: After-Hours Charging Station.

"When did she have time to go all Pinteresty on us?" I ask.

"Yeah, don't they have a couple of crises to solve?"

That's the problem. They do. me. No point in mentioning this to Roz, not when we're getting along. Before our devices had been corralled for the night, I had sent a few hasty texts.

> Me (to Aminta): *How about a bake sale for a program that feeds elementary schoolers with no food over weekends?*
> Me (to Caresse): *SOS. I need your fashion skills.*
> Me (to Josh): *Tech confiscated. Screens are burning me. Who knew?*

He's been incommunicado all day, according to my new schedule of periodic and timed tech usage.

> Tech Check, 8:00 a.m.: no text.
> Tech Check, 10:00 a.m.: silence.
> Tech Check, noon: crickets.
> Tech Check, 2 p.m.: boycotted afternoon check; bad for my self-image as strong, independent young woman.
> Tech Check, 4 p.m.: out of responsibility to my academic standing, I take a quick peek. Nothing.

Now, when I turn on the phone, my heart leaps at the sight of the alert: Josh has answered a minute ago.

> Josh: *Sorry, I've been cramming for tests all day.*
> Josh: *So. I have an idea.*

What could ten more minutes of unsanctioned and nonessential screen time possibly hurt, especially if my screen is permanently set on night mode?

> Me: *What?*

Instead of a text buzz, my phone rings, a sound I only associate with my parents, who are the only people to call me. It's Josh. What's with my nerves? It's as if Tuesday's FaceTime and phone calls never happened, and I'm speaking with him for the first time.

"Shh!" Roz is back to hissing. So much for our sisterhood détente. I quickly silence the phone. She drags me to the basement door. What? Is she going to shove me down the stairs? "Don't blow this."

Clearly, my little sister is more skilled in covert spycraft than I am, because the basement is the best place for a clandestine conversation: under the living room, out of earshot of our parents' bedroom, and no one ever dares to come down here unless it's to do laundry. As soon as I'm in the stairwell, Roz closes the door so gently, I don't hear it shut. That leaves me in the dark. With the wolf spiders. The phone vibrates again.

I fumble for the stairwell light, even as I answer the phone, but the over-head light is so bright, I can't chance any further skin reaction, especially since I'm not geared up in a hat or the right clothes. I cast a nervous glance up, over, and around myself. No spiders.

"Why are you calling?" I say, then flush as I flick the light switch off. It's too late to backtrack to a benign hello. Or even better, a casual hey, but to be honest, I'm a little miffed at his stuttering, on-again, off-again communication.

"How sick are you?" Josh asks just as preemptively as if we've both agreed to edit out the inconsequential bits of a conversation. Immediately, he swears and says — more accurately, barks, "Put me on speakerphone."

"But the screen is black."

"Remember, I'm not a science guy. So if it emits any kind of invisible rays, I don't want to burn you even more. Hey, speakerphone."

I sigh — loudly — into the speakerphone, then set it by my feet. I sit down warily on one of the top steps, where I'm within an arm's reach of the door and fast escape from any creepy crawlies.

"You don't sound so great," he says.

"It's because I'm in the land of spiders," I tell him.

"What?"

"Okay, so, when we moved in ten or so years ago, we found these three huge, super-fast spiders in the basement. I mean, these things could run."

"Wolf spiders."

"Yeah, and then Mom read that they can rise up on their hind legs!"

"No way!"

"Way! And show their fangs. And then Roz saw one pounce."

"Not even."

"It jumped. So we were all: roll out the red carpet to chemicals. Pronto."

"I take it your parents don't represent the Arachnid Humane Society."

"No! Wait, is there even such a thing?"

"Probably," he says.

"I am so not baking for that cause."

"Good, because how sick are you?" Before I can answer, he says, "And don't censor."

"I don't censor." (Much.)

"You actually do, but you don't have to with me. Just tell me what you're thinking, straight up. So on the sick scale: one to five."

"Two."

"Or a three. Or three and a quarter, right?"

Was he right? I frown, wanting to deny it, but what was the point of deny-ing the truth when he seemed hell bent on hearing how I was really feeling?

"Okay," I concede as I lean against the step behind my back. "A solid four after the poke shop. And a two and three-quarters today."

"I'm sorry."

"It's not your fault."

"It is. We talked way too long Tuesday night. I mean, I like talking with you."

"I know what you mean." I smile because his words run into each other like he's a little nervous-excited to be talking with me, too.

"So what'd you do today without your phone?" he asks.

"I planned: my college, our research expeditions, *Persephone*."

"Where are we researching this weekend?"

"We're not." I clear my throat, embarrassed. "I've been zombified. Blisters and everything all over my face."

"Okay, *World War Z* zombie would be alarming, but *iZombie*? I'm down with that." Which makes me laugh again, especially when he continues, "Plus, the perks of photosensitivity. You can only go out at night, dark, impossible to see anything, no makeup ever, not that you need to wear any, anyway. So, hey, how's Sunday night?"

Wait. Did he mean, "hey, how's Sunday night" as in "hey, editorial consultant, we could research Sunday night." Or did he mean, "hey, I want to kiss you Sunday night?" I rub my hands together, because the cold of the basement is now seeping through my pajamas.

"So Caleb and I used to run the staircases on Queen Anne, and I know that you miss trail running. So I thought, maybe, if you were interested, we could hit some of the staircases and run them by moonlight," he says, rushing through this invitation.

It doesn't matter if this is pure research, not romance. I am swamped with a big rush of yes. "I would love that."

"Awesome."

Then we become our own dark sky reserve of silence.

Finally, Josh says, briskly, all business, "Okay, Ultra, I should let you sleep. I'll text you the details."

"Yeah," I say.

A moment later, I'm back in the warm kitchen, glad to defrost, but the abrupt ending to our conversation keeps playing in my head.

"Your phone," hisses Roz from the nook, where she's been sitting.

"Oh, right," I whisper as I drop it back into the basket. She leaves the kitchen at the same time as I do.

At her door, she sniffs. "You're welcome for being your watchdog."

CHAPTER THIRTY-SIX

On Sunday night, at the official moment the sun sets in Seattle at 6:22 p.m., I escape. Everybody else—notably, my parents—is tethered to the game, watching the Seahawks pummel the Buffalo Bills. (That said, the Buffalo Chicken Soup is the clear winner on this Souper Bowl Sunday. Sometimes, all you need to turn adequate into awesome is one secret ingredient: sriracha sauce.) Perfect timing, the living room erupts in cheers as the Seahawks unexpectedly intercept the ball again in the middle of the first quarter.

I dash out of the back door to meet Josh in the driveway, just as I planned. According to my calculations, we have a good ninety minutes of sunset to get to Queen Anne, run a couple of the secret staircases in the fading light, and return home before the game ends.

"You don't need to tell your parents?" Josh asks, his hand on the handle but making no moves to open the door.

"Nah, they're busy." Which is technically true. Just as it's technically true that Josh picked me up. And that I'm not sneaking out so much as I'm not interrupting my parents, who are otherwise occupied, fist-bumping each other and everyone else in their matching jerseys and Seahawks logo painted on both their cheeks. As for my cheeks, while I look like a skin-shedding zombie, at least my blisters are gone. Just in case, my face is shaded in my spacecraft hat, and every spot of my body is slathered in SPF 100 sunscreen.

"Hmm." Josh looks unconvinced, casting a look over his shoulder like he wants to head inside and confess our plans.

I tell him the truth as we approach his truck, "I'm so unbelievably excited to run."

"Not what most normal people say," he tells me, grinning.

"I'm not most normal people."

"Thankfully."

As soon as we reach Queen Anne, a neighborhood perched on the highest hill in Seattle, I hurry out of his truck, bouncing in my trail-running sneakers. Nothing tastes better than freedom. Josh is still opening his carefully folded *Map of the (Oft) Pedestrian Public Stairs of Queen Anne Hill* when I take off.

He catches up, refolding the map hastily. "The first staircase is back that way."

"We're taking the scenic way around," I say, laughing.

"Definitely not normal."

"Thankfully."

I luxuriate at the feel of my legs stretching long and fast on this road, Josh loping at my side. I quicken the pace; he keeps up easily. When we finally hit the first set of steep stairs near Kerry Park, I feel at home. This may not be the wooded forest, meeting Darren on a dirt trail, but here on these man-made concrete steps, I'm still heading uphill. My muscles protest after days and days of being mostly sedentary, yet it feels good and right and real to be here, now, with Josh. Winded at the top of the stairs, my hands go to my waist and I suck in air.

"I'm out of shape," I gasp.

"I'm afraid to run with you in shape," he says.

"Really?" Without warning, I trot down the staircase, smiling as I hear his laughter.

"So which international dark sky park would you visit if you didn't have to worry about money or parents?" he asks, catching up.

"Oh, the one in South Korea. Totally," I tell him because, why yes, I did do my research, not just for *Persephone*, but for the next potential bake-sale beneficiary. Preserving pockets of land for their dark skies is a cause Geeks for Good could support, feeling even more convinced of that as we head one block over to hit a second set of stairs, even steeper than the first and surrounded on both sides with evergreens. We need spaces that are pristine and beautiful. "It's their firefly conservation area. So you'd get both stars and fireflies."

"In the meantime, we could grab some Bok A Bok chicken after dark — "

I interrupt him, stunned, "You know Korean fried chicken?"

"I've been doing some research."

"On food?"

"That I thought you'd like."

He has? My gasp is camouflaged by my panting as we run up a shorter set of stairs yet another block over.

"So maybe we could drive up to North Bend sometime and eat the Bok A Bok in the total dark," he tells me, too casually to be casual. The boy has given this some distinctly non-work-zone thought. "It's not exactly a dark sky park, but . . ."

"It's a great Plan B. I love it," I tell him truthfully. Work-zone, I tell myself. Work. Zone.

"So help me with a Plan B for another research expedition for *Persephone*. I thought Angkor Wat would be a great scene, but that's a little too *Lara Croft: Tomb Raider*, isn't it?"

"Yeah," I say, following him down the street as we draw toward a thick copse of trees in a cul-de-sac. In the middle of this urban greenbelt, a concrete staircase curves up the hill.

"I was worried about that."

"But there are ruins in Laos that predate Angkor Wat."

"Yeah? How do you know that?"

"Auntie Ruth." Just saying her name makes me feel guilty because it's been days since I've spoken to her, not since I left her auto repair shop without stopping inside. It's so stupid, but I can't help feeling angry at her for abandoning our travel plans so easily, like she was canceling a haircut, not cutting off one of my dreams.

Josh isn't even breathless, halfway up these stairs. "Does she travel a lot?"

"She's been ticking off the bucket list she and Uncle Amos made before he died. She takes each of us, her nieces and nephews, on a trip with her when we turn seventeen."

"That's so cool." Josh is quiet for a moment so all we hear are our footfalls on the concrete steps. "All the places I had Persephone visiting were ones Caleb wanted to see."

"So he's still part of the story."

"Yeah. You know what's weird, though?"

"What?"

He sidles an uncertain look at me, one that I can read clearly in the moonlight. The planes of his face are sharpened in the shadows like he's aged half a decade, chiseled whatever was left of childhood from his cheeks and jaw. "Caleb and I would have the same ideas at the same time, but us? You and me? We build on our ideas together."

Us. We. Together. Even if he's talking in purely professional terms, my smile grows. "I love that."

"Me, too."

"Hey, where are we?" I ask. "I mean, the map." (I mean, us, we, together.)

"I'll check." At the top landing, Josh unfolds his map, while I collect my breath. What he says next makes me lose my breath again. He taps the map as proof, while his voice drops an octave. "The Comstock Grande Dame. It says this is great for kissing."

Grateful for the darkening sky because I blush, I'm not sure what propels me to say, "I wonder what empirical evidence they have for that?"

Josh steps closer to me, then closer. "Who was telling me that she believed in primary source research?"

"I'm a great researcher." I match him step for step, drawing so near our bodies almost touch.

And then they do. With his arms around me, pressing me tight to him, he asks, "Yeah?"

"But it depends," I whisper to him, lifting onto my toes while he bends down to me, "on the research subject."

"Like this?" He kisses me hard and deep, a ferocious hunger, like this is what's been keeping him up at night, what's been haunting him by day.

Or maybe that's me because my breath goes short, fast like I've been running all this time in one direction: to him.

Josh whispers, "Or this?" His kiss softens, gentles, as he cups my cheeks tenderly.

"Or this?" I trace his lower lip, tasting him, deepening the kiss, slow and sure. I lean into him, tilt my hips against his.

I lose sight of time and place and planetary rotation until an alarm goes off. Literally.

I groan. "What's that?"

"Time for you to pumpkin," Josh says, silencing his cell phone.

"Seriously? You set an alarm?"

Mr. Responsible shrugs. "Yeah."

When we head back to his truck, the night is completely dark. He takes my hand, his fingers moving gently on mine like he wants to keep our contact. How weird is it that holding hands is even more intimate than a kiss? Empirical evidence of one girl, me, shows that I don't want to let go when we get into his truck.

This is doable, I tell myself, buckling my seat belt. This, us, the dark. We can go on night runs, play night golf, take up night skiing in the winter. In the summer, we can dive off the dock into the lake at midnight. And then there are movie theaters, the perfect (safe) place to make out even during the light of day. The street where we're parked may be deserted, but Josh checks, then triple-checks his blind spots. His hand squeezes mine, once, before he places both of his on the steering wheel.

Back at home, I kiss Josh in the driveway, breezily tell him that I'm an independent woman, I don't need him to walk me up to the door. In the darkness, I wave to him, hearing the raucous cheers from inside the house.

I let myself in. No one has noticed that I've been gone.

This will be doable. It has to be.

CHAPTER THIRTY-SEVEN

"I really and truly didn't believe that anyone our age could look like a soccer mom," Caresse says, shuddering as soon as she sees me two days later.

Aminta says, "I wouldn't show up to school either if I had to wear that."

"Tragic," agrees Caresse.

"Hence, my SOS," I tell them, relieved that my friends have arrived at my home. Here's the thing: If I don't prove to my parents—and to myself—that I can make it out in the world, then I will never be allowed to go to college, let alone outside. So I figure, why not dress for my future success? My chances of being a foreign correspondent might be higher if I can find the right clothes. I'm betting on more layers since that seemed to have kept me safe from the streetlights on my night run with Josh. So multilayers it is, ones that fend off the sun without making me look like I'm on a perpetual safari or a soccer mom in resort wear.

Just in case I'm burning without realizing it in a millisecond of natural light, I take a cautious step deeper into my home, then another two.

"Project Wynnter to the rescue," announces Aminta.

I choke up. They've named the mission after my middle name.

"I know, pretty great brand name, huh?" she says, beaming. "How long have you told us that we needed to design our own line of clothes? Now we are, and for a good cause."

"The world needs you guys," I tell them. "I need you."

"That's stating the obvious," says Caresse, plucking distastefully at my forest-green button-down shirt. "Who designed this stuff?" She holds out her hand to Aminta, then snaps a one-word order, as if she's already a practicing neurosurgeon with a clothing line on the side. "Keys."

"Are your parents here?" Aminta asks, glancing swiftly toward the kitchen while Caresse sashays back to the car.

I shrug. "No, they're in San Jose. Client meeting."

"Good, what they don't know won't hurt them." She bends down to pick up a box that I hadn't noticed outside the front door and maneuvers inside with it. "Well, good thing they aren't home for this special delivery for UltraViola Li."

"Huh," I say, taking the box from Aminta. It has mysterious heft, but I don't even care what's inside because this box says that Josh is thinking of me.

They follow me to the living room, where the shades have been permanently lowered. Aminta asks, "Does Josh from Planet X know he's been banished from your solar system?"

"More importantly," says Caresse, sidetracking to the kitchen to set down the sewing machine, "does he know you're not subservient? Does he know you don't eat with chopsticks? Does he know — "

"Caresse!" I say, laughing. "He's from Seattle."

"So? The ignorance of some people could astonish you, and you definitely do not want to be with a creeper who has a weird mixed race fetish. They exist, you know."

"Oh, I know," I assure them, even as Aminta sings out, "For sure!"

"Anyway, why would he be banned?" Caresse helps herself to the scissors stuck in the butcher's block to do surgery on the box.

I tell her, "My parents think he's a bad influence."

"Yeah, wait until they see how we're going to sex up your clothes. Then we'll talk about bad influence." Caresse smirks, tapping on the sewing machine, before slicing through the last side of the box.

"Hang on," says Aminta. "You aren't expecting anything naughty in there, are you?"

Naughty? I blush. "Uhhh . . ."

205

"Definitely, hurry then." Aminta waves both hands.

Once I've opened the box flaps, we all lean in, and Aminta sighs, a rhapsody of delight: "A mixtape!" She grabs the cassette tape and reads the label out loud before I can make out the handwritten word myself: "Nocturne."

Caresse looks around the kitchen. "Do you even have a tape player?"

I reach into the box and pull out the device. "You mean this?"

"I do like his style," Caresse says as she draws out three chocolate bars. "Dark chocolate. I really like his style."

"You know, most guys wouldn't think to do this. Can we time-share him?" Aminta asks.

Caresse wriggles her fingers impatiently for the tape player. "Gimme."

"Seriously, I could see him every other weekend, kind of like my schedule with my dad," Aminta says.

They're both so pushy that I laugh, feeling more relaxed than I have felt in the days since my parents laid down the Tech-Free Decree along with gerrymandering a nice, big Josh No Fly Zone. Some boundaries, I decide, are meant to be redrawn.

Caresse presses a button. The tape player opens, and she feeds the cassette into its mouth. "Let's see whether this boy knows you at all."

"But does it matter?" I bite my lip. "What guy would date me if I have to stay in the dark? Forever?"

"Okay, that's like saying, what woman would date my dad, who's in remission from cancer?" says Aminta.

True, that wouldn't deter my mom from setting him up with Auntie Ruth or any of her single friends, as long as he was kind, stable, and drank gallons of kale juice.

"Yeah, and trust me." Caresse taps the cover of the tape recorder. "No one makes a mixtape unless he's in serious wooing mode."

"Wooing," I say, and look at Aminta, both of us cracking up. "We're just working together."

"Yeah, right. The last time you got together, he held your hand," Aminta divulges.

"In public?" Caresse asks, eyes narrowing.

I nod.

"That's serious woo-age," Caresse says stubbornly. "Major significant woo-age."

"When was your last girlfriend?" I ask her.

Caresse answers, "A year ago."

Aminta laughs. "And we should listen to you because . . ."

"Wisdom over experience," Caresse says. "Okay, do the honors."

I press the PLAY button. A familiar chord strums, and I could be sitting with Josh in Ada's Technical Books as the lead singer of Death Cab for Cutie croons the first words.

Aminta shuts off the music. " 'Love of mine?' " Her eyebrows arch up.

"Wooing," pronounces Caresse. She presses REWIND. "Let's just listen to that again, shall we? Okay, *Project Runway* time. You cannot possibly look like a homeschool kid when you come back."

"And you better be coming back because we've been wearing these things and giving ourselves major hat head" — Aminta lifts off her hat to show her creased hair — "just to normalize hats for you."

"You have?"

"Yeah!" they both shout.

"So, seriously, go get all your clothes," says Caresse, "and I'm using that term loosely."

When I return, Caresse has taken off her hoody. I point to her black T-shirt flecked with silver thread. "That's what I want to wear."

"Oh, this?" She looks down at herself. "The Geminids."

"What are those?"

"The best meteor shower in this galaxy." I must look blank because Caresse drops one of my UPF-shirts distastefully on the breakfast nook table. "You've never seen them? Or the Perseids in the summer? Whoa. The ones in a couple of weeks, the Draconids, are supposed to be awesome this year."

Halfway through reconfiguring my wardrobe, we break into the chocolate to fortify ourselves against ugly. I don't remember a single bite. As it turns out, the way to this girl's heart is through her ears, because I melt, ever so slightly, with every delicious note of the nine songs Josh selected for me.

CONTENTS OF MY VERY FIRST CARE PACKAGE FROM A BOY WHO MAY OR MAY NOT BE WOOING ME

(I HOPE HE IS.)

1. Nocturne :: Mixtape

> I Will Follow You into the Dark — Death Cab for Cutie
> The Stars Blink Just for Us — Say Hi
> Even the Darkness Has Arms — The Barr Brothers
> Night Time — The xx
> Night Swimming — Cumulus
> Night Vision — Tennis
> Out of the Dark — Nada Surf
> Black Treacle — Arctic Monkeys
> The Sound of Silence — Disturbed

2. Tape cassette player.

3. Three chocolate bars, all dark: Coconut. Maple and Bacon. Potato Chip.

CHAPTER THIRTY-EIGHT

Composing a thank-you text to Josh takes longer than researching the number of elementary-age kids who go hungry every weekend. Thirteen million in America alone, according to some experts. Thirteen million is way too many according to me. There's got to be a better solution than sending fifty kids home with backpacks full of weekend meals, but my tech time is coming to a close. So after procrastinating on it all day, in my last two minutes, I quickly write Josh.

Everything feels fake—too chipper. ("Hey! Thanks for the care package!") Too somber. ("Hey. Thanks for the care package.") Too flirty ("Hey . . . Thanks for the care package . . .") Which leads me to three epiphanies. First, punctuation marks are way more important than I ever knew or imagined. Second, I'm glad there's not an app that divulges how many times a text gets rewritten before it's sent. And third, I don't want to work-zone Josh anymore.

Frustrated at myself, I check the time: six thirty. The kid I need to feed is about to come home from crew, hangry from her workout. Mom and Dad now text to say they missed their flight and will be back home closer to nine. Can you say de facto private chef? After I've fixed some chicken ravioli with pesto for Roz, I head to my bedroom, where I sit on my bed next to the pile of my newly tailored clothes.

"Still pathetic, but at least now you can tell you've got some curves" was Caresse's final verdict.

As I'm texting my friends another round of thanks, so much easier to write than Josh's, Roz finally deigns to inform me she's got a team dinner tonight.

Excuse me? Now she tells me that she's eating out?

Everyone else is moving on with their (normal) lives, my parents jet-setting on another last-second business trip, Roz hanging out with her team. Honestly, I should have asked Josh to go to Bok A Bok with me tonight. Everyone else made their plans without any regard to me. I need to make mine. I head outside to the patio, where the darkening evening awaits.

Me: *Persephone Research Trip #1 — Draconids*
Me: *In two weeks.*
Me: *Dress code: Warm.*

CHAPTER THIRTY-NINE

Exactly five minutes after I message Josh, post-text reality sets in along with the cool night air, which smells and feels like fall. I draw my legs up on the garden chair as I stare at my phone. What the hell have I done?

Hell, no is the Lee & Li Way since disaster can happen anytime, anywhere. So just say *hell, no* to risk of any kind that might harm you, heart or limb.

Risk like: Josh is not into me. (Never mind the care package.)

Risk like: He may or may not even want to first date, let alone date-date. (Never mind the care package.)

Risk like: He could be a confirmed, irredeemable player. (See: care package.)

My hands cover my face as a cold wind skims my skin, making me shiver. Innocent goose bumps may pimple my arms, but they worry me: Are they an early warning sign of impending hives? Proof that moonburns are possible? Evidence of girl stupidity for thinking she can lead a perfectly normal life that includes a boy?

And I repeat, what the hell have I done?

CHAPTER FORTY

The moment I leave the patio for my bedroom, my phone pings. I jerk, startled, and almost drop my phone on the concrete pavers.

> Josh: *"I am the leaf in the wind—watch how I soar."*

I push the kitchen door open and pause at the fridge to grab a glass of cold water and collect myself. I won't—I can't—*Firefly* flirt with Josh until I get answers. I need answers, concrete and undeniable, real and truthful.

> Me: *Is that a yes to the Draconids?*
> Josh: *Depends.*
> Josh: *Is that just a research trip?*
> Josh: *Or is that you asking me out?*
> Me: *What if I was?*
> Josh: *"Zoë, we're runnin' . . ."*

Wanting clarification about Friday night himself? Quoting *Firefly*? Curating the most awesome songs about the dark for me? Giving me three dark chocolate bars? Those are words and gifts that unlock my heart: I don't just want to work with Josh. I want him.

But where can we possibly go with this?

No matter what my *hell, no* Lee & Li training tells me, I say: Hell, yes, yes, yes.

CHAPTER FORTY-ONE

There is a time for everything. I believe that. "A time to weep and a time to laugh. A time to mourn and a time to dance." A time to stay safe inside and a time to dare the cosmic light show outside (with a cute guy in the complete dark). Tonight, I choose to laugh, dance, and flirt like any normal (healthy) girl. (Never mind that I'm casting anxious glances back at my slumbering house while shivering out on the curb, waiting for my clandestine ride with my clandestine guy to arrive: *Hurry, hurry, hurry.*)

I've waited for this night for what feels like forever, not chancing my skin for a single moment. Josh and I restricted ourselves to texting in short spurts throughout the day and talking every single night by speakerphone. The house behind me is dark, everyone tucked safe and sound in their bedrooms. Still, my parents and their keen sense of crisis means I should be rehearsing my excuse: *We're conducting research for a project that's going to impact people with photosensitivity, not to mention catch the eye of Georgetown's dean of admissions.* Plus, I have a backup scarf to wrap around myself, not to mention a hat and mittens, water bottle, and chocolate for stargazing outside of the truck. See? My life can change, but it's not ending. It will be even better than before.

My fists are freezing into half-moons, so I cup my hands in front of my mouth, breathing into them, while I crane my neck to scan the empty street. Maybe Josh isn't coming. Maybe Aminta is wrong about tonight. Maybe I should head back inside, where it is safe as a tomb.

But then a pickup truck rounds the corner and stops next to me, despite my being dressed in black (coat) on black (hat) on black (extra-warm power leggings). The better to hide from security cameras with, my dear. So fast, I could be Ultra, speedier than UV rays, I'm inside the truck with Josh.

Texting may keep us connected in small, bantering snippets, but being with him in person—when I don't have the luxury of editing and rewriting my comebacks, when he is so touchable, when he can see me up close—is nerve-racking.

I tell him, "Let's go for hard burn!" just as he asks me, "Your parents know about this, right?"

Perhaps standing out on the curb was a dead giveaway, but nothing is derailing my plan tonight. I tell him, "It's dark and it's research."

"Purely research?"

"Well, no." Why isn't he unbuckling his seat belt and kissing me?

Instead, Josh asks, "What time do you need to be back?"

I answer truthfully, "Tomorrow's Sunday."

"Souper Bowl?"

"Already made both soups, thank you very much."

"So not too early." He angles a quick look at me before he focuses on the road. Wait, why isn't he kissing me? Did he change his mind about the way he feels about me? Is this another Darren moment where he's just pretending to be interested in me? Josh tells me, "Okay, River, we're off."

"Zoë." My correction goes quiet—and my fretting silences—when he wraps his hand around mine. I imagine those hands on me, skimming my shoulders, smoothing down my bare back. I am, for once since my diagnosis, dressed to kill under my parka: a daringly low-cut (UPF!) T-shirt, care of Caresse, who pointed out, the dark is made for sexy.

Josh fact-checks me. "Didn't you shut down that jerk at school by threatening him with the FBI?"

"Maybe . . ."

"Maybe that's not Zoë or River. Maybe it's Persephone."

"Oh. I like that."

"She can't help but get involved. Kind of like you." He squeezes my hand. "So I've been thinking about what you said about me co-opting Caleb's plans."

"I didn't say co-opt."

"But that's what I was doing." Now he sounds nervous. "I've been thinking that I might want to study psychology. Maybe be a counselor."

"I can see that," I tell him, squeezing his hand back. "You're a good listener and insightful. Yeah, I can totally picture that."

"Me, too, especially if I study art therapy."

"That is brilliant."

"Yeah, you are. So, editorial consultant, any new brainstorms?"

"I'm so glad you asked." I tell him about how Persephone could arrive on Earth on a shower of Draconids. "I mean, just imagine a superhero who's able to surf the stars."

"Or stardust."

"Especially from the constellation of a dragon."

"So that would answer why Persephone gets stranded on Earth."

"Yeah, because it's not like our planet sheds meteors for her to surf back home to Planet X," I tell him triumphantly.

"That's so cool," he says with a grin before he lifts my hand to kiss it. Then he places both of his safely back on the steering wheel. "But I really liked your idea of the Necromanteion. Maybe there's a way to work them together?"

"Yeah," I say, but plotting is hard to do when my mind is fantasizing about his lips on mine.

"You warm enough?" Josh asks.

Actually, I'm sweating, but I don't think it has much to do with the cranking heater or the seat warmer set on high. It has everything to do with me wrapped like a surprise present.

"Boiling!" I move the seat belt out of the way without unclipping it.

"I can pull over."

"No need." I lean forward to strip off my heavy winter parka, which admittedly is a struggle since contortionist I'm not.

"I'm pulling over."

"Don't worry." I'm not sure who is more relieved when I toss my coat into the back and finally rest against my seat. "Now it's perfect."

"It really is." Josh blinks because it's probably the first time that he realizes that I do, in fact, have a chest under the protective covering of all my usual layers. He returns his gaze to the nearly empty highway before us as we leave the suburbs of Issaquah behind. Flanked on either side by dark woods, the night grows even darker with a low fog that shrouds the road ahead.

I ask, "Do you think we'll see anything tonight?"

"The weather said there should be a small clearing around midnight."

"What if there isn't?"

"What if there is?" A huge semitruck lumbers ahead of us, chugging up the incline. Josh signals us into the fast lane. We fly into the night.

CHAPTER FORTY-TWO

The night seems a thousand times darker atop Snoqualmie Pass, more substantial somehow. Two other cars have already staked out spots around the parking lot. When Josh stops right in the middle, ignoring the parking lines, I know what tonight's about: to live my own life.

"I didn't know this existed. So," I tease him, but really I'm fact-finding, "do you bring all your girls here?"

"Just one," he says. "You."

My heart stops at those unexpected words, words that can pierce the scar tissue of a broken heart.

"I came here a lot after the car accident . . ." Josh says, and his voice trails off.

I fill in the blank. "It's a good place to be alone."

"And to look at the stars and think that maybe he's up there somewhere." Josh shrugs. "It was the first place I drove to after the accident. I knew if I didn't, I might never drive again." Josh keeps his eyes directly on the night ahead like he can will himself into the stars. His hands slide off the steering wheel as though he's lost all control of the direction. "I just miss him," he says, "and part of me worries that I'm going to do something that hurts you, too."

"Hardly," I say, and flex my biceps. "Do you have any idea how strong I am?"

"I do."

As we gaze at each other, I hear my own words and hope he hears them, too.

"Hey, look," he says, pointing to the clearing in the sky. "You brought the stars. Persephone would be happy."

"She would be . . ." (In clothes.)

"I hear the 'but,'" he says. "But . . ."

"But she'd be happier wearing real clothes."

His fingers drum the steering wheel. "I just don't feel good about changing any part of her."

"I get it. Caleb drew her." (But . . .)

"I literally heard the *but*."

"Okay, fine. But she can't fight vampires in that uniform. Not to be too graphic, but logistically, the way she's drawn and everything, there's going to be a lot of bounce going on. A. Lot. Of. Bounce." I stop because Josh is frowning, and after years of watching Mom and Dad work with skittish clients who balk at their recommendations, I know I'm pushing him hard. So I shrug and back off. "I'm sorry, but it's true."

"Don't apologize," Josh says quietly. "I'd rather hear the truth. So bounce. Okay, then what should she be wearing instead?"

"To fight vampires?" I turn to face him, tucking one leg under myself as I warm to this topic. "Layers."

"Layers."

"If you have to keep the bikini, then toss on some layers. And channel Zoë. Revolutionary badass."

"But River Tam. She fought in a dress."

"Yeah, and combat boots. But River's in another category of badassery completely."

"So she could fight vampires in a dress."

"For sure."

"So increase Persephone's badassery —"

"And layer."

Before I can elaborate, a meteor flashes across the break in the clouds, a streak of gold that slices the sky open. I'm surprised stardust doesn't shower down on us. The meteor moves so fast, if I had blinked, I would have missed it. Even now, a split second later, still staring hard at the sky, I lose the tail.

As one, Josh and I slam out of the truck. At first, I don't notice the cold much, figuring I'll grab my parka in a moment. We stand side by side in the dark with his arm around me. I'm officially freezing now, but I don't want to risk missing the next meteor by getting my coat or my hat and scarf. I stare so hard at the sky that my eyes start to water, blurring the pinprick stars. I blink away the tears rapidly.

Josh calls, "There!"

Too late. In that blink of my eye, I've missed the fleeting meteor in another part of the sky that I hadn't been watching. I sigh, disappointed.

"There'll be more," he promises. "NASA predicted a hundred an hour. Give or take a dozen."

I shiver and wrap my arms around myself.

"Hang on a sec." Josh leaves for the truck and returns with a familiar blanket, the one I had forgotten after the poke restaurant. He hands me my coat, then hops onto the hood of the truck, holding his hand down to me. I don't even hesitate, shrugging first into my parka, then clambering to sit next to him. Josh maneuvers behind me so that he can enclose me against his chest, wrapping his legs around me. With the blanket snug around both of us, we are cocooned tight.

He murmurs, "Go ahead. Lean back."

I tilt my head against my new favorite pillow, his shoulder, as I stare up at the sky. I swear he can hear the thudding of my heart. I know I can. My body should be approximately negative thirty degrees of cold. Instead, I am a furnace of warmth and wanting. And then, then, Mother Nature acts, unleashing a comet-dragon, gold-streaked and long-tailed. The meteor bolts across the sky.

"Did you see that?" I ask him, myself, the stars. Maybe it took this very moment and that very meteor to appreciate the darkness. The night isn't a prison closing me in, but freedom. Here, outside in the dark without any fear of my body shutting down, I can breathe and shed protective layers and be me. "Did you see that thing?"

He leans down, his breath warm on my cheek. "It'd be hard to miss."

"It was so beautiful."

"It is."

We turn toward each other, untangling only to tangle again, now with my legs wrapped around him. He stares so hard down into my eyes that I don't think he means the meteors. Or even me, really. But this — this electricity, this comet of an emotion streaks from him to me, and back again.

"You want to kiss me," I whisper to him, this elemental fact seeping all the way into my bones.

"You say that to all your guys."

"Just you."

No more questions, no more replies, I know he's going to kiss me, the air is fraught with expectation. Anticipation. My lips tingle. He closes the gap between us, his hands tracing the edge of my low, low-cut shirt, his tongue gently following up the curve of my neck. Then, nothing, but his lips held a mere breath from mine. Not even a soft brush of his lips. Instead, he makes me wait, wait, wait.

I sigh, breathe, moan.

When I finally feel his lips hard upon me, I suddenly understand the workings of physics and reject its laws outright.

Because.

This kiss is pure action, reaction, reaction.

Reaction.

All I can do is trust that the Earth is still spinning, gravity still anchors us to the ground, meteors are still flashing across the sky. Eyes closed, pressing into this boy, all I know for sure are his kisses — soft, hard, slow, thorough — that dance across my lips. My skin has become his sky.

CHAPTER FORTY-THREE

Minutes, hours, light-years later, a single snowflake grazes my cheek. Its sister lands on my forehead. Little whispers sent from Mother Nature: Welcome back to my world. Josh kisses the wetness away, melted snowflake tears: not yet, not yet, not yet. We lose the competition with Mother Nature, which is no contest anyway. There's no way he can kiss all the snowflakes away when the snow falls harder. Stars, meteors, and moon disappear overhead, graying the night sky. Now, only now, do I feel the ice-cold air lash my cheeks and my neck. I shiver. Only then do I remember the time.

"It's midnight," Josh says. His voice is husky. "You really got to pumpkin?"

"I really got to pumpkin," I say, laughing.

Immediately, I regret my answer when he pulls away from me and jumps down to the snow-covered ground. He slips a little. "Careful. Weird, it wasn't supposed to snow."

"You checked the weather?"

"Of course."

I sigh, already missing his warmth, his arms, his chest. He holds out his hand, my knight in the snow. I take it and scoot off the hood. He catches me in his arms. One stolen kiss becomes two. Three. Four.

I shiver.

"You're freezing. Come on," he says in a distinctly take-charge way as he walks me back to the passenger side.

"Not yet."

"You've got to pumpkin."

By the time we are both inside the truck, the air has become insistent with snowflakes, heavy, thick, and fast. Inside our snow globe, Josh cranks on the windshield wipers to full speed. Mother Nature scoffs. These flimsy blades are nothing against the force of her snow.

"You buckled?" Josh asks, glancing over at me.

Even though I nod, he does a visual check, eyes dropping from my shoulder to my hip. I wait for his quip. I get none.

Kissed to near oblivion, I hadn't even noticed that a gray Tesla has joined us in the parking lot. It lurches forward, then skids. Josh pulls up to the driver's side, rolls down my window, and leans over me.

"You need any help?" he asks.

The gray-haired driver, with a golden retriever lying in the back seat, shakes his head. "No, I got it. Freak snow though, huh? I'm going to wait it out. You kids might want to, too."

That's not possible when I've got to be home before dawn. The early bird patrol awakes around five, and there will be a perimeter check at seven when I should be rousing for my heart-healthy breakfast.

As soon as my window is rolled up, Josh asks me (again), "You buckled?"

"Still buckled," I confirm.

Yet (again), his eyes sweep me, triple-checking.

"It wasn't supposed to snow," he tells me (again). "I'm sorry. This is my fault."

"You can't control the weather."

He doesn't answer. We turn out of the parking lot without a problem, but as we slow at the stop sign, the truck skids. I yelp.

"I've got four-wheel drive," Josh says, but whether he's reassuring me or himself is unclear. "This is the last thing my parents agreed on after the accident. They wanted me in something indestructible."

"Hey, we can wait it out."

"You've got to get home. Or can you call your parents? Let them know you'll be late?"

I could, but the problem is they don't know I'm out. I don't tell Josh that. Before he can detect my lie, he checks his cell phone instead and swears.

"No service. How about you?" he asks.

Thankfully, I don't have cell service either. The truth is safe in the dark with us.

"Okay. Home then?"

"Home." I can feel his impending question and answer preemptively, "Still buckled."

"Good," he says, gripping the steering wheel. "Home."

Easier said than done because the traffic is at a dead standstill at the on-ramp to the highway. We can't even get on I-90, stuck with the rest of these late-night travelers.

"Let me find out what's going on," I tell him, and jump out of the truck before he can insist on doing that himself. A Toyota sedan is ahead of us. I tap on the snow-speckled window. "Hey, excuse me. Do you have any idea what's happening?"

"They've closed the pass," the tiny woman with three passed-out tod-dlers in the back seat tells me.

"Entirely?"

"Yup. Nobody was expecting the snow. None of the snowplows are ready, and all the motels up around here are sold out for the night."

"When's it going to reopen?"

"Who knows?" She shakes her head, a mass of brown curls. "An hour? Two? In the morning?"

Shivering, I hurry back to the truck and report to Josh: We aren't going anywhere any time soon. Forget Cinderella and her pumpkin; I'm going to be Rapunzel locked in my room forever when my parents discover this. My windows will be welded shut, padlocks bolted on my bedroom door. What colossal stupidity to slip out tonight, to prove to them that I was capable of a normal life.

Josh's hand upon mine stops my spiraling. "Hey."

"Hey," I say.

"Your parents would rather have you safe."

Which is true. If they knew where I was in the first place. The snow continues its relentless fall from the sky, muffling all sight and sound outside.

"We can't suffocate in here, can we?" I ask. "I mean, like, if it dumps six feet by tomorrow morning?"

"Don't worry. I won't Donner Party you."

"And here I thought I was tasty."

"I better double-check that."

"I'm not buckled anymore."

With that invitation, Josh leans in to kiss me. I meet him halfway, slipping my arms around him. Time, parents, suffocation shrug off me, skin that I no longer want to wear. Our kiss deepens, then deepens more. I need to feel him, want him to feel me, but I am wearing a sleeping bag (rated to be weatherproof down to negative ten degrees). I pull away.

"Not yet," he whispers.

"I'll be back." I shrug out of the heavy parka, and Josh throws it into the back seat. And there is only my low-cut shirt and the steaming windows and Josh and me pressing into each other.

What feels like hours later, he drags himself away with one last touch, tracing the lines of the lariat I wear around my neck. "Wait a second."

"Now?" I say dubiously.

"It stopped snowing."

"Clearly, I need to step up my kissing game if you noticed that."

"Not a chance, but hang on." Josh rummages in the glove compartment and holds up an ice scraper like it's some he-man's trophy. When he opens the driver door, the cold slips inside. So does reality. Thoughts of Mom and Dad blast me. How much trouble was I going to be in this time?

Above me, Josh scrapes the snow off the sunroof. A patch of clear sky hangs above us, a second miraculous opening in the clouds.

"Your own personal theater," Josh says when he returns to me, shivering and breathing on his cupped hands. I take them into my own.

"Ice cubes!" I say, recoiling from him. "New rules: no touching, not until there's no possibility of secondhand frostbite."

"Huh." Josh pulls his hands from mine, rubs them together rapidly, breathing on his fingers hard.

I laugh. "Seriously?"

"Seriously wondering about going outside now."

"Are you kidding me? Watching a meteor shower from the comfort of my own private theater?" I lower my seat all the way back so I can look straight up through the clean sunroof into the sky. "My hero. Persephone would approve."

"Would she?"

"Yes, even in her teeny, weeny, tiny bikini that would give her frostbite in two seconds flat."

"You have a point."

"Say it again."

"You have a—"

Before I can kiss him, a meteor rockets above us. I gasp. He whirls around to stare out the sunroof in time to see the second one skimming the sky. For an instant, the twinned meteors streak together before they burn out. There are no words, or even kisses, after that. Josh's hand finds mine, and we both hold on tight.

CHAPTER FORTY-FOUR

Searing white. My skin is fire. A lava field of magma pours over me. I am a vampire, burning to death in the sun. I cannot open my eyes. They are dry kindling, combustible. There is a buzzing in my ears. Is that my skin sizzling? Broiling? I almost moan, afraid, but can't make a sound.

"Viola!" I hear from both far, far away and much, much too close.

I cringe.

"Viola." My name, three notes of panic.

A hand presses into my forehead. I frown from the pain, shrink from the touch. A moan escapes me, no light, come-hither sound. Even I'm alarmed by what I hear: injured animal trapped in biting metal.

A billion layers of heaviness are cast over me. Another moan. No skin contact, no contact, no. But I can't speak, and the cool fabric buries me. And I remember where I am: inside Josh's truck, watching the meteors, kissing each other. We must have fallen asleep. Sunlight presses against my eyelids. How long have we been here, out in the open? I am sinking through the leather seat, the metal frame of the truck, the dirty snow, the pitted asphalt below.

Josh, I can hear him struggling with the broken sunroof, trying, trying, trying to slide it closed inside. He grunts, but even his Thor muscles cannot fix this brokenness. The driver's side door opens and then slams shut. My parents are here. But no, I'm alone in Josh's truck, light surrounding me like I'm standing at the doorsteps of heaven. Or before the inferno of hell.

So much light, it is hard to tell.

I want the black of my bedroom. The blinds. The blackout shades.

My wish is granted. The interior of the truck dims. Blessed, blessed dark.

The car door opens again, and I welcome the cold to soothe my hot-fire skin. I know I am covered in welts.

"Mom," I whisper, wanting her so badly. She'll know exactly what to do. Then Dad will make it happen.

"We're getting you home soon, Ultra," Josh says confidently, even if he can't fulfill that promise. "The highway's going to reopen before long." He sighs. "I'm going to find a phone. Get help. Just hang tight. I'm sorry. So sorry."

"Me, too," I whisper to him. I'm sorry for coming up with this idea, sorry for leaving the safety of home, sorry to drag him down with me.

Pain and guilt, we burn in different ways.

CHAPTER FORTY-FIVE

I huddle in a makeshift tent in Josh's back seat, my parka thrown over my head and his coat curled over my body. The blanket, draped outside, blots out the sun from the roof and windshield. Even in the cold and dark, I burn. Josh plies me with the bottle of water from his emergency kit, refusing out of some unspoken Boy Scout code to break into mine in my messenger bag. Mostly to calm him, I take halfhearted sips in between slathering my skin with the aloe vera Mom had stashed in his emergency kit. He sits at my feet, lending me his presence and body warmth, but he has retreated soundlessly into his own Necromanteion.

I need an extraction, but will settle for a distraction, something other than my pain to think about.

"Talk to me," I whisper.

"About what?" Josh asks, a note of desperation.

I muster a shrug, which takes all my energy.

He remains silent, and I can feel him scanning and discarding topic after topic.

"Necromanteion," I say.

"Where we are so not going. Not a chance. This is all my fault."

First, Auntie Ruth, now Josh. Another swath of travel dreams are razed under the sun. My answering sigh is less winter wind than it is the remembrance of a summer breeze; it already feels like regret.

He starts rambling. "Okay, so I thought about what Persephone would be doing in the Necromanteion. Of all the places on Earth, what would draw her to that spot? I thought about how you said that the Oracle of the Dead resides there. So what would she want from the Oracle of the Dead? I can't figure that out."

"Answers," I whisper.

"Answers." His laugh is scraped up, a raw sound. "Like: What the hell, God? Literally. Like: Why this and why you?"

"Yeah."

"Like: Why Caleb and not me?" he continues, anguished. "You know, Caleb was the good twin, the one who got all As, the one everyone loved. Our parents would never have called him a mess-up. He was the quiet, smart kid who never got into trouble. He would never have gotten drunk at a stupid party. He would never have gotten anyone else killed. He would never have risked you like this."

Yeah, and Caleb also liked women in skimpy pseudoclothes (sorry, but true). He thought he was a better illustrator (he wasn't). I sigh.

"This was my fault," Josh says quietly. "What if this is about him reaching down from heaven to tell me that?"

"Josh, he doesn't blame you."

"How do you know?"

"Because I don't blame you."

He scoffs. I hate that scoff.

Then he says the damning words, "My parents blame me."

"Oh, Josh."

For all of my parents' crisis-controlling ways, I have never, ever once seen them blame each other. Whenever anything goes wrong, they'll dissect, micromanage, conduct extensive postmortem discussions afterward. But they never point fingers, never say, "It's your fault." That's how love works. I lower the parka to tell him so, but there's an inopportune thump on the driver's window. Josh rolls down the back window while I flinch from the sun that brightens the interior, withdrawing into the thick shelter of my coat.

"Viola?" asks my auntie, the woman I've been avoiding, punishing her for my skin condition, even though the doctors won't ever know for sure what triggered it. It was just easier to blame her deep down than to deal with my own grief and anger and responsibility. I want to tell him all of this, but Auntie Ruth calls again, "Viola!"

"Yeah," Josh answers for me, and opens the door. "She's here."

Then a man shouts, "Found them!"

Auntie Ruth says, "Viola! We've been looking all over for you."

On any other occasion, those words would be ominous, strike terror in a girl. But right now, they are balm. My parents have put together their own search-and-rescue mission, calling on their vast network of friends, colleagues, and clients — finding anyone and everyone who could get to Snoqualmie. Unbelievably for us, a friend of a friend of a friend has a cabin ten minutes west of the summit: none other than Silver Fox from Souper Bowl Sunday. He and Auntie Ruth deliver me via snowmobile down the still-closed pass and to the Volvo sedan where Dad waits. He's been on call for Mom, who had been manning Command Central in case I wasn't at Snoqualmie the way Aminta, my Plan B, told them.

Trust my parents to figure out a way to rescue me. Trust Auntie Ruth to be part of that rescue mission. I have never, ever been so happy to have parents who are crisis managers, and an auntie who is undaunted by any vehicle and any obstacle.

"Thank you," I whisper to Dad and Auntie Ruth after I'm bundled into the back seat. "Josh?"

"They're opening the pass in a couple of hours. He'll be fine."

I wasn't so sure about that.

"It's your mom you should thank." Dad smiles, but his forehead is furrowed with tension. "She was relentless."

I expect nothing less. "This was my idea."

"Save your energy, honey," says Auntie Ruth. (You'll need it.)

"It's not his fault," I say.

That absolution falls on deaf ears. The one who needs to hear these words is still trapped at the top of the pass, unreachable.

JUST THE FACTS, MA'AM

After the rush to get the immediate facts out, reporters are going to clamor for more information. Who found out about the issue? What is the scope of the problem? Keep to the facts. Do not speculate. Do not theorize. Do not overshare. At this moment, silence could be your best friend until you fully size the problem.

—Lee & Li Communications
Inside the War Room: The Crisis Management Playbook

CHAPTER FORTY-SIX

The drive to the Children's Hospital drains me of every bit of residual energy that hasn't already been sun-sapped. Once in the darkened room back inside the Emergency Department, I find no relief. Lying on the hospital bed, my lariat is strangling me. I struggle to unloop it, but my skin stings. I refuse to ask for help. My parents are outside in the hall with Auntie Ruth, dissecting my accomplice. Finally, I am free of the necklace's looping strands and can focus on eavesdropping as they replay everything they think they know about Josh.

"That Boy is teaching her to ignore her limits: the coffee shop. The poke place. And now this," Dad says, ticking off Josh's so-called transgressions. "Which might be fine if she was totally healthy, but . . ."

That but. Its logical conclusions slay me in a million different ways. But I'm not healthy. But I'm not normal. Therefore, I can never hope to have a healthy, normal relationship.

"Isn't testing limits a good thing? Yes, she's got a condition, but she's got to live, too," Auntie Ruth argues.

"Live? Did you see her? She could barely walk," Mom says. "And her skin . . ."

As much as I will myself to get out of the hospital cot, to join their conversation, to minimize whatever consequences are going to fall upon me, my muscles revolt. I stay under the weight of warm sheets and my guilt. However bad I was feeling, Josh was probably feeling ten times worse. How many times did he ask if my seat belt was buckled as if he could protect me from harm? I want to text him, but I have no idea where my phone is. Probably confiscated like my freedom.

Surprise, surprise, Dr. Anderson walks into my hospital room. My entourage follows behind. He looks insanely pleased, not to see me again, but Auntie Ruth.

"We have to stop meeting like this," Dr. Anderson enthuses, dimpling at her.

For the first time in the entire history of matchmaking, Mom isn't issuing invitations to Souper Bowl Sunday. Instead, she looks annoyed that a man is hitting on Auntie Ruth. She attacks with questions: "What is the highest dosage of antihistamines that you can give her? Does she need steroids? Can you prevent blisters?"

After answering Mom—a lot, perhaps, no—Dr. Anderson turns his attention to me and frowns. "Viola, it was quick thinking to throw the blanket over the sunroof."

"Josh did that," I whisper.

"You'll have to remember next time that the snow reflects the light. Let's get you something to take the inflammation down."

"That's it? That's all you can do for her?" Dad asks.

"It might be time for you to consider more aggressive treatments," Dr. Anderson tells me after reviewing my chart. "Photochemotherapy could be helpful."

"The research says the benefits are just temporary," I mumble. "Not worth it."

Dr. Anderson sits on the wheeled stool and scoots toward me. "I'm afraid your condition is a lot more pronounced than we first thought. I know this is hard to hear, and I wish I could tell you otherwise," he says with a heavy sigh, "but I think you need to let your body recover. Stay inside. Then, if you absolutely have to go out, try to keep it at night, or at dawn and dusk. Start with no more than five minutes or so. And get a lot more aggressive with the techniques we shared with you a few weeks ago, like always using a sun-blocking umbrella. And if it's really sunny outside, even consider using an umbrella at home since even with the film on them, UV light still makes it through windows."

"Umbrella," Mom echoes, but thankfully she doesn't say I told you so.

"And finally," Dr. Anderson says, "you might want to consider home-schooling. At least for the time being."

"That's a good idea," says Dad.

Horrified, I sit up. "But my friends, my bake sales, my college apps . . ."

In the imaginary theater in my head, the curtains rise. And . . . action!

THE EMERGENCY FAMILY MEETING

A Play in One Painfully Short Act
by
Lee & Li Productions,
a subsidiary of Lee & Li Communications

MOM

Dr. Anderson's right. Plus, given everything — the school's lackadaisical implementation of UV-protective window-ware . . .

DAD

Not to mention, how you have to take notes on your Mac in class.

MOM

And frankly — and I hate to say this — but, Viola, your irresponsibility with the safe boundaries that we've put in place for your own good — I —

DAD

We.

MOM

We agree with Dr. Anderson. You'll be better off finishing senior year at home as much as it hurts us to do this.

DR. ANDERSON

(not understanding that his role is to be a silent observer, not a complicit enabler)

You should stay inside and in the dark as much as possible.

MOM & DAD

(power nodding)

See?

ME

(dumbfounded, rendered speechless; then, in a voice that plumbs every punctuation mark known in the English language)

What. What? What!

DAD

(waving his hands as if he's at the podium of a contentious news conference)

Think of this as a hybrid solution. Some Liberty, some homeschool, some Khan Academy, and some Auntie Ruth. I'm sure she'd be happy to work with you on math and science a couple of days a week.

MOM

Plus, do you know how much time is wasted at school each day? If you're really productive—really efficient—you should be done by eleven, assuming a six a.m. start.

DAD

Think of everything you can do with all your free time.

MOM

(with the air of a queen bestowing a stay of execution)

You'll have time to do whatever you want.

ME

(BLACKOUT)

(END OF SCENE)

...

One small step to homeschool for senior year, one short leap to homeschool for college. Was that even possible? My parents and Dr. Anderson exchange a meaningful look, one that is resigned and resolved, one that says there will be no safe place left for me to live.

CHAPTER FORTY-SEVEN

"You," Mom's voice is blistering.

Before I open my eyes, I know it's Josh. Some people go on dates; others wait in the lobby of the Children's Hospital. I scoot to the edge of the wheelchair, order my feet to hit the floor, close the span separating us, and fall into Josh's arms. But the shocked look on his face cements me to the wheelchair. I wish I could unsee that expression, proof that I'm not the Sick Girl; I've become the Freak Girl.

"I wanted to make sure that Viola's okay," Josh tells my parents, not me. He's looking everywhere except at me.

"Okay?" Mom's voice rises to a glass-breaking pitch. "What you did — the two of you did — was highly irresponsible."

"Mom. Mom. He didn't know that I didn't tell you we were going out. He even asked if you knew. It's not his fault."

Dad should be calming Mom down with me, but instead he's glaring at That Boy, the one in his Seattle Central College sweatshirt, the one holding our blanket, folded neatly over his arm.

"I'm really sorry," Josh says quietly.

I can hear my parents thinking: *You should be.* Even worse, I can hear the phantom echo of his parents: *It should have been you.* I would run from all possibility of hurting anyone, too, if that judgment — that blame — was echoing in my head.

"It was my idea," I remind him, Lee & Li, everyone. "I made the decision to go. If it's anyone's fault, it's mine."

He shakes his head. "Your parents are right, Ul — Viola. It was a mistake to go out with you last night when I should have known better."

A mistake.

To go out.

With you.

A mistake to even use my nickname. My heart seizes each phrase, whittling away the unnecessary words. Reducing the message down to its essence. Each phrase is a tiny stab.

A mistake.

"No one — not even the weather channel — predicted the snowstorm," I say loudly, wanting everyone to know, wanting to grip Josh's hand, because I especially need him to hear me. I don't want him holing up in an even deeper cave because of me. "Everyone says it was a freak storm."

"Don't," he mutters.

A mistake. I should have known better.

"The car's outside," Dad reminds us now. "We need to go."

My eyes are watering and my throat is closing. I insist, "It was an accident."

"Accidents, mistakes. Aren't they the same thing?" Josh asks, ready for his own getaway. "You need to rest."

"That's a good idea." Genghis Khan singes the enemy with a sharp glare.

Auntie Ruth's jaw tightens as she frowns at Dad, disappointed. I'm even more surprised than Josh when she throws her arms around him in a big, Aminta bear hug, and my heart floods with gratitude for my auntie. "Thank you for doing everything humanly possible for her. You literally thought of everything."

He stands still, like even the smallest motion will break him. With an effort, he gathers himself for one last nod, then leans down to place my blanket on my lap, a peace offering. Then, my Josh walks away.

Let him go. Ask him to stay. The head wars, and the heart waffles. Not yet. Not when he hasn't heard me: It's not his fault. I throw out one last life buoy and stand up over my parents' protests. The blanket falls to the ground. I cry out, "Wait!"

Josh stops, his back still turned to me, still silent, still lost somewhere I can't see, somewhere I can't follow. When he turns to face me, his eyes don't falter. He sounds exhausted. "I'm tired of hurting people I care about."

"You didn't hurt me. And I don't regret it. Not at all."

"But I do," he says.

A mistake.

To go out with you.

I regret you.

"Stay inside," he tells me. The glass doors close gently behind him.

Guilt and grief overwhelm what could have been Us. I sob. I didn't just do this to myself; I did this to Josh, too.

A CRISIS OF TRUST

Studies show that customer trust declines by a full 12 percent after a security breach.

—Lee & Li Communications
Inside the War Room: The Crisis Management Playbook

CHAPTER FORTY-EIGHT

The sound of sobbing wakes me a few minutes before three almost every morning for the next week. Every single time, I think it's me, crying from a terrible dream, wispy remembrances of Josh walking away from me. But I touch my cheeks. They're dry. My eyes close, not that it makes much of a difference. It simply trades darkness for bleakness.

The ghost of a meteor darts behind my shut eyes now. The sight is mocking: *See? See? You thought you could be normal, but Freak Girl, what the hell were you thinking?*

That was no fragment of a dream I heard, but the sound of my fracturing reality.

CHAPTER FORTY-NINE

Even if all I want to do—all I feel I can do—is stay in bed, I haul myself out of my room. It's been a quiet week at home, and I'm only now beginning to feel my new normal. I trudge past Roz's bedroom, her door still shut. She's sleeping the blissful sleep of the healthy who can row themselves exhausted under the hot sun. From the kitchen, I can see the lights gleaming outside in the Shed, where my parents are conferring in secret, most likely about today's destruction for my life.

I know why I'm upright. The Basket of Doom draws me. There, I find a bombardment of texts from Aminta, Caresse, and Auntie Ruth. A week of silence from Josh.

"Viola," Dad says, stepping into the kitchen, startling me.

Mom follows, shutting the door behind them. I lower my phone hastily, guiltily, even though this is within my sanctioned fifteen minutes of usage. Her eyes lock on me as if by the sheer power of her stare, she can stop me from disobeying their No-Josh Mandate. Honestly, that mom death stare could be another superpower for Persephone. I make a note to tell Josh, except would he even answer? (No.) Are we even working together? (Unclear.) Does he want to see me ever again? (Unlikely.)

"Have a seat, honey," Mom says, gesturing to the breakfast nook.

Sitting across from me, Dad intones, "We need to talk about trust. You know how important trust is, between all of us." He gestures first to himself and Mom, then his hand moves back and forth between them and me.

"And we know how developmentally appropriate it is for teens to test boundaries. But when you do, you erode our trust," Mom says.

Trust, really? They want to start in on trust again?

I can't take this, not anymore. I slide out of the breakfast nook and stand in front of the kitchen island, glowering at them. "Do you mean trust as in being consulted about all your grand plans for me? Trust that I can figure things out, too? Trust that I actually know how to research? Trust that I want to get better, too?"

I've become Roz, whose every utterance creates yet more havoc to deal with later. Being messy is liberating.

"Honey," Dad says, back to his radio-talk-show soothing voice. "We think it's better for you not to go outside for now. Let's get your skin back under control, and then we'll take stock."

"You're locking me up?" I ask.

"No, not that at all," Mom says. "We've even remodeled—"

I won't hear it; I can't. I leave them, midplan.

"Viola!" Dad calls.

I ignore him for once. Out of habit, I touch my lariat, but it's not there. My reminder to be fierce, to fight for truth, to speak for the powerless is gone.

Of course it is.

I've lost my boy. I've lost my life.

And now, I've lost the last best part of me.

CHAPTER FIFTY

My parents may take the sky away from me, but they aren't touching my bake sale. Nothing is stopping me from raising funds to feed hungry little kids with food-stuffed backpacks, not even my shaky legs. Just the thought that any kid in our community, let alone the entire world, doesn't have enough to eat—eat!— makes me want to spend an entire week cooking. Aminta's promised to pick up the miniature cupcakes and bite-size brownies after Souper Bowl Sunday, and Caresse is printing out my (short) article on hunger in America. Two hours after my showdown with my parents, I throw open the freezer to look for the flour. It's no longer jammed full of Ziploc baggies of frozen soup from our canceled Souper Bowl last week; all of those are defrosting in our fridge. I cannot bring myself to care that the soup won't be custom-themed for the game this week.

Out of nowhere comes the familiar, searing heat of my sister's irritation. "Thanks to you," Roz snipes, "I'm not allowed to go to India with Auntie Ruth anymore. Now they're all paranoid about the malaria meds."

I shut the freezer door without removing anything. "But they don't know for sure if the drugs made me photosensitive. It could be anything, a freak of nature."

"Does it matter?"

Roz is right. When our parents are in serious lockdown mode, logic doesn't matter. I tell her, "I'm sorry."

Roz sniffs. "It's not fair that I'm being punished because of you."

"Welcome to my life."

"You've never been punished for me." Offended, she crosses her arms in front of her chest. Wait for it, wait for it. And there it is: the royal lift of her nose.

"Can you say, personal driver?"

"You were going to school anyway."

"At five thirty in the morning?"

"I have to go then, too."

"That's the point. I didn't." My thoughts, usually so tightly contained, burst through every lock I've bolted in place: Be the good girl, the good friend, the good big sister.

Roz narrows her eyes. "You're always so mean." Then, as always, the cry of the mortally wounded little girl who needs protection from the big, bad older sister: "Mom! Dad!"

To which, I dismiss her with a shrug and return to setting out my ingredients.

"Mom!" Roz hollers, since I'm not caving or apologizing, frantic to make it up to her. "Dad!"

The parent brigade rushes in to find Roz ready as always to air her complaints about me. With both hands on the back of her chair, legs spread wide, she could be addressing her crew team. "Why should I be punished just because Viola got sick?"

"It's called being prudent," says Dad patiently. "What if Viola's condition is genetic? There aren't enough studies to know. Why chance you getting sick, too?"

"But I didn't do anything," Roz wails. "This is all Viola's fault."

That is my cue to leave before Hurricane Rosalind gathers force, but I can't abandon those hungry kids. Silently, I turn to fetch the butter, but my legs feel weak. My hands shoot out to the kitchen island at the same time that Dad wraps his arm around me.

"Gotcha, princess," he says, which is just about the worst thing he could call me now, the nickname that had been mine until it was given to Roz as her birthright.

"You always need all the attention," she snarls at me. "Oh, I've got another bake sale! Oh, I've got another cause to support! Oh, I've got to make all the soup for Souper Bowl Sunday. Whatever."

"Rosalind!" Mom says, shocked.

Dad says to Roz in his best placating tone, "Princess, you don't mean that."

That *princess* is too little, too late, salt in my sister's wounds. She snaps, "I do."

Even Dad is looking at his little princess like he can't believe what he's hearing. While I should feel a spurt of vindication, I am woozy, something I won't admit. Dad must see it because he lifts me into his arms.

"No bake-sale prep today," Dad says.

"What do you need, honey?" Mom asks me. Again with the Mother Touch on my forehead like I have a cold or the flu, but this — this tender first responder attention for me before Roz is something that neither she nor I are used to.

"No, I've got to bake," I tell them, but, tired, I stay put in Dad's arms.

"Forget about that for now. Okay, honey, so we were thinking," Dad says, shooting a look at Mom, who nods at him.

A new phase in my crisis management plan is about to be rolled out. I brace myself.

"You can choose," Dad says.

I am literally shocked by those words. "What?"

"We finished the basement last week. It's all ready for you, and our strongest recommendation is for you to be down there because it's the safest place for you to be out of the light. But you can choose," Mom echoes Dad.

"She gets the basement?" Roz explodes as if anyone in their right mind would agree to live in a den of wolf spiders.

Dad asks, "Want to see it?"

"Yeah, I would," I say. There is nothing up here for me anymore.

No wonder they designated the basement as my final resting place. There is no chance of any light penetrating the windowless cement walls, now painted a warm shade of gray. Or of anything penetrating for that

246

matter—not a hint of fresh air or the lilacs blooming in spring or even the barking of dogs trotting by our house. The exposed overhead light bulb that could have been part of a set for a horror movie has been covered in a UV-protective shell, diffusing a vague suggestion of candlelight glow. As if that was the design intent, candle-filled lanterns of all sizes accent the basement.

In the corner, five throw pillows in varying gradations of pink cover the platform bed. The soft sheepskin rug from the Shed has been transplanted here, now topping a nubby carpet so plush under my feet, I've become Tigger, bouncing as I approach the back wall embellished with large decals of affirmations—"Wake up and be awesome!" and *Firefly* quotes—"Time for some thrilling heroics." My fuzzy, oversize beanbag chair occupies the back corner. Where the washer and dryer have gone, I don't know.

This is my dream room, the dorm space I've been designing on Pinterest for the last three years. I'm astonished my parents knew. I lift my eyes to Dad to find Mom at his side; both are nervous and expectant at the same time. How many hours did they pour into creating this room, the one that would have been totally perfect if it had been upstairs along with everyone else, or better yet, in a college far, far away?

"No fair," grumbles Roz, thudding down the stairs before gawping. "No Fair."

I'm about to say, "You take it, then," because no matter how beautiful the trappings, there is no masking that this is a glorified bunker. Then I read the quote above the landing:

"One day you will take my heart completely and make it more fiery than a dragon." —Rumi

My mind races to Josh and the dragon meteors and our fiery kiss.

If only that were true. I lower myself onto the bed. There, I find the blanket that Josh had wrapped around us, the one he had thrown over the sunroof to protect me.

"I'll stay here," I tell everyone.

"Oh, honey, that makes me so happy!" Mom says, and her face relaxes.

"It's the best choice," Dad agrees.

Roz clomps up the stairs: No. Fair. No. Fair.

So begins my stay in my very own Necromanteion.

CHAPTER FIFTY-ONE

My parents have nothing to worry about. There is zero possibility of me testing any limits, real or imaginary, especially when everything aches: legs, arms, skin, heart, soul. It's been a full week in the basement. So how the hell can I feel even worse?

I have a suspicion. Take your pick, any pick, of what's wiped me out in a way that the sun reflecting off the snow did not: Josh's continued silence, my solitary confinement, or my standing up to Roz for once. Heaviest of all, I flaked on yet another bake sale.

Awash at sea, I am tugged into deep waters of hopelessness. Even so, my hand reaches for the tape recorder that I have set on my bedside table.

If I can't have Josh, I'll take Nocturne.

Listening to the mixtape only makes me yearn for Josh even more. Call it compulsive and obsessive, but I tackle the stairs, a baker's dozen of them, just to pull my phone from the Basket of Doom.

One missed call, one voice mail, three texts. All from Aminta, Caresse, and Auntie Ruth.

"Honey," Mom says from out of the gloom in the breakfast nook. "I'm sorry, but you know what your dad and I said. You can't see That Boy."

Who knew that even more potent than hot rage is icy fury. Cold, my anger is pure iceberg, deep as a black sea.

"That Boy did everything possible to take care of me, not that you have to worry," I tell her, dropping the silent phone back into the basket. "That Boy doesn't want to see me. No boy is going to want to. So, no, you never have to worry about me seeing That Boy or sleeping with any boy or getting an STD or any of that anymore."

"That's not true."

"Mom, seriously? Do you honestly think that anyone is ever going to want to date a freak? A human vampire? A girl who can only go out in the dark? What man is going to sign up for a woman who has to sleep in the basement and never travel anywhere outside their home? Mom, I might never, ever get to fall in love. I might never get married. Happy now?"

"No, I'm not happy about any of this," Mom says, sniffling. I see the wads of tissue by her coffee mug. "But let's be perfectly clear. We don't want you to date That Boy because he's a rule breaker. He doesn't respect the rules that we have in place to keep you safe. It has nothing — nothing! — to do with you having a boyfriend or sleeping with a guy. Nothing." When I start to protest, Mom holds up a hand. "You have to listen to me about the second thing." Her voice gentles. "That Boy adores you, but he can't see you because he can't handle being responsible for yet another person."

"You researched him?"

Mom nods. "It's what we do."

It is true. I can't war against that truth. "So I'm too much to handle."

"No, your situation is too scary for any young man to handle, especially a young man who's already been in one major accident. It's just too much."

"But Dad stayed. He stayed with Auntie Ruth. He gave up going to Georgetown and went to UW to stay close to her. You've always told us that."

"That's because your dad is different." Her eyes widen and she gasps, holding her hand to her chest like she's having a heart attack.

That scares me. "Mom, what's wrong? Mom?"

Mom shakes her head, panting hard.

"Dad!" I yell. In the catch of the dim light, I finally see the puffiness around her eyes that she's concealed so deftly with makeup. The sobbing that I've heard for the past couple of nights, the hard, racking sobs, those weren't me or my dreams. But my calm, cool, collected Captain Zoë of a mother. She doubles over. I scream, "Dad!"

Dad races into the kitchen. "What? What's wrong?" Before anyone answers, Dad's dropped into the nook, scooping Mom into his arms. "Honey. What's going on?"

Tears are streaming down her face. "She didn't leave because she didn't love me, did she?"

Dad shakes his head, still holding Mom. "No, honey, no. It was just too much. Samantha was just a kid, too. She did her best for as long as she could. But she needed to survive herself."

Everything hurts: my head, heart, chest. Dad comforts Mom, assuring her that they won't leave me ever, they'll fix me, they'll figure something out. My fingernails scratch painfully against a fat, new blister on my clavicle. Scared, I place my hand on my pounding heart and feel the new topography bubbling on my chest. I am unfixable. I have become a hideous monster of the Underworld, wearing a lariat of blisters, too scary for any young man to handle. Before I'm discovered, I hurry back down to my lair, alone.

CHAPTER FIFTY-TWO

Lunch and dinner arrive on lavish trays, heavy with preservative-laden sandwiches and store-bought cookies. They return uneaten. On Sunday morning, I make my way upstairs to the odorless kitchen for my morning tech check. Without the scent of simmering soups, melting chocolate, and baking pies, the house smells dead.

"There you are!" Mom exclaims, as if I've been buried in an avalanche on Snoqualmie, instead of entombed in the basement they created without telling me.

"We missed you!" Dad echoes with such manic-elation, it'd lose clients.

"It's almost Halloween. When are you baking pumpkin bread?" Roz asks, expectant, as she spoons what looks like bland quinoa porridge into her mouth.

"That'd be a perfect snack. Your friends want to visit today," Mom tells me, matching Dad, joy for joy.

A bubble of irritation bursts. I tug my sweatshirt down to my new blisters. "Not looking like this." While my parents emergency confer in the bathroom about this new development, I check my phone unapologetically. Caresse has joined Aminta in showering me with insistent texts.

> Caresse: *HOW ARE YOU?!?!*
> Aminta: *YOUR FINGERS CAN MOVE.*
> Caresse: *SO: RESPOND.*

"We have all the ingredients," Roz offers as if this is another normal morning at Chez Lee & Li, where my main job is to be her short-order cook, not one where my heart has been pocked with yet another hole.

There is still no word from Josh.

I lower the phone without answering anyone. I have become That Girl, the one in an unrequited, long-distance relationship with her phone. I'm tempted to chuck my phone at the wall. Then, at least, I'd have the satisfaction of hearing it shatter, a response of some kind.

CHAPTER FIFTY-THREE

My one accomplishment so far in the dark isn't finishing the essay on Toni Morrison's *Beloved* that my parents assigned to me (yay, homeschool), but memorizing the lyrics of all the songs on my Nocturne mixtape, not that that is such a prize. Who knew Cupid could be so cruel?

"I'll follow you into the dark"—Josh hasn't even texted me once in the dark.

"Oh and the stars, oh, oh and the stars / Well, they just blink for us."— Maybe two weeks and a lifetime ago they did, but now they've burned out.

"Gets hectic inside of me / When you go."—Enough said.

CHAPTER FIFTY-FOUR

A few days later, I rouse from a late afternoon nap to the chorus of Aminta and Caresse's "Hey, Viola!"

Mom calls, "Can we send them downstairs?"

What is my mom thinking? Doesn't she understand that I'm maintaining a strict no-contact zone until my blisters burst, scab over, heal, and peel, which according to the dermatologist takes a good three weeks?

"Not today," I say.

Upstairs, Mom apologizes to my friends. Even if I (sort of) want them to protest, demand to see me, and barge down here, I'm glad they don't. I'm in no condition to be seen. As it turns out, Aminta and Caresse are a lot more stubborn than I knew.

"But we come bearing gifts," Caresse says through the basement door.

"Well, more accurately, we come bearing prototypes," Aminta corrects her. "From the 3-D printer you got us last year."

I draw to the bottom of the stairs. "I didn't get you anything."

"You baked," says Aminta. "And we bought the 3-D printer for the math department, remember? So we made you something."

Caresse says, "We wanted to call it the Deluminator, but that would have all kinds of trademark issues."

"So how does the DeLighter sound instead?" Aminta asks.

"Tell her that's still a little close," Caresse says.

"A lot close," I mutter.

Aminta says, "Well, you can't judge until you see the prototype for yourself."

Which is true. Despite my best intention to be blasé, I'm intrigued. "Okay, come on down."

The basement door opens. Even though my bunker is cast in dim candlelight, I yank my sweatshirt higher up onto my neck, wishing I'd worn a turtleneck, but it chafed too much. I tug my hat down.

"Well, this is very *hygge*," Aminta says.

"What?" Caresse and I ask at the same time.

"*Hygge*," Aminta says, gesturing around the basement. "Danish for 'cozy.' They don't get a whole lot of light in the winter, so they've embraced coziness."

"And you would know because?"

"I'm a geek. We know all kinds of arcane things. And" — she opens a slim, plastic box, the exact size of my iPhone — "we build things. Welcome to your DeLightor. See? Your phone is completely enclosed except for the home button, so you can make calls and use Siri safely." She clicks it shut. "Aren't you . . . delighted?"

Caresse groans. I echo that groan and raise it a snort.

"We are so not going to call it that. But look," Caresse says as she flips the case over. My name is inked in *Firefly* font.

I laugh and tear up at the same time. "This is amazing."

"It isn't yet," says Aminta. "But it will be."

"So now you'll be able to flirt with Josh safe and in style," says Caresse.

"I haven't heard from him."

"Today?" asks Aminta.

"In two weeks."

Aminta and Caresse exchange The Look, the one that confirms what I know: Whatever Josh and I had has died a quick and silent death.

"Maybe he's busy?" says Aminta, nodding. "He could be working on another issue of *Persephone*, or got slammed with tests."

"No, he did the drastic pullback," Caresse declares flatly. "The disappearing act. I hate that even more than the slow fade."

I hate it, too. What I hate more is that I start to cry, the weeping that makes you worry you'll never, ever stop. They go all "he's a stupidhead" on me. But the fact is, he isn't. It feels even worse to vilify Josh than to miss him.

"I'm sorry," I tell them in between sobs. "I need to be alone."

CHAPTER FIFTY-FIVE

The dark is not for the faint of heart. There, the primordial goop of tears turns into the primal fury of a dragon scorned.

What a fine fury it is.

He *is* a stupidhead.

Who does Thor think he is? Does he really think that his grief and his guilt and his fear are an excuse for plain old rudeness? Does he really think it's okay to share confidences and kisses and shooting stars one night, then vanish the next with a courtesy check-in to make sure I hadn't died?

News flash: Pullback, fade-out, and ghosting are pure cowardice.

I am done lounging in the purgatory of waiting: Will he or won't he text? I'm sure as hell not staying in some existential dithering: to text or not to text.

No, Josh does not get to stay in his tent, all safe and sound and silent. I have had it with being Little Miss Good Girl, sugar and spice and all things nice.

DEAR JOHN LETTER

VERSION 1

Dear (Dumb) (Boy)friend,

You promised me that you'd never ghost me. You said that was what cowards did. That Darren should have told me that he was moving on, instead of just fading out on me.

So what does that make you?

Angrily (too obvious for you?),

Viola

CHAPTER FIFTY-SIX

Hello, darkness, my old friend.

I shut down the mixtape and slide the tape recorder under my bed. As if hidden, I won't think of Josh. Who am I fooling? Every remembered note echoes of him.

The problem is: so does the sound of silence.

And the sound of Mom crying over her sister who left her. Josh wasn't ghosting me like some coward. He was surviving the only way he knew how: alone.

I trash the letter.

CHAPTER FIFTY-SEVEN

A few days later, I sneak upstairs when the house is quiet, and I can refresh my water bottle in peace without my parents enquiring about how I'm feeling and Roz hinting about everything I can (should) be doing (for her). Unfortunately, I've miscalculated. Roz is at the kitchen island, sitting with a book in her hand and a spoon in her mouth.

As soon as she sees me, Roz points the spoon at me and asks unexpectedly, "Hey, you want some Molly Moon's? Salted caramel?"

I begin to smile at her thoughtfulness until Roz tips her container in my direction, empty except for two, maybe three melting spoonfuls.

She says, "I'm done with it."

"You're giving me your leftovers?" I fact-check her, too sharply.

Even separated by granite and a cooktop, I can feel Roz's hurt. Instinctively, the surrogate mom in me wants to apologize for ruining her life, take the blame, volunteer to put myself at risk, and drive her back to the gourmet ice cream shop to buy her a fresh cup, any flavor she wants. Heck, get three!

"I was just being nice," Roz snaps at me.

"No, being nice would have been to bring me back some, too."

"You're always so mean."

"No," I correct her, "I'm honest. If I had gone to get ice cream without bringing you back your own, I can't even imagine how mad you'd be."

"That's not true!"

"Isn't it? If I gave you three leftover spoonfuls of my ice cream, do you really think you would have been okay with that?"

"Wow—"

"Excuse me? Did you just 'wow' me?" I say, stepping up to the island as rage courses freely in my veins. I may be five feet tall on a good day, and Roz might tower over me by eight inches, but that moment, I am Persephone in the flesh, a space Amazon ready to battle this time-sucking vampire. I slam both hands palm-down on the countertop and ignore the sharp stinging. "Do you even know how many times I went on pizza runs for you? And then you'd complain because, oh, horrors! It had olives. And oh, I need my rowing shorts. If I showed up empty-handed at the boathouse, I couldn't even begin to imagine . . ."

"What are you even talking about?" Roz actually asks me indignantly as if all of this is some bad fairy tale that I'm spinning. She is always Sleeping Beauty and Snow White and Cinderella, and I am forever the wicked stepmother.

"Oh, like your thirteenth birthday? I used an entire three months of my allowance to take you to Bumbershoot since your favorite band was playing, remember? Did I tell Mom and Dad? No, because they would have freaked out about all the secondhand pot smoke. And then I got you, yes, Molly Moon's in a huge waffle cone! And then when I only had enough money left for one slice of pizza for dinner, and all they had was the everything pizza, you looked at me and said, 'This is my birthday dinner?' I didn't even get myself a slice! I bet you didn't even notice that. So yeah, you pretty much do not ever get to 'wow' me."

"I was just trying to be nice," Roz says stiffly as she stomps away.

Run away, little sister. Run from the rage of your big, bad sister.

With a frustrated sigh, I head for the fridge, needing cold water since that rampage has left my throat raw, my emotions even rawer. But I stop when I see what Roz has left next to her cup of melted ice cream soup: her homework reading, the book of poems by Robert Frost, the one with the poetic lie about the "lovely, dark and deep" snow-filled woods. That poem should come with a neon warning about all that you can lose atop a snow-reflecting mountain pass. I shove the book across the granite countertop, a hockey puck on the frozen lake of my anger. It drops with a satisfying thud onto the floor. I refuse to pick the book up.

There's a movement in the dark hall. I steel myself for round two with Roz, prepare for her to play the victim when I have the weight of history and actions and miles of chauffeuring behind me. I swing around to find Dad, chagrined.

"I just didn't . . . know," Dad says.

"About Bumbershoot? What? Are you going to banish me?" I spread my arms out. "Sorry. Already done."

"No, I meant . . ." Dad looks toward Roz's bedroom down the hall. Yet, he says nothing. Nothing. Until finally, Dad drags his eyes back to me and tells me, "We — I — put too much pressure on you, honey. I'm so sorry."

My sigh is epic in its breadth and range — irritation, outrage, disbelief, sadness, regret, resignation. There are no further words, not even a breath of relief when my rage finally burns out. When Dad approaches me, though, arms outstretched for an apology hug, all I can do is shake my head and retreat downstairs.

Once in my bunker, I rest my back against the cement wall, welcoming its coolness, remembering the cold of another night. My hand reaches for my ghost lariat; it'd remind me of that long-lost girl, the girl who once was. I close my eyes, and the memory of stars dance in the darkness behind my eyelids, the memory of kisses dance across my skin. Vaguest of all, the lightness of hope when Josh's hand slid in mine just as a meteor shot across the night sky. No matter how hard I try to catch that elusive moment, it escapes my desperate grasp.

My balled fists release. I am alone, which is what I wanted, right?

...

Right?

NO NEW NEWS

By the time the reporters are talking with you, they already know the story. They are really only giving you the opportunity to explain.

—Lee & Li Communications
Inside the War Room: The Crisis Management Playbook

CHAPTER FIFTY-EIGHT

The darkness in the basement has weight and heft. Despair in three dimensions coils around me. My lungs are collapsing under its pressure.

Good, I think. Good.

It would be so much easier if I could drown.

...

I don't drown.

...

I have become Persephone, locked in a world not of my own.

CHAPTER FIFTY-NINE

My phone is no longer a lifeline to the world. It is the dead weight of a life that no longer exists.

I free the phone from its beautiful coffin and let go.

The phone drops to the kitchen floor. The screen cracks, forming a glass mosaic, splintered like my hopes and dreams.

Regret, that's all I can muster. I am too tired to grieve.

CHAPTER SIXTY

"Honey," says the trespasser in my bunker. The basement door opens wider so a little natural light creeps in. So does Dad. Mom's footsteps patter closely behind down the steps.

"I'm doing homework," I answer, glaring at the problem set as I work on my bed. Who knew that I'd miss being in math with everyone else? Who'd have thought I'd want to be at school on a Friday?

Do my parents listen? (No.) Are they uninvited? (Yes.) Unwanted as they are, Dad spins my desk chair around and plants it in front of my bed. He gestures for Mom to take the seat of honor. Sitting on the edge of my bed, Dad says, "Sweetheart, we need to talk. You. Us. Words."

Mom scoots the chair so close, her knees touch the mattress. "It occurs to us that maybe we went a little overboard."

"You don't need to sequester yourself in here," says Dad, waving around the basement that glows softly with my safety-proofed lighting. "We want you to live as normal a life as possible."

"We made a mistake. That's what we're trying to say," Mom says, and squeezes my foot. I draw it away. "We are really sorry."

Apparently, not all that sorry. Dad beams at me. "Ms. Kavoussi showed us your college essay."

"She what?" I fume, dropping my pencil on my math homework. "What happened to college counselor–student privacy?"

"There's no such thing," Mom corrects me and leans forward so she looks like she wants to dive into my future. "Anyway, more accurately, we went to Liberty to meet with your teachers about their curriculum for the next couple of weeks, and Ms. Kavoussi gave us her comments on your essay to work on at home."

"It's good. It's really good, honey," Dad enthuses. "You really thought through why you want to be a journalist. We just didn't know you were so serious about it."

Now, astonishingly, my parents become the professional cheerleaders for the future they've never wanted for me. Never mind the multitude of dinner conversations about the unenviable future of journalism: Newspapers are dying; magazines are dead; truth itself is being questioned. I say as much, even quoting them verbatim. A cold dose of their own reality does little to deter their newfound cheer.

GIVE ME A P! POTENTIAL! Mom: "So we were thinking that while, unfortunately, newspapers have all but cut their foreign desks, you could be a news producer for a morning show. Or," Mom says, lifting both hands up over her head. Dramatic pause. "A writer for a talk show! That is completely safe."

NOW, GIVE ME A D! DREAM! Dad: "How about going into academia? You could be a professor in a communications program. You could work in your own office, teach, and keep the classroom as dark as you want. Huh? Huh?"

WHAT DOES IT SPELL? POTENTIAL DREAM! Mom: "Yes! Or work in a public policy think tank. You could be a *researcher.* Someone who gets *quoted* in the news."

I am not making this up: My parents actually fist-bump each other, so pleased with their Viola Wynne Li Revitalization Program.

"Come on upstairs," Dad coaxes me. "I'll make popcorn, and we can brainstorm together."

"No, thanks." My voice is creaky from self-imposed solitary confinement.

"Now you're just being stubborn," says Mom.

Well, kiss my calm good-bye.

"This is what you wanted. You made this room without even telling me." Injustice fuels my exasperation, and I combust, reminding them, "You were the ones who left reams of research on my desk with all those scary pictures of all those photosensitive people with burned-up skin. You were the ones who lectured me on how irresponsible I was for going out." Did I or did I not just see my parents exchange a triumphant glance? I see their psychic high five: They got me to speak to them for the first time in days. I ignore them and their short-lived victory. "You were the ones who planned for me to live in this bunker."

"Basement," Mom can't help correcting me.

"And now you're actually telling me that I'm being stubborn because I want to stay inside?" I scoff. (So, please go away and investigate the pros and cons, advantages and dangers of me staying inside a basement-bunker like good little crisis managers, shall we?) I tell them, "Maybe you need to work on another crisis plan."

"Maybe you do," says Dad softly.

CHAPTER SIXTY-ONE

The decisive strikes of Auntie Ruth's Harley-Davidsons later that Friday morning announce her presence well before the basement door swings open and she barks, "Okay, girl, enough is enough."

I crank up the volume on my tape recorder, still playing and replaying Nocturne, and turn my attention back to my handwritten essay on *The Bluest Eye*.

Auntie Ruth drops her lipstick-red backpack on the floor, where it lands with a thump. She pulls out a stack of books from the backpack: *Unbroken*. *Seabiscuit*. "Laura Hillenbrand. Chronic fatigue syndrome. She still created." *When Breath Becomes Air* hits my bed, nearly grazing me. "Paul Kalanithi. Lung cancer. He still created."

"Shouldn't you be at work?"

"I'm having some work done at my shop. You should come see."

I don't respond. With a sigh, Auntie Ruth settles uninvited on the edge of my bed. Her voice gentles, as she rests her hand on my calf, the candlelight glinting off her wedding band. "You've locked yourself in your tent."

"This isn't a tent," I tell her.

"Are you sure?" She glances around in all of its candlelit wonder. "You're right. It's more like a yurt, but girl, there's a world outside."

"Have you talked to my jailers?"

"Have you?"

Here's the woman who's maintained a safe border between her militant singleness and her well-meaning friends and family who've wanted to set her up over these last few years. I call her on it now. "But don't you love your own tent, too, Auntie Ruth?"

Auntie Ruth flattens the rumples on the bedcovers, and I'm sure she won't reply. But she surprises me. "You know, I was perfectly fine on my own. After so many years being single, I thought that love wasn't meant for me. But then, along came Amos, barreling into my auto shop, Mr. Big Shot, Mr. I Own Every Dealership in the Northwest. I kept ignoring him, and he kept coming back. And then, one day he told me about his 1937 Bugatti 57S Atalante."

"The one he found in a barn." We all know this family legend.

"The one that was a rusted piece of mess. He presented it to me as a special project for us to refurbish together."

"Bait."

"Courtship."

"Wooing," I say, my eyes widening.

"Yes, wooing." The candles on my bedside table flicker. Her eyes grow misty. "That was just so, so . . . so specific to me. Like he knew the way to my heart would never be through a diamond bracelet or clichéd roses. Like he wanted me to know that he loved how I rebuild things. Like he wanted to get to know me. Honestly, I don't believe in a second big love like that."

"Do you want to be alone?"

That question startles Auntie Ruth into silence until, slowly, she says, "All of the men your mom's been setting me up with? They've all been — well, most of them — perfectly wonderful. I haven't been ready."

"You've been scared."

"That's right." She looks at me meaningfully. "I just don't know if I could ever recover if my heart got shattered a second time."

"What if it doesn't?"

"Exactly," Auntie Ruth says, leaning forward. "What if it doesn't?"

My own question, reflected back at me, cracks my defenses wide open. I liked my Life Before, my secret plan to be a foreign correspondent who tells the stories about the hardest places of our planet, and maybe, just maybe, in that way, helps the world. Blaming everyone else — my parental jailers, my princess sister, Auntie Ruth, Josh himself—is a heck of a lot easier than admitting I'm scared of Life After.

"What if I get that sick again?" I ask, tenting myself in the safety of my arms. I rest my chin on my knees. "What if my body really reacts next time?" (What if I die?)

"What if it doesn't? What if you're okay?"

There they are again, my words, used not against me but for me.

Auntie Ruth bends down to collect her backpack. "Gastrodiplomacy."

"Gastro what?" I ask, lifting my head.

"Diplomacy. Winning the world over one bite at a time. It's a real thing. NPR did a piece on it." Auntie Ruth whips out a printout of the story before I can make excuses: limited tech time, bad Wi-Fi connection in the basement, massive amounts of homework. "See? Studies show that people actually think better of a country after eating their cuisine. When Hillary Clinton was secretary of state, she created a program to send chefs to cook for foreign dignitaries. And"—she taps a section highlighted in hot pink—"some universities teach courses in gastrodiplomacy. Like American University, in DC."

"I cook soup."

"Even your Souper Bowl Sundays have meaning. You've done about a billion bake sales to get the word out about so many issues. And more than that, you try to get people involved."

I am absolutely still now, hearing the echo of Josh from weeks and weeks ago, pointing out that I didn't just report what happened; I wanted to change what happens. I hug my knees even tighter to myself, missing that boy fiercely. Missing myself even more.

Auntie Ruth continues relentlessly, "When you think about all that, isn't it funny how you're uniquely qualified for gastrodiplomacy? You know how to research issues, you know how to connect people to causes in a nonthreatening way through food, and you know how to tell a story."

"I doubt my parents are going to let me go away to college now."

"No. No. No." Auntie Ruth slams one booted foot on the ground, startling me. "Your family is all no-no-no. Can't. Won't. What if. It makes me wonder if I am literally and truly from a different planet sometimes. And you."

"I'm no better?"

"The absolute opposite. You were scared to be in the tent in the Serengeti when the lions sounded like they were surrounding us. But you went out first thing the next morning to get me coffee when I was scared to take one step outside."

"The tour guides told us it was safe."

"But did you see me going out? You did that all on your own, like the most intrepid war correspondent."

"Which I can't be anymore."

"Fine. I suppose, if you want, you can be the princess."

"Yeah, I'd take being Roz any day now."

"Princesses are locked in towers or put in deep sleep, waiting for someone to rescue them. I should know. It took years to convince your dad that I didn't want or need to be pampered. Being pampered is a prison in its own way, you know."

That's hard to deny when I look around my bunker, tricked out with everything a girl could want except for her freedom.

"So why not try this on for size?" Auntie Ruth holds up her article on gastrodiplomacy. "Or something else entirely? Give me one good reason."

I have no answer, but my traitorous stomach growls as if it's ready to be the first teen gastrodiplomat on this planet.

DEAR JOHN LETTER

VERSION 2

Dear Me,

Where'd you go, Viola Wynne Li? Where did
you go?

Viola

CHAPTER SIXTY-TWO

"Viola?" A tentative rap. Then Aminta asks more insistently, "Viola?"

I remain stubbornly quiet.

She does, too. When I'm wondering whether she's left, Aminta says one word, "Iceland."

I breathe out and engage despite my best intentions to stay wordless. "What?"

"They only get four hours of daylight in December . . . You can read about it here." Then I hear the soft patter of her light footsteps leaving my home.

I have zero hours of daylight in my bunker. Beat that. I stay on my bed.

CHAPTER SIXTY-THREE

Iceland.

I squelch the thought.

CHAPTER SIXTY-FOUR

Iceland.

The place beckons, silent and cold, dark and safe.

Even if those adjectives remind me a little too much of Snoqualmie Pass — locale of the infamous Singeing of My Skin, I can at least find out what Aminta has left at the top of the stairs.

GEEKS FOR GOOD CARE PACKAGE

1. *Lonely Planet Iceland*: pages about winter travel strategically flagged with green Post-it notes.

2. iPod Shuffle: loaded with podcasts from *Harry Potter and the Sacred Text* and *Talk Nerdy* to *The Narrative Breakdown* and virtually every single lecture given on Khan Academy.

3. Photosensitivity Prototype #2: The Astral Projection Hat[1]. Take one wide-brimmed, UPF-protective safari hat. Cover it with a veil made of sheer UPF protective fabric. Rig the crown with a UV-protected headlamp angled backward. Add a special FX filter that turns the light source into eight-point stars, and meet your

---

1 Prototype beta test is sanctioned and approved by Lee & Li Communications.

personal reading light that does double duty, filling the darkest of days with starlight.

4. A bag of orange and black foil-wrapped Halloween chocolate Kisses.

5. *Persephone*, special edition #1.

CHAPTER SIXTY-FIVE

I had no idea that Josh had reworked the first issue of *Persephone*. Without me. It is all kinds of ridiculous that I feel hurt, because what? He was going to crystallize his life and ideas and plans in amber, not moving forward just because we weren't speaking, his choice?

Then I read the title: *The Night of the Geminids*.

Persephone is surfing atop a meteor, a jet stream of gold stardust trailing across the cover.

Oh.

CHAPTER SIXTY-SIX

My rug is a galaxy of wadded-up wrappers from all the Hershey's Kisses I've inhaled. The new hat tops my head, the veil shrouds my shoulders, and my own constellation of stars sparkles above me. It doesn't matter that I've read this *Persephone* redux no fewer than seven times last night. The comic is back on my lap, and I'm studying it this time with the detailed attention of a forensic anthropologist sifting through bones. For good reason: I can't shake the feeling that I'm eavesdropping on all of my conversations with Josh. To fortify myself, I unwrap yet another Kiss and savor the sweetness that almost hurts my teeth.

First, there's Persephone, fully clothed on the cover. As in: Real clothes drape the entire expanse of her body. Granted, her uniform is body conscious, but so are Auntie Ruth's mechanic's coveralls, not to mention Superman and Batman's skintight bodysuits that leave exceptionally little to the imagination. This uniform turns Persephone into a revolutionary firefly: a blaze of bioluminescent light over a midnight-blue paratrooper jumpsuit. Modern and fierce in a way that would make both Zoë and River Tam from *Firefly* proud, this superhero glows.

Then there's the moment that Persephone discovers that devices — phones, computers, the laser she uses to communicate with Planet X — are hazardous to her strength. Near the middle of the issue comes the devastating moment when her isolation hits her: alone, in the dark, and five billion kilometers from her closest kin. She hides that kryptonite sadness from everyone, living on Earth like she is one of us, even though she's here to find her twin sister, who has gone missing in a meteor shower. Such are the perils of being twin intergalactic meteor-surfing sensations.

Along comes Oskar, a twentysomething, Thor-turned-astrophysicist who's been tracking the Geminid meteor showers for geomagnetic anomalies. (Well done, nonscience guy.) He finds Persephone, crashed on an ice field, burning hot, even though she's wearing a teeny, weeny bikini. He bundles Persephone into his superjeep, one with ridiculously oversize wheels, and slams over frozen lava fields and flies through rivers to get her to his home. Her head lolls back on the seat rest, her cheeks are flushed. She looks like she's dying.

(Did I look that bad on the night of the Draconids?)

Finally, they make it to Oskar's home while Persephone alternates between burning fire and freezing cold. To keep her warm, he tucks her under pelts of fur (which Josh will have to amend because if he thought the photosensitive were sensitive, just wait until the animal rights activists get ahold of this). (Seriously, the guy needs a crisis-trained editorial consultant.)

Josh (I mean, Oskar) tells me (I mean, Persephone), "It was my fault you almost died. I'm not letting you almost-die a second time."

"Now you're being idiotic."

"I wrote about Santorini. The vampires there almost killed you."

"Sorry to break this to you," she snaps at him, "but you're not the boss of me. I sent myself there."

"Why go back? The vampires have rallied. You might die . . . again."

"Because."

"Because you're more than a surfer of the stars."

Persephone looks stunned, then accepting. "I am. But what if I get sick again?"

There is one large box where the two of them stare at each other wordlessly, a long moment of silence. The one box turns into two smaller ones, then three tiny ones. It's an epic long staring match, almost as long as our twenty nights of silence. What neither of them expects is the magnitude of their geomagnetic disturbances whenever they're within kissing distance of each other.

See also: chemistry.

Finally, Oskar breaks the silence and says, "Well, then you'll need to wear more than that if you're going to save the world."

"Are you body shaming me?" Persephone says.

"Uniform shaming."

Even as my heart aches a little because the banter between them (us) is so familiar, I still snort. (Then, I wonder, logically, how the heck did Oskar procure a new light-up uniform for her, a mystery that remains unexplained in the comic for now.)

Then there's Persephone's last line to Oskar before they fall into each other's arms: "I've only felt this comfortable with one other person in the world." The next morning, Persephone traces the tattoo of the Gemini con stellation on Oskar's back while he sleeps. She is racked with guilt for being distracted from her mission, for replacing her sister even briefly, for falling for this man, for wondering if Oskar is who he says he is.

I pause right at this point to research the Geminids. These meteors originate from the constellation Gemini, Latin for twins. Twins, like Josh and his brother, Caleb.

The comic drops from my lap to the floor.

I've only felt this comfortable with one other person in the world. That's what Josh had admitted to me the night of our own meteor shower. Had he meant his twin? I flip back to the page where Persephone traces the Geminids on Oskar's back. Did Josh feel guilty because he thought I had somehow replaced Caleb? (And was he foreshadowing that Oskar might actually be Ultraviolent Reyes?)

In the last panel, Persephone slips into the starlit darkness. Unbeknownst to her, Oskar trails closely behind. She takes to the stars; he takes to the sky, following her into the dark.

CHAPTER SIXTY-SEVEN

Unable to focus now with *Persephone* orbiting in my head (what, exactly, was Josh saying to me and the rest of the world?), yet unwilling to have my heart recrack with false hope, I decide to do what I have always done best: research. There may not be many people on the planet with solar urticaria, but 1.5 million people in the US alone have lupus. So I get online on my UPF-covered Mac care of Aminta and Caresse, and within a minute, I find what I'm looking for: a chat room for people with lupus. Even better, there's an entire forum dedicated to managing photosensitivity.

Luluboo (new member): Can we just ask questions about how to deal with the sun and see what other ppl are going thru and see their answers so I don't feel so alone?

That single question makes me feel less lonely, especially when at least fifteen other members immediately welcomed Luluboo and reassured her that this is a safe spot. Below that, the questions and stories begin, interspersed with introductions of new members. There's Denali, who shares how she's had to stay inside for three straight months when the summer never set in Alaska and is now afraid to venture outside, wondering whether it's worth the risk. Then TheVault, who chimes in about how even sun-protective clothes aren't completely sun-blocking, how she got badly burned, how her body flared and ached for weeks afterward.

It's depressing, all these stories, all my whispers of "me, too." That is, until I scroll way down and get cyber-slapped in the face by a poufy-haired, silver-haloed grandmother.

Nana1947: *Yes, stay inside. Don't dare a flare. I understand that. I locked myself inside for the first ten years after my diagnosis, so worried that I'd be in pain.*

Yet there's smelling the first bloom of jasmine. Walking around the block with your dying husband. Throwing a ball with your daughter. Watching your grandson graduate from college. The cost of going out is high, but the cost of locking out life is much, much higher.

You can guess the price I choose to pay for those precious moments when my body feels up to it. Invariably, my body shuts down afterward, recovering is taking me longer and longer. For me, living is worth it. The only answer that really matters, though, is yours: Are you staying inside because you absolutely must or are you hiding inside because you're afraid to take a chance outside?

...

I rear away from the screen, as scalded with the truth as most of the responders. I haven't been running scared; I have encased myself in fear, the same as Josh. A few haters talk about how their condition was so much worse than Nana1947 and how dare she assume that everyone is staying inside because they're afraid. To which my new nana-hero responded with one line: There is still starlight.

CHAPTER SIXTY-EIGHT

I still don't have the heart to make soup.

...

Or do my calculus homework. Or reread *Persephone* for the thirteenth time. It's exposing, really, how Josh saw straight through to my fear that I refused to admit to myself—that I really am the Sick Girl. But if I felt vulnerable, what about him? He revealed himself to me through our conversations, too.

And now through this comic.

...

So I listen to a podcast and have a "no way" moment. The first thing I play happens to be the very episode on NPR that Auntie Ruth cited: *Gastrodiplomacy: Cooking Up a Tasty Lesson on War and Peace.*

Enemy, frenemy, friend, who knew that the way to people's hearts and minds—really and truly—is through their stomachs, just as I thought? Peace and progress can be served on a silver platter.

...

For a change of scenery, literally, I flip through the guidebook to Iceland, then look up the gastrodiplomacy class at American University, which leads me to one even closer to home at the University of Oregon. There are no fully dedicated gastrodiplomacy programs.

Yet.

...

There is still starlight.

SEVEN TYPES OF TENT-DWELLERS
YOU KNOW AND LOVE

(A PERSON WHO LACKS THE COURAGE TO
GO OUT AND EXPERIENCE THE WORLD.)

1. The Bunker Occupant. Keeps themselves cloistered inside safe from the sun, even though there is starlight.

2. The No-Thank-You Nondater. Keeps themselves single because they're afraid to break their hearts a second time.

3. The Crisis Planner(s). Keeps themselves from disaster with long, detailed contingency plans that obliterate crisis, but also any sense of adventure or fun.

4. The Princess. Keeps themselves in entitlement mode so other people will take care of them.

5. The Pity Partier. Keeps themselves locked in their problem, where every possibility is an automatic knee-jerk no.

6. The Player. Keeps themselves from true emotional connection with an endless number of romantic possibilities always on simmer. (See also: The Ghoster.)

7. The Ghoster. A kissing cousin to The Player except
    that their modus operandi is to keep themselves from
    any emotional entanglement with The Drastic
    Pullback, cutting off all contact with a preemptive
    good-bye.

I stare at this list in my day planner. Maybe we're all scared of something and just doing our best to live in what feels like a hard, unpredictable, and scary world.

And maybe, just maybe, when I stop placing myself in the middle of The Story of Us, I have to acknowledge that Josh isn't a classic Ghoster: Even after big, revelatory talks that lasted hours and hours, he kept returning to me. He met my parents. He hung out at Souper Bowl Sundays. He wanted to know me, and he wanted me to know him.

Perhaps his continued silence isn't because he's not interested in me. Maybe it's the exact opposite: that he's too interested in me, and like The No-Thank-You Nondater, he can't stand having another person be a casualty of his care. And maybe, just maybe, no matter what I said or didn't say, what I did or didn't do, no matter if I had solar urticaria or not, he would have eventually bolted. It is what tent-dwellers do, after all.

I should know.

CHAPTER SIXTY-NINE

Fairy tales are no innocent, sunny things. So I know better when I hear a tentative knock on my basement door in the afternoon and find Red Riding Hood in a maroon hoody, holding a brown paper bag. Just looking at the Molly Moon's ice cream logo on the bag gives me secondhand sugar high. My appetite stirs for the first time in days.

Roz says uncertainly, "I'm sorry! I got you some ice cream, but it's kind of melty! The bus stops, like, a billion times! I didn't know."

Of course she didn't know because she has never needed to take the bus. Maybe that's all I wanted from Roz though: a little effort on my behalf. She's hand-delivered ice cream to me.

So I tell my sister the truth. "This is so awesome!"

"They didn't have Earl Grey anymore," apologizes Roz, "but they had salted caramel and pumpkin, but pumpkin sounded disgusting, even though it's Halloween. So I bought salted caramel."

"It's Halloween?" I've lost track of my days.

"Tomorrow."

"Wow."

"Is this okay?"

"This is great," I assure her. I take a step, then two, out of my basement and into the kitchen. "That is awesome that you got there and back by yourself."

"I know." Roz sounds proud of herself. "You want to have it up here? I'll get you a spoon."

I shake my head and turn around, but when I look over my shoulder, my little sister, the gastrodiplomat, is gazing at me wistfully.

I widen the basement door because I believe in this peace process. "Get two."

Roz beams like that's all she has ever wanted: to be invited inside. I hear the clattering of cutlery behind me even as I stand at the door. There's no "wait for me!" She knows I will.

CHAPTER SEVENTY

"She's cooking!" Mom not-so-surreptitiously whispers from the hall on Sunday morning.

"Finally." Dad's relief, I bet, has more to do with his appetite than my return to the land of the living, not that I blame him. I've tasted what they've been "cooking" during my hiatus from the kitchen, and binge eating does not come to mind.

Their giddy delight surrounds me, but I'm too much in my zen spot to be distracted, especially now that I'm back where I belong. I slice into the tallest Rice Krispie Treats I've ever fixed, three types, including one drizzled with chocolate caramel sauce. I'm one hundred percent certain that Geeks for Good will sell out of these faster than at any other bake sale. They are so huge, the little kids who find their surprise treat in their backpacks aren't going to be able to hold them in their small hands. Perhaps I can't feed the world, but if I can feed fifty little kids for even a weekend, that is still good. Just like four hours of sunlight.

I've never been meant for broadcast stardom in front of a camera, and I've never aspired to be a celebrity chef. Behind-the-scenes baking to create understanding, crafting meals to communicate so much more than mere nutrition, highlighting issues with my writing, building goodwill in every meaningful bite and word?

That's a Plan B that I can get behind. So hand me a spatula. Stat.

"Real lives are at stake," I hear Mom saying as I now package the final Rice Krispie Treats, s'mores edition. "So we should wait to make the announcement, if we want to play it safe."

"Safe," agrees Dad. He opens the back door for my mom. The path lights up as they walk toward the Shed.

There are times when one single word triggers you, propels you into action, demands that you say something after weeks or years of silence. The one word that makes you say to yourself: no more. For Auntie Ruth, it was the word: *alone*. For me, it is: *safe*.

Instead of staying sheltered in the kitchen, I move the Souper Bowl Sunday soup (clam chowder, Seahawks vs. Patriots) to the back burner, then grab the document I printed after Roz left for crew practice. I am done with our nonslip, baby-proofed, outlet-covered lives. I head to my parents' sanctuary, their home office, the Shed.

Even as I give myself the Lee & Li preconfrontation pep talk, my heart is pounding. Roz may have mastered the Art of Saying Whatever to my parents, but I have not.

Out in the Shed, they are sitting at their oversize desk, facing each other. Lee & Li aren't just left brain and right brain to form the perfect business union; my parents are a perfect heart, left and right ventricles thump-thumping in perfect rhythm. No wonder they play it safe. Who would want to risk that once-in-a-lifetime love?

But I am mummifying in their good intentions.

"Mom, Dad," I say, standing at the door, feeling like I'm intruding as always on a special moment. "I want to talk to you."

Instantly, Mom does her laser beam eye scan over my body and asks, "Are you feeling okay? Did you overdo it by cooking? Why don't you sit down?"

Correction: I'm not mummifying. I have mummified.

"I'm fine." I take a deep calming breath, then another because the protective layers of their love are many and thick. I place my document in the middle of their desk. "I'm actually feeling great, so great that I have a plan I want to discuss with you."

"The Viola Li Best-Case Scenario Plan," Mom reads. "What's this?"

Dad cranes his neck to read the page upside down. "Move back to your bedroom? Oh, sweetheart, I don't know."

Studying my parents, I have absolutely zero doubt they would take my condition, a hundred times they would volunteer for it, a thousand times. My parents would place themselves at the center of every single crisis they've ever battled if it meant saving Roz and me, Auntie Ruth, and the world. No wonder reporting the truth isn't enough for me; I want to nurture the world, too, shape a better future truth for all.

"Mom, Dad, I totally appreciate everything you've done for me," I tell them. "But I have to reframe my condition. It's not like how I was yesterday is how I'm going to be tomorrow. So it's a lot healthier for me to think of everything as a test."

"Testing your boundaries," Mom says slowly.

"Testing is good," I tell them. "After the Draconids, now I know I can't tolerate hours of direct light, not even in the early morning. At least, for now. At some point, I should test that, right? Because what if I can go out at dawn sometime in the future? I want to know."

"Okay," Dad says slowly. "So you want to test yourself carefully?"

I nod and because sometimes, as Lee & Li know, you have to hear a new idea three times before you're willing to listen, I repeat myself, "Testing is the only way I'll know what my body is capable of tolerating. How am I going to get on a plane or go to college unless I test myself on the days I'm feeling good? Otherwise, I'll just stay in my bunker for the rest of my life. I can't be contained in a terrarium."

"So what you're saying is you want to live on your terms," Mom interprets for me.

"I've *got* to live my life," I correct her. "With the right tools. Like, I can't wait to test my new Wynnter wear outside."

"And school?" asks Dad, frowning, scanning the document. "This might be too much, too fast."

Mom chimes in. "And what about — "

"Just read," I tell them both, and tap the handwritten document complete with an action plan and an extremely conservative timeline. I have no desire to get sick ever again. When my parents bend over the pages, I play with the new pendant I bought myself online: a piece of Icelandic lava, black as a beautiful night. I tell them again, "Just read."

THE VIOLA LI BEST-CASE
SCENARIO PLAN

Over the past few weeks, we have lived out the Worst-Case Scenario for my condition: me descending into a bunker, living in the dark without knowing, really, how my skin will react to light today or tomorrow or months from now. Our assumption is I will always get sick.

Instead, I would like to propose Plan B: the best case for my condition. This doesn't mean that I don't acknowledge the real risks, but it does mean that I get to live on my own terms.

So.

First, I am instituting my Viola Li Security Advisory System, complete with five different alert levels, ranging from green (I'm good to go outside) to red (I'm bunkering inside). I'll always check the UV Index before I leave home. Even if the UV Index is at zero, I'll make sure to always carry an emergency kit filled with SPF 100 sunscreen, UPF-protective hat, UPF-barricading clothes, and even an umbrella. My cell phone will always be charged so we can reach each other in the event of emergency. I will always wear a necklace engraved with your numbers to call in case I'm incapacitated as well as a note that I am allergic to the sun.

Second, I am going to move back to my bedroom after I've earned enough money to install room blackening shades and room darkening curtains. (Plan B: If things get rough for me again, I will retreat to the bunker.)

Third, I'm going back to high school. I will work with the administration on ways where I can safely attend school without impacting the entire student body. Until I do, I will go to Auntie Ruth's office a few days a week as originally planned. (Plan B: I will homeschool.)

Fourth, I'm going to college. I will apply to Reed College, which is three hours from home. It has no grades. That should lessen my stress when my body doesn't cooperate and I have to miss class. I will also lobby for a single with special medical dispensation so no roommate has to suffer in the dark with me. (Plan B: If physical classes are impossible, then I will do all of my classwork online. I will move home if the dorm doesn't work out.)

And fifth, while being a foreign correspondent may be impossible for me now, the second best thing is for me to be an advocate, which is what I've been doing for the last three years anyway: using my writing and culinary skills to advocate for fifty different causes. So I will propose to Reed College to create my own gastrodiplomacy major in conjunction with Le Cordon Bleu, also in Portland.

I'm not sure where gastrodiplomacy will lead me: maybe working in the State Department or at an embassy, maybe teaching, maybe writing. While I know there are challenges and risks, I can't document or predict or protect myself against every single crisis. No one can, not even the perfectly healthy.

This is my plan.

For now.

...

"I don't know, Viola," Dad hesitates, frowning. "Your bedroom? Returning to Liberty?"

"No, honey." Mom abruptly leaves her side of the desk and plants herself in front of Dad, not me. Dad looks as startled as I feel, this no-honey is an unscripted deviation from their normal, in sync, dynamic duo-ism.

I'm ready with my counterarguments, the ones I've written and rehearsed earlier today.

"Plan B, honey. She thought of Plan B." Mom glances over her shoulder at me, incandescent with pride, before she places her hand on Dad's chest. "Plan B."

Dad automatically wraps his hand around hers and agrees slowly, "She did think of a doable Plan B."

"Not just doable, but thoughtful," Mom says.

"It's the Lee & Li Way," I tell them.

It's true. The hallmark of a truly great Plan B isn't that it's a loser's consolation prize, the next best thing. The power of a truly great Plan B is that it is pretty darn awesome, standing on its own.

"You'll have to give us some time to think this over," Mom says, picking up my plan. "We'll want to talk to Dr. Anderson to see if he has any suggestions for making this happen."

Dad sits down and leans back in his chair, thinking. "We could make a couple of calls, set up a couple of informational interviews, see what's really possible."

Already, Mom is mentally reviewing their database of contacts. "Remember that expert on foreign affairs we had to call for that European fiasco?"

"Thomas —"

"Kharim. Yeah, that's the one."

"Good thinking. He's an adjunct professor at Wesleyan now, I think."

They grin at each other, aglow with my possibilities. Plan B, I'll take. From my parents' heads, bowed together over my plan, so might they.

CHAPTER SEVENTY-ONE

Right on time, the next morning at breakfast, the doorbell rings. I rocket out of the kitchen, beating even Dad.

"Trick or treat!" Auntie Ruth says as she hands me her key fob. "Ready?" Dad asks, "Wait. What?"

"Are you giving Viola a car?" asks Roz, incredulous.

"I'm being homeschooled at Auntie Ruth's office," I explain to everyone, well-prepared for this moment. After all, I am armored with every conceivable argument and with every possible layer of sunscreen, undershirt, custom-tailored, long-sleeved Wynnter shirt buttoned to my neck, heavy jeans, riding boots, safari hat, driving gloves tucked into my back pocket, and my new necklace. "You did say that if I was highly efficient, I'd be done with homeschool by eleven every day, right?" I remind my parents. "And the UV Index for the next couple of days is supposed to be especially low at that time."

"Viola gave me a list of everything to do to make my office safe for her. I've changed out all my light bulbs," Auntie Ruth adds with a smile. "Plus, UV-protected the hell out of every single window. And I preemptively tinted all of my car windows, thanks to a medical note from that nice Dr. Anderson."

I lift the key fob as evidence, ignoring Roz's "no fair" for now.

"Don't you think we should have discussed this first?" Dad asks with not a little judgment in his voice.

"This was your plan. I just accelerated it to my timeline," I tell my parents.

Mom protests, "But—"

"Mom. Dad." I take a deep breath. "You guys said you wanted me to live as normal a life as possible. Well, I'm testing my limits."

My parents exchange aggravated looks, as I thought they would.

"We were thinking," Mom starts.

I interrupt, "Mom. Mom. You've prepared me my whole life for this, to be ready on my own. You heard the doctor about Josh's quick thinking." Mom flinches at that name, but I continue, "He thought to throw the blanket over the sunroof, but Mom, you thought of the blanket. You made sure I had it. Even when you're not with me, you are."

Mom blinks back her tears as Dad tugs her close to him. He says, "You really are."

I tell them, "And maybe if studying at Auntie Ruth's works out, Roz and I can drive to the boathouse together until March third. That's when the sun will begin rising before 6:45 a.m., which doesn't give me enough buffer time to get to Auntie Ruth's with the UV Index and all."

"Yay, a chauffeur again!" says Roz gleefully.

"No," I tell her, "you'll be driving us to the boathouse, then I'll drive by myself to Auntie Ruth's."

"You thought this through, didn't you, honey?" Dad says.

"I did," I say, proving there are more than two crisis managers in our family. There's also a diplomat.

CHAPTER SEVENTY-TWO

The full impact of Ruth's Auto Repair hits me at once: The shop has been pinkified. Bright splashes of raspberry pink, the same shade as the racing stripes on my aunt's Mini Cooper, tastefully accent the interior: the great, big welcome sign, the throw pillows on the tailored gray sofa, the new branded pens. The lobby could double for a boutique hotel except for the (pink) power tools and (pink) hydraulic system behind the (pink) garage doors.

"Do you like my test concept?" Auntie Ruth asks uncertainly.

"What's not to like?" I ask. "I love it! But test concept for what?"

Auntie Ruth pours so much almond milk in my (pink!) mug, it turns the chai tea a nutty beige. "All my friends kept calling me to double-check the quotes they were getting from repair shops — North Carolina, California, Virginia. And the panic when they'd break down on the side of the road! So I decided, why not make a repair shop more welcoming? Why not hold women-only workshops so we'd all know how a car works and how to do easy fixes ourselves, right?"

"Right." I suggest, "Maybe you could tie those workshops into fund-raisers for different causes, like breast cancer?"

I wait for Auntie Ruth to nod politely, but she tilts her head to the side and mulls. "October: Check your boobies and your batteries. I love that."

"I can bake sugar cookie bras and ice them in different shades of pink."

While we brainstorm, a vintage Mini from the '60s pulls up to the shop, which is thirty minutes away from opening. Automotive emergencies wait for no woman. Or silver-haired men. Getting out of the car is none other than Silver Fox from Souper Bowl Sunday and Snoqualmie Pass, wearing a sharply tailored gray suit. He looks crisp and polished and every bit the wrong man for Auntie Ruth. Yet she is blushing.

"Well, look at what the Mini dragged in," I mutter to Auntie Ruth.

Her blush deepens. "I don't notice anything but his car."

"Nice . . . engine."

"Viola."

"What?" I blink innocently at her.

"I'll be back in ten minutes. You okay on your own?"

"I love being on my own."

Her hand pauses on the double lock on the front door. Then Auntie Ruth whips around to face me, searching my eyes with concern. "It's okay to be with the right someone, too, you know."

"It really is, Auntie Ruth." I smile at her gently and hear the double locks on her heart release even as she fumbles with the ones on the door.

As soon as her door opens, Silver Fox says, "Ruth! My car's been making a funny noise again."

Again? My mouth twitches with amusement. Anyone with a working knowledge of flirtation can see what's been going on. Smiling to myself, I head for Auntie Ruth's darkened office, where I remove my computer, the one that the Geeks for Good have rigged with a UV-protective screen. My hands rest on the cover. Fifteen minutes — it'll be a test to see if I can tolerate that much screen time after days without my Mac. Before I lift the screen up, I plot my search in advance.

Iceland. Determine what (if anything) there is to do.

As it turns out: There's quite a bit, and quite a few fans of visiting Iceland in the dead of winter with its four fleeting hours of daylight. The ones who rave about the otherworldly beauty of layers upon layers of natural white: snow, ice, sky. The ones who love having the ice-locked country to themselves, devoid of tourists. The ones who relish the idea of flying over snow-covered lava fields in mammoth superjeeps outfitted with oversize wheels.

If Iceland and gastrodiplomacy were a few degrees away from my original plans, what else could I do? I pull my planner from my messenger bag, determined to find out.

ADVENTURES: THE BLACK LIST V1.0

1. Viewing the aurora borealis in Iceland. The country is a six-and-a-half-hour direct flight from Seattle. Not only has Iceland been named one of the safest places to travel on earth, but it is one of the safest for me with its lack of sunlight in winter. (Plan B: We go to the Methow Valley, a six-hour drive from Seattle in the winter.)

2. Kayaking in Puerto Mosquito, the brightest bioluminescent bay in the world. This trip will take a little forethought since we need to time it for the New Moon, when the night is at its absolute darkest, which coincidentally will be the safest time for me. (Plan B: We drive two hours north of Seattle to Bellingham to see its bioluminescent bay.)

3. Visiting the glowworms in New Zealand. Imagine boating the underground river in the Waitomo Caves with its thousands upon thousands of glowworms. (Plan B: Caverns of Sonora, in Texas, which are sans glowworms, but the caves look like they're straight out of the *Lord of the Rings*.)

4. Stargazing in the Atacama Desert. Chile has the clearest night skies on the planet, and we can join other astro-tourists at the ALMA Observatory. (Plan B: We could return to Snoqualmie Pass in August for the Perseids, and this time I will wear every possible UPF-protective garment known to girlkind.)

5. Night snorkeling with manta rays off the Big Island of Hawaii. You can swim with the rays at night when they feed, no diving experience necessary. (Plan B: the Night Zoo in Tasmania, featuring creatures that come alive in the dark.)

CHAPTER SEVENTY-THREE

"Hey, honey! More trick-or-treaters!" Dad bellows down the stairs a few hours after I return home from Auntie Ruth's. "Can I send them down?"

Before I can answer, Aminta floats and Caresse clomps down the basement steps, both of them wearing cowboy hats and carrying orange pumpkin buckets.

"This is way more *hygge* than I remember!" Aminta says, grinning at me, as my Halloween candles burn around the basement. Then, she frowns. "Except that music. You're not still listening to that mixtape, are you? That's, like, the opposite of *hygge*."

"That's the word!" I tell her, embarrassed because I have been listening to Josh's mixtape out of habit. "I'd been trying to remember it. Warm and cozy, right?"

"Like this?" Caresse holds up a black turtleneck silkscreened in silver with the word *wynnter*, the same as on theirs. "We're going as a K-pop band."

"Wynnter isn't a bad band name," I say.

"It's an even better brand name," Caresse answers.

I check the shirt more closely. The tag inside reads: WYNNTER. I grin at them. "You're so official."

"Well, it's a start, anyway," says Caresse. "In senior spring, we'll ramp up."

"We can do a bake sale to launch your line! Maybe raise awareness for — "

Caresse says, "We sold out of the Rice Krispies. The s'mores went first."

"Awesome, I'll give some thought to the Wynnter bake — "

"I can't stand this anymore!" Aminta cries. "My ears are bleeding."

Caresse and I look at her, worried. For a girl whose normal stride is a glide, Aminta now stomps over to the tape recorder. The song "Night

Time" chokes off. My room goes silent. "You need a new playlist for your life."

I laugh. "You're right. I do."

Caresse says, "So hurry up and change."

"My parents —"

"Are giving you your fifteen minutes of streetlights," says Aminta.

"We can get into a lot of trouble in fifteen minutes." Caresse grins naughtily. "So, yeah, hurry up and get your *hygge* on. I tailored the turtleneck extra super tight . . ."

Surprise, surprise, when I slip into my Wynnter wear, I feel like an exceptionally *hygge* version of me.

SAY YOUR PEACE

The truth is: You cannot control anyone — not their feelings, not their inexplicable silence, not their wackadoo decisions. Sometimes all you can do is cobble together your own peace process.

— Viola Wynne Li
The Gastrodiplomat's Guide to the Galaxy

THE VIOLA WYNNE LI PEP TALK

Okay, Viola girl.

It's seven at night and dark outside. Time to slap on your Astral Projection Hat and get thyself to a kitchen.

There is comfort in finding the perfect recipe and collecting the ingredients: flour, sugar, vanilla extract. There is comfort in peeling and chopping apple after apple. The best culinary fix for a broken heart is Caramel Apple Cobbler, a salute to the end of a season.

CHAPTER SEVENTY-FOUR

Even more than the peace I feel from cooking, I thrill at the mysterious transformation that happens in the heat, turning flour and sugar and apples into comfort food. Even so, while the cobbler bakes, I measure the flour for the backup just in case the first comes out a disappointing, gooey mess.

Half-baked has been known to happen.

I tell myself, *Viola girl, you can't force him to text or email*. With a deliberately light hand, I whisk the flour with sugar and milk and vanilla: *You may never know what he was thinking*. I rap the whisk sharply on the rim of the mixing bowl. *Ever*.

Here's the thing: *You can stay second fiddle to your fears for the rest of your life*. The apples, tucked nice and snug in the baking dish, await the batter topping. *You can stay stuck in a tent*. After I slide the second dish into the oven, I set the timer. *A full three weeks have tick-tocked by, and (his) life is continuing without you*.

As I clean up my mess in the kitchen, warm apple cobbler heavily scents the air. *You, girl, are scared to say your peace. But if you don't, you're going to be afraid to risk your heart, like Auntie Ruth for five whole years*.

Out of habit, I creep down to the basement. Halfway there, my muscles boycott. I am paralyzed on the stairs. Moving out of the basement is part of my plan. It's not just my parents who've been reluctant for me to make progress on that plan; I've been clinging to my basement. There's no possibility of burning down here. But no matter how comfortable my safe room is with its decal affirmations and plump throw pillows and soft sheepskin rug, it is still a bunker.

Reinforced, underground bunkers are meant for surviving, not for living.

What do you say, Ultragirl? Princess or Persephone?

With my Astral Projection Hat and my sunscreen, my lava pendant and outfit by Wynnter, I reemerge. The living room flickers with firelight. Up there, I put pen to paper. As it turns out, I have a lot to say.

THE RESOLUTION PHASE

The Resolution Phase marks the end of your crisis. Sometimes, even the bitterest of stories deserve the sweetest of endings.

—Viola Wynne Li
The Gastrodiplomat's Guide to the Galaxy

CHAPTER SEVENTY-FIVE

"I'm heading out," I tell my parents as if they've approved my Best-Case Scenario Plan, as if this is life as usual — except I'm wearing a sunhat at night, every inch of my body is hidden in sun-defensive fibers, and I'm carrying a still-hot baking dish of Caramel Apple Cobbler.

A mix of silent calls-and-responses pass between my parents while they try to formulate a solution to this small but unexpected crisis.

"I'll be gone for forty-five minutes," I say, sticking closely to the script I've prepared. I nod to Josh's address already on the kitchen table. "I'm driving just three miles away."

Mom doesn't look at the piece of paper but at the apple cobbler, and she knows where I'm going. "Honey, are you sure about this?"

"This is how I'm saying good-bye. I'll call the moment I think I need you. Plus, I'll bring Roz."

Knowing that her eavesdropping skills are even keener than mine, I counted on Roz to chime in from her bedroom, "Can we go to Molly Moon's after?"

Together, as one voice, my parents and I say, "No."

Though she grumbles, Roz rushes out to our Subaru. I'm glad for our sister time, too, not just because I need this first semi-solo test run into the outside world to go flawlessly. Not even because this is the exact moment my parents have been picturing since Roz's birth: sisters in blood and spirit. The truth is: I need my sister. I'm scared to go by myself.

"You've thought this through," Mom says slowly.

"It's a good plan," Dad agrees.

With that endorsement, I leave my Necromanteion for the dark outside.

CHAPTER SEVENTY-SIX

"You look like you're going to have a heart attack," Roz says, ignoring her phone for the first time on our drive to Josh's home. "Are you?"

"I wish. It'd be better than this," I tell her truthfully. Vulnerability is so overrated. My hands are taut on the steering wheel, my mind taut on the letter in my back pocket, mentally reviewing every word, every admission, every good-bye.

"For the record, I think this is really stupid. He's ghosted you. The last thing you should do is chase him. All the power is his now."

"I'm not sure it works that way."

"Says the girl who's never had a real boyfriend."

"I had one."

"Darren? The guy who could only be monogamous with himself?"

"That's so true!" My laugh twines with my sister's.

Josh's home is located on a dead end street, not where I'd imagined him living. On the far edge of the driveway is a portable moving pod. A FOR SALE sign glows white in the dark near the curb. If it weren't for the rhythmic bouncing of the basketball, I would have missed Josh entirely on the driveway.

"You sure about this?" asks Roz as I turn off the ignition.

Sure or not, I don't have much of a choice because Josh notices us. He hugs the basketball to his chest. My heart squeezes. I have missed this boy so much.

"I'm just giving him something," I tell Roz, but mostly I tell myself.

"I don't know, Viola."

Frankly, I don't either. I'm not even sure if Josh will actually stay to see why I'm here. He doesn't just stay; he swaggers toward me, all superhero confidence, whisking me right back to MoPOP. My throat clogs with pre-tears. I so much prefer the hello of *Firefly* to this good-bye.

No matter how many times you play a hard conversation in your head, practicing your side of the dialogue, predicting the other person's responses, what actually comes out might be garbled to this:

"I missed you."

I know, I know, I know. (Head bangs against an imaginary wall.)

Prepare, prepare, prepare. And then prepare some more. That is the Golden Rule of Lee & Li crisis communications. Death by mortification will happen later — approximately five nanoseconds after driving away — but for now, in this moment, all I feel is the ending of us.

"You have a new necklace," he says.

An (astute) observation, not an emotion.

Clearly, I am a finalist for the Darwin Award because my first instinct — the death instinct — nudges me closer to him. I want to feel him against me again, filling my arms.

Just as swiftly, he steps back to do a quick perimeter check of his house, frowning at the blazing lights on his garage. Josh is already swiveling to his house as he says, "Wait a second."

"No, don't," I tell him, and reach for his arm, unthinking. *Not now. Not yet. Not again.* That innocent touch is like getting zapped by an electric fence, an invisible but effective repellant. Instinctively, we jerk away from each other, sending yet another fracture line in my heart that I thought had already shattered. Apparently, there is room for more breakage.

"Wait, I've just — " I start to say just as Josh tells me, "Wait, it'll just — "

Once upon a time, talking over each other would have only been uncomfortable, the awkwardness of a new acquaintance: "You first," "No, you." Now that we're living in the Land of After, this is yet one more sad proof that we've lost our syncopation. We're off-sequence, arrhythmic, one heart beat too fast, the other too slow.

...

THE WARNING SIGNS OF AN ATTACK
OF THE HEART

Light-headedness: check.

Shortness of breath: double-check.

Chest pain: always.

...

Weeks and weeks of silence have attacked my heart. 911 won't help me now.

"How're your parents?" Josh asks.

I reply, "I think they used the words, 'House arrest lifted.'"

"Good."

That's it? That's all I get? Good? "Yeah."

"Do you need anything?" he asks.

Duh. You. Knocked uncertain, I keep my answer to a single "Nothing."

If I needed another reason why I could never be a crisis manager, I get it now. Suddenly, inexplicably, unpredictably, I see red. Angry, enveloping, destroying flames of red. Actually, I don't just see red. I feel red: The heat races up my neck, burning my cheeks. I'm mad at myself for chickening out of the conversation I've played and replayed in my head. I'm furious at him for his one-word "good" treatment. You don't end a relationship by fading away and punctuate it with a single "good." Whether the (dumb) guy admitted it or not, we had a relationship.

"You know," I say (spit), "I'm the one living with this. I'm here to help you with Caleb; I didn't run from that. That's what a relationship means: We help each other through stuff. So you can't use my condition to run."

Josh says pretty much the only thing that could defuse my anger: "But it was my fault we went to the Draconids."

"We settled that weeks ago. I asked you to go there with me. I asked you."

"You could have died."

"I didn't. I could be hit by a car."

His body jerks at that.

"I could be in Paris when a bomb goes off. I could get cancer. I could slip down a cliff trail, running. I could have a weird allergic reaction to something I don't even know I'm allergic to. Life is so unpredictable, my parents think living itself is dangerous. But what are you going to do? Never love anyone or anything ever again?" I breathe out and hear the incessant danger-thrum of the Serengeti that is unpredictable, chaotic, beautiful Life. I watch myself unzip the tent door, risks be damned. "I don't regret it." (Or you.) "Or you."

Even without a crisis plan for this moment, I know it is too much, the moment too fragile to sustain the weight of all this unfettered emotion.

"We're moving," Josh says — an explanation for his silence or a deflection from a hard conversation, I can't tell.

Whatever it is, I ask, "Where? Why?"

"My mom wants a fresh start. Mazama."

"Mazama? Where's that?"

"Central Washington. It's a small town. No traffic."

I know a crisis management plan when I see it: Yeah, sure, escape to a small town, and flee the specter of another fatal car accident. But let me be the first to tell you this: No place on our planet is completely safe. Not bomb shelters, not underground bunkers no matter how tricked out they are, not even a girl who refused to look at another guy until Thor trooped his way into her life. Hurt can seep into even the most reinforced places.

So can love.

"But you're doing okay?" he asks, looking straight at me. For the first time since we've spoken, I feel like Josh is really and truly present and locked in on me.

"Yeah."

"Okay, then, I should — "

The car door opens, slams shut, reminding me that we have an audience. Roz approaches with the apple cobbler that I've forgotten in the station wagon.

"Here," she says, thrusting the dish at Josh. So much for gastro-diplomacy. The cobbler is less a kiss good-bye than a kiss-off. "Hey, Viola, we need to get going."

She's right, of course. My first real outing, and I should be home, not just on time, but early.

"Here," I tell Josh, holding my letter to him, but his hands are occupied with the cobbler. His hands that I can feel on me, skimming my shoulders, running along my clavicle, curving on the small of my back. He lifts the crook of his arm, and I tuck the letter snug next to his body where I once belonged.

"I'll talk to you later," he says to me.

I could simper the corresponding lie: "Yeah, for sure."

I don't because we won't. For as long as I can, I look deep into Josh's eyes, memorized long ago so I can see the sunlit blue despite the blackness of the night.

"'She understands.'" I start to quote River Tam, but for once her words slay me. I will myself to speak through that lump of grief lodged in my throat when I want so badly to go back, not to MoPOP when my skin was still my ally. But to the meteor showers when Josh was my Thor. No tears, not yet. I try again, "'She understands. She doesn't comprehend.'"

Roz takes that as her cue to tug me back to the car. I'm grateful to follow her lead.

CHAPTER SEVENTY-SEVEN

Grief, sharp and keening. Grief that makes me gasp, the pain of an excised heart. I rub my chest even as I hear my parents: *Both hands on the steering wheel. At all times.*

How the hell did heartache literally hurt so much?

"You okay?" Roz asks.

I nod, a silent lie, and keep focused on the road. I hadn't felt this demolished when Darren faded away. But Josh? I miss him at a soul-deep level.

"He isn't worth it," Roz says.

"He was," I tell her.

~~Auntie Ruth signed up for death-do-us-part until death came to col~~lect early. I can finally understand why she has placed herself in a self-imposed exile. I can't even bear the thought of being shattered like this again. But Josh showed me what lay outside my (post-Darren) tent: a true connection, so much more than mere physical lust. Although that was good, too.

I correct myself, "He is."

As I press my foot on the gas pedal, I spot an orange hazard sign: ROAD WORK AHEAD.

No truer words. Josh has his work ahead of him.

So do I.

And now I laugh.

"Should I call Mom and Dad?" Roz holds her phone, ready to emergency dial them.

I refuse to be a tent-woman, someone who remains hermetically sealed and who keeps her pain in mint condition. I refuse to take tidy, polite, no-thank-you bites when the next right guy asks me out. Our universe is way too large, populated with way too many unexpectedly cool people not to cough up or hand deliver the next right one, even if I want Josh.

"You sure you're okay?" she asks.

"Not yet," I say, "But I will be."

Dear Josh,

So.

You've been on my mind. First, rewatching *Firefly* (actually, relistening since, well, screens and UV rays and tech curfews). Also: I'm feeling unsettled because we didn't get to talk. So I hope you'll let me say my peace.

Our hearts are a renewable resource, according to Auntie Ruth. I believe that. But could yours still be somewhat depleted from everything that happened pre-Us? All this to say: If this is where you are, I understand. Of course you could have simply lost interest. It happens. I just wish you had told me.

I've decided to officially quit my consulting job with *Persephone*, hang up my Muse shoes. I've overstayed in my own Necromanteion, and there are other places in the world I'd like to see. I hope you get to Chile, too.

Zoë's right (as usual): "She's torn up plenty, but she'll fly true."

Take care,
Viola

P.S. I did have one last idea. What if Persephone seeks out the Oracle of the Dead? She thinks she can find the answers to her twin sister's fate, but instead, the Oracle of the Dead (always the cryptic) tells her to live it all—the good, the bad, the deeply awful, and the extremely joyful. Sometimes, we are never given the answer to why.

P.P.S. And now your own mixtape.
STARLIGHT
Another Sunny Day—Belle & Sebastian
Sunday Morning—The Velvet Underground, Nico
See the Sun—The Kooks

Everlasting Light – The Black Keys
Rise to the Sun – Alabama Shakes
Mornings – Tica Douglas
Sunburn – Ed Sheeran
Pocketful of Sunshine – Natasha Bedingfield

REANIMATION

When the past direct dials you, sometimes — not always, but sometimes, it's possible to turn leftovers into something even more delicious, like Caramel Rum Banana Bread Pudding, the best use for day-old banana bread.

Viola Wynne Li
The Gastrodiplomat's Guide to the Galaxy

CHAPTER SEVENTY-EIGHT

My Astral Projection Hat casts a warm halo of light in the kitchen. Even though I'm tired from baking, I can't help but admire the *vinaterta*, my first attempt at the multitiered Icelandic celebration cake, which is a fancy way of saying: prune cake with the shelf life of freeze-dried astronaut food. Gastrodiplomacy has to start somewhere, and this is a surprisingly delicious invitation to my parents to migrate from "we should go" to "we went."

After a few hours of smelling sugar, I need fresh air. Mom's maternal radar may be a fine-tuned security system, but Dad is our designated night guard. Before going to bed, he's the one to check the perimeter, testing the locks and latches on all the doors and windows. That's what I'm counting on when I press the four digits of our security code — the month and year of my parents' anniversary. The alarm beeps, then disengages. I wait.

Sure enough, Dad patters down the stairs.

"Where are you going?" he asks in a calm voice, taking in my armful of coats and the front door, still locked shut.

"Waiting for you," I tell him, and hold out his down jacket.

"For what?" Dad asks, but he's drawing to me, halfway to maybe.

"To look for Planet X."

"There are only eight planets in our solar system."

I suppose, one day, innocent statements won't trigger memories of Josh, but for now, it does. Hello, again, memory. I must wince because Dad asks, "You okay, honey?"

"Yeah, I'm going out."

"At night? Why do you have to? I never snuck out at your age."

"Maybe you should have."

It's true. If I was my sister's keeper for fifteen years, how has it been for Dad, who's been everyone's keeper since he was my age? I tell him, "Since I'm asking you to go with me, it's technically not sneaking out. Besides, it's testing. And besides that, Dad, you need to play more."

"I play."

"With crisis containment strategies, maybe."

At that, Dad chuckles. I don't want him to wake my mom or my sister. It's rare to have him all to myself.

"Come on, Dad, let's go," I whisper to him, and wonder whether he'll follow. But then Dad opens the front door, which chimes. Like me, he glances swiftly toward the stairs and then mutters to me, "Hurry."

Our attempt at skulking is amateurish at best because we start cackling, then staggering down the driveway.

"Seattle emits too much light to see the stars," Dad says, tilting his head back. I knew that even before I lured him outside. There's no way we could have found Planet IX or X with our naked eye, not even if they existed, not even with our best intentions.

"Come on," I say, heading for the street.

"And where are you going?"

"Dad. Dad. Spontaneity."

That is such a foreign concept to my father, the crisis manager whose timelines have timelines. The thought of a single unpremeditated action freezes Dad. In the moonglow, he looks so youthful in his indecision: unguarded, unsure, unbalanced, the way he must have felt when he sacrificed his Georgetown dreams to go to UW to stay near Auntie Ruth.

"It's glacial out here," says Dad, shivering, but he rubs his hands on my arms, warming me, not himself. As always. "You okay?"

There are so many ways to answer that. Like: This is nothing compared to how cold it's going to be, shivering in the middle of Iceland when we watch the northern lights.

I settle for this: "Freezing will make us appreciate going back inside."

"Have you appreciated enough yet?"

"I can still play." I head into the dark, alone. One moment of silence spills into the next. And the next.

Then I hear Dad at my side a moment before he tags me on my Astral Projection Hat and races ahead into the dark: "So can I."

CHAPTER SEVENTY-NINE

Three minutes after Dad and I start to defrost inside our home, four nights after I have said good-bye to Josh, I get the text that Aminta has been adamant would come.

Josh: So.

According to Lee & Li, response time matters. It signals something. Even now, as Dad reads over my shoulder since I must have made a strangled sound, he says, "Hmm. Let him wait."

"Says the man who says I can't date That Boy."

"Says your father, who thinks That Boy should work hard if you're giving him a second chance."

"With you?"

"With you." Dad kisses me on top of my head. "Good night, kiddo."

"Hold on, where are you going?" I whisper-hiss to him as he heads upstairs. Now would be a good time to have some male interpretative help or to make it easier for me to opt out of responding to Josh. "Aren't you going to lecture me about him? Or my tech curfew?"

"I trust you," Dad whispers back, rubbing his cold hands together. "Just remember . . ."

"What?"

"Do you know why I try so hard to make sure your mom never questions where she stands with me?"

"Because you love her."

"Because being left is her worst fear."

With that, my dad heads up the stairs. I know I won't be able to sleep, not with that cryptic parting thought in my head, and not with Josh's dangling proposition on my phone. While I figure out whether (when) to respond, I begin to prep tomorrow's second Souper Bowl Sunday dessert as quietly as I can. I coarsely dice the loaf of banana bread I had made for breakfast yesterday. Then I taste-test the caramel rum sauce that's been chilling in the fridge: The waiting time has magnified its rumminess. Delicious.

Maybe Dad has it right. Maybe waiting time is good for a girl's soul, making sure I know what I want before Josh offers anything.

So I let Josh wait, but not too long. Twenty-three minutes seems the right amount of time to signal a casual, noncommittal, *Oh, hello, friend.*

> Me: *Story time?*
> Josh: *Yes.*
> Josh: *The story of an idiot.*
> Me: *Is it good?*
> Josh: *Depends on you.*
> Josh: *Depends on if you'll accept my apology.*
> Josh: *Depends on if you'll hear me out.*
> Me: *Depends on how long I'll have to wait.*

There is a soft knock on the front door.

CHAPTER EIGHTY

"Semicolon."

Josh's first words to me after so many nights of silence, and I get, semicolon? That settles it: This boy is staying right there at the front door with the cold wind blasting his back. I whisper, "Excuse me?"

He mansplains in a low but urgent voice, "Two main clauses — two complete thoughts — separated with a pause."

Sorry, confusion. "I don't understand."

"Like us."

"Are you talking about your running away, and this is you coming back again? Because I don't do mysterious pauses anymore. I'm not a toy you pick up when you're bored and put down when you're scared."

Josh breathes out. While I can see and feel his struggle to strip down to the scary, revelatory truth, I can't help him. I won't. This, he needs to say all on his very own, if he wants me. I don't just need his words. I deserve them.

He says, "Semicolon, like us. We don't just have the same thought; we're part of the same thought. You and me. Put together, we're more."

Ah. Semicolon.

My mouth twitches into an almost-smile. His mouth tightens into an almost-grimace. He asks, "Stupid?"

"No." I open the door and let him in.

It actually makes perfect sense. Mom and Dad are semicolons; Auntie Ruth and Uncle Amos were ones, too. Who wouldn't want to protect that rare and precious semicolon at all costs? Who wouldn't preemptively want to stay behind a perfectly functional, self-sufficient full-stop period after losing their perfect half?

And who wouldn't be scared to find a perfect half they never expected to exist?

"Semicolons are my new favorite," Josh says.

"Mine, too."

It's a start, a good start. Yet I need to hear his full and complete explanation, every last word. My bedroom is too personal, the basement too tempting. So I lead him to the living room and ask him in a very Lee & Li fact-finding way, "Why are you really here?"

We sit shoulder to shoulder, hip to hip on the sofa, too close for comfort and way too close for conversation. Reluctantly, I scoot a few inches from him, a physical pause that I need. I have to see his eyes, watch his expression. After all, I am Lee & Li trained, and eyes and bodies can communicate what our words cannot.

"So," I say. "You hurt my feelings."

Listen to him, I tell myself. Watch him. Don't back-fill the nervous space with my own monologue. I shut my mouth (literally, physically, and figuratively).

"I know," Josh answers, and turns completely on the couch to face me. He takes both of my hands in his. "I'm so sorry that I hurt you. I never want to do that. I guess I was scared. My brother died because of me. I just couldn't handle that I almost made you die, too. So I ran. But when you came to me that night, that was just about the bravest thing I've seen. I don't want to lose this, you, us, just because I'm scared."

"I get that," I tell him, "but for the record, I do have a condition. You can't always blame yourself if I get sick when we're together. I mean, you just can't." I sigh because what I have to say next is hard, but it has to be spoken. "Otherwise, this will never work, and you have to know there are easier girls to date."

"Easier, yeah. But date? I only want you."

There it is again, that melting of my heart. Yet melting is easy; staying is hard. Look at my mom, still hurt thirty years after my mystery aunt abandoned her. This was what Dad was talking about, after all.

"This — me — I might be too much, and this might be too unfair for you. The truth is, if you aren't there for me, I'll probably be crushed. And it's a lot to ask of anyone, Josh. I might be able to only go out in the dark. And then there are times when I might not be able to go out anywhere." I take his hand now and lead him down to the basement, keeping the door open in case my parents do an inspection check. Every step down is an invitation for him to bolt again, but I'd rather know now if he's got real staying power. I have nothing more to hide. "This is where I might have to live. Here." I turn on the UV-protected overhead light. "For months, maybe."

"I've been researching solar urticaria," Josh says, sitting on the edge of my platform bed, "and if we take even more precautions, we should be able to keep you safe in the dark. Some people only get a little rash when they go out."

"And some people can't even go outside," I counter, lowering myself down on the far edge of the bed. "Ever. No beaches, no bikinis, no running in the sun together. No picnics, no — "

Almost as if he's been coached by Auntie Ruth or Nana1947 from the lupus board, Josh tells me, "That's a lot of no, and there is such a thing as moonlight. Plus, not to brag or anything, but I have a lot of confidence in my creative problem-solving ability."

"But your job isn't to protect me."

"I thought that's what people who love each other are supposed to do: have each other's back." And then he reaches all the way over to take my hand.

Melting. Again. All I want to do is kiss my Thor. Yet I know this is one of those historic moments, the ones where everything hinges on one misplaced word. Or one well-placed semicolon. Without meaning to, I clench his hand, never feeling so urgent about wanting to understand someone and wanting that same someone to understand me.

"What?" he asks. "Tell me."

So I do.

"Okay, here's the thing," I say. "We can research the hell out of my condition. We can read every little study done around the world. We can write the world's best plan to protect me. But studies are just guidelines and plans always change. Everyone has a slightly different reaction, and every single time I go out, my reaction might be different. And that's not even the point," I say, and I'm heartened because Josh is paying exquisite attention to me like he's actively storing everything I'm saying into his memory. I gesture around my bunker. "This might be it. This basement might be the entirety of my life."

"Are you asking me whether I like being in the Necromanteion with you?" he asks softly, his gaze unwavering. "Because the answer is yes."

"Actually, do you like Iceland?" I whisper.

"For the volcanos?" He touches my lava necklace. His voice deepens, husky, and he says, "This is very Persephone: lava rock and silver. Light and dark."

As if he knows what I'm yearning for, Josh traces my lava-hot skin. Then he smiles the smile of the Thors of this world, a guy who knows the distracting effect of his touch. "So what about Iceland?"

I clear my throat and ignore the deepening of his knowing smile as his finger continues to trace small infinity signs underneath my shirt(s).

"Iceland?" he prompts me.

"NASA is predicting the best aurora borealis in years in December. So Iceland. Six-and-a-half-hour direct flight. You should go research it."

"Central Washington. Six hours' drive. You should come."

"Are you inviting me to your lair?"

"Yes."

"I don't know."

Josh pulls back, stunned, worried, no trace left of the he-man smile. "What? Viola, I want to be with you."

"No, I mean, yay! But I mean, Helgafell."

Somehow, he tracks what I'm saying and asks, "What's that?"

"The Holy Mountain in Iceland. Legend has it that it's a portal to life after death."

His eyes grow as wide as mine must have when I did my extensive research on Iceland. "Persephone and the Vikings."

"Exactly, and according to Icelandic folklore, if you hike up the mountain without turning to look back once, you'll be granted three wishes when you reach the top of the hill." I blink up at him. "Can you even imagine what Persephone would wish for?"

"A kiss."

"Finally."

He immediately flushes (a lot and adorably); I flush (a lot and sweatily).

Semicolon, indeed.

My lips part, and let me tell you, a wish has nothing on this kiss. Tender, raunchy, soft, hard, all of the above, and everything in between—the right kiss can express a thousand emotions. And this one does. Enveloped in Josh's arms, his lips upon mine, we run the full gamut: apology and forgiveness. Separation and reunion. And homecoming. So much homecoming.

CHAPTER EIGHTY-ONE

As much as I want to revel in my bedroom and cozy up in my old flannel sheets, I lean against my pillows in bed and consult my planner. There is too much to check off on this Souper Bowl Sunday morning to lounge around, even if it's to relish the memory of Josh's (many) (many) kisses last night. The motion-sensing night-light flashes on, casting just enough light so I can make it to my desk without stubbing my toes. Or so I thought. My knee bangs hard against the desk leg. I yelp.

Immediately, my bedroom door flings open, and ninja-mom leaps in to the rescue, ready to karate-kick any intruder foolish enough to invade her daughter's room.

"Good morning," I say, rubbing my throbbing knee.

"What're you doing in here?" Mom asks, bewildered. Without waiting for my answer, she becomes my personal tour guide of the dangers lurking in my bedroom. "Honey, even that night-light can hurt you." She's already bending down to remove the offending 0.3 watts of light bulb. "We haven't safety-proofed your room yet."

"I feel great. Just ask Dad."

Mom straightens abruptly, leaving the night-light in place. "Did you guys really sneak out to the park last night?"

"Yeah, way past his bedtime, too."

Mom chuckles. "You didn't hear it from me, but he's still groggy after two cups of coffee."

I laugh. "Yeah, I bet. He's not used to breaking rules."

"He said he had fun," Mom says, gazing at the curtains, which don't just black out the sun. They block out every hint of the world that lies outside.

"Full moon. It was beautiful."

"I wish I had been with you guys."

"Well, you could watch the northern lights with us in the Methow Valley." I sidle a look at her. "Josh's mom is moving there. He invited us."

"He did?" Mom asks without sounding surprised. Of course she isn't. Dad's already filled her in on last night, always her partner. "I've always wanted to see the northern lights."

While I don't test Iceland with Mom, since Josh and I only sketched out that research trip last night (in between kissing), I tell her how we would use our time in his new hometown to research *Persephone*, complete with moonlight snowshoeing.

"That sounds like fun," Mom says thoughtfully. "But it's a long way from home with a boy."

If I've learned one thing from my parents, it's to pounce on the right openings because opportunities don't just wait around. Either you're in or you're not. Either you seize the moment, or you don't.

I seize; I seize. I sit down on my desk, surrounded by my favorite articles and my most treasured photos. "Come with us, Mom."

A denial shapes on her pursed lips until Mom's eyes rest on the photo of Auntie Ruth and me, outside our tent in the Serengeti next to the one of our family at Disneyland.

"Hmm," Mom muses, and I know that we're on the path to yes.

CHAPTER EIGHTY-TWO

The benefit of crashing in the hotel room while everyone else went cross-country skiing all day is that I'm well rested at midnight. Everyone else, not so much. Yawns, yawns sound everywhere when we venture out into the cold, dark snowfield to watch for the northern lights. Far beyond us, in a haze of dark are the snow-filled woods where Josh and I plan to snowshoe in the dusk tomorrow, if my body is up for it.

"Well, this is certainly bracing," Mom says, shivering, after we've huddled on the red Adirondack chairs around an unlit fire pit for all of five minutes.

The innkeeper joins us outside to make sure "we" have everything we need, but the way he's studying Auntie Ruth, I know who he's concerned about. Who wouldn't be? Her silver parka is going to inspire Persephone's entire Wynnter wardrobe.

"Oh, wow. Would you look at the northern lights. So awesome," Roz says flatly as we all stare at the cloud-dense sky. There is not a trace of the aurora borealis, not even a hint of pale honeydew green on the black canvas above.

"Sometimes they're there. Sometimes not," the innkeeper responds.

"How long is this going to take anyway?" Roz's whine shades the contours of every consonant and vowel in her question. How should I answer? In a minute, two hours, twenty days, an eternity, unknown. "Whose idea was this?"

"Mine," I tell her, and when she aims a death glare at me, I can't help but add, "And we're doing this again tomorrow night."

"Again?" Roz demands. "Why?"

"Clouds tonight," Josh says, tilting his head back.

"Then why are we here now?" Roz asks, but meets my eyes as our parents answer in tandem: "Just in case." She sighs. "I so did not win the family lottery."

Oh, but little sister, you have. When we get home, I plan to convince our parents to let Roz go on her seventeenth-birthday expedition with Auntie Ruth. That will be this big sister's parting gift before I leave for Reed College. (Application submitted — and surprise of surprises, my campus interviewer loved my three-page researched and footnoted proposal to create my own gastrodiplomacy program with Le Cordon Bleu. Afterward, Ms. Kavoussi gave me a high five.)

Meanwhile, the innkeeper sidles even closer to my aunt and asks her, "Hot rum toddy?" After Auntie Ruth nods eagerly, let's just say a grown man has never run so fast in snow. (See also: gastrodiplomacy.) And let's just say I smile, watching Auntie Ruth absently rub her ringless finger, feeling the wedding band that is tucked away safe, somewhere.

We sit outside for so long, without so much as a delicate lightening of the sky, that everyone else, even Mom and Dad, dozes, neglecting their sentry duty of scanning the horizon for any possible sign of danger. As they made sure we all knew (repeatedly), just a few days ago, a cougar had snatched a pet cat off a porch nearby. The only sound now is the soft wind, the drift of snow from the mounds around us. I press my lava pendant lightly to my chest. This, right here, right now, is all I need.

In this peace, my eyelids droop, even though I napped earlier, but I refuse to fall asleep now, not when Josh takes my mittened hand and stands. We walk a few feet from everyone else.

Cocooned in our embrace, I whisper up to him, "So."

"Story time?" he asks. I can feel Josh's dimpled smile before I see it.

"I had an idea for my next gastrodiplomatic effort." The clouds shift, clearing an amphitheater overhead, sparkling with stars. "A moonlight bake sale at the last tailgate at school, featuring mooncakes and information about photosensitivity. And we can sell *Persephone* there. I think it'll make it easier for me to go back to school if I'm the one who tells everyone about my condition."

"Or I could just impale the guy who was a jerk to you in the next issue."

"I'd rather educate him."

Josh squeezes my hand: *My gastrodiplomat.*

I squeeze back: *I know.*

So many divergent roads have led us to this very moment: a trip to Africa that may or may not have triggered my allergy to the sun, a condition that added depth and meaning to a comic, a comic that's given me a place to use my voice for others, and a boy who is my semicolon.

"There it is!" exclaims Auntie Ruth, jabbing her finger due north.

The innkeeper, I notice from my peripheral vision, is hurrying back (to her) with a steaming carafe and an enormous camera with the largest lens I've ever seen. He takes that opportunity to stand (body-warmingly) close to my aunt as he hastily sets up a tripod.

I squint and see nothing but stark black. I blink, then stare even harder at the sky. Even more nothing.

"This is it?" I say to Josh. All that's visible is the most unimpressive smudge mark on the dark sky. Seriously, this is what people ooh and aah over? This is what people fly to Iceland and trek thousands of miles to Norway to observe? This?

Josh starts shoulder-laughing, trying hard (and failing) to squelch his chuckles. I do, too. I don't want to hurt the innkeeper's feelings because he's (excitedly) adjusting his camera lens here, fiddling with the tripod there.

"Look here," the innkeeper says, beckoning all skeptics to his camera.

I trudge over the snow to his elaborate setup. He taps his finger on the screen on the back of the camera. The camera catches what I have missed completely with my naked eye: a green-blue light splashes across the dark sky. It is glorious.

"Sometimes you need a little help," says the innkeeper.

·

Sometimes? I glance at my parents, who have force-fed heaping piles of help on me, Roz, Auntie Ruth, their clients. They had good reasons, namely, Love.

Roz gasps. "No way!"

In the blink of an eye, some atmospheric conditions have changed without us even sensing it. Now, as I look skyward, the universe premieres a ballet of light for us. The aurora dances in the night sky, light that is lovely only because the sky is so dark and deep. I gasp. Darkness is the prerequisite condition. My heart expands as the wild green light dances free and bright.

With his arms around me, Josh sings in my ear softly, "Take my love, take my land / Take me where I cannot stand . . ."

My voice rises to meet his: "I don't care, I'm still free."

Together we end, our voices all twangy strong: "You can't take the sky from me."

"You guys are really and truly—" Roz starts to say, but then stops the way I have, hundreds, thousands of times before.

"Weird, I know," I fill in the censored blank for her.

"No," she says, "perfect for each other."

The shelter of the night may conceal my grin, but it can't contain it. Good thing, because I don't think I'm hiding my happiness from anyone, least of all Josh, who squeezes my hand. I stare up at the northern lights, stare until I can almost believe that my eyes will never miss another miracle that bursts around me. Stare until I know with absolute certainty that I will remember every contour of this radiant moment when my eyelids finally close.

In one blink, I am lit with possibility.

Starlight, moonbeam, sunray, I glow.

"If light is in your heart, you will find your way home."

— RUMI

Light surrounds me, my heart, my life, my faith, notably from my personal constellation of wonderful people who are beloved waypoints into this story.

Steven Malk, my agent, who has unfailing belief in me, and Cheryl Klein, who graciously brought the idea for this book to me and shaped it so intelligently. Nick Thomas for his insightful editing and compassionate worldview. Arthur Levine and Elizabeth Parisi, who made me feel at home at Scholastic, as well as Rachel Gluckstern, Ann Marie Wong, and Anna Swenson. Lorie Ann Grover for being this story's muse, first reader, and bestie. And as always, Janet Lee Carey for her loving feedback of every last word, sentence, and emotion.

A special note of gratitude to Bethany Strout for our fateful dinner in Denver, where she told (commanded) me to continue writing. Dr. Margarida Goncalo and Dr. Keen Lawlor, my medical go-to team on two continents, who shared their thoughts and research on all things photosensitivity. Dr. Tsippora Shainhouse and Dr. Kathryn Boling for their close reads and feedback on solar urticaria. Any medical errors are wholly mine. Nicole Miller and George Stathakopoulos for helping me with all things cybersecurity, crisis management, and the stars. Ryan Penagos for sharing his love of Marvel and storytelling with me. Katie Williams for the fabulous playlists in this book. Deb Cragen-Larsen for enabling me to write everything in my heart. Sue Bevington for our memorable adventure in Iceland. Sue Lim for being my steadfast non-Roz of a sister. And finally, Paul Taylor and Josh

Selig, at long (long) last, the proper thanks for your heroic protection in a hard, sad time.

As ever, my children, Tyler and Sofia Headley, light my heart. So grateful that we found our way home to Dan, Alex, and Zoe Johnson, our dearest sequel.

ABOUT THE AUTHOR

Storytelling runs in Justina Chen's blood. After all, her middle name means illuminate, which is what story does: It throws light on life. Her debut novel, *Nothing but the Truth (and a Few White Lies)*, won the Asian/Pacific American Award for Youth Literature, and her novel *North of Beautiful* was named one of the Best Books of the Year by *Kirkus Reviews* and was a finalist for nine state book awards. Justina is also the co-founder of Chen & Cragen and a story strategist to leaders. While her home is in Seattle, she feels at ease wherever she goes so long as she has her coconut black tea, journal, and pen. Please visit her at justinachen.com.

This book was edited by Cheryl Klein and Nick Thomas. Jacket and case design by Elizabeth Parisi. Interior design by Maeve Norton. The production was supervised by Rachel Gluckstern. The text was set in Bulmer MT Standard, with display type set in Century Gothic and title type hand-lettered by Baily Crawford. The book was printed and bound at LSC Communications in Crawfordsville, Indiana. The manufacturing was supervised by Angelique Browne.